Patrick Maloney had diverse jobs before settling down as a writer: Court Assistant, Computer Programmer, Systems Analyst and Actor. He is an active volunteer archaeologist and amongst other sites, has excavated at the 1066 battlefield at Fulford. He lives in Lancashire with his wife, Toni.

For more information about the author, the books and even some free stuff, go to

www.ThegnEdgar.com

THE LOST LAND

Patrick Maloney

www.ThegnEdgar.com

Copyright © 2020 Patrick Maloney

All rights reserved.

ISBN: 979-8-65-644349-4

This book is a work of fiction and except in the case of historical events and characters, any resemblance to actual events or persons, living or dead, is purely coincidental.

No part of this publication may be reproduced, stored in a retrieval system, or transmitted, in any form or by any means without the prior written permission of the publisher, nor be otherwise circulated in any form of binding or cover other than that in which it is published and without a similar condition being imposed on the subsequent purchaser.

For Toni, with love and thanks.

1

Dunholm

January 1069

Fat snowflakes fell from the overcast night sky, spitting and hissing as they landed in the campfire. A slender man, made large by the heavy animal skins in which he was wrapped, poked at the fire with a stick.

He put the stick down and wrapped his hand in a thick band of leather. Cautiously, he reached into the edge of the fire and withdrew a pot full of boiling liquid. With great care, he poured some of the liquid into a beaker pressed into the snow by his feet. The snow around it immediately began melting.

The man replaced the pot on the fire and picked up the beaker with his mittened hands. He held it to his mouth and blew gently across the surface of the liquid. He sipped gingerly at the steaming brew.

He sucked cold air over his lips as the hot drink stung. The hot liquid followed by the cold air entering his mouth sent a spasm of pain through his head. He reached up and felt above his ear under his thick woollen hat. The scar felt tender. A Norman sword had sliced across the side of his head over two years before, leaving a long wound. Even though now healed, it looked red and angry, lacking in hair. He rubbed his fingers up and down the scar, feeling the little lumps where chips of bone had settled under the scar tissue. A more competent healer would have removed the chips when he was first tended to, but there were none present at the battle where he had been injured. His friend had cleaned the wound effectively enough as he lay bleeding on the ground and had probably saved his life.

He patted his hat back into place and looked around. Other low fires burned nearby, and in their feeble light he could just make out the shapes of leather tents and more ramshackle shelters made from woven branches. He heard snatches of conversation from around the fires, but nothing other than the smallest of small-talk. At the fire closest to his, a young man with shoulder-length blond hair was running a whetstone along the length of his sword, from hilt to tip.

Scrape, scrape, scrape.

He looked at the young man; barely more than a boy. His glassy eyes watched the stone travel down his blade over and over again.

Footsteps crunched in the snow behind him, and a man in a thick woollen cloak squatted down on the ground beside him.

'Well, Brihtwulf, a fine brew you seem to have there,' he said.

Brihtwulf smiled at his old friend, the man whose imperfect ministrations had left a lumpy scar, but saved his life. 'Help yourself, Artor, but have a care, it's bloody hot.'

Artor gathered his cloak around him and sat down beside Brihtwulf. He picked up the leather band and wrapped it around his hand. He poured the steaming brew into his own beaker. He lifted it to his mouth and blew across it.

'What is it?' he asked.

'Mead, mostly, but with some dried berries and roots.'

Artor sipped. 'It's good,' he nodded approvingly.

They sat in companionable silence for a short while.

'What's the word?' asked Brihtwulf, offhandedly, as Artor had known he would, eventually.

'Some of the scouts have returned. They believe that the enemy will reach Dunholm tonight. They'll be fairly confident that they've crushed all opposition on the way north. God knows, they might as well have done. Hundreds dead, whole villages put to flame,' he shook his head angrily and took another sip.

'They also have a name for us,' he added.

'Oh yes, what's that?'

'The enemy commander is called Robert de Comines.'

'Poncy name.'

Artor chuckled. 'Poncy name or not, he's the Bastard's choice as earl of Northumbria.'

'Well,' drawled Brihtwulf idly. 'You know we have a history of dealing with earls we don't like around these parts.'

The scraping of the whetstone continued. Artor turned to look at the young man sharpening his blade.

'Lad!' he called, softly.

The sword-sharpener made no response. Artor picked up a handful of snow and threw it at the man.

The Lost Land

'Lad!' he repeated as the snow hit him in the face.

The young man looked up as if awoken from a dream.

'Huh, what? Is it time?'

'It's sharp enough, lad,' said Artor, indicating the sword. 'Sharpen it any more and there'll be no blade left at all.'

The youth looked down at his sword as if seeing it for the first time.

'Oh, sorry,' he said.

He put the whetstone away into a bag lying by his side.

Brihtwulf heaved himself to his feet. 'I'll take my turn with the watchers,' he said, and walked towards the rise to the south of their camp. The path was barely visible in the moonless night, and he walked with care. A feeble torch flickered close to the top of the rise, visible here in the lee of the hill, but not to the south, where they were watching. He headed for it.

Once at the top, he grunted greetings to two or three others who stood on the exposed ridge. He couldn't tell who they were in the dark, but he was aware of their presence by the sound of their shuffling feet as they struggled to fight off the cold.

Below him, in the unseen valley, wandered the River Wear, on a particularly rocky bend of which stood the town of Dunholm, seat of Bishop Aethelwine, a man known to have bent the knee to the Bastard.

Nevertheless, Aethelwine had ridden south to meet the newly appointed earl, to warn him against attempting to reach Dunholm.

As Brihtwulf peered into the darkness to the south, a low cry came from his right.

'There! Torches!'

Brihtwulf strained to see, the bitter wind making his

eyes water. He caught a flicker. Yes, now he was sure, two pinpricks of light, three, four, more. In a moment a whole column of torches could be seen, snaking its way northward towards the point where Dunholm sat broodingly over the Wear.

'It would appear that my lord Bishop has failed utterly in his mission,' muttered someone next to Brihtwulf.

'I don't think the Bastard's men take advice from the English, no matter who they are,' replied Brihtwulf.

'They'll learn.'

'By God, I hope so.' Brihtwulf held back his true feelings. It seemed to him that killing, raping and destroying was in the Normans' very nature. He doubted that they would ever, or could ever, change. He sighed.

As they watched, the torches disappeared one by one like distant, faint stars.

'They've gone into the town. The gates must have been opened to them,' said the watcher to his left.

'Can you blame them?' asked Brihtwulf. 'They know what's happened in dozens of villages. Capitulation is the only way to survive, that's the Norman message.'

The torches had all disappeared now. The watchers remained on station, checking for any further movement of the enemy force.

'How many men do you reckon there were?' asked one.

'Don't know,' replied Brihtwulf. 'How many would be carrying torches?'

'One in ten? Maybe one in twelve?'

'Alright, at a rough guess that would put their number at six or seven hundred.'

'We can take them,' said a voice, confidently.

There were muttered agreements from the gathered

The Lost Land

watchers. Brihtwulf held his tongue. He sometimes thought that false optimism was all they had left. There had been so many defeats.

Just then, a gasp and oaths of disbelief and fury arose from the watchers around Brihtwulf. He looked back towards Dunholm, where a small patch of bright flame had appeared. As he watched, two more fires flared up, then a fourth.

'Sweet Jesus, they're torching the town,' said the man to his left.

Within minutes, countless fires had appeared. The watchers could do nothing. They simply looked on mutely as Dunholm burned.

A deep voice rumbled from behind them. 'What's happening?'

The watchers turned towards the instantly recognisable voice. It came from Aelle, an ealdorman formerly of Bebbanburg, but now leading the English forces of Northumbria. He stepped forward as no answer came.

'Shit!' he muttered. 'How many are they?'

'We estimated six or seven hundred, my lord,' replied Brihtwulf.

'Is that you, Brihtwulf?'

'Aye, my lord. There were about sixty torches, one in ten or twelve would make six to seven hundred.'

Aelle grunted. 'If that's all there are of them, then we should be able to overcome them, given a good deal of surprise and a smile from God.'

He watched the flames flickering over the rooftops of Dunholm for a short while then turned to the watchers.

'Return to your troops. Tell them to get some sleep now, we'll advance during the dark of the morning and arrive there shortly before sunrise. We'll make the bastards pay for what they've done.'

The walk to Dunholm was difficult. To describe it as a march would give it a dignity that it did not deserve. The troops stumbled through the dark, guided only by the glow of the burning town ahead of them. They dared not carry torches themselves, for fear of giving their presence away to any Norman guards who might have been positioned around the walls of the town. Aelle had cautioned them to beware of any out-riding skirmishing parties, but they had encountered nobody on the snowbound roads. Seven men had fallen by the wayside during the journey, mostly with twisted or broken ankles. The injured were assisted back to the camp by their fellows, who then had to return to the English army on their own in pitch darkness.

Brihtwulf tripped over something covered by the snow. The man next to him caught him and stopped him from falling.

Ahead of him, Aelle strode purposefully at the head of his war band. Aelle had spoken to his lieutenants privately before they started to move towards Dunholm. This was not a trained army as he was used to from his days serving the earls of Northumbria, he had said. This was a ragtag army, made up of dispossessed thegns, ceorls and a large contingent of peasants, both free and unfree. He had over a thousand men of all types, though, and he considered that the great advantage of surprise that he was sure they had would more than make up for the inexperience of his army.

Brihtwulf had been slightly dismayed by Aelle's poor opinion of the army they had mustered, but grudgingly agreed that he was probably right.

Seven twisted and broken ankles seemed to be a small price to pay for the advantage of surprise that he hoped to gain over the smaller but more professional army of the new earl.

Aelle whistled softly as they came within sight of the walls of the town. Small fires persisted, flickering from some rooftops, but most had now died down.

Brihtwulf hoped that not too much damage had been done to the town. The people who lived there did not deserve that.

In response to Aella's whistle, the column of men came to a halt, unevenly and not without a few bumps and muttered curses.

Brihtwulf, Artor and three other senior thegns made their way to the front of the column.

Aelle whispered a few words of command. The army was split into four groups, each led by a thegn. Aelle would remain with Brihtwulf's group, whilst the other three separated and made their way around the base of the town walls until each was gathered at one of the town's main gates.

Brihtwulf's party of three hundred men moved towards the walls, stopping within sight of a wooden gate, guarded by a low, stumpy tower, which was presently unoccupied.

They waited. The birds were starting to sing and soon the first stain of dawn would appear in the south-east.

His men stood silently behind him. He had impressed on them the necessity of absolute quiet. A rattle of weaponry or an unguarded cough at this point might mean death for all of them.

'Right, that's long enough. The other groups should have reached their gates by now,' whispered Aelle and gave a low call. Aelle had planned this attack well in advance, and at the call, the gate they stood before swung open.

Inside stood a peasant, shoeless in the snow and clad only in a light tunic and ragged leggings.

'You look cold, Glaedwine,' said Aelle to the peasant.

'It's been warm enough in here this night, my lord.'

'So we saw. What do we need to know?'

'There are about seven hundred and fifty of them,' began Glaedwine. Brihtwulf smiled inwardly. Their estimate had been close. Aelle would be pleased at that.

'They've billeted themselves in houses throughout the town,' continued Glaedwine. 'Those that they haven't burned down, anyway. The leader and his elite guard are in the Bishop's house. It's made of stone, so it may be difficult to breach if they decide to make a stand.'

'Right. Thank you Glaedwine,' said Aelle. 'There's a man called Elfhelm at the back of this group. He has your clothes, armour and weapons. I will not have my thegns going into battle dressed like that,' he indicated Glaedwine's poor clothing.

'No, my lord.'

'Good work.'

'Thank you, sir.'

Glaedwine walked away from the gate and towards the back of the group. Brihtwulf heard him calling softly for Elfhelm.

Aelle gave a curt order and his men drew their weapons and advanced slowly and quietly into the devastated town.

All around them, smoke rose from the burned buildings into the cold morning air. Within many of the buildings, Brihtwulf saw objects that were unmistakably charred human bodies. He seethed as he looked on the destruction.

Useless, pointless destruction. The only message is 'submit or die', or in Dunholm's case 'submit and die anyway'.

'I'm taking a hundred men and heading for the Bishop's house,' said Aelle to Brihtwulf. 'Join me there when you've cleared this area out.'

'Yes, sir,' said Brihtwulf.

The troops split and Aelle led his hundred away up the hill towards the centre of the town.

Brihtwulf and his men carried on into the devastation. They came across their first Normans on what used to be a street corner. Eight men, dressed in mail shirts, but without helmets. They were staggering heavily, clearly having been drinking all night. One of them pulled up short when he saw Brihtwulf's war band.

He said something that sounded like 'Whoops,' and tried to draw his comrades' attention to the danger they were in.

Brihtwulf hissed a command to the front row of his men. Four warriors stepped forward and killed the men instantly with axe blows to the head.

The next street had not been destroyed, so Brihtwulf and his men began kicking the doors open.

The first house he entered was an expensive, two-storied one, probably a rich merchant's house, he thought. As he entered the lower room, a middle-aged woman with fresh cuts and bruises on her face, and tear marks down her cheeks looked up in alarm from her seat at a table. Lying on the floor of the room was the richly dressed body of a man. His skull had been split open and blackened blood had congealed in a large sickly-smelling pool around his head.

The woman relaxed a little when she recognised English warriors. With a flick of her hand, she indicated that they should go upstairs.

Brihtwulf raced up the stairs, two at a time, in the hope of catching the Norman unaware.

He needn't have bothered. Lying on a wrecked bed was a naked man, Norman arms and armour on the floor beside him. He was snoring loudly, and still in his hand was a beaker, from which had dribbled the last of his evening's drink.

Brihtwulf strode forward and grabbed him by the hair, which the man wore in the peculiar Norman style, shaved from the crown of the head back. The hairstyle of the thug.

The man woke blearily, and began frantically scrabbling at Brihtwulf as he was dragged to the stairs. With a powerful kick to the back of his knees, Brihtwulf propelled the man down the stairs. He fell forwards, hitting the first step on his knees and then crashing face downwards to the bottom of the stairs where he lay in a groaning heap next to the woman.

Brihtwulf descended, lifting his axe, but the woman stood and held out her hands to stop him.

'What?' demanded Brihtwulf.

'Please,' she said, imploringly. She held out a trembling hand to take Brihtwulf's axe. He handed it to her and she nodded thanks to him.

Slowly she turned round to face her rapist, who was struggling to get to his feet, his hands holding his head.

As he rose, the woman brought the axe down fiercely into his groin.

The man screamed. She had missed her mark, but the axe embedded itself in the top of his inner thigh. He collapsed and lay on the floor, rolling and gasping. She yanked the axe out of his leg and brought it down again and again and again. She worked herself into a frenzy, hacking and hacking first at his groin and then at the rest of him.

Aelle could see that the man had died at the second or third stroke, but the woman was crazed.

Brihtwulf stepped forward and deftly caught hold of the handle of the axe as she brought it up for yet another hack.

'Enough,' he said simply.

She stared angrily at him, and then burst into tears and collapsed back onto her chair.

Brihtwulf walked forward and placed his hand on the side of her head, gently caressing it for a moment. Then he dragged the corpse of the Norman out of the house and dumped it in the street.

All around him he could hear screams of pain and shouts of fury. The other parties were approaching the centre of the town. Bodies were piling up on the street, the snow that had fallen during the night turning red with Norman blood. The townspeople of Dunholm, shocked from the burning of their town and the murder of its inhabitants, had willingly joined in the slaughter.

The Norman contingent was completely outnumbered and even now, those who were not drunk were only just starting to organise themselves into some form of effective resistance. But it was too late. Too many of them had been killed, and their attackers were growing in number by the minute.

Brihtwulf watched as his men dragged Normans out of their accommodation and butchered them in the street. This had been too easy. Yet he knew that the most difficult fight lay ahead. Aelle had headed towards the Bishop's house, where his spy had said that Robert de Comines was holed up. He knew where that was, he had known Dunholm in happier times. He headed off in that direction.

As he approached, he could hear the commotion. The Bishop's house was one of the only stone-built buildings in the town and, as such, it was a defensible location for Robert de Comines and his principal officers.

Brihtwulf saw that Aelle's men had encircled the building and were facing determined opposition from a troop of Norman footmen, who stood between the English warriors and the Bishop's house. Over a hundred Normans stood defiantly around the house as the English raiders shouted abuse at them. Brihtwulf knew from experience that the Normans would fight to the death. They gave no quarter and consequently expected none.

He strode over to where Aelle stood in front of his men.

'Brihtwulf, just in time,' smiled Aelle cheerfully. 'We've pushed the guards back to here. Now to get the little turd.' He raised his arm. 'Hold!' he shouted.

The order was repeated around the building.

Aelle turned to one of his deputies, who stood nearby, his axe at the ready.

'Is Comines definitely in there?' he asked.

'Yes, sir. He came out a short while ago, but when he saw how badly his men were being defeated, he fled back inside.'

Aelle nodded. In a loud, commanding voice he shouted 'Robert de Comines!'

There was no reply, and the Normans looked uneasily at each other.

'Robert de Comines!' repeated Aelle. Again, his call was greeted with silence.

'If you give us Robert de Comines, your lives will be

spared!' he called, addressing the others within the house.

An arrogant, angry voice called back. 'Who are you and on what authority do you commit this atrocity?'

Aelle smiled slightly to himself.

'I am Aelle, an ealdorman of Bebbanburg. My authority is that of the people of Northumbria whom you have taken it on yourself to slaughter and rape and whose property you have destroyed indiscriminately.'

'I am the earl of Northumbria, appointed by our lord the King. I am within my rights to punish rebels as I see fit.'

'These are not rebels, you piece of Norman shit. The gates were opened freely to you. But I am not here to debate the niceties of decent behaviour with you. Come out and your men will be spared.'

'My men are loyal to the King and to me,' called Comines. 'Surrender now and your deaths will be merciful.'

The English axemen laughed out loud.

Aelle shook his head and called to his men.

'Take them.'

The shout went up around the house and the English walked slowly forward towards the Norman guards, who in turn began to step back, tightening their circle around the house.

Brihtwulf readied his axe and stepped forward with the men.

With a loud shout, the English axemen drew up their shields and axes and ran towards the Normans. With a thud of shields and a clang of weapons against armour and against each other, the battle was engaged. The Norman guard fought bravely, and Brihtwulf had to admit to himself that he was impressed by their discipline and ferocity. He saw three of his men fall in quick succession, next to each other. As they fell, he saw the Normans responsible, two giants, swinging their swords mightily and with an ease that spoke of immense strength and years of constant practice. Probably on innocents, thought Brihtwulf bitterly.

He started a rough sparring with a guard next to the two giants. The man was strong but unskilled.

Beside Brihtwulf, Aelle pulled his axe from his belt and leaped into the fray, facing the two giants with a defiant roar.

Brihtwulf groaned inwardly. Aelle was a fine leader and a brave fighter, but even he could not defeat these two single-handedly.

Both of the huge men turned on him, and immediately Brihtwulf saw that Aelle was fighting for his life. They set about him with powerful sword strokes, which he parried with his shield and his axe, always on the defensive, never able to make an attack himself.

Brihtwulf, whilst concentrating on his own fight, kept a watch on Aelle, noticing that his leader seemed to be losing strength. He was going to lose the fight.

Drawing on fury from deep within, Brihtwulf whipped his axe low down across the front of his enemy. The blade smashed into the very bottom of his opponent's sword blade, just above the hilt.

The blow wasn't strong enough to dislodge the sword completely, but it must have numbed the Norman's hand and loosened his grip on the sword. Brihtwulf slashed his axe upwards and into the side of the Norman's face.

His opponent yelped, blood streaming from under his helmet. This time he did drop his sword, and Brihtwulf brought his axe sweeping round into the Norman's neck, nearly severing the head.

Maintaining the momentum of the blow, Brihtwulf, in

a lightning-quick move, swung round and brought his axe down on the shoulder of the nearest giant to him. He heard a muffled grunt, and the giant's shield dropped.

Aelle had just parried a blow from the second giant, and in a continuous swing, brought his axe up and smashed it into the nose guard of the wounded man's helmet. The iron of the nose guard buckled and Aelle's axe smashed into the giant's face, at the top of his nose. The man dropped to the ground and Aelle swung back to face the second giant.

Too late, he raised his shield to deflect the returning sword blow, and the sword smashed into Aelle's axe arm, splitting the mail armour and biting deep into his forearm. The axe dropped from his hand and he staggered back. The giant grinned and stepped forward, raising his sword for the death blow.

As he did, an arrow whistled over Aelle's shoulder and embedded itself in the giant's cheek. The man stopped, stunned, and at that point, Brihtwulf brought his axe across the giant's neck. The man moaned, and his sword fell from his hand. Slowly he toppled and fell to the ground.

Aelle stumbled backwards, Brihtwulf following him. Nausea threatening to overcome Aelle. He gripped his arm tightly above the wound.

'Back. Sit,' ordered Brihtwulf, and lowered him to the ground behind the battle line. Aelle looked up to see how the battle was progressing. His men were in total command of the fight. More and more Normans were falling.

Brihtwulf wrapped leather thongs tightly around Aelle's arm to stop the blood loss. As he did so, a great cheer rose from the English ranks. The last Norman guard had fallen.

'Tell them to fall back,' Aelle said to his deputy.

Brihtwulf looked up and yelled 'Back!'

The English warriors fell back, carrying their dead and wounded with them. Norman bodies piled up around the Bishop's house like a barricade.

Aelle looked up at Brihtwulf again.

'Archers,' he said. 'Prepare fire-arrows.'

Brihtwulf passed on the order and a party of archers ran from behind the lines of the axemen. Others brought pots of oil and rags.

'This bastard likes to burn people and property,' Aelle said to Brihtwulf, between gasps of pain. 'Seems fitting that he should experience it himself. Give the order.'

Brihtwulf looked towards the archers.

'Light arrows!' he called.

The rags were wrapped around arrows and dipped in oil. One man from the far right of the line ran along it, a flaming torch in his hand. As he passed each archer, he lit the oily rags on the ends of their arrows.

'Draw bows!'

Brihtwulf faced the house, hearing the creaking of the bowstrings. Oily smoke rose from the line of archers as they readied their aim.

'Loose!'

Twenty fire-arrows arced across the sky, falling almost simultaneously on the thatched roof of the house.

'Again!' called Brihtwulf. 'This time the windows.'

The windows of the ground floor were narrow and closed tight with wooden shutters. The arrows thudded into the shutters, igniting them. Two arrows bounced off the stone walls of the house, drawing jeers from some of the English axemen. The arrows fell backwards, into the piled-up bodies of the Norman guard, where they started to smoulder, catching the leather and linen shirts of the fallen guards.

More arrows thumped into the window shutters, which were now smoking and catching. The roof was firmly ablaze, the thatch igniting easily. Even though the outer layers had been dampened by the recent snow, the arrows penetrated to the dry layers beneath.

One shutter, wildly ablaze now, fell backwards off its hinges and into the house. It was followed by a volley of fire-arrows through the window, catching the Bishop's expensive furnishings and tapestries.

Shouting could now be heard coming from within the building, and the door crashed open. A man staggered out amidst a belch of dark grey smoke, bent double, his arm across his eyes. Six arrows flashed from the English ranks, and he fell to the ground. The door of the house slammed shut.

'Cease!' called Brihtwulf.

He sat down next to Aelle, checking his arm.

'It's no good,' whispered Aelle. 'I've lost too much blood.'

Brihtwulf grunted and pulled Aelle's mail shirt off. With his knife, he tore open the arm of the linen tunic beneath.

'Hold on,' he said. He turned and bellowed at one of the nearby archers to bring him a lit fire-arrow. The archer removed his arrow from the bowstring and ignited it. He hurried across and handed it to Brihtwulf, who without hesitation thrust it into Aelle's wound.

Aelle screamed and passed out. Unhurriedly, Brihtwulf rolled the flaming arrow round and round Aelle's wound, cauterising it.

He shouted to some of the foot soldiers. 'Take Lord Aelle into a good house. Be careful with him, and when he wakes, bathe his wound with clean rags wet with melted snow.'

The men hurried to obey, and as they carried Aelle away, Brihtwulf turned to watch as the Bishop's house began to collapse.

2

Roskilde

Spring, 1069

Osfrith Edwinsson, former king's thegn and friend to Harold Godwinson, king of England, looked up from his silent reverie. He had been staring into the small fire, for how long he did not know. Outside the door to his rooms, he heard the deep, booming voice of the guard, one of his men, a tall, mostly Danish man called Hallvindur.

'Get away from here, you brat! Lord Osfrith is resting.'

Osfrith could hear the piping voice of a child. He could not make out the words.

'I don't care,' said Hallvindur, slowly. 'Go away or I'll make you regret disturbing us.'

The child's voice returned, sounding insistent. Osfrith stood and walked to the door. He opened it to see the broad back of Hallvindur. His hands were placed firmly on his hips as he blocked the door to Osfrith's rooms. A small boy stood in front of him, staring defiantly up at Hallvindur.

'What is it?' asked Osfrith.

'Now see what you've done!' exclaimed Hallvindur. 'I'm sorry, sir, this brat won't go away. I'll beat him.'

'It's alright, Hallvindur, let's hear what the lad has to say.'

Hallvindur reluctantly took a sideways step, allowing the boy to look at Osfrith.

Osfrith looked back and addressed the boy in Danish.

'What is it, boy? Didn't you hear Hallvindur tell you that I was resting?'

'I'm sorry sir, but I have an important message.'

'And what is it?'

'You are summoned to the guest lodgings at the King's hall.'

'By whom?'

The boy looked puzzled. 'It is the King's hall, sir.'

Osfrith sighed. 'Very well, you've delivered your message, off you go.'

'Will you be going, then, sir?' asked the boy.

Hallvindur took a step towards him. 'Go away!' he growled.

The lad turned and ran off back towards the hill on which the great hall stood, the local residence of Sweyn Estrithson, king of the Danes.

'I'd better go, Hallvindur, it might be something important.'

'Do you want me along?' Hallvindur asked.

'No, no. Why don't you sit by my fire and keep it stoked until I get back?'

'Yes, sir. Thank you, sir,' replied Hallvindur, happy to have the opportunity to sit by a fire on this chilly late Spring afternoon.

Osfrith returned to his chair and retrieved a heavy cloak that hung from the back of it and a stout walking stick. He swung the cloak round his shoulders and walked out, leaving Hallvindur within.

As he walked up the hill towards the King's hall, Osfrith cursed the wound in his leg that caused him to limp so heavily. The pain got worse the further he walked, and going uphill was the worst of all. The wound had been inflicted on him during the great battle at Senlac, where William, the bastard duke of Normandy, had defeated the army of the English and claimed the throne of England for himself.

Ahead of him, Osfrith saw his comrade Wigmund, another king's thegn injured in that battle. He called after him and Wigmund turned. He waited whilst Osfrith hobbled up to him.

'Going to the hall?' asked Osfrith.

'I am, I've just received a mysterious summons.'

'So have I. Any idea what it's about?'

Wigmund shook his head. 'No, I don't even know who the summons came from.'

'We'd better go and find out then.'

The two warriors continued up towards the hall.

Once there, they made their way to the sumptuously appointed guest quarters, as they had been instructed. A servant opened the door to them and they walked into an audience chamber, used by visiting dignitaries to conduct essential business. At one end of the room was a chair, raised on a low dais.

Osfrith looked around the room. Two or three dozen men were already present, and Osfrith noted the presence of several senior English thegns. He nodded at one or two when they caught his eye. Also present were some of Sweyn-king's advisers. It was quite a gathering.

A door beside the dais opened, and an armed warrior entered, followed by a small, elderly woman, dressed in rich fabrics and with a thin fillet of gold around her head. Her grey hair was pulled tightly away from her forehead and hung down her back in a short pony-tail.

A stifled mutter ran around the room as those present recognised her. Osfrith knew her well, and with everyone else, he bowed his head briefly as she ascended the dais and sat on the chair.

The Lady Gytha acknowledged the respect in the room with a graceful wave of her hand. Osfrith suddenly realised how important this meeting must be, for Lady Gytha was the aunt of Sweyn-king, and mother of Harold Godwinson-king, the man whose life Osfrith and the other thegns had failed to protect at Senlac.

'Gentlemen,' began Gytha. 'Thank you for answering my summons. I apologise for bringing you here under such strange circumstances, but as you can probably imagine, I am not visiting my dear brother-son simply out of familial love.

'I will not waste time here, because I need to hear your views on what I have to tell you, even before I tell the King himself.

'As you will have heard, the conquest of England by the cursed Normans is not going well for them. The Bastard is having real difficulties in consolidating his control over the kingdom, particularly in the north.'

Muttered affirmations came from the assembled men.

'You will have heard that the Bastard appointed one Robert de Comines to the earldom of Northumbria. This

The Lost Land

brutal thug burned and murdered his way to Dunholm, where he was utterly defeated, and killed in his turn.'

Mutters of approval ran around the chamber.

'This was three months ago. You may not be aware of what happened after that.' She looked quizzically at the faces in the room. Seeing nothing to contradict her statement, she continued; 'Then as it's clear that you don't know, I will tell you.

'Following the defeat of Comines, the English leaders in exile in Scotland were moved to join forces with the resistance fighters. Earls Gospatric and Maerleswein headed south into Northumbria under the leadership of Edgar Atheling.

'The combined forces attacked Eoforwic, where the new Norman castle was breached. The Norman governor of the city was killed, and the city sacked. The Bastard himself marched north to face our forces, and I'm sorry to report that he managed to drive them back. Fortunately, the leaders escaped. The earls are with our men in the Northumbrian hills, and the prince has for now returned to the court of Malcolm-king in Scotland.

'The Bastard put in place another governor in Eoforwic. This time no less a man than the butcher William fitzOsbern. FitzOsbern is rebuilding the castle there and now has a much stronger garrison. Since then there have been three more raids on the town, only partly successful.'

She paused, looking around the room. Drawing a breath, she continued; 'I have within the past month heard from our people placed close to the court of the Bastard that he has sent his wife back to Normandy.'

There were loud mutters around the room at this news.

'Yes. The Bastard fears enough to remove his wife from

England and send her to a place of safety.'

The tension in the room became palpable.

'I have been in conference with my grandsons, the sons of Harold-king, whom some of you know. They have been gathering strength in Ireland, and now we feel that it is time to strike from that direction as well.'

Loud cries of approval arose from the men in the chamber. Gytha held up her hand for silence.

'With your support in this matter, I intend to advise my brother-son that there has never been a better time to launch an invasion of England than now.'

Shouts of joy filled the room. Gytha smiled a small smile and allowed the noise to subside.

'As you will have noticed, my brother-son has been... reluctant, shall we say, to launch a full invasion of England. Never, though, has such an opportunity presented itself like this. Success is virtually assured.'

'What do you need from us, Lady?' called one of the exiled English thegns.

'I require assurances from you that you will join the expedition. That you will make contact with your people back home and ensure that as many armed men as possible are ready to meet us when we arrive in England.'

'You shall have all that!' cried a man at the back of the room, to cries of approval.

'There is one more thing,' said Gytha quietly. She paused and looked searchingly at the men gathered before her.

The room fell silent. Gytha drew herself up. 'You must swear your loyalty to Sweyn-king and support his rightful claim to the kingship of England.'

The air in the room suddenly seemed thick and cloying.

The Lost Land

The silence stretched uncomfortably. Eventually, a voice from the back of the room broke through the barrier of silence.

'What of Edgar Atheling, my lady?'

'Something will be worked out. I swear that the prince will not be harmed. My preferred choice is a sharing of the kingdom as has happened in the past. Sweyn will rule the traditional Danish lands; Edgar will have Wessex.'

The silence took on a more thoughtful texture.

'You will need to talk about this amongst yourselves. I understand that,' said Gytha. 'I will leave you now. When you have made your decision, send a messenger to me. I will be waiting for your response. But know this, my lords; without the support of a huge Danish army and the enthusiasm of my brother-son the King, the Atheling will never reign at all.'

'My lady,' ventured a thegn. 'What is the basis of Sweyn-king's rightful claim on the throne of England?'

Gytha narrowed her eyes. 'The right is twofold,' she replied slowly. 'Firstly, his mother Estrith was sister of Cnut-king, making him also first cousin to two other kings of England, Cnut's sons Harthacnut and Harold. He is also cousin to my murdered son, Harold Godwinson. Sister-son of one king of England and cousin to three more, who better to succeed to the crown?'

The thegns began to mutter to each other.

'What of the second right, my lady?' persisted the first thegn.

'Ah yes. That is by promise.'

'Promise, my lady?'

'Indeed. My brother-son was promised the succession by none other than Edward-king himself.'

Osfrith narrowed his eyes. There had been some sharp intakes of breath around him at that. If this claim was true, and Osfrith did not believe for a moment that it was, then old Edward-king had been somewhat profligate with his promises. The basis of Duke William's invasion of England had been that Edward had promised him the kingdom. When the crown was taken by Harold Godwinson, it was said that Edward, on his deathbed, had handed the safe-keeping of the kingdom to him. Now it transpired that the old king had made a third promise.

A voice from the back of the chamber asked a question. Osfrith missed it, but it was clear from Gytha's response that the man who asked the question was thinking along the same lines as Osfrith himself, and, it seemed, of many others in the room.

'The crown was never promised to the Bastard, you know that. And my son certainly never promised to support him in that claim. The crown was promised to Sweyn, who also has a very solid blood claim. His claim is far better than the Bastard's ever was.' Gytha stood up from her chair.

The clamour died down as the gathered company bowed to Gytha's retreating back.

'I shall be waiting, my lords,' she said as she passed out of the audience chamber.

3

Plans

Stormleaper had been dragged out of the water of Roskilde Fjord. She lay on her left-hand side – the side Loki referred to as the backboard – to the west of the busy landing stages. Her crew was spread along her length, carefully inspecting the planks of which she was made. Even beached like this, the sight of the great ship caught the breath in Edgar's throat. He stood next to her owner and commander, Captain Loki, and admired the elegant sweep of her hull. The seductively feminine lines of her exposed steerboard side brought a smile of wonder to Edgar's face.

'She looks good even out of the water,' he commented to Loki.

Loki grinned. 'Becoming quite the waterman aren't you, Edgar?'

Edgar laughed. He had only boarded Stormleaper with considerable reluctance as his escape route from England because a troop of Norman soldiers commanded by no less a character than Robert de Barentin was in hot pursuit of him. He had never sailed on a sea-faring longship before and had been dreading the experience. The voyage to Denmark had taken eight days, during which he had discovered that the swell of the ocean and the wild tossing of the ship had not bothered him at all.

His principal housecarl, Guthrum, had spent the first two days throwing up violently at every pitch and dip in the passage, only to gain his sea legs on the third day of the crossing. His other carl, Halfdene, had looked a little green for the first few hours, but had rallied well, and eventually admitted to having enjoyed the crossing. Edda, his young ward, had never flinched, despite having initially been terrified of boarding the ship. She, like Edgar, had been pleasantly surprised to find that an ocean crossing did not actually make her ill. The final member of Edgar's party, the somewhat mysterious spy, Alaric, had never batted an eyelid at the prospect or the actuality of an ocean crossing and had become a useful member of the crew during the journey.

'Well,' said Edgar. 'It's not as bad as I'd thought, but give me a horse any day.'

Loki laughed. 'You would exchange *that*,' he gestured proudly at the ship, 'for a *horse*? One of those mad-eyed, skittish, shit-spreading, insane animals? You're mad.'

'I can control a horse. That wave-rider can't be tamed by the likes of me.'

'It doesn't have to be. I am her master. She obeys me, sings my song, dances to my tune. All you have to do is sit there.'

Edgar snorted. 'And put my back to the oars when your precious wind is not sufficient to belly her sails.'

'Of course, my friend, that is the nature of a sea voyage.'

'You don't need wind to ride a horse.'

'You don't need to feed Stormleaper bales of hay.'

Edgar sighed. 'Alright, let's agree, different horses for different passages.'

'Agreed.' Loki took a deep breath of the salty air. 'You have to admit, though, she's beautiful.'

Edgar waited a moment before answering. 'Oh, yes,' he said with a smile.

'What are your men looking for?' he asked.

'Weakness,' Loki said, simply. 'Although the planks of her hull are fitted very tightly together by the shipwright, there are always some gaps that need filling, even before the ship first feels water beneath her keel; tiny gaps that can only be seen when looked for very carefully. No matter how small, the water always finds its way in. These little gaps are tightly packed with coarse wool, soaked in resin from pine trees. Sometimes, this can work loose and needs replacing. Also, the constant rolling of the waves can cause new gaps to appear between the overlapping planks which need similar packing. The ship twists and rolls all the time at sea. It's no wonder that tiny gaps appear, the planks are being pulled and stretched every moment she's at sea. It's a regular maintenance task that all ships' crews have to perform.'

One of Loki's crew stepped forward and raised two thumbs towards Loki. Loki raised his hand in the air. 'Alright, lads, let's do the other side,' he called.

The crew moved to the backboard side of the ship and cautiously began to tip the ship over. A party remained on the steerboard side – so called because the steering-board, or rudder, was on that side – and eased the ship down as she was pushed over.

The crew now all gathered around the newly exposed

backboard side of the ship and began an intense scrutiny of her exposed timbers. A pot of pine resin sat a short way from the ship, sitting over a low fire. A young man was feeding large balls of wool into the pot and stirring it in with a long stick. He was concentrating no less than those examining the ship. He kept poking at the wool, forcing it under the surface of the warm resin, twisting and turning it to ensure that all the air trapped within the wool was replaced by the thick, sticky liquid.

Further up the bank, a small contingent of women carefully pored over the sail, sewing and patching where necessary.

'I've ordered a spare sail,' said Loki. 'There's a group of women – and some men – in the town who make fine quality sails. A spare is a luxury, I know, but when you need a new sail, you really need it.'

He suddenly turned to Edgar, his eyes alight with passion and excitement.

'I have plans for this summer,' he said.

'Oh yes?' said Edgar.

'I'm going to trade with Micklagard.'

Micklagard! Edgar reeled at the thought. The greatest city in the world. Home of the world's richest people, ruled over by their great Christian emperor. Apart from the fabulous tales of the vast city with its huge buildings, impenetrable walls and fantastically wealthy inhabitants, Edgar knew nothing about it. It was beyond the bounds of his imagination to think that one day he might actually see the city for himself.

'Where is it?' he asked.

'At the ends of the Earth,' said Loki. He smiled. 'South, through the Rus lands and beyond the Euxine Sea.'

Edgar paused. He knew nothing of Rus lands or the Euxine Sea. 'Isn't that a long way away?'

'It's a very long way, but there is a well-known route from right here all the way to Micklagard itself. There's a river system that will take us there. It's by far the most profitable route for traders in the entire world.'

'What would you take to trade with them?' asked Edgar, interested.

Loki looked around him to ensure that he was not being overheard.

'One of my agents has secured a large number of high-quality bear pelts. I also have a fair quantity of amber that I've been accruing for the last few years. Bear skins and amber are two of the most profitable items to deal with at Micklagard. They can't get enough of them.'

'And what will you bring back?'

'Fine jewellery, gold and silver. Also, fine materials, even silk, both in bales and in ready-made clothing. The profit will be tremendous. I've been waiting many years for the right time to make the trip. I think it is now.'

'Is the journey dangerous?' asked Edgar.

'There are dangers on any trip, and this is not an easy one. Although the river system will take us all the way, the rivers don't all flow into each other. There are points along the journey where we'll have to lift the boat out of one river and drag her across the land to join another. These points are well-known, however, and there are always people there to assist, for a suitable consideration, of course. But the profits make it all worthwhile.'

'What of bandits?'

'There are areas that are more prone to it than others, of course. These places again are well-known, and we'll be well prepared.'

He paused and looked at Edgar. 'Especially if you and your two men would join us. You are fine fighters. I've seen that. You would, of course, be entitled to a share in the profits of the trip.'

Edgar felt a small rush of excitement course through his body. What an adventure this could be. It would be a great opportunity to boost his coin supply, which was beginning to look somewhat desperate.

'It sounds interesting,' mused Edgar. 'I'll discuss the matter with Guthrum and Halfdene. I take it they, too, will have a share in the profit?'

'All the men who serve under me receive a share of the profits. That is what keeps them loyal. That and the history they have with me.'

Edgar nodded. 'Alright, I'll talk with them this evening.'

'Good. I've noticed a certain restlessness in them of late.'

It was true. As Guthrum and Halfdene no longer had an easily recognised role in life, exiles as they were, finding gainful employment for them was not easy.

Edgar, as an exiled minor noble, had little influence on events around him, and although they were all loosely associated with the court of Sweyn-king, their placement within that court was only very vaguely defined.

Edgar nodded. 'That's very true,' he said. 'I think we'd welcome the opportunity to sail with you. Only Guthrum may be a little uneasy.'

'He got his sea legs eventually, and it has to be said that most of the journey to Micklagard is by river, we only cross the sea at the start of the journey and at the end. The rest is relatively calm.'

Edgar smiled. 'Good, I'll speak with them, then.'
He fell silent as a thought occurred to him.
'What is it?' asked Loki, sensing Edgar's hesitation.
'Edda,' he replied.
'What of her?'
'What will we do with Edda? She's still a child, and my responsibility for her is binding on me.'

Edda was eleven years old, maybe twelve, if her father's estimate of her age had been correct. Edgar thought her a bit younger. She had been rescued by Edgar when her village of Osmundestun was destroyed by the Normans and all its other inhabitants slaughtered, including Edda's parents. Osmundestun was within the estates of Rapendun, and as its last thegn, Edgar felt an unbreakable responsibility for her, the last of his people.

Later that evening, Edgar, Guthrum and Halfdene sat together around a table in the guests' hall. Several of the other English exiles were sitting around, drinking ale and conversing in low tones.

'I received an interesting proposition this afternoon,' began Edgar.

Guthrum raised one eyebrow. 'Oh yes?'

'Was it from Freygird? Who works in the kitchen?' asked Halfdene. 'I would.'

Edgar and Guthrum ignored him.

'I was speaking with Loki, and he suggested that we accompany him on a trading voyage.'

'Ah. Well…' said Guthrum, placing his hands on the table and leaning slightly back.

Edgar stilled him with a gesture. 'It's not going to be a great sea voyage. Most of the journey will be along rivers.'

Guthrum relaxed visibly. 'Well, that might be alright.'

'Where would we be going?' asked Halfdene, interested.

'Micklagard.'

'Micklagard! Great gods that must be thousands of miles away!' exclaimed Guthrum.

'I don't know how far away it is,' said Edgar. 'But Loki tells me that it's a well-travelled route and probably the most profitable in the world. He has a cargo of bearskins and amber to trade, items he says are always in high demand amongst the Romans.'

'Why would he want to have us along?' asked Halfdene suspiciously.

Edgar smiled. 'Well, there's the rub, of course. The journey is not, apparently, without its dangers. There is some danger of banditry and there's also some heavy shifting that needs as many hands as possible. Apparently, the ship has to pass over land to get from river to river.'

'Over land? Sounds difficult.'

'Loki assures me that it is, but it's not impossible. Look at Stormleaper now. She's right up out of the water for maintenance. The crew just dragged her up onto the shore. It seems that many ships cross from river to river every year. The porting places are so well used that a local industry has grown up of men who assist in the movement of the ships, for a price.'

'Like a toll?'

'I suppose it must be like that.'

'What's in it for us?' asked Guthrum, clearly still not appeased about having to travel in the vessel that had made him so ill the last time.

'Well, by my reckoning we're all just about out of money by now. Loki tells me that the profits from this voyage should be substantial, and we'll get a fair cut. You never know, we may even enjoy the trip. If it's truly profitable, we may wish to do it again.'

Guthrum looked sceptical. 'It would have to pay off spectacularly for me to want to travel in that damned thing.'

'Would you do it the once?' asked Edgar.

Guthrum and Halfdene exchanged a silent glance.

'You are our thegn, Edgar,' said Halfdene. 'Wherever you go, we go.'

Guthrum nodded. 'Aye,' he said. 'That's the thing of it.'

Edgar sat back on his stool and regarded his two housecarls. 'Thank you, lads,' he said.

'It's our strength and axes he's after then?' asked Halfdene.

'That's about it, we're three carls up for hire and he's offered to hire us, and pay us well.'

'Seems fair enough. Never thought I'd be a traveller,' said Halfdene.

Guthrum grunted. 'Never *wanted* to be a traveller. Still, we seem to have little say in our own lives. Nothing new there, then.' He paused and stared up at the far wall before continuing, quietly, 'and I *would* like to see the city these people call Micklagard. They say it's the greatest city in the world, and a mighty Christian emperor lives there, all dressed in jewels and cloth of gold, and he has thousands of guards, each of whom is richer than an earl in England.'

Edgar laughed. 'I doubt guards are paid that much anywhere, Guthrum. Carls are carls the world over.'

'Aye, maybe you're right. Let's go and see for ourselves, eh?' He raised his beaker of ale and they all clinked their vessels together and took deep swigs from them.

'There is one problem, though, that I have to consider,'

said Edgar.

'And what's that?' asked Guthrum, his eyes narrowing in suspicion.

'What about Edda?'

'Edda is no problem. She stays here,' said Guthrum.

'I can't leave her here, Guthrum, you know that,' said Edgar. 'I can't leave her at all.'

'But she's just a child, she can't come on a dangerous journey to the ends of the Earth! We'll have enough to think about protecting ourselves and the ship without having to worry about a girl all the time. Not to mention what Loki's crew would think of having a girl-child on board with them. Very superstitious lot, sailors, you know. Coming over from England we only got away with it because she wore that cloak and hood all the time, so none of the crew had to look at her.'

'I'll sort something out with Loki. There has to be a way.'

'It would be different if Edda were a boy,' said Halfdene.

Edgar nodded. Young boys frequently travelled on long trading voyages; it was how they learned the ways of the longships. Some even went on to become merchants themselves.

Just then they heard the sound of a deep bell. Everyone in the hall looked up at the sound. Loud and resonant, it was the bell in the tower that stood beside the King's residence, summoning the members of the court to attend the King in his great hall.

As an exiled noble living within the royal precincts, Edgar was an honorary member of the King's court, as were all the other exiled English nobles who had emigrated to the court of Sweyn Estrithson-king.

'You two stay here, I'd better go,' said Edgar, draining his cup and placing it on the table as he rose.

Edgar walked up the hill towards the great hall. Walking up from other directions, he saw several former English thegns that he had met since arriving in Denmark. Also amongst them were Danish nobles, permanent members of the court.

The great doors of the hall, thick, solid oak covered in intricate bronze tracery, were flung open to admit the gathering members of the court. Two long tables stretched along the length of the hall, with benches provided on both sides of each table. The men who had arrived first sat down, while the late arrivals stood around the walls of the hall.

Edgar managed to find a seat between a large, fat, sweaty Dane whom he did not know and a dispossessed English thegn, like himself. He nodded briefly at the thegn, whose name he couldn't quite recall. Across the hall, he caught sight of King's Thegn Osfrith Edwinsson, whom he had met in England the year before. Osfrith looked up and saw Edgar. His face broke into a wide grin and he winked knowingly at him.

Ah, thought Edgar. This announcement may be very interesting indeed.

Once everybody had arrived, the doors were closed, and without fanfare, the King walked in through a door that led to his private audience chamber. He was a tall, well-built man, but a damaged leg gave his gait a slightly cumbersome swagger.

Everyone stood as the King entered and stepped up onto a raised dais at the far end of the hall. On the dais was a large, plushly-upholstered chair, and several small ones, no less comfortable, on either side of it. The King sat on the throne, whilst four other men and an elderly woman sat on the smaller chairs around him. Edgar looked with interest at the elderly woman, who had seated herself at the King's left hand.

At the King's right hand sat a tall, muscular man with long dark hair and a lush beard. His resemblance to the King was striking, and Edgar assumed that this must be Sweyn's younger brother, Jarl Asbjorn, whom he had heard of, but had never seen before.

Once the King and his council were seated, the nobles of the court resumed their seats amid much shuffling and scrapings. The noise settled quickly and the King began to speak in a deep, gravelly voice.

'Certain urgent matters have recently been brought to my attention. I have been in conference with my council, and a decision has been reached which will affect many of you here present.

'It is well known to all here, especially our honoured English guests, that my beloved cousin, Harold Godwinson, rightful and God-appointed king of England, was these two years past, viciously and unlawfully slain by the murderous and Godless Bastard of Normandy, against the laws of God and man. This treacherous creature now calls himself king of England by right of some imagined promise made to him by Edward, then king of England and my cousin Harold, then earl of Wessex.'

Angry mutters rippled around the hall. The King let them settle before he continued.

'My notice has been drawn to the fact that the rule of the Bastard is not sitting well with our English brethren.'

The Lost Land

Small pockets of bitter laughter broke out amongst the audience.

'In fact, so badly does the iron hand of the Norman lie on the peace of England, that the rule of the Bastard is continually disrupted by rebellion and acts of destruction. Though as the Bastard's rule is unlawful and sinful, we should refer to these acts not as rebellion, but as resistance.'

Mutters of approval greeted the statement.

'You have heard, I know, of the slaying of the Bastard's man in Dunholm and that of his entire retinue earlier this year. This was followed by a powerful attack on Jorvik, which the Bastard only just managed to defeat. Further attacks have taken place on Jorvik, and it cannot be long before the Norman hold on the whole of Northumbria is lost forever. Resistance is strong in the south, too. The Bastard's grip on his unlawful territory is slipping.'

He paused and looked round at the eager faces in the hall in front of him. The looks on the faces of the English nobles were particularly intense. They knew, or at least hoped they knew, what was coming. Sweyn continued.

'In what I am sure you will all agree is a significant development, it seems that the Bastard is now so unsure of his own safety and authority that he has sent his wife home to Normandy. If he was confident in his victory over the resistance, he would not have considered doing such a thing. He grows afraid, it seems. And with good cause.

'I am informed by my deeply beloved aunt, Gytha, mother of the slain Harold Godwinson,' he indicated the elderly woman with a graceful wave of his left hand, 'that her grandsons, Godwin, Edmund and Magnus, the sons of Harold the King, are about to launch a massive attack on the south-west coast of England, further shattering the authority of the Bastard.'

Edgar listened eagerly to what the King was saying. Was this it? Was this what Edgar and the other exiled nobles of England had hoped for?

'My aunt reminds me that the throne of England would legitimately fall to me if this Norman upstart were not in the way.

'As the throne of England is mine by lawful right and by the will of God, I have decided to stake my claim on the throne. I am now ordering my faithful brother, Asbjorn, here present,' he indicated with his right hand, 'to assemble a large fleet of ships that will carry my forces, under his leadership, to the shores of Northumbria to begin the process of extricating this vile usurper from my realm.'

The hall erupted with cheers, especially from the English nobles, who stood and hugged each other.

The King held up his hand for silence and the clamour died down.

'I can see that this will be a popular expedition. As of now, I am placing Jarl Asbjorn in command. You will obey him as you would obey me. Now go, and prepare yourselves for conquest!'

The guest hall was alive with rowdy conversations, and the ale was flowing freely. Edgar was sitting again with Guthrum and Halfdene, both of whom had received the news of the forthcoming invasion with great joy.

'One of the Danish nobles was telling me on the way back from the King's hall that not only does the throne pass naturally to Sweyn-king by right of succession, but he was also promised the throne by Edward-king himself several years ago.'

'Isn't that what William claims?' asked Guthrum.

'It is, but we know that isn't true. It's just the Bastard's way of legitimising his invasion and regicide.'

'Hold on,' said Halfdene, his cup stopping half-way to his mouth. 'Doesn't that beg all sorts of questions?'

'Like what?' said Guthrum.

'If the throne is legitimately Sweyn's, and Edward promised it to him, doesn't that make Harold a usurper?'

'Harold always said that Edward passed the kingdom to him on his deathbed,' said Guthrum.

'So three different claimants to the throne all say that Edward promised the throne to them?'

'So it would seem,' said Edgar carefully.

'I can see another problem,' said Halfdene.

Edgar nodded. 'Edgar Atheling. If Sweyn's claim to the throne is legitimate, then the Atheling's cannot be. That has the potential to split the forces and we'd be in a much weaker position against William.'

They sat silently for a few moments, looking glumly into their cups.

'Sweyn Estrithson is not a stupid man,' said Edgar eventually. 'He will be aware of these potential conflicts, and the Lady Gytha must also know of them. Perhaps she even holds out some hope that her grandson Godwin Haroldson may yet succeed to the throne.'

'Well don't chuck another name into the pot!' exclaimed Guthrum in exasperation.

'Look, the main thing is to get rid of the Bastard and his murderous thugs. Who reigns afterwards, Edgar, Sweyn or Godwin doesn't matter. They're all preferable to the Norman.'

'Aye,' said Guthrum and Halfdene in unison.

'These matters are above us. They are for kings and princes to settle between them. For now, all factions seem united in a single purpose, and that's one that we three can wholeheartedly support, yes?'

He looked questioningly at Guthrum and Halfdene.

They both nodded in agreement.

'Well then, to the invasion,' Edgar raised his cup of ale. The other two touched cups with his, and they drained them.

'At least it solves the problem of Edda,' said Edgar. 'Or at least puts it off for a while. She most certainly cannot come on a voyage of conquest with us.'

'You're leaving?' asked Edda in a hurt voice.

'We have to, Edda, and it will only be for a short time, a few months at most.'

'But why?'

'The King has ordered that an invasion force be sent to England to dispose of the Normans and to get rid of William. This is very important, Edda, we are going to get our country back.'

'But why do you have to go?'

'It's my duty. I am a thegn. I have to fight for my rights and for my people. When we've won, I'll come back for you and we can return to Rapendun. Wouldn't you like that?'

Although Edda was just eleven years old, the look that crossed he face was that of a much older person, one who had seen terrible things.

'Well there's not much left there for me now, is there?' she demanded.

Edgar knew that one day he would have to sit down with Edda and discuss with her what had happened to her family and her village. As it was, the right time had not arrived, and all the horror and anger and grief and guilt were still screwed up into a poisonous ball somewhere inside her young body.

'I'm sorry, Edda, I didn't mean it like that. You'll stay with me at Rapendun. I told you that I would never abandon you, and I meant it. I will come back for you, I promise. You believe me, don't you?'

She stared hard at him for a while and then wrapped her thin arms around his waist and buried her head in his chest.

'Of course I believe you, Edgar.'

She began sobbing silently and he placed his hand gently on the back of her head.

After a few moments, she pulled away from him and wiped her eyes irritably on her sleeve.

'Well, if you have to go then you have to go,' she said, not looking at him. 'Don't forget to take your good sword, will you?'

Edgar grinned at her and pulled her into another hug.

4

Preparation

July 1069

Once again, Edgar was looking at Stormleaper. This time, however, the situation was very different. The ship, now fully overhauled, was sitting proudly against a jetty in Roskilde's dock. Loki's crew swarmed over her, preparing her for her next voyage. It was not, however, the voyage that Loki had planned.

Loki stood next to Edgar, stoically watching as his profits receded into the distance. All ships within recall distance had been summoned to Roskilde by the King's messengers. All were to take part in the great invasion. Looking out over the sparkling sea of the harbour, Edgar could see close to three hundred ships, riding the gentle swell like sleek beasts of prey; silent, waiting to bound forward and snatch their unwary victims.

'I'm sorry that you won't be able to travel to Micklagard this year,' said Edgar, knowing how inadequate his words

The Lost Land

must sound.

'We can go to Micklagard next year,' said Loki. 'For now, England calls. That's not so bad. A successful raid will reap a good profit.'

'This isn't a raid, Loki, this is an invasion. If successful, England will be ruled by Sweyn, and you wouldn't want to annoy him by raiding his new kingdom, would you?'

Loki smiled lopsidedly. 'Don't be fooled by the rhetoric, Edgar. All Viking voyages are raids. Don't think that this will be any different.'

Edgar remained silent. He knew the tales of former times, when Danes and Norwegians plied up and down the east coast of England, plundering and killing. The stories were horrific. Loki was implying that this voyage would be the same as those and that Edgar himself and his companions were about to inflict the old terror on their own people. The thought did not sit comfortably with the young thegn, and he unconsciously rubbed at the scar tissue on his damaged face.

'Edgar!'

Edgar turned as he heard his name being called. Leaning heavily on a stout walking-stick and limping awkwardly, Osfrith Edwinsson walked up the path towards them. Following a pace behind him was his faithful housecarl and bodyguard, Hallvindur.

'Good morning, my lord,' responded Edgar, bowing slightly as the older man pulled up beside him, slightly breathless.

'Impressive, isn't it?' said Osfrith, waving his stick towards the gathered fleet.

'Very,' replied Edgar. 'May I introduce Captain Loki, of Stormleaper? Loki, this is King's Thegn Osfrith Edwinsson.

I told you about him.'

'Ah, Captain Loki, a pleasure,' Osfrith reached out his hand and Loki shook it. 'I've heard so much about you.'

Loki snorted softly. 'I'm sure you have,' he said without warmth.

Edgar was puzzled. There was an undercurrent here that spoke of things he was unaware of.

'It's fortuitous that I find you both here together,' continued Osfrith. 'There is a matter of some importance that I need to speak to you both about.'

'Oh?' asked Loki, one dark eyebrow raised in sardonic enquiry.

'Yes,' said Osfrith, apparently missing the tone of Loki's response, or choosing to ignore it. 'As I'm sure you're aware, the forthcoming invasion is going to rely very heavily on reliable information. Details of enemy troop numbers and deployment, town defences and perhaps, more importantly, the mood of the people.'

'Sweyn has many informants along the eastern coast of England. This much I know for a fact. I've carried messages between them and the council for many years,' said Loki.

Although he hadn't known it before, this news did not particularly surprise Edgar. Loki was a very active trader between England and Denmark, he was a natural conduit for information.

'Indeed,' said Osfrith, nodding. 'Your service is highly spoken of at the court.'

'Do you need Loki and his crew to gather information from these informants?' asked Edgar, tiring of the two men, or at least Loki, dancing to a tune that he could not hear.

'Yes, but I've been instructed by Jarl Asbjorn to recruit further informants for a more active role.' He paused to let

The Lost Land

the words sink in. Edgar looked at Loki, who showed no surprise at all.

'These teams will be small, no more than four or five men each. They will be dropped along the coast and collected an appropriate time later. This work is of vital importance; it could mean the difference between success and failure.'

'Is Asbjorn not confident in the size and readiness of his army?' asked Loki.

'It's more subtle than that, as I'm quite sure you are aware, Captain,' said Osfrith.

'Subtlety is not a trait I have come to associate with the Jarl,' said Loki.

Osfrith looked taken aback.

'Loki...' began Edgar.

Loki shook his head. 'Forget it,' he said.

'Of course numbers are important, vital even. But good information can make a bare victory into a decisive one. You know this,' said Osfrith, reasonably.

Loki nodded and sighed. 'Very well, go on.'

'Edgar, I would like you to lead one of my new teams. You still have your carls with you? The ones I met in Bortone?'

'Two of them, my lord. We lost Eric during our flight to the coast. Without the help rendered by Captain Loki here and his crew, I doubt any of us would have escaped with our lives.'

Osfrith nodded slowly. 'I am sorry for the loss of your man. Take the two you have then, and I shall assign Hallvindur here to your party to make up the numbers.'

'I have a third man, sir. We captured him as a Norman spy, but it turns out he's not a Norman at all. He is, however, a first-class sneak.'

'You trust him?'

'He has done good work for us and even saved our lives in the past, sir. Yes, I trust him.'

Osfrith still looked doubtful.

'I have had opportunity to assess the character and worth of this man of whom Edgar speaks,' said Loki. 'I consider him trustworthy.'

Osfrith's expression softened. 'In that case, you shall take him, too.'

'Alright. I'll try to find him, then,' said Edgar, puzzled by Osfrith's total acceptance of Loki's words when he had seemed to doubt Edgar's own.

'You don't know where he is?'

'I hardly ever know where Alaric is. He will somehow know that he's wanted and will appear.'

'Remarkable.'

'That he is, sir.'

Osfrith nodded, pleased.

'Good. Well, you must inform your men. You will need peasant clothing. You've spent time travelling under the Normans' noses before. I'm sure I don't need to tell you how to go about it. Captain Loki,' Osfrith turned to the small sea captain.

'You are requisitioning my ship and her crew to transport these spy teams of yours.'

'I'm glad we understand each other, sir.'

'Well, let's say that I understand you, shall we? And that I understand Asbjorn.'

Osfrith frowned slightly.

'Alright. I'll be in contact with you both in due course with more details.'

Edgar bowed slightly to the king's thegn.

Loki did not reply.

'Thank you,' said Osfrith. 'Until later, then.'

He turned and limped away.

'What was all that about?' demanded Edgar.

Loki shook his head angrily. 'Another time, Edgar.' He stomped away towards his ship, leaving Edgar puzzled and concerned.

Guthrum and Halfdene received the news of their assignment with considerable enthusiasm. The opportunity to return to English soil so quickly was unexpected and very welcome.

'We'll pretend to be refugees; our village and fields having been destroyed by Normans. That will explain why we're moving from settlement to settlement.'

'Sounds familiar,' said Guthrum.

'Quite. I think that's why Osfrith has chosen us to perform this task. We've already had to live off our wits whilst travelling through the country. We've done it before; we can do it again. This time there'll be no need to find a place to settle, we just gauge the mood in each settlement and then move on. We can live off the land as we go.'

'Hopefully, we can incite more to rebellion as we travel, or at least encourage them to join the invasion when it begins in earnest,' said Halfdene.

'I think incitement could easily be seen as part of our mission,' replied Edgar.

'We need Alaric,' said Halfdene, thoughtfully.

Edgar smiled. Halfdene had been the most inclined to kill the supposed Norman spy when he had first been captured by them. Edgar now realised that the capture of

Alaric had been an illusion. If Alaric had not intended to be captured, there was no way that he could have been. It had been Eric who had captured him in the first place, along with Osfrid, a carl of Thegn Godric of Deorby, who had accompanied Edgar during the months of his search for his abducted wife.

Edgar nodded slowly. 'I have a feeling that Alaric will know when he is needed.'

The other two mumbled their agreement through mouthfuls of ale.

'There is one issue we have not addressed since we got here, and I think it is time we did,' said Edgar.

He sensed, rather than saw, Guthrum stiffen beside him.

'My lord,' began Guthrum, formally.

'No, Guthrum. No. It has been long enough. Halfdene.'

Halfdene picked up all three men's cups. 'To start, we need more ale,' he said. He walked across the hall to the buckets of ale. He dipped the serving spoon in and filled each of the cups. Whilst he was there, he picked up a fourth cup and filled that one also with ale. Then he returned to the table. He set one cup in front of each man and then waited in silence until Edgar turned to him and nodded.

'Eric,' began Halfdene, 'was my friend. He was stout of heart and strong in battle. The strength of his arm was legendary, the power of his shield unbreakable. His devotion to his friends was total, his hatred of his enemies terrible to behold. His loyalty to his thegn was a lesson to us all, it was complete and it was selfless. I grieve deeply for my friend. I wish he were here.'

Silence followed as the three men contemplated Eric's life and death.

The Lost Land

As the silence stretched out, Edgar spoke.

'Eric was my friend. As a servant and carl to my grandfather, the thegn, he was without par. His arm was strong, his heart was huge. He was as loyal a friend as a man could wish for. He was as loyal a carl as any thegn could desire. I miss his laughter, I miss his voice, I miss his strong arm. I wish he were here.'

The silence stretched out for some time. Gently, Edgar said 'Guthrum, will you not speak for our friend?'

Guthrum breathed deeply. 'Aye, my lord,' he answered, eventually.

'Eric was my friend. Eric was my brother. When first I saw him, he was practising with the axe. Clumsily. I took the axe from him and I showed him how to use it. From that day, he never forgot. We managed our thegn's estate together, we fought together, we protected our young master together, we ate together, we drank together, we laughed together, we attempted to flee the accursed Norman together. He fell fighting with us. There is no nobler way for a friend and brother to fall.' Guthrum's eyes were moist with unshed tears. 'Farewell, my friend. Farewell, my brother. I wish you were here but you are not, and so we drink this drink for you. Farewell, our friend. Farewell, our brother.'

Guthrum took up the fourth cup of ale that Halfdene had brought to the table and drank from it. He handed the cup to Edgar, who took a second swig. Edgar then handed the cup to Halfdene, who finished off the contents.

Edgar stood and addressed the whole hall. 'My friends!' he called. 'My friends!' The conversations in the hall subsided as each face turned towards Edgar. 'My friends, tonight my carls and I drink to the memory of our dear brother Eric, who died on the end of a Norman arrow as we were making our way to this place. Will you drink with us to the memory of Eric of Rapendun, faithful carl and friend?'

All eyes in the hall were on Edgar.

'Eric!' they shouted, 'Eric!'

This was a regular ritual amongst the English exiles. One individual was being recalled by name, but the atmosphere was heavy with other, unspoken names.

Edgar raised his cup in thanks to those present and sat down again.

Guthrum stared bleakly at something far away, and a single tear slid down his cheek. Edgar looked away, and Halfdene carefully studied the bottom of his ale cup.

The following morning, Edgar was once again down by the dockside, watching as Stormleaper was provisioned with materials for her voyage to England. A small army of labourers carried sacks of food and sealed skins of water, all under the watchful eye of Captain Loki. Loki looked up from his labours and noticed Edgar, but he did not call him down to join him, merely returned to his work.

Edgar had a strong sense that now was not the right time to try to get to the bottom of Loki's strange hostility towards Osfrith Edwinsson yesterday, so he turned and walked towards his quarters.

He passed a practice field as he walked, and noticed Halfdene and Guthrum, practising axe and shield work. The axe was still the preferred weapon of the Englishman and the Dane; the small, single-bladed type being lighter and much cheaper than a sword. Most experienced practitioners believed that the axe was a more versatile weapon. An axe could be used to strike an opponent, of course, but it could also be used as a hook to drag and pull at an enemy and his shield. An accomplished axeman could disarm an opponent in two swift swings of the axe. A good pull on an axe hooked around the top of an opponent's shield could break your enemy's arm and leave him vulnerable to a fatal blow on the return stroke.

Edgar watched his men practising for a while, impressed with their aptitude. Guthrum was a supremely skilled fighter, and Edgar noticed how he was pushing Halfdene to his limit, occasionally stopping to correct Halfdene's stance or timing.

Edgar was proficient with the axe, mostly due to Guthrum's training regime, which he had kept up to this day. Now, however, he was working more with the sword. Before Edgar left his home in Rapendun to face the invading Norwegian army at Stanford nearly three years ago, his grandfather, then thegn of Rapendun, had given Edgar an exceptionally fine sword. Edgar mostly kept this sword sheathed, using plainer models for his practice. Whenever the sword was unsheathed and on display, it always attracted a small crowd of admirers, eager to look at its fine craftsmanship. Occasionally, Edgar would demonstrate its cutting ability – for the blade held an edge like no other sword he had ever known. He sometimes came across people who had seen a sword like his before. They carried the name 'Ulfberht' on the blade, and all were believed to be very old, though nobody claimed to have seen a finer one than that which hung at Edgar's side.

Edgar turned onto the practice field, loosening the loops that held his sword within its scabbard. He positioned himself in front of one of the large wooden poles set up for sword practice. With ease, he slipped the sword from its scabbard and swung it experimentally in his hand. The balance was astounding, the sword seemed to weigh far less in the hand than it actually should. He swung the sword at the wooden post, not putting a great deal of force behind it, yet it still embedded itself half its own width into the post. He pulled it out and swiftly spun round, bringing the opposite side of the blade down in a sharp chopping motion into the post's other side. The swing sliced through the side of the post, removing a thick wedge from it. Edgar brought his sword blade up to his face to examine the blade. There was no damage, the blade was incredibly hard.

He heard a cough and looked up. In front of him stood a squat, thickset man with wild greying hair and an unkempt beard. He was wearing well-worn leather armour.

'Care to practise on something a little less docile?' asked the man.

'Certainly,' replied Edgar.

The man smiled and handed Edgar a round shield. 'Harek,' he said, introducing himself.

'Edgar,' replied Edgar, taking the shield from him and threading his left arm through the leather strap on its back.

Harek watched him. 'You've damaged that shoulder in the past,' he commented; a statement, not a question.

'Yes, I broke it in battle two and a half years ago, it's fixed now,' said Edgar, somewhat surprised.

'No, it isn't. You're still compensating for the pain, even if the pain itself has gone. You've got into bad habits. We'll start with that.'

Edgar nodded. 'Alright.' He lifted his sword and stood ready.

Harek raised his eyebrows at the fineness of Edgar's

blade but made no comment. He hoisted his shield onto his arm and stood face to face with Edgar.

'Are you ready?'

'I'm ready.'

'I don't think you are.'

'I tell you I'm ready,' said Edgar tetchily.

'Alright,' said Harek and launched himself at Edgar. Edgar was thrown instantly onto the defensive, but could not withstand the fierce onslaught from Harek. In just four blows from Harek's sword, Edgar was on the ground, his own sword flipped from his hand and the tip of Harek's sword at his throat.

Edgar half laughed. 'Well, I thought I was ready.'

Harek held out his hand and helped Edgar to his feet. 'I told you you weren't,' he said, seriously.

'How did you do that?' asked Edgar.

'Your weakness is fairly obvious, and it's easy to take advantage of. What did you notice about the blows I was making on your shield?'

'They were all downward, and heavy.'

'Exactly. If your left shoulder had been at full strength, and if you weren't unknowingly protecting it from further damage, I would not have found that so easy.'

'How did you flip my sword out of my hand so easily?' asked Edgar, looking in some surprise at his empty right hand.

'That's a lesson for another day. For now, we need to concentrate on that left shoulder. If we don't fix that, it may very well be the death of you.'

'Yes, I see that now. Though I've had a few fights since I broke it and nobody else seems to have noticed it. Even I hadn't noticed it.'

'It only takes one,' said Harek. 'Again. This time, be conscious of your shield position, lift it higher than you think you can. You'll be weak at first, but with sufficient practice that will improve.'

Edgar retrieved his sword and again took up the ready position. Harek launched himself again at Edgar, who tried to lift his shield higher than before. He felt the weakness then, and the battering of Harek's sword brought his arm down again and he once more found himself with Harek's blade just inches from his throat.

'Again,' said Harek.

This time, Edgar fended the blows off for a little longer.

'Better,' said Harek. 'But before we do much more on this, I want you to work this muscle really hard.' He gripped Edgar's left shoulder as he spoke.

'Look,' he searched the ground around him, eventually picking up a large stone. 'This isn't big enough, but it will do for a demonstration.'

He held the stone in his left hand and lifted it up and down above his head. 'Like this, and like this,' he held the stone away from his body in front of him and then to his left, each time lifting the stone high above his head.

'Then this,' he rotated his fully extended arm in front of him and then to the side.

'Find a stone that you find fairly difficult to lift with one hand and do these exercises as much as you can. We'll practise more with the shield in a week when the strength has built up a bit.'

'Thank you, Harek,' said Edgar, rubbing his shoulder.

By this time, Guthrum and Halfdene had made their way across the field to watch.

'Your technique is unusual,' said Guthrum. 'I would like

to learn more, if you would teach me along with my young master here.'

'Harek, this is Guthrum, and this is Halfdene, my housecarls,' said Edgar.

Harek bowed slightly to each in turn.

'You bested Thegn Edgar quite easily then,' said Guthrum. 'That's something of an affront to me personally, as I have been his trainer since he was old enough to pick up an axe. Would you care to try your arm against mine?'

Harek grinned. 'It would be a pleasure to match skills with you, Guthrum.'

Guthrum took Edgar's shield and held his axe ready. Harek raised his shield and held his sword loosely in his right hind.

Without warning, Guthrum leaped forward and swung his axe down onto the rim of Harek's shield, intending to drag it down. With a speed that astonished Guthrum, Harek dropped his shield very slightly, just enough to loosen Guthrum's grip on his shield edge. Then with a fast and surprisingly strong movement, he thrust his shield up, taking up the temporary slack in Guthrum's arm and snapping it upwards. The axe was forced from Guthrum's grip and was sent spinning upwards and away from them. Harek then thrust forward with his shield, forcing Guthrum onto the back foot. Harek's sword stopped as it began pressing into Guthrum's jerkin just beneath his belly button.

Guthrum stopped and stared open-mouthed at the sword touching his jerkin.

'How…' he began, but he couldn't finish the question.

'I've been doing this a long time,' said Harek gently. 'I practise every day with sword and axe. I've developed methods of using the shield as an effective offensive weapon rather than simply a defensive one. When I'm not practising with my weapons, I'm working to strengthen every muscle in my body. You could call it my passion.'

Harek stepped back from Guthrum and lowered his sword.

He raised his voice slightly. 'I see you are all English exiles. I take it then that you will be joining Jarl Asbjorn's expedition to England?'

'Yes, we will,' said Edgar.

'Then we have little time. I will teach you what I can in what time we have, if you wish.'

'We do,' said Edgar, without even glancing at his carls. He knew what their answer would be. Guthrum and Halfdene both muttered their agreement.

'Good. Guthrum, you should retrieve your axe.'

For the next two weeks, Edgar, Guthrum and Halfdene trained constantly with Harek. His teaching was rigorous, and he gave none of them any quarter. Even when all three of them attacked him at once, he could beat them back, usually disarming at least two of them. The man's skill and strength were prodigious. Edgar had always considered Guthrum to have been his finest tutor in the arts of warfare, but even Guthrum agreed without any hesitation that Harek's skill and teaching ability far outweighed his own.

Edgar had taken Harek's advice to heart, and even after a long training day, he had returned to his quarters, where he had picked up his heavy stone and performed the exercises that Harek had shown him on the first day. Even after only a week, he had felt the benefits. His shoulder was stronger and he could react faster. Harek had declared himself content with Edgar's progress and pushed him to greater and greater efforts.

One evening, after a tough day of constant practice and exercising, the four of them sat down beneath a tree at the edge of the training field. The sun was dipping towards the horizon, though there was still heat left in it. It had been a mercilessly hot day, and the training had been difficult, but at long last, Harek had grunted and declared that they had done enough for the day.

They were sitting silently, leather jerkins removed to allow their sodden undershirts to dry. Edgar turned to Harek.

'How old are you, Harek?'

Harek frowned briefly. 'I'm not altogether sure, but it's somewhere between fifty-two and fifty-four years.'

'You put us to shame,' said Edgar.

'Less so with each passing day. You are progressing well,' he looked round at them. 'All of you.'

They watched as a column of armed men marched past the practice field, heading towards the temporary camp on the far side of Roskilde. The armour they wore was unfamiliar to Edgar, and they called to each other in a strange language as they marched. Their tongue seemed totally unlike Danish or English. He turned a quizzical face towards Harek.

'Poles,' said Harek. 'Sweyn-king has many allies, and all are sworn to help him in his great matter. We have contingents from Denmark, England and Scotland, and from Poland, Saxony and Frisia. The Saxons and the Frisians speak languages close enough to ours to be understood, but these lads,' he waved his hand towards the retreating Poles. 'I don't know. God knows how we're going to communicate with them. Bloody good fighters, though.

I've seen 'em in action.'

'What's in it for them?' asked Guthrum. 'What part of England are they going to claim when it's all over?'

'It's not like that,' replied Harek. 'It's politics and diplomacy. They help us now in our battles, we'll help them later, in theirs. Like I say, they're good lads to have on your side in a scrap. I suppose they must think the same about us,' he laughed shortly. 'And they'd be right.'

That evening, the leaders of the expedition were called into conference with Jarl Asbjorn. Osfrith had requested that Edgar accompany him.

As the Jarl entered the room, everyone rose.

'Be seated,' said the Jarl curtly. Without waiting for everyone to sit, Jarl Asbjorn began speaking.

'As you know, my aunt's grandsons, Godwin, Edmund and Magnus Haroldson, sons of my murdered cousin Harold Godwinson, were due to make an incursion into south-western England at around this time. News has now reached us of their attack.'

Excited stirrings rippled round the room. Asbjorn held up his hand for silence and continued.

'The sons of Harold sailed from their fastness in Ireland at Midsummer. Their fleet consisted of around sixty-five ships, each carrying between thirty and fifty warriors. Initially, they raided along the Avon. They laid siege briefly to the port of Brycgstowe. The siege does not seem to have gone well for the Haroldsons, and it was apparently lifted after only a short time. Further raids took place along the north coast of the territory known as Defenscir, culminating in a landing near a town called Barnestaple.'

A mutter of recognition arose from a couple of the

exiled English thegns. Asbjorn continued.

'There they were met by a small army raised from the local levies. Although under Norman leadership, we should all take note that the men fighting in the defence force were English.'

Mutters of discontent and disbelief arose from the assembled nobles.

'Now it must also be borne in mind that the invading force was probably seen as an Irish raiding party, and may not have been recognised for the liberating army it was supposed to be.'

Asbjorn's face took on a look of barely disguised disgust. 'Which is hardly surprising considering the amount of loot they are said to have taken in their raids. Although the Haroldsons are claiming victory over the defenders, they took to their ships immediately and returned to Ireland.'

Edgar felt a rush of disappointment at the failure of the King's sons to secure a foothold in England. It sounded like nothing more than a mildly irritating raid, not the start of a concerted campaign to restore the throne of England to its legitimate succession.

'The Haroldsons' army was, we feel, too small and too undisciplined. However, it has served to distract the Bastard, his eyes will now surely be on the west coast at least as much as the east. His forces will be split. We have five times as many ships as the Haroldsons had, and more disciplined and motivated fighters. We also have the lawful claimant to the throne, which must be in our favour. We need to act before the Bastard has chance to rethink his defence policy, and whilst his forces are still split. We will sail within the month.'

A cheer arose from the assembled commanders. There

was clearly disappointment in the room at the feeble nature of what had been intended to be the first blow in the reconquest of England. Yet the Jarl's words had found their mark. The joint forces of the Danes, the English and their allies would surely succeed where a few Irish raiders had failed.

5

Voyage and Landing

August 1069

As part of one of the advanced information-gathering groups, Edgar set sail with Loki two weeks ahead of the main task force. Stormleaper glided gracefully out of the harbour, powered by her oarsmen until they were clear of all the other ships of the fleet. Loki then ordered that the sail be raised. Edgar joined the crew as they pulled on ropes attached to wooden pulleys at the top of the mast. The sail was heavy, but soon it was secured in position and it filled with the moderate breeze. The oars were stowed and the great sleek vessel ploughed its way through the waves towards the north.

The wide bay of Roskilde lies well protected from the open sea. Roskilde Fjord, a narrow strait, more like a broad river, heads north for more than twenty miles before it meets open water.

Guthrum sat amongst the rowers amidships. Edgar

watched him with some concern, knowing his friend's intense dislike of sea travel, and the illness that the swaying of the ship brought to him. Sure enough, within a few minutes, Guthrum had struggled past the oarsman to the edge of the ship and now hung his head over the side of the vessel.

The oarsmen around him cheered cruelly and slapped him on the back. Edgar looked around the ship to check on the other members of his team.

Halfdene sat with the rowers, having taken his place pulling with them. He was chatting amiably with a couple of men around him. He had no problems getting his sea legs. Sitting behind him was Harek, who along with Osfrith's housecarl Hallvindur had also been rowing. They, too, seemed unconcerned by the rolling of the ship as it moved on into more open seas.

He looked round as he felt someone sit down beside him. It was Alaric, the inconspicuous little man whom Edgar and his carls had captured as a Norman spy. No, Edgar corrected himself, Alaric was the inconspicuous little man who had allowed himself to be captured whilst playing the part of a Norman spy. In the months after his 'capture', Alaric had proved himself a loyal and invaluable ally. Edgar still did not understand Alaric's true motivations, and perhaps he never would, but for now, he was a singularly useful member of Edgar's band.

'How does seafaring sit on your stomach, Alaric?'

'My stomach is unconcerned, my lord,' replied the little spy. 'In fact, I find the rolling motion to be quite soothing. Being too small and weak to man the oars, I have much time to think. And snooze a little.'

During planning sessions with Osfrith, Alaric's role had

The Lost Land

been clearly defined. As Edgar's team was to land in advance of the main invasion force and ease the route for them, so Alaric was to land in advance of Edgar's team. A single man can hide more easily and gauge the lie of the land, preparing the way for the larger group. Alaric would make landfall two days in advance of the rest of them and would find the best landing place for Edgar and his men. To this end, a small skiff was being towed behind Stormleaper. Hallvindur had volunteered to row Alaric ashore and then return with the skiff to Stormleaper. Two nights later, Alaric would light a fire at the place he had selected, and Stormleaper would beach at that spot. The rough landing area was already decided on, a length of coastline about five miles long. The area was called Heldernesse, and Edgar had first heard of it when it was ravaged by the invading army of Harald Sigurdson in the lead up to the fateful battle at Stanford, where Edgar had received his horrific facial injuries.

'What's your plan of action?' asked Edgar.

'I have several alternative strategies, depending on what I find when I get there, and what people I meet. Some strategies I like better than others, but my best plans usually form at the moment that I need them. Initially, I intend to remain hidden, or at least very inconspicuous. Finding a suitable landing spot is my priority. Anything else would be a bonus.' He paused, looking along the length of the ship. He looked sidelong at Edgar. 'I'll let you know the details of my plan when it's happened.'

Edgar laughed. Alaric's display of calm confidence was an inspiration. He sometimes thought that was one of the most important things that Alaric brought to the table.

He slapped Alaric on the back and stood up. Gingerly, he stepped between the men sitting in the boat and made his way to the stern, where Loki stood, his hand on the tiller.

'You look better,' he said.

It was true. On land, Loki was often grim, sullen and uncommunicative. Now he looked relaxed, and a contented smile played around the corners of his mouth.

'I'm always better at sea,' he said. 'There's nothing like the feel of the ship beneath your feet and the pressure of the tiller in your hand. The wind in the sail and the bracing sea spray in your face.'

'I'm not sure Guthrum would agree with you,' said Edgar, nodding towards the still puking man.

'He'll be alright. He got his sea legs eventually on our flight from England. He'll do so again on our return. Don't worry, I've never heard of anyone who actually died as a result of seasickness.'

'At least we have a moderately calm sea.'

'It should remain so for the full voyage. Look at the sky.'

Edgar looked up. The sky was a clear, pale blue, marred only by some distant thin clouds over the land behind them.

'I hope you're right, for Guthrum's sake if nothing else.'

'I'm right.'

As Loki had promised, the weather remained calm for the full voyage.

Early on the eighth morning, a line of haze on the horizon ahead of them announced their arrival in English waters. Loki ordered the sail to be dropped. Edgar walked to the stern to stand beside him.

'The coasts will be watched,' said Loki. 'It would be foolish to announce our arrival by waving a huge sail at them.' He raised his voice and shouted down the ship.

The Lost Land

'Ready oars!'

The crew leaped into action, picking up the oars from the bottom of the boat and lowering them into the rowlocks ready for use.

Once the oars were all in place and the oarsmen set, Loki ordered them to begin rowing.

'This way we'll be much less visible,' he said.

Within an hour of the oars being deployed, Edgar could make out a dark line on the horizon ahead of them, and an hour after that, the coastline could be clearly seen. Thin tendrils of smoke rose from settlements along the coast.

'This is quite a busy coast, there are small ports all along here, dealing with local and more far-flung trade,' said Loki. 'As we have nothing to trade, it would be very suspicious if we were to arrive at a port and dock there. Too simple. We'll stay out here and your men can make their own way. Nobody would suspect a simple skiff like this,' he pointed at the skiff behind them with his thumb.

'Alaric, Hallvindur, your time is now,' he called.

Obediently, the two men rose from their seats and proceeded to the rear of the boat. An ill-matched pair, it seemed, Alaric small and trim, Hallvindur tall, broad and shaggy.

A crewman leaned over Stormleaper's stern and began pulling at the thick rope that connected the skiff to the ship. The skiff drew alongside the backboard side, and with many helping hands, first Hallvindur and then Alaric were lowered into it. Oars were passed down to Hallvindur, who carefully fitted them in place. Alaric untied the knot holding the skiff to the connecting rope and Hallvindur began pulling at the oars. Alaric waved cheerfully to the crew as the skiff pulled off towards the distant shore.

Edgar watched as the skiff grew smaller and smaller, a knot of anxiety growing in his stomach. He was keen to assist in the reconquest of England, but he did not relish the thought of facing the Normans in battle. He had fought and killed many of them before, but mostly on a small scale, rarely exceeding two dozen combatants. A pitched battle was another matter. The Normans were tough and disciplined fighters. This was not going to be easy.

The skiff vanished into the coastal haze, Hallvindur never letting up from his rowing. It was a good two miles to the shore and would take him at least two hours to complete, but he was strong and determined.

It was not easy to keep Stormleaper in place as they waited for Hallvindur's return. Currents tended to move the ship away. Loki kept careful watch on the distant shoreline, locating tiny details with his hawk-like eyes, and passing instructions to the oarsmen to pull first this way, then that. It was intense work, especially for Loki, whose concentration could not waver for a minute. It therefore came as a great relief when one crewman cried out that he had seen a small boat some way to their south. Instantly, everyone strained to see what the crewman had seen. Just visible rolling up and down was a small craft. It dipped in the trough of the waves and was lost, then crested on the next wave and was seen again.

Loki called out his orders, and Stormleaper swung rapidly round and darted across the swell towards the vessel. Was it Hallvindur? From this distance, there was no way to tell. But who else would be out here this far from shore in a boat of that small size?

In ten minutes, Stormleaper pulled up by the small craft. It was indeed Hallvindur, looking exhausted and plastered with sea spray and sweat. Loki threw the rope to him and he caught it. They pulled the boats together and with help from the crewmen, he climbed up into Stormleaper.

Loki strode over and began to quiz him.

'Did you see any other boats?'

'No sir.'

'Was there anyone on shore to see you land?'

'No, the whole area seemed deserted. If anyone saw us, we certainly did not see them. Alaric seemed content that he was unseen.'

'How far were you from settlement?'

'I cannot say, I saw nothing as we rowed in and we landed at the foot of a steep embankment. I didn't leave the boat, so I never got to see what was beyond it. There were no signs of habitation in the area we landed in.'

'Sounds good,' said Edgar.

'So far,' agreed Loki. He turned his back on Hallvindur and returned to the tiller.

'Well done, Hallvindur, get some water and rest,' said Edgar.

'Thank you, sir,' replied the big man and struggled to his feet. He wobbled down the ship where he sat down and took a skin of water that was handed to him by a crewman.

Edgar stood beside Loki.

'We must make landfall before dark,' said Loki. 'We don't want to draw attention to this part of the coast so we'll head south to the great river mouth. We can land there and make camp.'

Swiftly, Loki turned to his crew and shouted orders. The oars were put in place and soon they were heading south-east. Once the coast was out of sight, Loki ordered the sail to be raised, and they took advantage of a stiff northerly breeze.

After an hour, Loki steered the ship towards the west, back towards the coast. A short while later, Edgar saw a long spur of land ahead of them, the miles-wide mouth of the great river beyond it.

Loki nodded his satisfaction. 'We're on a good tack, we must round this spur and then we can make landfall on the far side of it, though first we'll move a little further upriver and drop off a hunting party. We'll make a camp down at this end of the spur, but we must have fresh meat first.'

As they made their way up the southern edge of the spur, Edgar watched the changing landscape with interest. The end of the spur just seemed to consist of piles of stones, whilst the further upriver they went, the lusher the vegetation. The area seemed to be quite uninhabited.

'This land used to belong to a Danish warlord,' said Loki. 'I heard tell of him from a very old sea-captain when I was just beginning my explorations of this coast. The warlord's name was Hrafn, and so this strip of land is known as Hrafn's Spur. This would have been at the time when a Danish kingdom was still ruled from Jorvik. Hrafn settled here as an old man. At least that's what I was told. Who knows?'

'It looks deserted now. I suppose this Hrafn left no followers behind to keep his place going.'

'I've rarely seen anyone along here. It's a good resting spot. Here,' he swung the tiller and the ship turned in towards the muddy shore. 'Landing!' he shouted, and his men took up their landing positions.

Stormleaper grounded on the soft mud a few feet from the shore and Loki's men leaped out into the water, taking ropes with them. All those left on the ship hurried to the stern so that the prow was high as it was pulled further up the shore with the ropes.

'Welcome home,' said Loki.

Edgar snorted. He walked to the prow of the ship and jumped down into the soft mud of the shore. Guthrum and Halfdene had volunteered for the hunting party and were gathering hunting bows and arrows from the ship's stores.

'Take it easy, lads,' Edgar said to them. 'Loki says this area is uninhabited, but we can't be too careful. Those bloody Normans will be sticking their snotty noses into every corner of the kingdom, no matter how remote and deserted.'

'We'll take care,' said Halfdene with a smile. 'After all, we're just a trading concern, yes?'

'Yes. Nevertheless…'

'I'll look after the lad,' said Guthrum, looking only too pleased to have his feet back on solid ground once more.

The six men who comprised the hunting party slipped away into the brush-covered land and were gone.

Stormleaper was re-beached further down towards the end of Hrafn's Spur, and eight cooking fires hissed and crackled along the beach. Kindling for the fires was to be found in great abundance at this end of the spur. Dead bushes stood all around, their branches dry and whitened by the sun. It burned quickly, though, and large quantities had to be gathered.

Pots rested on iron tripods in the fires, and the plentiful game killed by the hunting party boiled and roasted on each fire, sending enticing smells wafting amongst the hungry crew.

'What's it like back there?' asked Edgar as Guthrum

poked his fire with a stick and added more dried wood.

'Solid vegetation. There are no roads, not even animal tracks. It's a very narrow strip of land, only a hundred or two yards across. If the Normans want to investigate this area, they'll have to do it by boat. We barely made our way through the bush as it was. It's just as well that the place is teeming with hares. We couldn't have travelled far.'

'Loki was right, then. This is a good resting place.'

'Seems so.'

Guthrum resumed his fire-tending.

'You seem out of sorts,' said Edgar.

Guthrum slowly placed his stick down.

'Sorry,' he said. 'It's just that where we dropped Alaric off this morning isn't that far from where we lost Eric. I'm just aware that we had to leave his body where he fell. We never had the opportunity to give him a proper burial, to say our farewells by his graveside.'

Edgar sighed. He had been thinking the same things as he watched Alaric disappear towards the coastline.

'I know. Some day we may have the opportunity to find where he ended up.'

Edgar thought back to the terrible day of Eric's death. They had been assisted in the fight by some local carls, working against the orders of their thegn, a weak and desperate man who had reported Edgar's presence to the Norman baron, Roger de Barentin.

'I'm sure that Cendred and Agra will have given him a decent burial, they were honourable men and knew and liked Eric. They wouldn't have left his body where it fell.'

'What if they had no choice? The Normans weren't far away, they would have had time to regroup and come back.'

'I don't think so. I was watching their leader, de

Barentin. I saw him recognise defeat. I saw him turn and go. His men would have followed.'

'I hope we get the chance to find where he is,' said Guthrum.

'We have other priorities at the moment, but if we get the opportunity, I promise we'll look.'

'Thanks,' mumbled Guthrum.

'I wish I could find out where Gifu is buried, but I don't see that happening either, do you?'

Guthrum turned round to face Edgar.

'Oh, Edgar,' he said, his face filled with grief. 'I'm sorry, I didn't mean…'

'It's alright, Guthrum. I've come to terms with that.'

Edgar's wife, Godgifu, had been abducted by Norman raiders and had eventually poisoned herself, having taken several of her abductors to the grave with her. Edgar had never learned where she had been buried, or even if she had received a proper burial at all.

'God knows his own,' he quoted an oft-repeated saying amongst soldiers. Many of those killed in battle received no proper burial and no priestly rites to help their passing. Even the priests admitted that the lack of the correct rites was probably no bar to the soldiers receiving their eternal reward. It was a special case, they said, and God did not mind.

Edgar wondered how the priests knew what God thought, and why they believed that he did not mind in this case when apparently an unshriven man or woman in any other case would go straight to hell without the intervention of a priest. Edgar suspected that the priests allowed God to think only in the way that would best suit their purposes. Unconsciously, he rubbed the small raven amulet that hung around his neck, a gift from the mysterious old woman who had lifted much of the grief he felt over the death of his wife. She had made him drink a strange concoction which had given him exceptionally vivid dreams and had finally drained away the last vestiges of belief he had had in a loving God who personally intervened in men's affairs.

Guthrum watched Edgar's hand as it reached for the amulet. He had noticed Edgar doing this many times, an unconscious gesture, like when he reached for the lines of scar-tissue on his battle-ravaged face and stroked them.

'I've been meaning to ask you about that amulet,' said Guthrum.

'What, this?' Edgar lifted the amulet away from his neck.

'Yes. I first noticed it after you went missing in the woods that time.'

'There's nothing to it.'

'I think there is.'

'I said there's nothing to it, Guthrum,' said Edgar sharply.

'As you wish, my lord.'

Edgar instantly regretted his harsh tone. Guthrum was the closest thing to a father-figure he had in this world.

'I'm sorry, Guthrum. It's not a subject I'm ready to talk about, that's all.'

'Alright.' Guthrum picked up his stick and began prodding the fire again.

Late the following evening, as the sun dipped deeper towards the north-western horizon, Loki gave the order for the camp to be struck and for Stormleaper to be refloated.

With an efficiency that was a credit to their captain, the

The Lost Land

men gathered their equipment and stowed it in the ship in bare minutes. The burnt patches where the fires had been were kicked over and covered with fresh sand and stones until no trace could be seen.

Half the crew climbed into Stormleaper and made their way to the rear of the ship, lifting the prow as the other half pushed the ship back into the water. They splashed through the shallows and hoisted themselves on board. The oars were deployed and soon Stormleaper was headed out towards the open sea.

Once clear of Hrafn's Spur, Loki ordered the sail up and they set off eastwards as if heading out to sea.

Loki's timing had been excellent. They were about a mile from shore when the sun slipped behind the land, a fiery orange ball extinguished behind distant hills. Once the shore became difficult to see, Loki turned the ship north, back towards the spot where Alaric had been dropped.

'We'll have to sail up and down the coast until we see the signal. We don't know where he'll have ended up, so we don't know exactly where to look for his fire,' explained Loki. 'So we'll head up and down the coast for an hour or two until we see it.'

They headed north for half an hour until they were considerably further north than the point at which they had dropped Alaric off. Loki gave the order and Stormleaper swung around and headed south again.

A cry went up from one of the crew. 'I see a light!' he called.

The others all strained to see through the darkness. Edgar could just make out a tiny pinprick of light, just on the edge of visibility.

'No,' said Loki. 'Too small. That must be a good way

inland. Alaric will be making his fire very close to the shore, so it should appear quite bright.'

Edgar squinted into the darkness. Without any means of measuring the passage of time, Edgar had no idea of how long they sailed back and forth. He was just beginning to feel the first stirrings of concern when he heard several quiet cries of relief around him. It was Alaric's signal. It just seemed to blink into appearance very suddenly, bright and unmissable. Edgar was puzzled, the coast was fairly flat and featureless along here, there were no appreciable headlands, so how could they not have seen the fire from a greater distance?

'Has he just lit it?' asked Edgar.

'No, that's been going for some time. He's a good man, that spy of yours. He's done exactly what I told him to do.'

'What's that?'

'He's constructed two long baffles, one on either side of the fire, pointing out to sea.'

'Why did you tell him to do that?'

'Two reasons. Firstly, they will shield the light of the fire from any watchers who may be about. A fire can be seen a very long way in the dark, and we don't want to announce our arrival to any Normans who may be patrolling the coast. Secondly, with the fire baffled on each side, we can only see it when we are headed straight towards it. As we can see it now, I know that we are looking right down the corridor formed by the baffles. As long as we keep the fire in view, then we know that we are going to land precisely where Alaric wants us to. If we deviate from that line, the fire will fade and disappear.'

Edgar nodded. 'Ingenious.'

Loki grinned. 'An old smuggler's trick,' he said.

The Lost Land

The sail was lowered and the oars dropped carefully into place. The crew rowed with great care, making as little noise with the oars as possible. As the fire faded out in one direction, Loki called orders for the ship to veer in the other direction, and soon Edgar began to hear the faint sounds of waves dashing up the shingle beach and dragging pebbles noisily back towards the sea. The fire was no longer a tiny point of light, but visible for what it was, and standing to one side of it, Edgar could see a single figure.

Loki called out softly to his men and they started rowing harder. Edgar felt a surge of acceleration as Stormleaper sped towards the shore.

Then with a loud grinding noise, the prow of the ship lifted and ploughed up the beach. The men sitting at the front end of the ship now leaped out into the churning waters of the beach, pulling at ropes to secure Stormleaper. Edgar ran forward and followed the men down onto the beach. The corridor of baffles had worked perfectly. Stormleaper was exactly where she should be. A few dozen yards north, large boulders obstructed the beach. Had Stormleaper hit those, she would surely have broken up.

Alaric was busy throwing sand and soil from the beach onto the fire. Edgar grabbed handfuls of sand and did the same. Once it was extinguished, and without speaking, they both set about dismantling the baffles and spreading the pieces around the beach, to look just like the flotsam and assorted beach-rubbish that it had started as.

Loki joined them. 'Excellent, Alaric. I couldn't have done it better myself.'

'Thank you, Captain. I'm glad to see you safely ashore again, all of you.'

'What's the situation here, Alaric?' asked Edgar. 'How

far is the nearest settlement?'

'About three miles from here there is a small farm, and two miles beyond that there's a fishing village. Probably not more than a hundred people in total. I doubt there will be anyone about to observe us.'

'Nevertheless, we'll sleep on the ship tonight. There will be no camp,' said Loki. 'And before first light, you and your team can leave the ship and we'll set off to join the fleet.'

The ship was made ready as a night shelter. The sail was draped over the crossbeam, turned so that it lay along the length of the ship, making a long tent under which the men could sleep. They ate sparingly of their rations of dried meat and fruit. Two crew members were detailed to stand guard until midnight when they would be relieved by two more.

Being late summer, darkness was very brief, and Edgar was woken after less sleep than he would have liked. The horizon to the north and east was bright, though inside the shrouded ship it was still dark. Edgar woke his men in turn. Guthrum, Halfdene, Hallvindur and Harek pulled on their peasant clothes, reluctantly leaving their armour and weapons behind in the ship.

Edgar handed his sheathed Ulfberht sword to Loki.

'Don't worry, Edgar. Nobody but me shall touch this sword in your absence. I'll store it beneath the deck plank here,' he tapped the removable plank by his tiller position. 'It will be safe.'

'Thank you,' said Edgar. He turned to see his men all standing behind him, ready to go.

'Alright, let's go. We'll meet you back here in seven nights' time.'

Loki nodded and clasped Edgar's arm.

As they left the ship, several of the crew slapped them encouragingly on the backs and shoulders.

The section of the beach where they had landed was similar to the location where Alaric had originally been dropped by Hallvindur. There was a low cliff of crumbling stone, only twenty feet or so high, broken into gullies in many places making it easy to climb up. Alaric was waiting for them at the top. As they reached the top, Edgar looked back to see that Stormleaper was already pulling away out to sea.

He turned back inland, to find his men all standing waiting for him.

'Right lads,' he said cheerfully. 'Let's get our country back.'

6

The Lost Land

The six men walked away from the shore, across a sea of tough, thick grass and patches of gorse. The land appeared uninhabited.

'Which way to the nearest farm, Alaric?' asked Edgar.

Alaric pointed to his left – south.

'That's where we'll head first, then.'

As they walked across the heavy grass, the sun broke free of a bank of low cloud on the north-east horizon. A small bird flitted along in front of them, flashing white tail feathers. High above them, skylarks sang their fluting, tremulous song as they hovered and then fluttered their way back down to the ground.

After a few minutes walking, Alaric led them to a track passing through the long grass. Parallel ruts of dried mud indicated the occasional passage of wheeled vehicles. There was no sign that anything had passed this way for some time. Alaric pointed ahead of them.

The Lost Land

'There,' he said.

A thin column of wispy smoke rose behind some trees in the distance. 'That's the farm I told you about. I visited there yesterday. The farmer and his wife live alone. It's a small concern, but I think they must be able to support themselves reasonably well. They certainly aren't starving.'

'Who's the local thegn?' asked Edgar.

'There doesn't appear to be one. The farmer, Leofwine by name, told me that he expected the tax collector from the thegn to call over two months ago, but he never came. The thegn used to reside at Colton, a couple of miles further on, but the mead hall is abandoned and in a state of some disrepair.'

'Like Rapendun,' said Guthrum.

'I expect Colton is like that for the same reason. The thegn has been chased off by Norman upstarts. They're probably so busy grabbing land that they haven't had time to consolidate what they've already stolen. Leofwine may think he's got away with paying his taxes this year, but I fear he may have a very unpleasant surprise in store. What are his feelings towards the Normans?'

'He seems indifferent, though he hasn't had any personal experience of them as yet. It may be well to speak with him yourself, sir.'

Edgar shook his head. 'No, I'm too recognisable, and my features are well known to the Normans. Don't forget that Roger de Barentin was active here himself less than a year ago. I can't risk being recognised. It'll put us all in danger. Guthrum.'

'Yes?'

'I want you to go to the farm with Alaric. Gain the farmer's confidence. Speak with him about how he really feels and what his neighbours have been saying about the Normans. See if you can find out what their reaction to a reconquest would be. I know he's not important, but we need to know the quality of any groundswell that we may be able to raise.'

'Very good, my lord,' replied Guthrum.

They walked on until they were almost at the trees. Edgar sent Alaric and Guthrum ahead to speak to the farmer. Then he ordered the other men to sit down and await Alaric's return. They moved away from the path and settled amongst the trees.

'Once Guthrum and Alaric return, we'll head into Colton, see if we can find out exactly what happened to the thegn, and who professes to be lord there now.'

As Edgar was speaking, Halfdene held up his hand.

'Shh!' he said. 'Listen.'

They stopped and listened carefully. Behind them, in the distance but getting closer, they could hear the sound of galloping horses' hooves on the path.

'Get down,' hissed Edgar.

The four men lay flat in the long grass and awaited the horsemen.

'Let's hope Guthrum and Alaric have heard them,' whispered Halfdene.

'We have company. Get off the road!' said Guthrum, urgently tugging at Alaric's sleeve.

'No, I heard them. Running would only make them chase us. They're like dogs. If something runs from them, they chase it. Stay your ground and look suitably awed as they pass.'

Alaric shuffled Guthrum over to the side of the road

The Lost Land

and then stood staring in wonder at the horsemen as they approached.

There were four of them, in mail coats and wearing helmets. As Alaric had predicted, they rode straight past, not acknowledging the presence of the two men at all.

Guthrum watched their retreating backs and grunted. 'Well, well,' he muttered.

'You see?' said Alaric. 'One of the first things I learned as a spy is that usually the best place to hide is right out there in the open where everyone can see you. Those riders saw two weak and useless peasants walking along the road. They did not see the vanguard of an invasion. People see what they expect to see. If they had caught a glimpse of us running then they would have seen something suspicious. Just wandering along the road, we didn't look suspicious, just everyday. The secret is always to look everyday.'

'I get it,' said Guthrum, looking thoughtfully down the road after the horsemen. 'Come on, we need to get to that farm.'

They walked another half-mile until they reached the farmhouse. It was a poor thing, nestling in a small fold of land, surrounded by fruit trees. Chickens squabbled in the stamped earth courtyard.

As they approached, a crook-backed man walked round the side of the house. He was maybe forty years old, thin grey hair surrounded a large bald patch. He looked up in surprise when he saw the two men approaching him. His face relaxed when he saw Alaric.

'Back again, Medwin?' he called.

'As I said, Leofwine,' replied Alaric. 'This is the friend I told you about. Guthrum.'

'Welcome, Guthrum. Won't you both come in and

share a beaker of ale with me?'

Alaric and Guthrum thanked the man and followed him into the shabby cottage. It was dark inside, light only coming in from two narrow slit windows, one on either side of the single room. A rough table stood in the centre of room, with a wooden bench at each side.

On the table was a jug and a single beaker. When Leofwine had offered to share a beaker of ale, he had been speaking literally. He sat and indicated the opposite bench to his guests. He poured a thin stream of cloudy beer into the beaker from the jug and handed it to Alaric.

Alaric thanked him and took a mouthful of the beer, making appreciative noises.

'That is very welcome on a warm morning like this,' said Alaric, passing the beaker to Guthrum.

Guthrum took a mouthful of beer and had to stop himself from spitting it right back into the beaker. It was very sour, like a mouthful of vinegar. The ale lingered a moment in his mouth until he forced himself to swallow. It burned as it went down, leaving an unpleasant acidic aftertaste.

'Thank you,' he croaked.

Leofwine took the beaker and finished it off, clearly relishing every last drop.

'I'm afraid that I'm not in a position to be able to offer you any work,' said Leofwine apologetically. 'As you can see, my holding is very poor. I can barely grow enough to feed myself and Aelfthrith, and a little left over to pay my taxes.'

'That's all right, Leofwine, your generosity is more than enough for us,' he indicated the jug.

'Oh,' said Leofwine, taking this as a prompt to refill the beaker. Guthrum gave a barely audible groan.

As the beaker was passed round again, Alaric began gently questioning Leofwine.

'Have you seen nothing of the Normans who now hold this land?'

'Sometimes horsemen pass by. They never stop. It's as though I'm not worth taking any notice of. Long may that remain so.'

'Have you had no tax demands at all recently?' asked Guthrum, grimacing slightly as he swallowed a sip of Leofwine's acetic ale.

'Nothing. Normally one of the thegn's men would have come around a couple of months ago, but this year – nothing. I've been to Colton, because not paying your tax can get you in a lot of trouble, even if it's not your fault. I went to see the thegn, but the hall is empty. Didn't look in too good a shape to me, either.'

'Hmm...' said Alaric. 'Well, thanks for your hospitality, Leofwine. We'll be off now.'

'Alright. Safe journey, wherever you're going.'

Alaric and Guthrum thanked Leofwine again and emerged from his cottage, blinking in the bright sunlight.

As they walked away from the farm, Guthrum looked askance at Alaric.

'Is that all you wanted to know?' he asked.

Alaric shook his head. 'No, I want to know far more than that, but that poor wretch can't provide the answers I'm looking for. What would he think of a Danish invasion? Who cares? He hardly speaks for the kingdom, does he? We need to get to Colton for starters.'

As they walked away from the humble farm, their colleagues emerged from cover a hundred yards down the road.

'Nothing to report from here,' said Alaric to Edgar. 'The little people seem to be ignored for the time being, though that won't last, and I fear those like our poor friend Leofwine there will feel the strangulation of Norman taxation before long.

'We need to find out what happened to the thegn. If he's been thrown off his land then he may be out in the wilds somewhere just waiting for an opportunity to join up with some organised resistance. We could do with finding him. He may have a party of followers we can sign up for the invasion.'

Colton appeared ahead of them a short while later. A small huddle of houses with a tiny chapel and bell tower. The thegn's residence was a little further on, a modest hall within a protective palisade.

'Alright, remember our story, everyone,' said Edgar as they approached the village.

The main street led down to the shoreline and was lined with dwellings, each with a strip of land behind, in which Edgar could see vegetables and grain growing. Fields to either side of the main street contained a few cattle and sheep. There was little activity visible as they walked towards the shore.

Here there was a well-built wharf with jetties for half a dozen large boats. Only two were occupied.

'Let's split up,' said Edgar. 'Halfdene and Harek, you speak to the lads on that boat,' he pointed at the more distant of the two ships tied up at the wharf. 'Guthrum and I will take this one,' he indicated the nearer, smaller vessel. 'Alaric and Hallvindur, try the thegn's hall.'

The men split up and Edgar and Guthrum walked

The Lost Land

casually along the wharf, stopping a few yards from the smaller boat. Edgar pulled out his water skin and took a draught from it. He then offered it to Guthrum.

Next to the boat was a blanket on the ground, covered with items for sale. Edgar and Guthrum walked up to it and started looking at the merchandise.

'It's all got to go,' said a voice.

Edgar looked round and saw a man emerging from the boat. He was dirty and dishevelled, and his hair stuck out wildly round his head. He looked despondent.

'What's the matter?' asked Edgar.

The man shrugged. 'There's no trading any more along this coast,' he said, shaking his head. 'Here at Colton there used to be a well-organised market. The thegn's men ran it all without a hitch. Oh, they took their share, of course, but it was a small price to pay for being able to set up in safety in a proper market. Now look at it. Reduced to peddling my fine wares on the quayside.'

He waved his hand towards the blanket as if revealing a vast array of treasures.

'What happened?' asked Edgar.

'The bloody Normans happened, that's what,' said the man sourly. 'I don't know why, but after they came the thegn disappeared. I expect he got a huge tax demand and couldn't pay. So rather than face being thrown off his land, he just upped sticks and left. Can't say I blame him, but it's left the traders in the lurch.'

'Where have you come from?' asked Guthrum.

'Wuelle, in Nordfolc. Used to be a nice profitable trip up here and back. I could usually manage half a dozen round trips in the year. I don't think I'll be coming back here again. I'm thinking of trading to the south from now on.'

Edgar looked at his boat. 'Where are your crew?' he asked.

'Out hunting and scavenging whatever food we can get before we have to head back. Apart from Uric there,' he pointed at a large heap of animal skins from which a gentle snoring issued.

'He's my guard.' The man grinned sheepishly. 'Of course, this has been coming quite a long time,' he said, staring at his wares.

'What do you mean?' asked Edgar.

'This coast. There's something wrong with it. The tides get higher every year. Colton is frequently flooded. I don't know why that happens. There's a story about a lost village. It used to be round here somewhere, out there,' he pointed out towards the sea. 'The story says that it was overcome with the waves and was lost beneath the sea. On still nights, they say you can still hear the church bell ringing. Now it seems the same fate is to befall Colton. People are moving away. As I said, it was only a matter of time. I think this will be my last trip.'

He looked sadly towards the town.

'I like this seax,' said Edgar, stooping to pick up a short domestic knife in a supple leather sheath. He pulled the blade out and saw that it was well made, and the handle was firmly fixed to the tang. It was perhaps a little small for a man used to carrying a longer, fighting seax.

'Yes, it's nice. I had a few of those from my local blacksmith back home. That's the last one.'

'I'll have it,' said Edgar. He reached into his scrip and brought out two cut silver halfpennies.

'Too much,' said the boatman, 'just one.'

'Take two,' insisted Edgar.

The Lost Land

'Thank you, sir. I appreciate that.'

'Safe journey home,' said Edgar.

'Thank you, sir. God bless you.'

Edgar and Guthrum turned away from the boatman and walked back across the wharf and into the town. They turned off the main street and headed along the road that led to the thegn's hall. The gate stood open, and Edgar and Guthrum stepped cautiously inside the palisade. A solitary chicken pecked at the ground. The hall certainly looked abandoned. They approached it warily. The door was closed, but it opened as Edgar pushed at it.

They peered into the gloom of the hall.

'What do you men want?' boomed a deep voice from behind them. They whirled to face a solidly-built looking man brandishing a long seax.

'We're looking for the thegn,' said Edgar.

'He's not here,' said the man, not taking his eyes off Edgar and Guthrum nor dropping his seax at all.

'We mean no harm. We need to speak to the thegn. Where is he?'

'He's gone, and you're looters,' said the man, raising his seax.

Edgar dropped to his left side whilst Guthrum swung his right leg round, catching the man behind the knees with his foot. He fell backwards as his knees gave way, the seax dropping from his hand. As it hit the ground, Edgar snatched it up and held it to the man's throat.

'Get up,' he said. 'Inside.' He pushed the hall door open and followed the man in.

There were no torches in the hall, and it was quite dark within. As the door closed behind them, Alaric and

Hallvindur peeled themselves away from the wall behind them.

The man turned round. 'More of you,' he spat. 'Now you kill me and steal anything you can find in the hall.'

'I don't want to kill you,' said Edgar, passing the man's seax to Guthrum. 'We are not here to kill, and we are not here to loot. We really do want to see the thegn. It's hard to explain, but we're here to help.'

'Help? What help can you offer?'

'I can't say for now, but we genuinely mean you no harm. Can you take us to the thegn?'

The man looked round at his captors. He nodded his head.

'Follow me,' he said.

He walked back out of the hall into the sunlight. He crossed the courtyard of the thegn's residence, towards the tiny church that sat close to the gate in the palisade wall. He grasped the brass ring handle of the stout wooden door, twisted and pushed. The door opened with a slight creak. He entered the church and the others followed him inside.

The church could not have served a congregation of more than thirty, even if they were all standing shoulder to shoulder. The walls were plain stone, undecorated and the altar at the west end was a simple flat slab of stone on two crudely carved pillars. The ground was of beaten earth.

The man walked up to the wall just to the left-hand side of the altar. He indicated a patch of recently disturbed earth by the wall.

'There lies Gundar, my thegn, whom I was not here to protect,' he said bitterly.

Edgar and his colleagues looked down on the fresh grave.

'Normans?' asked Edgar.

'What else?'

'Tell us what happened.'

'It was about three months ago. The Normans had made a ridiculous tax demand and were threatening to throw the thegn off his own land. The land that his family had owned for a hundred years and more. The thegn managed to raise the tax, and when the Normans returned to take it, he handed over the money. They had no cause for complaint.

'Now I wasn't here, I was away on the thegn's business to the north, but I was told afterwards what happened. The money was counted out by a Norman cleric. It was all there, and he told his master so. The leader stayed on his horse in the courtyard the whole time. He said something to the cleric, and although my witness couldn't understand their heathen tongue, it was clear that there was some argument going on. Eventually, the leader barked an order at the cleric, who told my thegn that there was not enough money. The thegn showed the cleric the tax demand and proved that he had paid it to the last penny. The cleric seemed to be trying to explain this to the leader, but the leader shouted him down, and the cleric then told my thegn that because of the delay, the amount of tax required was now double what the thegn had paid.'

The man paused and took a deep breath. 'The Normans had a party of about a dozen foot soldiers. The thegn began to shout at the Norman leader, and the three housecarls who were in the residence at the time ran up to support him. The Norman leader called a single word to the soldiers, and they drew their swords and advanced towards the thegn and his carls. All four were killed there and then. The leader shouted out something at the people gathered in the courtyard, and the cleric repeated it in English. He said that his master was now the lord of this land and that he would return in time to claim it. I understand that the cleric, Norman though he was, was visibly shaken by the events he had seen unfold. He attempted to give the last rites to those who had just been killed, but the Norman leader dragged him away.

'I got back from the trip north the following day. My colleagues and I arranged for a priest and we buried our thegn and our friends. We took too long coming back. We should have been here.'

'It wouldn't have made any difference,' said Edgar. 'We've heard this story up and down the kingdom. The Normans don't really want the tax. They want the land. Our land is being carved up by the invaders. Even if you had been here your thegn was doomed. You would have gone to your grave with him.'

'That would have been preferable,' said the housecarl stoutly.

Hallvindur grunted his agreement.

'That's as maybe. But you still live. How many of your colleagues are still here?'

'There are six of us. We don't stay here. We've moved out of the town.'

'Take us to them.'

'Why, what could that possibly achieve?'

'My name is Edgar, formerly thegn of Rapendun in Mercia. More or less the same thing happened to me. My grandfather, the previous thegn, was killed by the Normans. My wife was kidnapped, raped and killed by them. We have lost colleagues and friends. We've seen the same thing all over the kingdom. Now there may be some hope. I would speak with your colleagues. Maybe we can fight back.'

The housecarl stood in contemplation.

'Edgar, you say?'

Edgar nodded.

'I'm Swithun.'

He held a meaty hand out. Edgar grasped it. 'I'll take you to meet my friends.'

They walked out of the church, following the man called Swithun until they came to a wood bordering a sheep field. Swithun led them through a gap in the hedge, which was closed by a loose gate. They walked through the woods and down into a shallow valley, at the bottom of which ran a wide stream. The banks of the stream were covered in mossy boulders and the long, pointed leaves of wild garlic, which gave off a heady aroma when crushed underfoot. They walked along the bank of the stream for some time until Swithun stopped and gave a loud whistle.

From behind a large pile of rocks, two men cautiously approached.

'It's alright, lads, they're with me,' called Swithun.

The men relaxed and came forward. Edgar found himself comparing the way Swithun and his men did things with the methods of the Wildmen with whom he had stayed the previous year. These men were clumsy and noisy by comparison. They would not have seen the Wildmen, nor recognised their signals as anything other than normal bird calls.

'Come on,' said Swithun, leading them around the back of the rocks. There they saw the camp. A fire burned in the middle of a clearing, with four hares roasting on spits over it.

Guthrum grunted. He, too, was making the comparison with the Wildmen.

'What's this about, Swithun?' asked one of the men who had met them.

Four other men closed in and faced Swithun.

'This here's Thegn Edgar, he's faced a similar situation to our own. Lost his land, family killed. He has something to say to us.'

'He doesn't look much like a thegn,' commented a wiry, curly-haired man with a thin nose.

'How far do you think I could travel through this Norman-infested land if I looked like a thegn?' asked Edgar.

The man shrugged. 'Don't know,' he said.

'About as far as you could throw Hallvindur here,' said Edgar, indicating his giant companion.

'Want to try?' rumbled Hallvindur.

Now Hallvindur was speaking English, Edgar noticed that he had a pronounced Danish accent.

Edgar held up his hand to Hallvindur. 'We come to bring the possibility of hope, not to fight.'

Hallvindur stepped back immediately. 'Yes, my lord,' he said.

Hallvindur's instant obedience, as much as Edgar's words, seemed to convince the men that Edgar might well be what he claimed.

Swithun cleared his throat in the awkward silence that followed.

'Sit, everybody, please sit,' he said. They sat in a circle around the fire, and the wiry man who had issued the mild challenge to Edgar turned the spits on which the hares were roasting.

The Lost Land

Edgar began talking. He spoke softly, causing the men to lean forward slightly to catch his words.

'We've heard tales like yours told all across this lost land of ours. I lost my home and my wife to the Normans. Guthrum and Halfdene here are the last two of my housecarls. We have lost others. Hallvindur is carl to a king's thegn and fought with Harold-king at Senlac when the Normans first came. Guthrum, Halfdene and I fought at Stanford, also with Harold-king. We have travelled far through the land. We have seen what the Normans are doing. It isn't a subtle plan. They demand monstrous taxes, and if these are not paid, or even if they are, they throw the rightful lord off the land, or more usually, simply kill him. You are not alone. The kingdom is full of men such as yourselves. Do you know of others like you? Other thegns who've been evicted?'

Swithun spoke. 'Aye, we do, alas. The thegn of Pridby, just to the north of us, was killed as he tried to protect his hall from the invaders. Alfred of Swaddleton, a few miles to our west, was driven off his land and his hall burned. I don't know where he went or if he still lives, but his carls remain in the village, which makes me think he must be dead. They're not the only ones.'

'So what are you prepared to do about it?'

'What?'

'Are you just going to allow this to happen? Just going to sit by your campfire for the rest of your lives? Because believe me, if nothing is done, then these Normans are going nowhere. They're here to stay.'

'But what can we do? There's no communication with other evicted thegns and carls. There doesn't appear to be any resistance at all.'

'Did you not hear about the events at Dunholm at the beginning of the year?'

'No. What happened?'

'The new Norman governor sent there by the Bastard was slaughtered, along with his entire company of soldiers. Eoforwic was sacked and the Norman fort there thrown down.'

The men around the fire looked up at this, a spark of interest in their eyes. Edgar continued.

'The sons of Harold-king brought a fleet to the south of England and brought the Normans to battle there just weeks ago. In the Great Forest, there is a group calling themselves the Wildmen. They kill Normans and disrupt the Bastard's lines of communication all the time. In fact, there are so many revolts that the Bastard has sent his little Norman wifey back home out of harm's way. He's worried. This is the time to act, but we must all act together.'

'How can we know when to act and what to do?' asked one of the men.

'The Danes are coming.'

There was a collective intake of breath. The phrase Edgar had chosen to use had in the past brought terror to the people of this coast. More recently though, the terror had passed as the Danes who initially came as raiders and plunderers settled down and became integrated into the local populace. As in Edgar's home of Rapendun, most of the men here would carry some Danish blood in their veins. The Danes had ruled more or less peacefully here for over a century from their capital at Eoforwic until the land was reunited under a single English king the previous century.

'What do the Danes want with us?' asked the same man.

'They want to throw the bastard duke of Normandy out

of England. Sweyn-king would become king of England.'

'Better a Dane than a Norman,' muttered one man, to universal approval.

'The fleet is on its way. I know this because I sailed ahead of them. There are three hundred ships poised to land on these shores in a very short time. There is a huge army waiting to smash its way through the Norman scum and retake this kingdom.'

The men around the fire began talking animatedly amongst themselves. Swithun turned to Edgar.

'What can we do? How can we help?'

'Take us to meet your neighbours, we'll let them know that the time to rise up against the oppressor is here and that they should be ready for action. It's important that the Normans be kept busy. Let's distract them away from the coast, make them move their forces inland. This will give us time to assemble our army and march inland. Can you do that?'

All the men agreed loudly and with great enthusiasm.

Alaric suddenly held his hand up. 'Quiet!' he hissed.

'What is it?' asked Edgar.

'Horses. We must clear the fire.'

'Quickly!' whispered Edgar. 'Put out the fire, cover it up. Then hide.'

One man pulled the hares off the flames whilst three others stamped at the fire, one emptying a large flagon of water over it. It hissed, steamed and smoked.

'It's too late,' said Halfdene. 'They'll have seen the smoke.'

Edgar cursed.

'Give me one of the hares,' said the wiry man urgently.

'What? Why?' said Swithun.

'Just give me a hare.'

Swithun handed him one of the part-cooked hares.

'Right, get out of here, all of you. If they find one man here with a fire, they may not suspect there were more. Go!'

'We can't leave you, Ecgfrith, we won't,' said Swithun, looking puzzled.

'Just go, you fool!' snapped Ecgfrith urgently.

'He's right,' said one of the other men.

'Quickly!' called Alaric. 'They're almost on us!'

Hurriedly, the men ran away from the still-smoking fire, leaving Ecgfrith crouching beside it, holding the hare. They ran deeper into the woods and threw themselves down just as a party of two dozen armed horsemen entered the clearing. They approached Ecgfrith at a trot and encircled him.

One of the men, apparently the leader, though they all wore the same arms, shouted a question at Ecgfrith.

'What?' he replied. 'I don't understand you, what do you want?'

The leader shouted back at him in the Norman tongue.

'I don't understand. Can you speak English?' asked Ecgfrith, sounding desperate.

One of the riders pulled out a spear and poked Ecgfrith with it.

'What's that for? Stop it!'

The man pushed his spear into Ecgfrith's buttocks.

'What? You want my meal? Here,' he pushed the hare towards the man who was prodding him.

With disdain, the man thrust his spear into the hare and flicked it out of Ecgfrith's hand.

'Hey!' he called.

Then they all had their spears out. Ecgfrith started to

bolt, and they playfully let him run between two of the horses.

Lying on the ground next to Edgar, Swithun reached for his seax, but Edgar grabbed his arm.

'No,' he hissed. 'We must remain hidden.'

'They're going to kill him.'

'I'm sorry. He knows what he's doing. He's keeping the rest of us safe.'

'No, we must go,' said Swithun and began to climb to his feet.

'Hallvindur,' said Edgar urgently.

Hallvindur jumped up and threw himself over Swithun, forcing the smaller man to the ground, where he struggled to no avail to escape from under the giant's body.

Meanwhile, Ecgfrith had broken into a run and was heading away from his hidden colleagues. The Normans trotted casually after him. He ran across the clearing and disappeared into the woods on the far side. The Normans followed him in, and from their hiding-place they could hear the sound of the Normans laughing and jeering.

After a few minutes, the sound died down and they heard the horses' hooves thudding off into the distance at a gallop. Presumably, they had had their fun and were now making up for lost time.

Edgar shoved at Hallvindur's shoulder. 'Alright, let him up. We need to find Ecgfrith, see if there's anything we can do for him.'

Hallvindur rolled off Swithun and then helped him to his feet.

'Sorry,' said Hallvindur. 'But Lord Edgar was right. If you'd run, we would all be dead right now.'

Swithun was purple with rage. 'As it is, only Ecgfrith

died, so that's all right I suppose?'

'No, it isn't alright,' replied Edgar. 'But these are the realities that we face at the moment. This is war, though the Normans may not yet realise it. We may all be called on to make sacrifices. Ecgfrith's sacrifice wasn't the first and it most certainly won't be the last. I'm just sorry that it had to happen at all.'

They walked cautiously across the clearing and into the woods on the far side where they had last seen Ecgfrith.

The ground plants were crushed in a path away from the clearing. They followed the path and came to a circular flattened area, where the Normans had had their fun. Towards the edge of the area lay Ecgfrith. His tunic was covered in blood and he was unmoving.

Swithun ran over to him, followed quickly by the others.

'Ecgfrith!' called Swithun as he reached him.

He was lying on his right-hand side, his knees drawn up defensively towards his chest. Swithun carefully took hold of him by the left shoulder and gently rolled him over onto his back.

'He's still breathing!' exclaimed Swithun.

'Here, let me look,' said Alaric, pushing his way to the front of the men. He dropped down onto his knees and carefully lifted Ecgfrith's tunic. His chest was slick with blood, and Alaric hurriedly inspected the body with eyes and fingertips. He looked over his arms and legs with quiet efficiency.

'He's lucky we're here,' he said. 'If he'd been on his own, as the Normans clearly thought he was, then he would almost certainly have bled to death. As it is, we should be able to save him. I need wrappings.'

Two men immediately stripped off their tunics and began tearing them into strips, handing them down to Alaric.

'Fetch water, plenty of it,' ordered the little spy.

A man ran off in the direction of the fire, where the flagon still lay.

When the water arrived, Alaric dipped one of the strips of tunic into the flagon and swiftly washed Ecgfrith's body down. The men breathed a sigh of relief when they could see that the wounds were not as bad as the quantity of blood seemed to indicate. There were three wounds in his side, but none was deep. His arms had four wounds and his legs three. There were two stab wounds to his buttocks.

Quietly and efficiently, Alaric bound up all the wounds. The blood flow was slowing quickly in any event, and in a few minutes, it seemed to have stopped.

Ecgfrith groaned. Alaric held the flagon of water to his mouth and let a small trickle out. Ecgfrith swallowed and then spluttered a little. He opened his eyes.

'Norman bastards,' he muttered.

'You've been wounded, Ecgfrith, but you're going to be alright. Just lie there for a moment,' said Swithun.

'Do you have any shelter?' asked Edgar.

'No, we've been sleeping in the open.'

'This man needs to be under cover. Is there anywhere in Colton where we can take him?'

Swithun looked round at his friends. 'Anyone?' he asked.

One man stepped forward. 'My sister's house. We can take him there. It's away from the main settlement and her husband is a good man. Ecgfrith can stay there for a few days.'

'Good, Daeglaf, that's good.'

'Leave him to rest for a couple of hours,' said Alaric. 'We can move him to Colton under cover of darkness. You, Daeglaf was it?'

The man nodded.

'You'd better go to your sister and prepare her for her visitor. We don't want any problems when we arrive.'

The man Daeglaf looked at Swithun, who nodded his assent. He loped off into the woods in the direction of Colton.

Alaric looked up at Edgar. 'This man needs a stretcher,' he said.

'Right,' said Edgar. 'Harek, Hallvindur and Guthrum, cut withies for a stretcher. Swithun, half your men are in their loincloths, you need to get tunics for them.'

'There are some clothes in the mead hall.'

'Good. Halfdene, go with him,' he turned to the remaining four men. 'You men come with me. I'm going to teach you how to build a fire that will leave a far smaller trace than the one you made.' He looked at Swithun. 'Then you can take us to meet your neighbours.'

7

The Fleet Arrives

The six companions waited patiently on the beach. As darkness fell, they gathered driftwood and flotsam and constructed a pair of baffles as Alaric had done on his earlier visit. More driftwood, dry after the hot days in the sun, was piled up to form a low fire. The fire could not be taller than the baffles, because of the danger of it being seen. The low cliffs at the edge of the beach prevented it from being seen from inland, but there was still the possibility that a watcher north or south of them on the coast could spot the bright flames.

They sat outside the baffles, so as not to damage their night vision with the glare from the fire. They sat in silence, each with his thoughts, as they waited for the arrival of Stormleaper.

To Edgar, it felt like they had been waiting much of the night. Although near midsummer, with its long twilight and very short night, it still seemed very dark when he heard

Halfdene shuffle slightly on the pebbles.

'Edgar,' he said softly.

'Yes, I see it,' added Alaric.

'I see nothing,' said Edgar.

He squinted into the darkness, but all he could see was a faint change in the density of the gloom where the sky met the sea. No, wait, was there a darker shape?

The great horse's head prow of Stormleaper loomed suddenly out of the darkness, illuminated by the firelight and coming in fast. The ship surged forward on a mighty pull of the oars, and with a hiss of sand, gravel and small pebbles, lurched up the beach directly in line with the two baffles.

Loki's crew immediately started jumping from the prow, pulling ropes with them with which to secure the ship.

Edgar and his men leaped to their feet, rushing to extinguish the fire and to collapse the baffles. Edgar heaped sand and fine gravel on the flames, dousing them quickly. The baffles were spread around the beach, returning to their constituent parts.

Loki dropped from the prow of his ship onto the beach, the pebbles crunching under his stiff mariner's boots.

Edgar stepped forward to greet him.

'Right on target, Loki,' said Edgar, smiling.

'A well-constructed target always helps,' replied Loki, taking Edgar's hand. 'Have you had an interesting week? You all seem unharmed, at least.'

'We are unharmed. I'm afraid I can't say that for the local population, at least the thegns and housecarls. It seems there's been much harm inflicted amongst them.'

'Is there anything about the enemy presence here that I need to know?'

'No. There's no local stronghold. We've seen patrols. Usually only four or six horsemen, but sometimes up to two dozen. They don't seem to have got their claws deeply in here yet.'

'That's good, but we must still make haste.'

'What news do you have of the fleet?' asked Edgar.

'The fleet's made landfall at the mouth of the Humbre,' replied Loki. 'Defences are being raised and the troops are being offloaded in stages. They should all be ashore by the time we arrive.'

'Ah, that's good news.'

'So, did you find much out?'

'Yes, I think we gathered some useful information. We encountered several groups of homeless carls, some even had their thegns with them, those that haven't been killed already. The mood is of great bewilderment and anger. Almost everyone we spoke to would be more than willing to fight back if the opportunity arose for some sort of coordinated attack. They're scared to fight back individually, as you can imagine, but an invading Danish army is a huge incentive.'

'Almost everyone?'

'There are some thegns who believe, or at least when speaking openly say that they believe that nothing will change with the Normans in charge. They think that if they just sit tight and cause no trouble, then they'll be ignored and life will eventually settle back down to how it's always been.

'Speaking quietly with the housecarls of those thegns who are reluctant to make a move, however, I think that if there was a really good opportunity to strike back, we'd get even their support.

'I have every reason to believe that when we do begin our reconquest, we'll get a huge groundswell of popular support.'

'That sounds good,' said Loki. He smiled, but the smile looked forced, somehow, insincere.

'What?' said Edgar, tersely. Loki had never exhibited the enthusiasm for this venture that Edgar would have expected from him. 'You seem less than certain about all this, Loki. What is it? Is there something you're not telling me?'

Loki looked around at the activity on the beach, harder to see now that the fire was extinguished. Taking Edgar by the upper arm, he led him away from the bustle, out of sight and out of earshot.

'What is it?' asked Edgar, concerned.

'Look, Edgar. All this may amount to nothing. Gods, I hope so.'

'Tell me,' said Edgar, insistently.

'You're not Danish. I am. I've spent my life around Danes, talking with Danes, working with Danes, living with Danes. I've spent more time in Sweyn-king's court than I care to think about. The thing is this. I know the Danish mind. I know the way Danes think.'

He paused, looking back along to where his ship and his Danish crew lay hidden by the night's dark.

'Go on,' prompted Edgar.

Loki took a breath. 'The days of great Viking armies carving out kingdoms and empires are long gone, Edgar. In days gone by, in the time of Cnut-king, then maybe. But now there just isn't the heart for it any more. Raids, yes. Loot-taking, yes. But the effort of running kingdoms on foreign soil? No. Not any more. We lost England, we lost Norway. The Rus have gone native. Running an empire is

The Lost Land

just too difficult. It's so much easier to return to the old ways of looting and pillaging.'

Edgar felt a cold pulse course through his body.

'So what are you saying?'

Loki took another breath. 'I know this means a lot to you, Edgar, really I do. And to your companions. This is your country, and I understand your anger and sense of loss and injustice, and I feel it with you, I do, but I think, truly, from my heart, that this invasion will come to nothing. Sweyn appears very enthusiastic about the venture, but his enthusiasm will wane, and quite quickly. His attention will be diverted by something else. He doesn't really want to be king of England. He's not even here. If his heart was truly set on the English crown, he would be here to lead the army himself. He wouldn't have left it to his inadequate brother. Asbjorn is not a born leader of men, for all his size and bluster. He's not one of these politically motivated modern leaders. He's an old-style Viking through and through. He's a raider and a plunderer, pure and simple, and Sweyn is no Cnut.'

He looked down at his feet, kicked the sand and pebbles around.

'Edgar, let me give you some advice, unwelcome though it will be. Don't set your heart on this reconquest of England. It won't happen. Not now, anyway, not with this army. If I know Asbjorn, and I think I do, then this will be nothing more than a glorified raiding trip.'

Edgar could not believe what he was hearing.

'Loki,' he said. 'You're talking nonsense. Why would Sweyn-king gather such a vast army simply to go on a raid? There are three hundred ships in the fleet – three hundred! The King has called on his allies for hundreds of miles around. There are troops from all over northern Europe here. That's a ridiculous amount of effort to put in for a raiding trip. And how many favours did the King have to call in with his allies? For a raiding trip?'

'I know, I know, but trust me. You shouldn't build your hopes up about this expedition. I know what I'm talking about.'

Edgar felt a wave of acidic anger growing within him.

'How? Tell me Loki, how do you know what you're talking about? How do you know more than anyone else? How do you know more even than the King?'

Edgar's anger was rising now, feeding itself on the back of his own words.

'You've been against this expedition from the start, haven't you? Don't deny it. It's because you've had to put off your precious trading trip to Micklagard isn't it?'

Loki shook his head and raised his hands to placate Edgar.

'Edgar, please listen…'

But Edgar was having none of it. 'There's something between you and Asbjorn isn't there? And yet how can that be, Loki? He's a mighty jarl, the King's brother, no less. The man the King trusts so much that he's sending him as the leader of an invasion to claim an entire kingdom. And you? You're just a common-or-garden trader. What would you know, Loki? What would you know? I bet Jarl Asbjorn doesn't even know you exist!'

'Edgar, enough!'

'No!' shouted Edgar. 'I don't want to hear it, Loki. If you can't get behind this expedition for whatever reason, then that's your concern, not mine, not my companions and not this army's. And let me warn you, you'd be well advised to keep your treacherous thoughts to yourself and your treacherous mouth shut!'

'My thoughts are far from treacherous, Edgar,' said Loki, his own voice rising with anger. 'I have a clearer view of this than you do. You must believe me.'

'Believe you? Why should I believe you? The whole of the King's court is behind this expedition. Everybody but you thinks this will succeed.'

'Edgar, you're investing too much in this.'

'And why shouldn't I? This is my home, damn you! The home that's been ripped away from me. My family that's been murdered. My wife abused and killed. My inheritance snatched away. How could I not invest so much in it?'

'Alright Edgar, calm down.'

'Calm down? Calm down? Fuck you, Loki!'

Edgar turned and strode purposefully away, back towards the beached ship. Loki could only watch his retreating back in anguish.

Early the following morning, Stormleaper rounded Hrafn's Spur, the waves slapping loudly against her hull as she crossed the confusing currents of the mouth of the great river Humbre. Edgar pulled at an oar, looking at the estuary of the river that had for countless generations marked the boundary between the earldoms, and earlier the kingdoms, of Northumbria and Mercia.

Ahead of them, south of the river, a host of ships sat bobbing on the waves just off the coast. As they drew closer, Edgar could see that a great ditch was being dug, and a bank within it, the defences for the army as it disembarked itself and all its provisions.

'I can only see about a hundred ships,' said Guthrum as

they approached the shore.

Edgar did a quick count of the masts and came to the same conclusion.

'The rest of them are up and down the coast, raiding,' said the oarsman next to Guthrum. 'This is just too good an opportunity to be missed. It'll soften up the opposition for when we decide to move inland.'

Edgar looked astonished. 'The Normans are the opposition, not the English!' he said angrily.

The oarsman shrugged. 'It's what we've always done in the past before a major attack. It always worked then, so why change a winning policy?'

Edgar sat back in disgust. 'I don't believe this,' he muttered.

Harek, sitting just behind him, laid a hand gently on Edgar's forearm.

'It's proved a good policy in the past, Edgar. It may not be to your liking in this instance, but it works.'

'It works? What do you mean? We're not supposed to be attacking the English! We're supposed to be attacking the Normans! What is the point in "softening up" the very people we hope to attract to our cause?'

Stormleaper beached softly amid several other ships and Edgar made his way to the prow to disembark. He did not even glance at Loki, who remained at the tiller.

Edgar and his companions jumped down into the shallow surf and, with their packs over their shoulders, walked up the beach onto the grasslands beyond, where the army was pitching its tents. The tents were mostly for the expedition leaders. Most of the others would be sleeping on board the ships that had brought them here.

Edgar scanned the banners fluttering over the tents that had already been pitched, and recognising the banner of King's Thegn Osfrith Edwinsson, led his men towards it.

As Edgar approached the tent, he saw Osfrith sitting on a bench with another man Edgar did not know. They were deep in conversation, but when he saw Edgar, Osfrith stood up from his bench, leaning heavily on a stick. He smiled at Edgar and held out his free hand towards him.

'Edgar, good to see you. Come and join us. Harek, you too.'

He indicated the bench next to himself. 'There's food and drink available for your men over there.'

He pointed to a spacious tent about fifty yards away, where a large gathering of men stood.

'Hallvindur,' he added. 'I'm glad you're back unscathed. Go and eat with your colleagues and then report back to me when you're done. No great hurry.'

'Aye, my lord,' rumbled the big housecarl.

Guthrum, Halfdene, Alaric and Hallvindur walked off in the direction of the gathering, where something was being roasted over a roaring fire.

Osfrith turned back to Edgar.

'Well, Edgar, what did you find out during your little expedition?'

Edgar gathered his thoughts.

'North of the river,' he began, 'the Normans seem not yet to have such a tight grasp on the country as they have further south, but I think this is changing. Several thegns have been evicted from their lands, as they have further south. Some have also been killed. We've met a few bands of housecarls, who have no thegn to serve any more. They're living rough, mostly in the wooded areas. The thegns who've been thrown off their lands but who still live are generally with their housecarls, who have gone into voluntary exile with them. The mood is very angry, confused and resentful, and from what we've seen…' he glanced at Harek, seeking confirmation. Harek nodded encouragingly. 'From what we've seen, we can rely on a popular uprising to support our attack.'

'Excellent!' exclaimed Osfrith.

'However,' cautioned Edgar. 'It's also apparent that without clear and definite action from our army, there will be no uprising. We will have to act first to show that we mean it.'

'Yes. I understand. Well, that all sounds very promising. What have you learned of the disposition of the Norman forces?'

'As I understand it from the people we were able to talk to, there are as yet no permanently fortified Norman stations in the area where we were dropped. Regular patrols, but nothing of a more substantial nature. My information, of course, comes from some way north of here. I don't know whether that is true for here.'

'That's alright, we have reports from other teams that were dropped in this area. It seems that even though we're south of the great river, we're still a good way from any Norman fortifications. This is just a staging area; we'll be operating mostly from the ships.'

'Surely, we should remain on land now that we're here?' asked Edgar, puzzled.

'That's not the way the Danes do these things, Edgar, and you must remember that we are here as part of a Danish army.'

'Speaking of the Danish army, my lord, I can't help but

be disturbed by the fact that over half the fleet is currently engaged in raiding up and down the coast. That doesn't seem to me a policy that is going to gain us much favour with the very people that we hope to be getting support from.'

Osfrith tapped his finger on his lips thoughtfully.

'There is more to these raids than you may be aware of, Edgar. The targets of these raids are mainly Norman holdings. Information from small groups like yours have pointed out where the Normans actually are, and it's these places that we're hitting. Norman troops are being engaged all along the coast. The object is to spread the Norman forces out as thinly as possible along this section of the coast. If the Bastard doesn't know where the next attack is going to come from, he'll have to spread those troops out. Then, when we march in force, as we will, there should be little resistance, no matter where we decide to land our army. I understand your misgivings, and I accept that there will be some damage and loss to some Englishmen. This is a war, some damage is inevitable, I'm afraid.'

'I see,' said Edgar, not quite convinced. 'So where will our first main thrust be directed?'

'We've just been discussing that. The word from Jarl Asbjorn's messenger is that we are going to make our first strike at Eoforwic.'

Edgar immediately felt heartened. That was more like it.

'It's the obvious choice, really,' said Osfrith.

Edgar frowned. 'If it's so obvious, then surely the Bastard will have a heavy concentration of troops there, won't he?'

'That's possible, but this is where the raiding comes into

its own. It will draw troops away from their major centres, like Eoforwic. And don't forget, our army is huge. It's all been worked out quite carefully, Edgar, truly.'

'Here,' said the slender man sitting next to Osfrith whom Edgar had not recognised. 'Have some ale.'

Edgar looked across at the man, who was holding a beaker out to him. He took the cup from him and took a swallow of the ale. It was good, and he was grateful for it.

'Thank you...' he let the implied question hang in the air between them.

Osfrith stirred. 'This is Thegn Brihtwulf. He's been appointed as my deputy and will be the leader of the battle-group in which you will be marching. Sadly, my condition,' he slapped his battle-damaged leg in frustration, 'prevents me from leading a group myself, curse it. Brihtwulf was at Dunholm when the Bastard's puppet and his entire garrison was put down. He was also with us at Senlac. He copped a nasty clout on the head from a Norman sword. Didn't wake up for four days.'

Brihtwulf smiled and turned his head so that Edgar could see that much of the hair on the left side was missing, and a shiny red scar nearly two inches wide snaked across from his left eye to the crown of his head.

'Ouch,' said Edgar, with feeling.

'I could say the same to you,' smiled Brihtwulf.

Edgar brought his left hand up to the side of his face that had been shattered by a Norseman's axe during the battle at Stanford.

Brihtwulf raised his cup to Edgar. 'We wear our scars of battle with pride, Edgar, for they say far more about us than a pretty face ever could.'

Edgar grinned back at him. They touched cups and

drank their ale.

'I'm going to be needing lieutenants,' said Brihtwulf. 'I hear from Thegn Osfrith that you have no little experience in fighting the Normans in… less orthodox ways than straightforward battle.'

'Yes, I was involved with a group who called themselves the Wildmen. They were all exiles, like me and my men. They lived in the Great Forest, causing as much disruption as possible.'

Brihtwulf leaned forward on his bench.

'I only know what you have told Osfrith of your time with these Wildmen. I'd be very interested in anything else you could tell me about them and their methods, if that is acceptable to you.'

Edgar nodded. 'Of course, that would be more than acceptable. I would suggest that you also talk to my men Guthrum, Halfdene and Alaric. They also fought very successfully with the Wildmen.'

'I will,' said Brihtwulf.

'The Wildmen are led by a man called Alfweald, he used to be the reeve of Warwic before the Normans came.'

'Alfweald,' muttered Brihtwulf softly, as if trying to recall if he already knew the name.

'Alfweald is a fine leader and has organised the Wildmen superbly. They are all dedicated to causing as much trouble as possible to the Normans. Their actions have resulted in the Normans trying to avoid the Great Forest whenever they can. It's very unsafe for them there.'

Brihtwulf looked thoughtfully down towards the ships.

'Do you think these Wildmen would be amenable to assisting us in our aims?'

'I'm certain of it. They exist purely to bring about the

overthrow of the invader.'

'That's good. Very good,' mused Brihtwulf. 'In that case, Edgar, I appoint you as my lieutenant. Your first task is to make contact with the Wildmen and enter discussions with them, bring them into the fold. How many men will you need?'

'Just my own; Guthrum, Halfdene and Alaric. They all have experience with the Wildmen, and perhaps even more importantly, would be known and recognised by them,' replied Edgar.

He looked at Harek, who had been sitting in silence during the discussion. 'Oh, and I could use Harek, as well,' he added. 'If nobody minds, that is.'

Brihtwulf turned respectfully to face Harek.

'Would you mind, Harek?' he asked.

'I wouldn't mind a bit, Brihtwulf. In truth, I'd relish the opportunity to see these Wildmen for myself.'

Edgar felt puzzled. As he had been told no differently, and as Harek had remained silent on the subject, Edgar had assumed that Harek was an ordinary, if exceptionally gifted, warrior. Now to see Brihtwulf, a senior thegn, acting with deference towards him gave Edgar pause for thought.

'Thank you, Harek,' he said. 'I would greatly value your presence.'

Harek grinned, enjoying Edgar's obvious discomfiture.

'Nice catch, lad,' he said.

Osfrith clapped his hands together. 'Excellent. That's all settled, then. Edgar, Harek and their men will make contact with the Wildmen as soon as possible and bring them into our confidence. I'm sure their contribution will be most valuable if what I've heard about them is anything to go by. All we have to do now is decide exactly what we want them to do.'

Guthrum, Halfdene and Alaric were brought into the discussions about how to employ the Wildmen. Guthrum brought back platters of food for Edgar and Harek, and they both tucked in hungrily.

Osfrith was explaining the strategy that he had worked out.

'I envisage our army pushing the Normans back towards the Great Forest, and a wave of troops already in the forest – the Wildmen – engaging them from the rear as they retreat,' he said, bringing his hands together in front of him.

'Trap the Normans between two armies, you mean?' asked Edgar.

'Precisely,' said Osfrith. 'It makes sense.'

Edgar looked at his men, seeing alarm on their faces.

'It might make sense here and now, my lord, but it will make no sense at all to the Wildmen.'

Brihtwulf looked puzzled. 'I thought you said they would certainly be with us. Would they not do what we ask?'

Guthrum cleared his throat.

'If I may?' he asked.

'You may speak freely here, Guthrum,' said Osfrith.

'Your question is a difficult one to answer, my lord,' said Guthrum. He stared up at the sky for a few moments.

'Getting rid of the Norman invader is the very reason for the Wildmen's existence. Remember the stories they told us, Edgar? Every one of them had been abused by the Normans in some way. Thrown off their land, family killed, thegns killed or exiled. Threats hanging over them. They will want to help, yes, certainly, there can be no doubt of that.

But the methods that your plan calls for are just not theirs, and I'm afraid that it is something they simply will not agree to. They are not battlefield fighters. Their strengths lie in a different kind of warfare; the sort that the Normans are not good at. No matter what you think of those bastards, there can be no denial that they are good – very good – at battlefield warfare. So why deploy the Wildmen in a battlefield situation which they are not good at, against an enemy who is very good at it? It makes no sense. We should use the Wildmen where they are strong and the Normans are weak.'

'So you think that we should abandon our plans and devise something more to the liking of the Wildmen?' asked Brihtwulf.

'It's not that the plan has to be to their liking, my lord. The plan must be to their strengths and abilities.'

'Guthrum's right,' said Edgar. 'A simple two-pronged attack with the Wildmen attacking from behind might appear sensible, but the Wildmen are not trained for that type of warfare. Many are simple farmers, not all of them even burwarran. They've developed their own methods of fighting the Normans, and they are all supremely good at that. If we use them to their strengths, I think they should have a far greater impact. To use them as regular troops would simply be to throw them away.'

Osfrith looked at Halfdene and Alaric, who had each remained silent.

'What about you two? Do you agree with Edgar's appraisal of the situation?'

'Yes, my lord,' said Alaric.

'Completely,' said Halfdene.

Brihtwulf's face creased into a frown and he turned to

Osfrith. They conferred privately for a few moments.

Osfrith turned back to face Edgar and Guthrum.

'Alright, you know these Wildmen and we don't. You're in a better position to understand their strengths and weaknesses, and I agree that we should not present their weaknesses as a gift to the Normans. We need to formulate another plan, one which the Wildmen can agree to, and we'll have to open some means of communications with them. From what you've told me, communication with them could be something of an obstacle.'

'They can be difficult to contact, yes. By their nature, they are in hiding all the time. They have to be hard to find.'

'Agreed, but not by their allies. We have to be able to communicate with them quickly and easily.'

'I understand,' said Edgar.

'Do you think that you would be able to persuade them to allow an easier line of communication with us? It would, after all, be to the advantage of all of us.'

Edgar nodded. 'I'm sure they'll agree to that. They really are very keen to rid the kingdom of the Normans.'

By dusk, which fell late on a bright, clear summer's evening, a new plan had been devised, one which worked very much to the strengths of both the Danish army and the Wildmen. Edgar now knew exactly what was going to be proposed when they eventually found the Wildmen again.

It was decided that a very small party would be less conspicuous as it travelled south to the forest, and would also be less likely to scare off the Wildmen, or even be attacked by them. Halfdene and Alaric would go as former Wildmen, and Harek would go as a representative of the Danish army. Between them, they would make the initial contact.

Meanwhile, Edgar and Guthrum would join Brihtwulf's battle group in the march on Eoforwic.

The deliberations finished for the night, Brihtwulf produced another flagon of ale, and they all filled their cups thankfully. Talk continued until the last gasp of twilight and the fall of a near-darkness.

Edgar and his companions retired to a clear patch of ground close to Osfrith's tent. It had been a hot day and the night remained warm, with little chance of rain so they did not bother to pitch their tents, simply throwing blankets down on the grass.

Edgar lay on his back, watching the summer stars brightening against the darkening sky.

'Do you think we'll be able to find them again?' asked Halfdene, softly.

'I think that you'll have more chance than anyone else,' said Edgar. 'You know where they are, more or less. You know the calls, and hopefully they'll remember you. Like I say, if you can't find them then I don't suppose anyone can.'

'I hope we can persuade them to join us.'

'That may be the easy part,' said Edgar.

8

Eoforwic

September 1069

Brihtwulf, Edgar and Guthrum rode at the head of a group of two dozen horsemen, all fully armoured. The horsemen carried long cavalry shields and spears, whilst axes and swords hung from their belts. All day they had been riding as part of the great army's vanguard, though they had met no resistance on the road. Occasionally, a peasant farmer would watch with a stony glare as they rode by. The faces Edgar saw were those of a people resentful of the constant hardship of being in the midst of a war that was none of their making.

They passed through an area of heavy woodland, and Edgar wondered how Halfdene, Alaric and Harek were progressing in their search for the Wildmen. If all had gone according to the rough timescale they had worked out, contact should have been made by now. If only they could persuade the Wildmen that the plan was good, that it would further everybody's aims.

Edgar and his superiors were relying on Halfdene and Alaric's familiarity with and to the Wildmen. Alaric's talent for getting people to agree with what he wanted them to do, Halfdene's popularity as a former Wildman troop leader, and Harek's presence as a representative of the Danish court should all increase the likelihood of them obtaining the agreement they wanted.

Edgar softly whistled a bird-call that had been used when he was with the Wildmen.

'You too?' asked Guthrum.

Edgar snapped out of his reverie. 'What?'

'You're thinking of the Wildmen, and of Halfdene's mission. You just whistled the "friend approaching" signal.'

Edgar laughed. 'Yes, yes I did. I can't help thinking about how they're doing.'

'They'll be doing just fine,' said Guthrum confidently. 'I can't imagine three men better equipped with the talents needed to see them safely through this land.'

They rode on until they cleared the wooded area. Ahead of them, Edgar saw a smudge of black on the horizon.

Brihtwulf held up his hand. 'Halt!' he called.

The riders all came to a stop.

'Is that what I think it is?' asked Edgar, pointing towards the black cloud.

'Dear Lord, Eoforwic's burning,' said Brihtwulf.

'How far ahead of the main army are we?' asked Edgar.

'About an hour,' said Guthrum.

'There may not be anything left to besiege,' said Brihtwulf. 'Maybe local resistance has started the process for us. Come on, let's see what's happening.'

He ordered his troops forward at a gallop and they thudded along the road towards Eoforwic.

When the town came into sight, it was clear that much damage was being done. Nearly the whole town was ablaze, including the great minster church which stood in the northwest quarter. Brihtwulf pulled up his troops just below a low ridge a mile from the town walls. They dismounted and waited, out of sight.

From the burning town, a small group was winding its way along the road towards them.

'Can you see if they're soldiers?' Edgar asked his men. They all squinted into the distance.

'It looks like a family group to me, sir. There's a handcart and what looks like two children,' reported one of his men after a few moments. Others muttered agreement as the party grew closer.

'Very well, we'll wait for them and then see if they know what happened.'

The weary-looking party approached their resting place, unaware of the horsemen behind the low rise ahead of them. As they trudged over the rise, the man pulling the handcart looked up and saw the horsemen. His eyes opened wide and his mouth dropped.

At Brihtwulf's signal, Edgar stepped forward, holding his empty hands palm out towards the man.

'It's all right, we won't hurt you,' he said loudly.

The man let go of his handcart and stood upright. A woman appeared next to him with the two children spotted earlier. She hastily gathered the children protectively into the scant safety of her skirt. The man nervously placed himself between his family and the armed men.

'Are you them?' asked the man fearfully.

'Are we who?' said Edgar.

'The soldiers in the town think that a huge Danish army is advancing on them.'

'Really? Do we look like a huge Danish army?'

The man peered round Edgar, assessing the size of the band of horsemen.

'You could be an advance party,' he said, defiantly.

Edgar looked at Guthrum, who simply stared at the man.

'Why do they think a Danish army is on the way?'

'I dunno. Spies, I suppose. There are spies everywhere these days.'

'Who started the fire?'

'Them. The Norman guards. They said that there were houses too close to the outside of the walls, and they set about burning them so the enemy wouldn't have any materials to build siege weapons and ladders.'

'So they decided to burn all the houses outside the walls?'

'Yes. But it got out of control. Now the whole town is on fire. I got my family out before the flames reached our house. It'll be burned to the ground by now,' he said bitterly.

'It seems we'll have little to do here,' said Guthrum.

The nervous man stepped forward a little. 'Who are you then?' he asked timorously.

Edgar smiled. 'We're the advance guard for a huge Danish army,' he replied. 'I would get off this road if I were you, head west. The army will be coming through here in an hour or so, and you don't want to get in their way. Go on, off you go.'

The man worked his mouth slowly. Then he picked up the handles of his handcart again and began pulling.

'Thank you, sir,' he muttered as he passed Edgar.

His wife followed; eyes averted from the horsemen. The children stared, wide-eyed, at them until their mother hurried them along.

Brihtwulf watched the family retreat and turned to his men.

'Did you hear that lads?' he said in Danish. His men shook their heads. Maybe they couldn't understand the Eoforwic man's English.

'It would seem that the Normans, in trying to defend Jorvik, have set it alight themselves.'

The men burst out laughing.

'If we keep going at this rate, the Normans will kick themselves out of the country before we even get to them!' More laughter followed.

'Right, saddle up. We're heading back to report to the commanders what's happened here.'

The men climbed back on their horses and turned back down the road up which they had just ridden.

On their return to the main body of the army, Edgar and Brihtwulf were taken to speak with Jarl Asbjorn himself. The army marched on along the road as the jarl and his closest council pulled aside to listen to the report by Brihtwulf and Edgar.

The jarl looked resplendent in his gleaming mail, sitting over well-fitted leather armour. His long hair was drawn back from his face and tied at the back.

Brihtwulf gave his report. The jarl looked astonished.

'What kind of people are these?' he rumbled.

'With respect, my Jarl,' said Osfrith, who rode in the jarl's party. 'They are fierce, brave warriors who fight like demons. It does appear, however, that they can make mistakes.'

'We could do with them making a few more mistakes like that,' replied Asbjorn. 'How severe is the fire?'

'The whole town seems to be ablaze, my lord,' replied Brihtwulf. 'As you know, there is a fine minster church within the walls, and even that can be seen to be burning.'

'We need to get there as soon as we can. The place will be in panic.'

He turned and called back into the party of his immediate followers.

'Order an increase in pace, I want to be at Jorvik within the hour!'

Six of the jarl's council turned their horses towards the marching column of men and passed the order along. The men picked up the pace in response, quickening towards the distressed town.

The Danish army drew itself up in battle order quarter of a mile from the eastern gate of the burning town. Jarl Asbjorn's great banner was unfurled and it flew defiantly above the heads of the army.

One horseman, a member of Jarl Asbjorn's party, rode forward towards the gate.

Above the gate, a single Norman guard called out urgently along the wall. More guards appeared next to him. The herald waited as the guards called down to their colleagues below. After a short time, a new figure appeared at the battlements.

The guards deferred to him as he arrived, indicating to the herald that he was a senior man, capable of taking his words to the leaders of this place.

The Lost Land

'In the name of Sweyn Estrithson, King of the Danes and the English, Jarl Asbjorn Estrithson hereby demands the immediate surrender of this place. The governor and his lieutenants will submit to the authority of Jarl Asbjorn, and all your troops will surrender their arms,' called the herald.

'I must confer with my superiors,' called back the man on the battlements. 'I will bring you their reply.'

Edgar surveyed what he could see of the town from his position on the right flank of the Danish army. He and the rest of Brihtwulf's troop were still mounted on their horses. The fires were slowly being brought under control, though many areas of the town were apparently being left to burn themselves out. The roof of the minster still burned in places, but buckets of water were being hauled up in an attempt to save the venerable building.

Edgar could see soldiers scurrying about on the walls, which themselves had been severely damaged by the fire.

'They've got to surrender. They must be able to see that they haven't got a hope of winning this,' said Brihtwulf.

Edgar glanced at him. 'I'm not so sure. Surrender isn't the Norman way. You were at Dunholm; wasn't it just as plain then that they didn't have a hope? And yet they fought to the last man.'

'Aye. I suppose that's true,' conceded Brihtwulf. 'All the same, a surrender would be very welcome at this stage of the invasion.'

The man at the battlements reappeared short moments after he had disappeared. The herald smiled to himself. The man's superiors were obviously close at hand.

The man drew himself up. 'This town and this kingdom

are the property of William, King of England and Duke of Normandy. You have no authority here. You are ordered to withdraw at once and return to where you came from. Failure to comply with this order will result in your complete destruction. That is all.'

The herald turned and walked his horse slowly back to the Danish lines. He made his way unhurriedly round to where Jarl Asbjorn sat patiently on his black stallion.

The herald relayed the Normans' response word for word to Asbjorn.

Asbjorn sighed. Like Brihtwulf, he had hoped for a quick surrender but wasn't unduly concerned at the prospect of a battle which he believed would be quick and decisive.

'So be it, then,' he said. He gathered up his helmet from where it was fastened to the saddle of his horse. He held it aloft so that all in his party could see it, then brought it down onto his head.

All the members of his immediate party did the same.

Watching Asbjorn from his position, Edgar saw the Jarl place his helmet on his head.

'Looks like we're in for a fight,' he said, loud enough for everyone in his troop to hear.

He unstrapped his helmet from his saddle and pulled it onto his head, fastening the chinstrap tightly. All the horsemen did the same. The footmen, in turn, saw the action, and drew themselves into tighter formation, ready for the fight.

The gate in the wall ahead of the waiting army swung open and a column of Norman soldiers emerged, some on horseback, but mostly on foot. Edgar counted them as they filed out of the gate, and the two opposing forces lined up to face each other. No more than a thousand. An unequal fight, but Edgar was well aware that numbers were but one factor in deciding the outcome of a battle.

He looked across at the straggly Norman lines. They looked nervous and ill-prepared for battle. The fire had obviously been a terrible mistake and had left many of the men shocked. They had been fighting the fire for hours now and were not in the best physical condition for a stiff fight.

Looking over the Danish army that was facing them, Edgar saw fresh troops, clean armour and weapons, the faces beneath the helmets unflinching.

Brihtwulf climbed down from his horse. Edgar and Guthrum followed suit and indicated to the other riders that they should do the same. The men led their horses to the rear of the battle lines where they would be looked after during the battle. The Danes had no more love for cavalry battles than did the English, and like them, preferred to fight on foot.

Brihtwulf, Edgar, Guthrum and their men joined the rear of the infantry ranks, ready to take their turn in the fighting when the time came.

They watched as a party of eight Norman knights galloped out to the disorganised Norman lines and started barking orders. The Norman footmen immediately began pulling themselves into smarter lines and soon looked more the fighting force Edgar had come to expect.

The armies faced each other. Edgar scanned the front row of the Norman lines. He saw soot-smutted faces, tired eyes, some with red skin. He also saw a grim determination, and he knew this was not going to be an easy fight.

Apparently without a signal having been given, the

Danes started clashing their axes and swords in unison against their shields. Edgar spotted some nervous glances amongst the younger faces in the Norman lines, but the older, more experienced fighters remained resolute.

At a cry, archers at the rear of the Norman lines loosed a volley of arrows which arched high above the ground and then plummeted down onto the heads of the Danish army. Shields were quickly raised, but not before several men had fallen, pierced by the deadly shower. Arrows thudded into the ground around Edgar, and in front of him, he saw a man dropped by an arrow that hit him at the base of his throat, dropping almost vertically from the sky. The man made no sound, killed instantly. Two men to his side caught him as he fell and dragged him out of the line. They dropped him where they stopped. There was no time now for decorum, the battle had begun.

A shout arose from the huddle of royal housecarls around Jarl Asbjorn. The order to advance at a slow walking pace. As the Danes began moving forward, a second volley of arrows lashed down from the skies. This time the Danes were ready, and the arrows found only shields to embed themselves in. Those with pierced shields quickly pulled out the arrows, or if they were too deeply embedded, they snapped off the wooden shafts behind the deadly iron tips.

In reply to the second volley, a massive wave of arrows shot from the rear of the Danish lines. Not as ordered as the Norman volleys, the arrows kept coming constantly, flashing out of the sky and into the Norman ranks.

Edgar watched in satisfaction as dozens of Norman footmen and one of the heavily-armoured knights fell to the ground, transfixed by the iron rain.

One of the Norman horsemen shouted something over

the din of the clattering of arrows on shield and mail. Unable to escape the fury of the Danish arrows, the Norman footmen began running towards the Danes, it was the only way to get away from the arrows. The Danes, without needing the order, stopped advancing and stood their ground. Edgar shook his head to himself. The Norman commander had fallen for an old trick. He had been pushed into a headlong dash at the Danish lines.

At a shouted command, the Danes brought their shields up to form a solid defensive wall. Axes and swords hung menacingly above the shields as the Normans advanced.

In a matter of moments, the Normans crashed into the shield wall of the Danish army. Dozens fell to the ground, felled by the axes that bore down on them the second they arrived. The shield wall flexed backwards as the Normans hurtled into it, but it did not break. Edgar could see Danish axes hacking away at the defenders, but he saw no Dane fall, and no gaps appeared in the shield wall.

At a cry from the front, the rear of the Danish army began moving outward, curling round to enfold the sides of the Norman lines. Edgar found himself at the front of this new attack, on the Danish right flank.

The Normans at the flanks turned to face the new threat. Edgar saw ahead of him a young man, not much more than a boy, turn to face him. His helmet was too large for him and his eyes were filled with fear. Edgar tossed his axe in his hand, bringing the head to the rear. He swiped the weapon round and brought it squarely onto the loose helmet of his opponent. The boy dropped to the ground, and Edgar offered up the briefest of prayers to whoever may be listening that he had judged the power of the blow correctly and that the boy would recover his wits enough to crawl away from the battle.

An altogether different foe now faced him. A large, broad man with heavy stubble and a snarl on his face. His sword thrust fiercely over Edgar's shield towards his face. Edgar ducked his head to his right and the sword glanced harmlessly off the cheek-piece of his helmet.

As the man withdrew his sword for a second blow, Edgar smashed his shield into the man's body, putting his full weight behind it, as Harek had taught him. The man staggered back, momentarily losing his balance. Edgar took advantage, smashing his axe into the side of the Norman's head. The axe hit the strengthened rim of the Norman helmet which buckled under the blow. Edgar's opponent's head changed shape subtly, and his left eye bulged from its socket.

Edgar stepped back. His foe would fight no more, but the crush of men around him meant that he would not fall to the ground, either.

The Norman second row was crushed and unable to bring their weapons up. Guthrum spotted the advantage at the same time Edgar did, and the two men set about slashing and hacking at the helpless foot-soldiers. On Edgar's left, one of the men who had ridden to Eoforwic with him was laughing loudly as he dispatched more Normans, unable to defend themselves.

The morale of the Normans, which had never been good, was now dropping like one of their own plunging arrows, whilst the Danes were riding a wave of growing confidence and battle-joy.

Shouts from the mounted Norman knights could be heard above the battle-din. The Norman foot soldiers began to move outward, releasing those trapped by the crush. The

The Lost Land

fight suddenly became more equal.

The soldiers who had been unable to bring their weapons up were now free to do so. As they pulled apart from each other, the terrible results of their earlier situation became clear. Dozens of Normans in the second line dropped to the ground, no longer supported by the crush. The front and second lines of the Norman force had been badly mauled and had no option but to close up again to fill the gaps left by their fallen comrades.

A new determination seemed to grip the Normans, and they fought ferociously. Edgar found himself on the back foot as a skilled swordsman battered mercilessly at his round shield. Edgar found no gap to bring his axe down into. He felt himself being pushed backwards, where the pressure from the second line behind him forced him forward again.

As the Norman's sword slashed down again, another sword jabbed out over Edgar's shoulder, deflecting it. It gave Edgar the briefest of moments, when the Norman was startled, to bring his axe round. He caught the Norman in the side. The Norman's mail armour held, but the blow was a heavy one, and the loud grunt from his opponent told Edgar that he had made a useful hit.

The Norman's sword wavered in his hand, as he reeled in the after-effects of Edgar's blow. The sword hovering over Edgar's shoulder stabbed forward again, hitting the man hard in the collar bone. He gasped again, dropping his sword. His shield fell from in front of him, leaving him open to the killing blow to the chest that Edgar now delivered.

Edgar never learned who saved him that day – he was sure that he had been saved – he was losing the fight at that point.

Edgar dropped back to the second row and was

immediately replaced by another fighter in the front row. He glanced round to assess the battle. The Danes were not having it all their own way but were winning the day. The flanking manoeuvre had worked, with the Danish lines now forming a closing crescent around the Normans.

The Normans were losing men at a far greater rate than the Danes, and soon there would be too few of them to continue any sort of meaningful fight.

Another shower of arrows flew from the behind the Norman ranks, but this time many fell short, killing more Normans than Danes.

Edgar heard an angry shout from the Norman rear, and although he did not hear the words, nor could he have understood them if he had, the sentiment was clear. No more arrows were fired from the Norman ranks.

A group of Danish archers were working together to pick off the Norman knights now. As Edgar watched, one of them was simultaneously hit by three arrows as several more flashed past him. He toppled slowly from his horse. Another horseman galloped past, also to be felled by several arrows. The Normans were losing their leaders. Only one result could follow.

The rear of the Norman lines began to break, and soldiers at the rear began streaming back towards the perceived safety of the town walls.

A huge cry of victory arose from the Danish army as they pressed home their advantage. More and more Normans fell, and more and more of them turned and fled.

At last, there were no Normans left standing on the field. Piles of dead were scattered around, whilst all those still alive were back within the ravaged walls of Eoforwic.

A cheer arose from the Danish lines, and once again

The Lost Land

they began beating their weapons in unison on their shields.

Asbjorn's voice carried across the field, and the clatter died down. The Danes reformed into a tight column. They marched resolutely over the fallen bodies of their enemies, up to the walls themselves and through the gate that none of the Normans had thought to close behind them.

Inside the town walls, the Danes found scenes of devastation. The fire had been very fierce and large areas lay as blackened, smoking waste. There were no people to be seen. The fire had started the process of evacuation, and the sight of an all-conquering Danish army had completed it. The citizens of Eoforwic had fled.

The Danes spread out and began the inevitable looting process. Edgar looked on with distaste as the town was stripped of what valuables remained. Small pockets of Norman resistance were met but were easily crushed.

The Danes cheered rapturously as Jarl Asbjorn and his party of royal housecarls rode in through the gate. The jarl rode through the devastated streets, looking in interest at the carnage around him. Eventually, he stopped in the open area before the minster. He looked up at its high stone walls. The roof had finally stopped burning, but blackened rafters stood starkly against the sky. Edgar and Guthrum had followed the jarl, not wishing to be involved in the desecration of the ancient royal town.

'We will camp here for the night,' declared the jarl. 'Tomorrow we will hold council to decide on what we do next. Until then, this town is yours!'

A great cheer arose from the assembled Danes as they accepted the largesse of their leader, who had just granted them licence to sack.

The following morning, Asbjorn sat with his council in the open air in front of the minster. The night had passed riotously, with the troops looting and pillaging into the small hours.

Now the leaders of the expedition sat together before their troops, looking very pleased with themselves.

To Asbjorn's right sat a pale young man, his fair hair bounded by a thin band of silver.

'Is that who I think it is?' asked Edgar quietly.

'I've never seen him before,' said Guthrum, 'but my guess is that it's Edgar Atheling. Look, beside him is Earl Maerleswein. Now him I have seen before. I thought he must surely be dead.'

He fell silent as Jarl Asbjorn rose. The jarl waited until the excited chatter had died down.

'We have won a great victory!' declared Asbjorn, to cheers. 'The Norman dogs ran before us. Is this the best that they can do?'

Edgar turned uncomfortably towards Guthrum.

'No, this bloody well isn't the best that they can do. They can do a damn sight better than this. What's all this self-congratulation? The Normans burned their own defences down for God's sake.'

Asbjorn continued. 'We have taken many prisoners. Many high-ranking Normans slept last night in our chains. And yet we must not think of this as a great victory, merely as the start of a campaign to take this land once and for all out of the hands of these barbarians. We have sent a message to the bastard duke of Normandy, who dares to call himself king of England.'

'Yes, and he'll be on our arses before we know it,'

muttered Guthrum.

'We will return to the ships this morning. Prepare yourselves for the march,' declared Asbjorn.

'What?' Edgar shot the question at Guthrum. He wasn't alone, surprised mutterings erupted amongst the gathered troops, especially the English contingent.

'My lord!' shouted an Englishman near the front of the crowd. 'Why return to the ships when we have a town to call our own? Is this not exactly the bridgehead that we were hoping to create?'

Asbjorn looked down calmly at the bold man who had the effrontery to challenge him in front of all his troops.

'Who are you?' asked the jarl calmly.

'Ricebehrt, my lord, late thegn of Tilford.'

'Well, Ricebehrt, late thegn of Tilford, have you seen the state of this town that you wish us to call home? Over half the houses are destroyed and the walls are damaged beyond our ability to repair within the time it will take the Bastard to get here with his army. We cannot defend this place. If we stay, we will lose our advantage. The Normans will be here in great force within days. It will be better for us to destroy what defences remain,' he waved his hand towards the two wooden motte and bailey castles that had been hurriedly erected by the Normans in the past year.

'There will be no sanctuary for the Normans here. When they arrive and find their town and castles thrown down, and that they have no walls to cower behind, then they will know fear. Meanwhile, we will return to our ships to make us safe and highly mobile. Our great mobility is our best advantage.

'Now, do you have any more questions? Any of you?' His question was met with muttered negatives.

'Good, you may all go and prepare for the return.'

9

Other Searchers

Halfdene, Alaric and Harek walked their horses slowly down the rutted road through the forest. Halfdene was searching for a track that he remembered from his last visit. He knew they were in the right area; his time with the Wildmen in the previous year had instilled in him a deep knowledge of the forest. He knew it was here, somewhere. It wasn't easy. They rode along the highway that passed through the forest from north to south, stopping occasionally as Halfdene squinted into the trees, trying to identify the track. Finally, he gave a subdued cry as he spotted what he was looking for. It was an insignificant-looking pathway, no more than may have been left by the regular use of a hare.

'I think this is it,' he said.

Alaric looked down at the track. 'I think you're right,' he said.

He turned round in his saddle and examined the trees

and bushes behind him.

'Yes, I'm sure of it,' he said. 'Well spotted.'

Halfdene led his two companions off the main road and they threaded their way carefully through the forest ground cover. On the journey, Halfdene had been coaching Harek on making his passage as inconspicuous as possible. Now Harek followed Halfdene's advice and directed his horse accordingly.

After ten minutes, Halfdene halted and made a low whistling. He paused and strained to listen for a reply. Hearing none, he whistled again, a little louder.

Birds made small sounds all around him, some barely-heard pipings, the occasional rustle in the undergrowth. Despite listening with all their attention, Halfdene and Alaric could again detect no reply.

They moved on for another quarter of a mile, Halfdene repeating his calls. Once more, no reply was heard. Halfdene looked quizzically at Alaric.

'When we left them, they had moved further west. They may not be operating this far east any more,' said the spy.

'Then we need to move further west ourselves. Let's keep going.'

They pressed on through the forest, taking small animal tracks so they left no sign of their passage through the woods.

As it started to get darker, Halfdene called them to a halt. Once more he tried the call of the Wildmen, to no avail.

It was getting harder to see when they arrived at the edge of a clearing. Meadow grasses spread ahead of them for about a hundred and fifty yards.

'We'll have to stop for the night. We can't carry on in the darkness.'

The Lost Land

They dismounted and unstrapped the saddles from their horses. Alaric took the horses to a nearby small brook for a drink, and then tied them to trees where they could graze and drink with ease.

They decided not to make a fire. The night was warm and they had dried meat to eat and fresh water from the brook to drink. Halfdene was uneasy about the apparent absence of the Wildmen and did not want to advertise their presence any more than was unavoidable.

They sat quietly at the edge of the clearing and chewed on their dried meat rations. Alaric brought three thin blankets from the horses' saddlebags. As darkness fell, Alaric and Harek rolled themselves into the blankets whilst Halfdene took the first watch.

He listened to the night sounds of the forest. The night was still, and in the absence of rustling leaves, he could hear the faintest sound. For long periods there was absolute silence, then from a long way off he heard the call of an owl, and it was answered by another, closer this time. He listened very carefully to the cadence of each call. He was convinced that they were genuine owl calls, not the calls of the Wildmen. Occasionally a roosting bird would awaken and issue a quiet piping call, but again this was quite natural. Halfdene had slept outside hundreds of times in his life and was intimately familiar with the sounds of the forest.

His eyes registered very little. The sky overhead was a deep blue. It would turn quite black fairly soon. He could see stars above him, bright and constant. He looked at the strange sky-river that was called the Milky Way, looking exactly like a river of thin milk arching over his head. He puzzled for a moment, wondering what it actually was. Was it a celestial river? Did heavenly creatures row and punt their way along it, way, way above this solid earth? Would anyone ever know for certain? He put such thoughts out of his head. This life, he had learned long ago, had no certainties, other than death.

A sound caught his attention. Something was walking through the undergrowth, maybe fifty yards away. The sound made him tense, and he consciously forced himself to relax his muscles. He reached slowly for his axe, which lay on the grass beside his right hand.

The noise continued. It was quiet but seemed careless, as if whatever was moving out there was not deliberately hiding the sound of its passage. Halfdene relaxed his grip on the axe. This did not sound like a man.

A shockingly loud bark sounded in that instant from where the sound of movement had been coming. Deep and resonant, it echoed round the little clearing. It was followed by another, and another.

Although the first bark had made him jump, Halfdene released the axe and sat back. Just a deer. One of the big males, he thought, probably declaring his territory.

The thought comforted Halfdene considerably. If men were stalking them, the deer would not be anywhere near here. For now, then, he could relax.

Harek grunted in his sleep, roused slightly by the deer, but he did not wake. Alaric made no noise at all when he was asleep. Halfdene wondered if the little man ever actually slept. He would wake fully alert. He never needed time to shake off the sluggish bonds of sleep as Halfdene did.

It was the end of his shift. Time for sleep. He whispered into the darkness 'Alaric.'

'I'm ready,' said Alaric immediately, sitting up. 'Good night Halfdene, sleep well.'

The Lost Land

Halfdene lay back where he had been sitting and stared for a few moments at the starlit sky. He noticed fingers of blackness creeping up in the west. Stars were winking out and then brightening up again. Clouds. The weather was probably about to turn.

Halfdene rolled over onto his side and fell almost immediately to sleep.

Alaric looked up at the sky that Halfdene had recently been contemplating. He looked along the Milky Way and not for the first time remembered a view of a large town in his homeland that he had seen from the top of a distant mountain at night. The town was clear to see, illuminated by the torches and candles scattered throughout its streets and buildings. He had not, however, been able to distinguish a single torch or candle individually. All together, though, they produced a glow that he could see. Now he looked at the great river of light in the sky. Stars, he thought. Many, many stars. So faint and far away that they could not be seen individually, but produced a smooth, even glow. He could conjecture no further. Why so many stars would be gathered together like that he had no idea.

He sighed and looked down. All was darkness. Small birds made themselves known to his hearing, as they had for Halfdene. He settled himself into a state he had been honing for many years. He sat perfectly still and concentrated all his thoughts on the tiny sounds of the night. The birds piping, a tiny rustle of leaves, the quiet sound of a small twig falling from a tree. His breathing grew shallower and shallower and soon he found himself in the warmth of his still-awareness, as he called it. His thoughts clarified and his hearing became more acute.

After sitting motionless like this for twenty minutes, he

heard it.

It was very quiet indeed. If he had not been totally focused on listening, he would have missed it. Without any immodesty at all, he thought that it was fortunate that it was he and not either of his two companions who was on watch at that moment.

It was a metallic clink. Not close, and immediately hushed, but that one tiny noise could mean only one thing. There was a man, or men, relatively nearby. And moving.

Alaric strained to hear, becoming very aware of the constant whistling in his ears. It was not loud, and from conversations with others, he believed it to be perfectly normal. He had once known a man who could barely hear anything over the high-pitched squealing in his ears.

Just over his ear-whistle, he heard the sound again. Once he had latched onto the sound, he knew exactly what he was listening for, and this made the hearing of it much easier.

Slightly more distant this time, he thought. Then there again. Definitely further away, in amongst the trees on the far side of the clearing. The man or men were not, then, aware of their presence.

He did not hear the noise again, but it concerned him that somebody was moving through the forest at night, and striving to remain totally silent as they did so. Why would anyone do that if their business was legitimate? It was almost impossible to see in the woods, especially on a moonless night such as this.

The only conclusion that Alaric could arrive at was that it was a Wildman. There was nothing for it, Alaric would have to investigate. He leaned over and gently shook Harek, who woke silently.

The Lost Land

'What is it?' he whispered.

'I need to investigate something. It may be nothing but it would be foolish to ignore it,' breathed Alaric into Harek's ear. 'Take my watch until I'm back.'

Harek nodded and sat up.

Alaric paused, then added 'Until I return, both of you must remain silent.'

Harek nodded again, understanding immediately.

Alaric got to his feet and bent into a low crouch, set off across the clearing towards the source of the noise. He was soon amongst the trees, and not being intimately familiar with this part of the woods, he slowed down so that he could feel the ground beneath the thin soles of his shoes. He did not want to alert his quarry to his presence. Slowly and carefully, he picked his way through the undergrowth, not putting a foot down until he knew that nothing would snap, rustle or make any other sound when he did.

Progress was slow, and Alaric stopped occasionally to listen for any further sounds that gave away the location of his quarry.

What he heard convinced him that whoever had been moving around in the forest earlier was now at rest.

He continued creeping forwards towards where he had last heard the noise. It took him an hour, but his care was eventually rewarded when he saw a shadow move slightly about thirty yards in front of him. He stopped, barely daring to breathe. He could just discern the sound of a whispered conversation ahead. More than one man, then.

About half-way between himself and the men was a thick-boled tree. He moved sideways, placing the tree between himself and the men. He walked carefully towards it, even more cautiously than before. When he reached the tree, he placed the flats of his palms against the gnarled bark, feeling its comforting solidity. Slowly, he eased himself down onto the ground and poked his head out so that his ear was pointing in the direction of the men.

He could not make out any individual words, but he identified five different voices. The conversation was very quiet, stilted and slow, but from the rhythms of the speech, Alaric had no doubt that the language was Norman French.

In the tree above him, an early thrush burst into song, announcing that dawn would not be long.

Alaric cursed silently to himself. The gloom in the woods would not protect him once the sky started brightening, and it would take him too long to return to his friends. His best course of action would be to remain exactly where he now sat.

The Normans were unsuspecting of his presence. If he remained silent and unmoving that situation would continue. In the best of worlds, the Normans would simply continue on their journey at dawn, remaining unaware of the presence of Alaric and his friends.

He heard one of the Normans mutter something to his colleagues. A quiet creaking of leather suggested to Alaric that one of the men had risen. Now he heard careful footsteps. From the way they were increasing slightly in volume, Alaric inferred that the man was walking towards where he was hiding. There was a rustle of clothing, followed by the sound of a torrent of splashing water.

Alaric allowed himself a small sigh of relief. The man was just relieving himself, and none too cautiously. The sound of his water could probably be heard for hundreds of yards around, suggesting to Alaric that the party of men were being habitually silent and that they were not actually

The Lost Land

stalking anyone at the moment. He had puzzled over why a group of Normans, armed as they must be, were moving so quietly in the dead of night. The answer now came to him. These were special troops, not common-or-garden Norman foot soldiers.

Answers and more questions flooded into Alaric's mind with this insight. They must be deep in the woods for a specific purpose. What could that be? The answer presented itself immediately. They must be hunting the Wildmen. That may also explain why Alaric and his colleagues had failed to make contact themselves with the Wildmen. Either the Normans had successfully driven them from this part of the forest, or they were keeping silent, not returning calls that may now be outdated. The possibility occurred to Alaric that the Normans themselves might now be aware of at least some of the Wildmen's calls, and may have been using them to trick the Wildmen into giving themselves away.

Alaric made a mental note to stop using calls that now may suggest to the Wildmen that they were Normans. It could be a very dangerous thing to do.

He decided to remain in his hiding place until the men moved on. He prayed fervently that his final instruction to Harek to remain still and silent would hold.

The Danish army and their allies were preparing to depart from Eoforwic. The town lay in ruins, an indefensible pile of smoking rubble. The citizens of the town were nowhere to be seen. The streets were deserted apart from the occasional roaming band of soldiers, searching for anything of value that may have been left behind or which still lay unnoticed amongst the devastation.

Edgar and Guthrum rode silently out of the battered

city gate and joined their troop. Brihtwulf sat on his dappled grey horse and looked behind him at the smouldering town.

As Edgar and Guthrum drew up beside him, he turned round to face forward and without comment gave the order to begin the march back to the ships.

Outlying farms stood largely intact, and even now, farmers and labourers were out, guarding sheep and cows. Edgar wondered what the poor bastards thought they could do if the army decided that it wanted to eat their herds.

They passed close by the boundary ditch of a harvested wheat field, and a farmer, braver than most, stood and stared at the passing horsemen, his face a mask of contempt. Edgar could not meet his eyes.

After some time, Brihtwulf began to speak, without turning his face.

'Not exactly the beachhead we were hoping for, but a message to the Bastard that can leave little room for interpretation, I think.'

Edgar snorted. 'Are we not past the time for messages?' he asked. 'This looks like nothing more than a raid, and now we're rushing back to the protection of our ships, rather than waiting for the Bastard to bring up his army so we can face them in one final, decisive battle.'

'Eoforwic is no longer available to him as shelter. That in itself is something to celebrate.'

'Eoforwic is a ruin. An English town.'

'We'll rebuild it, don't fear. Better and stronger than ever.'

'But for now, we are retreating to the ships,' Edgar growled.

'Only briefly. We're using the ships to transport us to our permanent base as soon as we get back. It's time to

The Lost Land

make our true beachhead, get the army on land and settle in for the fight.'

His eyes sparkled with enthusiasm as he spoke. Edgar looked confused.

'It was decided in the council at Eoforwic that the time had come for landfall. The ships will continue harrying up and down the coast to keep the Bastard's eyes away from the larger force as we set up our camps.'

'Where are we going?' asked Guthrum.

'The Isle of Hakrholme, south of the great river.'

'I've never heard of it,' said Edgar.

'No reason why you should have, unless you've studied the history of the Danish raids,' replied Brihtwulf, a smile flickering around the corners of his mouth.

'Hakrholme is an area of land, maybe ten or twelve miles long by five or six wide. It's mostly marsh and waste, but there are some areas of higher ground, several with small settlements on them. The Isle is cut off from the land to the north by the rivers Ouse, Don and Torne, to the west and south by the Idle and to the east by the Trent. It's rich in game and fish, so we won't starve whilst we're there. There is a precedent for its use. The raiding Danish armies of years ago used to overwinter there occasionally.'

'Skulking in a marsh?' muttered Edgar.

'Oh come on, Edgar! This is the landfall you've been craving. It's well-protected and gives us access to the north and centre of England.'

Guthrum looked more enthusiastic than Edgar. 'Look at it like this, lad,' he said. 'We'll be like Alfred-king on the Isle of Athelney. That's in the middle of a marsh and he conquered the Danes from there, threw them right out of Wessex,' he said enthusiastically.

'Yes, yes. Well said, Guthrum, it'll be just like that.' replied Brihtwulf.

They rode on in silence for a few moments, until Brihtwulf turned thoughtfully to Guthrum. 'Though I wouldn't remind our Danish friends of that fact if I were you.'

The ships made their way cautiously through a thin, ragged mist. At the prow of Stormleaper, close to the front of the flotilla, one of Loki's crew clung to the great carved horse's head at the bow, leaning forward to peer into the mist. The boat ahead of them began slowing, oars dipped into the water. The crewman called softly back to the crew and they also began a gentle backward sculling to slow the ship.

Thick reeds parted as the sleek prow of Stormleaper ploughed through them. A gentle hissing announced that the keel had run aground.

'Can't see a bloody thing,' muttered Guthrum. The reeds hid everything around them from view.

'The water can't be deep here or we wouldn't have grounded. Is this it? Do we get out now?' asked Hallvindur.

'We wait for Loki's order,' said Edgar.

As he spoke, they heard Loki call quietly to his crew. Half a dozen of them stood up and walked to the front of the ship, drawing their axes. They dropped over the side and proceeded to hack away at the dense reeds until a clear path through was made up to the riverbank ahead of them.

To either side of Stormleaper, other ships were grounding and men were dropping into the river with muted splashes. All along the riverbank, men started moving ashore.

The Lost Land

When Loki called for disembarkation, Edgar and his men stood and joined the press to get to the bank.

Immediately they were ashore, the army spread out to form a defensive perimeter, though there appeared to be no immediate threat.

Ahead of them was an area of dry land, though all around it was a vast expanse of marshes and water meadows. The land before them rose to a low plateau. At the top, Edgar could dimly make out three thin columns of smoke, barely distinguishable from the mist. They were rising, he assumed, from the nearest settlement to their landing place, which Brihtwulf had called Gerulftoft.

An advance party was already making its way up the shallow incline towards the settlement. Ahead of them, over the crest of the plateau, three men were walking purposefully towards the advance party. The men looked unarmed, so Edgar assumed that one of them was the headman of Gerulftoft or his representative.

The two parties stopped when they met, with no animosity being shown on either side. The men talked for a short while, then the village men and the Danes continued up the hill towards the village. The order had come down to all the troops in the army to inflict no harm on the local populace unless absolutely necessary, but the village had to be secured. From what he had just seen, Edgar inferred that an agreement had been reached in advance with the inhabitants at least of this village to that effect.

The troops were pouring off the ships now, and once all their passengers had alighted, each ship pulled back from the beaching to make room for the next. The troops began setting up tents and shelters. The horses were led off the flat-bottomed transports and another party of men, armed with wood-axes, headed towards a stand of tall trees to collect timber.

Edgar and Guthrum set about erecting leather tents which would sleep eight men each. Further up the slope, a series of larger tents were being put up, to house the expedition's leaders in somewhat more luxury than was afforded to the bulk of the men.

A cheer arose from the men as Asbjorn stepped ashore and began walking towards where his tent was being pitched. He stopped and chatted to the men as he walked. Edgar watched him carefully. He was a large, powerful man, and yet he found it easy to maintain a friendly tone with even the lowest of his soldiers. It was an enviable trait in a man with the power of life and death over every one of them.

As they worked on putting up the tents, Edgar and Guthrum were joined by Osfrith Edwinsson, struggling up the shallow slope and leaning heavily on his stick.

'Edgar, Guthrum, glad you made it here in one piece. Once you've finished here, come and join me at my tent and we'll share a flagon of ale.'

Osfrith waved his stick up the hill, to where Hallvindur and four other of Osfrith's housecarls were setting up his spacious tent.

'Thank you, we will,' said Edgar.

The tents were finished and set up in roughly parallel rows. Edgar and Guthrum dropped their travel bags inside one of them and walked up towards Osfrith Edwinsson's tent, his banner hanging limply in the still air above it.

As they approached, they saw Osfrith sitting on a rough bench, his mouth full as he chewed his way through a tough-looking piece of meat.

Unable to speak, he waved them towards a second bench. With another wave of his hand, he indicated to one of the nearby housecarls that they should provide Edgar and Guthrum with ale.

Finally swallowing the food, he turned to look at them.

'Tell me all about it,' he commanded.

Edgar cleared his throat.

'It was not all that I could have wished for, my lord,' he said.

'Oh? How so?'

'As you have probably already heard, the Normans were panicked by the approach of our army. So much so that they set fire to the buildings outside the walls to deprive us of materials to build siege ladders and so on.'

'Yes, I heard that. It all got a bit out of control, though, didn't it?'

'That's an understatement. By the time we arrived, the whole town was alight. The Normans were in disarray, but they still came out to fight. We won, of course, easily.'

'So what's wrong with that?'

'Jarl Asbjorn then ordered the town sacked. Almost completely destroyed though it was, the rubble and smoking remains were put to the sack. We are supposed to be throwing the Normans out of England, not plundering it.'

'Ah, Edgar.' Osfrith looked at the ground between his feet and shook his head gently.

'Sweyn-king's troops hail, as you know, from all over northern Europe. Do you think that the King is paying them out of his own purse? Do you think even a king like Sweyn can afford that? Of course he can't. These troops need paying, and plunder and loot is the only way that can be achieved. The riches of this nation far exceed even what this army can hope to take away. It is, I'm afraid, the price we have to pay.'

'I don't have to like it.'

'No, you don't. But ask yourself this question; would you rather serve the king of Denmark or the man who calls himself king of England?'

'Sweyn, obviously.'

'Yes, so remember that. This land is currently William's land. In the regaining of it, I'm afraid we have to inflict some damage. Now be aware; Asbjorn is not above executing dissenters. I would keep your thoughts on how he chooses to perform his tasks to yourself, or at least very quietly amongst us. Fair warning, Edgar. Let's see how it unfolds from here.'

10

Wildmen Found

Harek woke with a small grunt. He silently cursed himself for an old fool. He had fallen asleep after Alaric had disappeared silently into the night. He flicked his eyes all around, trying to assess the situation. Had anything changed that might indicate that they were in danger?

The sky was turning blue as the autumnal sun clawed its way from beneath the horizon. Clouds were building to the west, but the east remained clear. Birds were singing loudly, heralding the dawn of the new day. Nothing moved in the clearing. Harek estimated that no more than an hour had passed since Alaric had gone. He cursed himself again, viciously. He extended a hand towards Halfdene and gently placed his hand over the other man's mouth. Halfdene awoke with a small start but remained quiet.

Harek raised a finger to his lips, telling Halfdene to stay silent. Halfdene slowly and carefully rose to a sitting position. Harek leaned in towards him and breathed into his ear.

'Alaric heard something. He went to investigate about an hour ago. I've heard nothing and there's no sign that anything has happened. Alaric must still be over there,' he nodded his head towards the trees in the distance.

'What did he hear?'

'I don't know. He just said that he needed to investigate something. I'm afraid I fell asleep after he went. I'm sorry.'

Halfdene snorted quietly. 'Doesn't look like any harm's been done. I'll stay awake with you now.'

They sat in silence under the brightening sky. With the birds singing so loudly, there was no way that they could hear the tiny sounds that were audible at night. As the land around them lightened into visibility, Harek and Halfdene lay down on their stomachs, heads facing the direction that Alaric had gone. In this position, they were as hard to see as they could make themselves without leaving their overnight spot.

'What about the horses?' whispered Halfdene.

'Nothing we can do, just be ready if we hear them. They'll start making noises if anyone approaches. If that happens then we might as well make ourselves known, it wouldn't be long before we were found.'

Halfdene loosened the axe from his belt and felt its comforting weight in his hand.

'I'll be ready,' he said.

Still hiding behind his tree, Alaric remained motionless as he listened to the sounds of the men he was stalking as they stirred and prepared for the day.

With the coming of the morning, the men had become less cautious about the sounds they were making. The virtually silent whispered conversations of the past night were now replaced with more normal levels of talk, though still quiet. Alaric, however, could now make out much of what they were saying. Hearing the words confirmed that they were speaking Norman French, which he understood perfectly.

The men were discussing plans for the coming day.

'We continue east,' said the first voice.

'How far?' asked a second.

'One mile at a time. You're on our northern flank today, so be aware.'

The second voice grunted.

The first voice continued, speaking to the other men. He was describing a very detailed search pattern, and it seemed that this was not the only band involved in the search. There was mention of other bands to the north and south. Alaric was now in no doubt that they were searching for the Wildmen. This was not good news.

He sat in silence, despite beginning to cramp from prolonged stillness. Eventually, he heard the men begin to move away. Fortunately, he had secreted himself to their west, and they were searching to the east. Once the sound of their footsteps had faded away, he waited a further thousand heartbeats, before painfully raising himself to his feet. He rubbed his calves and thighs vigorously to get the blood circulating again and then walked slowly and carefully back towards Harek and Halfdene.

'We were lucky,' he said as he lay down next to them. 'There are five of them, and they're just one team. There must be others, though I don't know how many.'

'What are they doing?' asked Harek.

'Same as us. They're searching for the Wildmen.'

'We could have stumbled into them at any time,' said Halfdene.

'Yes. Fortunately, we seem to have been behind them, it was just luck that we stopped a few hundred yards behind where they stopped. If we had gone any further, they would have had us, especially if we'd been making Wildman calls.'

'Shit,' muttered Halfdene. 'This is going to make our job a hundred times more difficult. If what you say is true, then these woods will be crawling with Normans. The Wildmen will have gone to ground and won't show themselves. Just looking for them is probably a dangerous thing to do. If the Normans don't get us, we're just as likely to be attacked by any Wildmen, as they'll probably assume we're Normans.'

Harek grunted his assent. 'I would if I were them,' he agreed.

'We have to come up with a new and better strategy,' said Halfdene. 'Anybody got any suggestions?'

After a few moments of silence, Alaric spoke. 'I suggest that I go on alone. I think we're about five miles from the Paddock. I imagine that the Normans are still unaware of it. The search teams will already have passed by there. I'll go there and see if any Wildmen are using it at present. If you can follow at least quarter of a mile behind the Norman search teams, we can meet there in a day's time.'

'We abandoned the Paddock because the Normans had found it,' objected Halfdene. 'Don't you remember?'

'No, they didn't find it. Folcwine led them there, but he didn't know quite where it was, and none of the Normans actually got to it. They were shooting fire-arrows more or less randomly at every bush and tree they saw. What's more, before he was executed, Folcwine told us that nobody knew of the rough location of the Paddock except the leader of that group of Normans, and he died that day along with all his men. I'd be confident that the Paddock is still secure.'

Halfdene nodded. 'Harek?' he asked.

'Seems as good a plan as any to me. As long as we take all precautions, then we should be alright.'

'I'll go on foot,' said Alaric. 'Take my horse with you when you go, and give me a good start. Don't head off after me until midday.'

'Good,' said Halfdene, looking at the newly risen Sun, now beginning to rise above the trees on the far side of the clearing. 'We'll set off at about noon, then.'

'If I find the Wildmen, I'll warn them to expect you. Don't attempt to contact them as you travel, and don't use their techniques for remaining silent. Be quiet, but don't give the impression that you are experienced in that regard, any Wildmen who see you may decide that you're part of the Norman search party and dispatch you on the spot.'

Halfdene and Harek signalled their understanding.

Alaric stood. 'I'll go, then. I'll get some dried meat for the journey from the saddle-bags as I go.' He stooped down and picked up a water skin from the ground.

Once back amongst the trees, Alaric made good progress. He remained quiet, yet not quiet enough to be mistaken for a Wildman by the Normans nor a Norman by the Wildmen. Every hundred paces or so he would stop and listen intently for a few minutes, before continuing on his way.

After he had walked what he estimated to be about halfway to the Paddock, a little over two miles, he stopped for his regular break to listen carefully to the sounds around him. Birds were singing and chattering, nothing unusual could be heard amongst their calls. There was a gentle pattering of small pieces of detritus falling from the trees, and the careless scuffling of a small animal a few yards away to his right. Suddenly, amid the natural chatter of the woodlands, he heard an alien sound. It was small and some way off, but he dropped swiftly to the ground nonetheless. He had heard a twig snap twice. He recognised the sound as almost certainly the result of a human footfall. He crept cautiously behind a large patch of bracken and let the wide leaves cover him. Listening intently, he heard more sounds. He estimated that there were at least three men, moving carefully but not over-cautiously. He began to hear their quiet conversation as they approached. They were Normans, that much he could tell from the pattern of their speech. He could also tell that they were moving towards him.

Peering between the leaves of the bracken, he could see them now. Four men, dressed in peasant garb, staffs in hand. They spoke quietly amongst themselves, but were too quiet and too far away for Alaric to catch the words. They were, however, still approaching his position, a fact that was starting to cause Alaric a little concern.

Without any warning, the four men all fell to the ground together. Alaric had caught the flash of something hurtling towards the men. Arrows! Their white flight feathers now stood out starkly against the green undergrowth. Alaric froze, knowing that his own life was now precariously in the balance.

'You can get up now,' said a voice alarmingly close to him. A figure rose from the ground just ten feet from where

The Lost Land

he lay.

Alaric stood.

'I remember you,' said the figure. 'You're the spy who ran with Thegn Edgar.'

Alaric looked at the figure, though it was still hard to make out that this was a man. He was covered with leaves, moss and branches. His shape was confused by pieces of foliage that stuck out at strange angles. His face was just visible as a dark black and green patch amongst the leaves. The effect was extraordinary. If the man stood still, he would pass as a long-dead tree stump. If he lay down, he would look like no more than a heap of forest litter.

'Alaric,' offered Alaric.

'Alaric, that's it,' the forest-man replied. He made a short clicking noise with his tongue and four more similarly disguised figures rose from the forest floor.

Alaric was shocked. He prided himself on his covert skills and yet he had walked straight past these five men, and the gods knew how many others.

'I can see that your camouflage skills have improved somewhat,' observed Alaric.

'Yours haven't,' he replied. 'We've had to get better. These Norman hunting parties are already almost as good as we were. We have to stay as many steps ahead of them as we can.'

'Yes, I can see that. My friends and I have been looking for you.'

'Yes, we know. We had to get rid of these scum before we made ourselves known to you.'

'There's another party a little way ahead of me,' said Alaric, 'I found them last night.'

'Already dealt with. You nearly ended up dead yourself.

Good job I recognised you. Now, we need to dispose of the evidence here. You can help and then we'll go back for your friends.'

The Wildmen produced wooden shovels and between them, they had the four Normans in shallow graves within an hour.

The leader of the Wildmen, who had introduced himself as Todda, surveyed their work and nodded with satisfaction.

'Good,' he said. 'We want to let the Normans know that any of them who enter our forest will simply disappear without trace. The wild stories are already spreading nicely amongst the locals. This forest is haunted, you know. There are evil things here. Boggarts. It won't be long, we hope, before not a single Norman will dare to enter the forest.'

'What of the other hunting parties?' asked Alaric.

'They will all be dealt with today. Each of the parties – there are fourteen of them – has a group like us attached to it, though of course, they are unaware of that. Not a single member of any team will survive the day.'

'That's very impressive.'

'It's essential, that's what it is.'

Alaric nodded. 'We need to speak to your leadership. Is Alfweald still in charge?'

Todda nodded. 'He is, we could be with him within the day if necessary.'

'I think it is, there have been significant developments that you will not be aware of.'

'We'd better get to your friends, then.'

As it would seem that the woods were now free from

Normans, Alaric did not attempt to be silent on his approach to Halfdene and Harek. The two men had moved away from where they had slept, and were concealed within dense bushes.

'Harek, Halfdene! It's alright, you can come out,' he called softly.

Carefully, Halfdene stepped out of the shrubbery.

'It's all clear,' said Alaric. 'I've found the Wildmen, or to be more accurate, they found me. Come on, let's get the horses.'

Harek joined Halfdene and the three men walked back the way Alaric had come. As they approached the area where their horses waited, Alaric halted them, and to Harek and Halfdene's astonishment, five men suddenly unfolded themselves from the forest.

'Sweet gods!' said Harek. 'Now there's a skill!'

'Todda here assures me that every Norman in the forest will be dead by the end of the day,' said Alaric.

'I don't doubt it,' said Harek.

Halfdene was looking carefully at Todda. 'Blood and guts, man, I would never have recognised you in there,' he said admiringly.

'Hello Halfdene, it's good to see you again.'

'We must get to Alfweald as soon as possible,' urged Alaric.

'Of course,' replied Todda. 'Come on, let's get to your horses.'

They walked together towards where the horses had been tied up the previous evening, Halfdene and Todda chatting like the old comrades that they were. The horses whickered in greeting as Halfdene approached them.

Todda walked up to the horses, and dipping his finger

in a pot that hung round his neck, he made curious marks on the horses' chests and flanks. They looked like random mud splatters.

'With these marks, you'll pass through the Wildmen patrols with no hindrance. You won't see them, but they will see you. You know your way to the Paddock, of course?'

'Yes, we were headed there in any event.'

'Good. Alfweald is there at the moment. It's now a temporary camp rather than the full-time home that it used to be. We've made many changes.'

'Those changes were already under way when we left you the last time.'

'Well, I wish you safety and success in your onward journey. It was good to see you again, Halfdene.'

'Thank you, Todda. I hope we meet again.'

'Who can say? Now, off with you. No need for caution, it sounds to me as if speed is more important.'

Alaric spent the journey scanning every piece of shrubbery and loose litter that he could on the way to the Paddock, and yet he saw no sign of the Wildmen. They had indeed matured into a most formidable and effective force.

Shortly after noon, the Paddock appeared before them, and they halted. The Paddock was only recognisable to them as their destination through long familiarity with it. To untutored eyes, it appeared simply as a very densely packed region of undergrowth with tall blackthorn and hawthorn bushes.

Slowly, Halfdene approached the point where he knew the entrance to be. He guided his horse between the almost invisible gap, turned sharp right and followed the tight gap between the branches of the hedge that would lead out into

The Lost Land

the open ground within the Paddock. The passage through the thick bushes had been carefully cleared of all the thorns that might catch a man or a horse as they passed through.

Behind him, Halfdene could hear Harek muttering in wonder as he passed along the all but invisible passage through the bushes.

As they emerged into the open central area of the Paddock, a small group of men walked forward to meet them.

The land inside the Paddock was mostly clear, and beginning to return to the wild. Halfdene remembered it as a busy, almost bustling place and yet still very quiet. Tents and a few temporary structures had been strewn almost haphazardly across the open space, but now there was nothing across most of the area. The grass stood long and untended.

One corner, however, was cleared and tidy, and four or five dark green tents stood there, presumably to provide sleeping quarters for the tiny garrison that still maintained a presence here. To one side, and not in alignment with the smaller tents, was a much larger one. Halfdene guessed this was where the council of the Wildmen held its deliberations. It was in the same location that the council's meeting place had been when he was resident.

Halfdene dismounted and indicated that Alaric and Harek should do the same. The three men walked towards the party who now stood watching them. Alaric did not feel at all surprised that they showed no concern about the riders. With the rapid advances in the Wildmen's methods, Alaric was sure that these men knew exactly who they were.

'Halfdene, Alaric, welcome.' A broad-shouldered man with shoulder-length brown hair stepped forward.

'Godwin, I'm pleased you have survived,' said Halfdene, taking the man's hand.

Godwin looked over Halfdene's shoulder. 'This man I do not know,' he said.

'This is Harek, a good man and a fine fighter. He's part of the reason we're here. We need to speak with Alfweald and the council.'

'Alfweald is here, as is some of the council. Come.'

Godwin led the way through the long grass to the cleared area where the tents stood. He strode up to the larger tent and lifted a flap at the front. He stuck his head inside and spoke briefly with the occupants.

'Go straight in,' he said, withdrawing his head.

Inside the tent was dim, but they could make out half a dozen men sitting on stools around a low table. One man stood as they entered. A big man with a long beard.

'Halfdene, Alaric, it is good to see you well. Come in, take a seat.'

'My lord, we are grateful,' said Halfdene, recognising former King's Reeve Alfweald.

'You had better introduce me,' said Alfweald, indicating Harek.

'I can introduce myself, Lord Alfweald. I am Harek, thegn to Sweyn Estrithson-king.'

Halfdene missed a beat. Harek was a king's thegn? How had they all missed that?

'Ah,' rumbled Alfweald. 'That explains much. I take it your visit has something to do with Danish interests?'

'Indeed it does,' answered Harek.

'Then you are welcome indeed, Lord Harek. Please join us.'

Harek, Halfdene and Alaric pulled up spare stools and

The Lost Land

joined the men around the table. They nodded greetings to each other as they sat. Some of the men around the table were familiar, others were not.

'We are representative of the council of the Wildmen,' began Alfweald. 'We have longed to hear from the court of Sweyn-king. Please tell us your news and how the Wildmen may be of service.'

Halfdene deferred to Harek, who began to speak.

'I am here as the personal representative of Jarl Asbjorn, Sweyn-king's brother. I speak with his authority. I have spent much time in the company of Thegn Edgar, Guthrum, Halfdene and Alaric here, whom I believe you know well.'

Alfweald nodded. 'We do. They were a fine addition to our band and acquitted themselves with great honour. I note with not a little distress that one name is missing from your roll-call. Where is Eric?'

Halfdene spoke up. 'We lost our comrade to a Norman arrow as we were about to board a longboat to Denmark. We were betrayed by a weak man. Eric fell honourably.'

'I don't doubt it. I grieve for your loss. Our losses mount by the day. I hope you are about to give us good news.'

Harek continued. 'I have been given very impressive reports of your actions and abilities by these men and their comrades. My task is to ask you for even greater effort, with the inevitable greater losses that will lead to.'

The men around the table remained silent. 'Go on,' rumbled Alfweald.

'Three hundred ships have arrived in Northumbria, carrying the largest Danish army assembled in a generation. Amongst them are many Englishmen, thegns, carls and others who have been forced off their land by the Normans.'

Mutters of surprise and relief greeted Harek's words.

'Jarl Asbjorn is in personal command of the army. We intend to destroy the Norman presence in England and place Sweyn Estrithson on the throne.'

Gasps of relief and joy escaped from all the men in the tent.

'God be praised,' exclaimed Alfweald.

'What of Edgar Atheling?' asked one of the men.

'The young prince is with us, and all his men, such as they are. There is some agreement between our king and the prince. I am not privy to the details, but the general belief is that the kingdom will be split as it was in the past, between Wessex and the Danelaw. The banished earls of England also stand with us. By now, our army should have retaken Jorvik.'

A low cheer arose from the men around the table.

'How may we be of service? For this is the moment we have been waiting for these three long years,' said Alfweald.

'We will ask much of you,' warned Harek.

'We will give much,' replied Alfweald.

'Good. Well said. The Wildmen's most important task will be keeping this forest clean of Normans, a task I see you are already most efficient at.'

'Aye, that we are!' exclaimed a large man to Alfweald's left.

'The Bastard will be drawn north by our harrying actions. His armies will inevitably pass through the forest. Whilst we do not expect you to face the armies in open combat, we would ask you to keep constant pressure on them at all times. Night raids on their camps would inspire terror amongst them. Stay well clear and do not engage them directly, but thin their numbers as much as you can in whatever manner suits you best.

'Supply trains will also be passing through in greater numbers than before. These mustn't get through.'

'They will not,' promised Alfweald. 'There are those amongst us who are trained warriors. I see that you understand our methods of fighting and that those methods are not conventional, but we could gather a force of maybe sixty?'

He looked round at his companions for confirmation. They all nodded at him.

'Sixty former thegns and carls who would gladly join your army and fight the enemy face to face.'

'Your offer is appreciated, Alfweald, and it may yet come to that. For now, though, I would like you to continue fighting to your greatest strength because your greatest strength is also the Bastard's greatest weakness.'

'Then that is how it shall be. I cannot begin to tell you how your news gladdens our hearts. I will convene a great council here in the Paddock, our old base, and give everyone the news and their new orders.'

'We appreciate your enthusiasm, Lord Alfweald. The attacks by our army have already begun, so your great council should be assembled with the greatest possible haste.'

Alfweald turned to the other men around the table.

'You heard Lord Harek,' he commanded. 'Back to your sections immediately. I want everyone here by the morning of the day after tomorrow. Go now, the forest has just been conveniently cleared, so you may make good speed. Tell no one of the reason for the council. This news must be heard by all at the same time.'

The men arose immediately and made their way out of the tent.

Alfweald turned to his three guests.

'I was pleased to see your return, but this is beyond my most optimistic dreams. Come, dine with me and tell me all that has passed since we last met.'

11

Caedmon's Tale

October 1069

The autumnal nights were getting noticeably chillier, and Edgar, Guthrum and Brihtwulf huddled together around a low fire. All three held horn beakers, and a bucket of ale sat between them, from which they regularly refilled their cups.

It was over a week since the sacking of Eoforwic, and there had been no word on their next target. To his great anger and disappointment, Edgar had learned that the raids had continued up and down the coast, indeed that they had been increased. Many towns had been raided, but the Normans themselves had not been met in battle except outside the walls of Eoforwic itself.

Edgar had taken Osfrith's warning to heart and had kept his counsel, but Brihtwulf and Guthrum were also becoming frustrated and confused by the apparent pointlessness of Jarl Asbjorn's plan of attack.

'The men will be getting restless,' said Brihtwulf quietly.

'There's nothing more dangerous than an army with nothing to do. We need to do something, anything, even if it's just digging ditches.'

'Asbjorn must know what he's doing,' said Guthrum. 'Maybe he's allowing the frustration and boredom to build up to make the men even keener to get stuck into the Normans.'

'We need to face them now,' said Edgar. 'When will there possibly be a better time? Our men are fit and ready. We have a very formidable force here, and it's just sitting on its arse.'

The three men were interrupted by a shout from one of the sentries down by the river's edge a few dozen yards from where they sat. They heard the sounds of the footfalls of another couple of sentries as they ran towards the shout, then some scuffling and splashing.

Brihtwulf looked over his shoulder towards the noise.

'Looks like the sentries have caught another poacher,' he said.

'You can hardly call them poachers,' said Edgar, testily. 'These people were here long before us. This is their land, their livelihood. They're just hunting for their tables, that's all.'

'There are clearly defined limits to where they can and cannot go, and this was all agreed in advance with the village headman. It really isn't difficult.'

Edgar shrugged. Brihtwulf was right, he knew. He was allowing their situation to needle him. He took a swig of his ale. The Danish army's presence on Hakrholme wasn't a great burden on the people who already lived on the Isle. Cooperation had grown up quickly, with many of the locals profiting nicely from the occupation. An army requires many products and services, several of which the locals were able to provide, at considerably inflated prices, of course.

The struggle by the water's edge had finished now, and Edgar saw two soldiers dragging a third man backwards up the slope.

'Evening, lads,' said Brihtwulf, affably. 'What have you got there, then?'

'We found this lurking in the reeds, my lord,' replied one of the sentries.

The sentries dropped the wretched man to the ground in front of Brihtwulf. He was small and soaked. Blood was seeping from a fresh head wound. His thinning hair was matted to his face, and laced with a frond of thin, green weed. He looked up, the firelight flickering in his terrified eyes.

'N... not lurking, my lord. Looking.'

'Looking?' asked Brihtwulf, 'Looking for what?'

'I seek King's Thegn Osfrith Edwinsson, my lord.' The little man peered past Brihtwulf towards the camp, as if hoping to catch sight of Osfrith in the gloom. 'I was hoping he might be with the army, though I have not seen him in many a year.'

Brihtwulf took a drink from his horn. 'And what would you want to find a king's thegn for?' he asked.

'I have news for Lord Osfrith, my lord. I worked in his household in... happier times. I haven't seen him since he rode away to the great battle. After... afterwards, the Normans came, killed everyone. I didn't know if Lord Osfrith lived or not, I... I don't know what became of him, but I have heard that many great men went to the court of the King of the Danes, and as you are a Danish army, I thought...' he shrugged helplessly. 'I thought he might be with you.'

'What is your name?'

'Caedmon, sir. Lord Osfrith will know the name.'

Brihtwulf looked at one of the sentries. 'Fetch Hallvindur,' he ordered. The sentry bobbed his head and headed off towards the centre of the camp.

The bedraggled man's face broke into a smile of relief and he nodded enthusiastically. 'Hallvindur is here, oh thank God! Yes, Hallvindur will know me.'

'You know Hallvindur?' asked Edgar, intrigued by the little man's tale.

'Of course, my lord. He is one of Lord Osfrith's most stupid housecarls.'

A few moments later, the sentry returned with a puzzled-looking Hallvindur in tow.

The Dane's deep voice rumbled, 'You sent for me my lord?'

'Yes, Hallvindur,' replied Brihtwulf. 'I have a question for you. Do you know this man?'

Hallvindur glanced down at the small man in his sodden clothes. The man looked back at him beseechingly.

'No, my lord.'

Brihtwulf sighed. 'Pick him up,' he ordered the sentries.

They hauled the man to his feet. 'Hallvindur, it's me! For pity's sake, man!'

Hallvindur peered more carefully into the man's face.

'My God! Caedmon, is that you?'

'Of course it's me, you dim-witted oaf. Tell these great lords who I am!'

'Hallvindur?' asked Brihtwulf, amused by the feeble little man's haranguing of the huge warrior.

'This is Lord Osfrith's steward. A bumptious prig by

the name of Caedmon. He's lost a lot of weight and a lot of hair since I saw him last, which is why I didn't recognise him at first. What are you doing here, Caedmon? I had hoped you were dead.'

'I have news for Lord Osfrith.'

'What news could you possibly have for Lord Osfrith?'

'It's for the Thegn's ears only. It concerns Master Cyneheard.'

Hallvindur stiffened.

'Who?' asked Edgar.

'Cyneheard is, or was, Lord Osfrith's sister-son and heir,' said Hallvindur. 'He was killed by the Normans along with all of Lord Osfrith's family and household in the weeks following the great battle. I think Lord Osfrith will want to hear what this man has to say.'

'Very well, Hallvindur,' said Brihtwulf. 'I'll release him into your custody. Take him to Osfrith and he can decide what needs to be done with him.'

'Aye, my lord.'

Hallvindur took hold of Caedmon by the upper arm and marched him off in the direction of Osfrith's tent.

'Thank you, lads,' said Brihtwulf to the sentries, who then returned to their duties by the river.

'Any idea what that might be about?' asked Edgar, as he watched Hallvindur and his charge disappear into the gloom.

'No. None at all. Osfrith has never talked about his family in my presence. I just assumed that they had all been killed, as with so many of us. It seems I was right.'

'What news could that man have about Osfrith's dead sister-son?'

'If we need to know, then I'm sure Osfrith will tell us.'

They continued drinking to keep the cold at bay. Although the beer was weak, Edgar found that it was having a mellowing effect on him, and the conversation had turned to lighter matters when Hallvindur returned, Osfrith leaning heavily on him as he limped along.

'Ah, good,' said Osfrith as he approached. 'You're all here. Got a spare beaker? I could do with some ale. I need to speak to you.'

Guthrum got up and reached inside Brihtwulf's tent, returning with a horn beaker which he filled with ale.

Hallvindur assisted Osfrith as he sat heavily beside Edgar. Guthrum passed him the ale and sat on the other side of him.

'The man that you saw before, the one Hallvindur brought to me, is called Caedmon, a steward in my household.' He paused, grimaced. 'My former household,' he corrected himself.

'I have never spoken of my past life. We all have past lives, and it is still too painful for most of us to talk about them. I'm no exception. It will not surprise you to learn that I did have a family, though not a large one. My wife died shortly before the Normans arrived, and we never had any children. My heir was my closest male relative, my sister's son. His name was Cyneheard. A clever lad, though maybe not as much a warrior as I might have liked him to be.'

He paused and stared into the fire, pain and regret washing over his face for a moment. He looked up again.

'As you know, I was at the great battle when the Normans came, and I received this,' he thumped his damaged leg impatiently. 'It took me two weeks before I was fit to ride after that. As I made my way home, I had to walk the horse slowly, so the journey took me four days instead of the one it should have taken.'

He looked stricken. 'It just hurt so much, you see,' he whispered.

He shook his head. 'By the time I got home it was too late. The Normans had already visited. I found my hall partly burned. Those of my housecarls who had survived the great battle and had been at home when the Normans arrived had put up a fight, but all had been slaughtered. One of the only members of my household to survive the attack was an old cook. She told me the story. It took a long time to get it out of her, she was weeping so much. She told me that my sister, her husband and all their household had been killed. There was nobody else left to speak to. And so matters stood from then until now.'

He paused and looked back at the fire. Different emotions played on his face this time. He raised the horn beaker to his mouth and drank the contents in one.

Guthrum reached out and took the horn from him, refilling it and handing it back to him.

Osfrith smiled weakly at him. 'Thank you, Guthrum.'

He took a more modest sip.

'Caedmon says that he was present when the Normans attacked. He has told me the names of those of my housecarls who stood and did their duty, and I will be honouring them in due time. He says that he tried to hide during the attack. That much has the ring of truth, Caedmon is not blessed with great courage; he would never get involved in a fight if he could avoid it.

'However, as he raced for safety, he says that he was run over by a Norman on a horse, and was rolled into a ditch.

'When he came round the fighting was over. My

housecarls lay dead and the Normans were looting, burning and making use of the women.

'He says that he saw the Normans dragging several bound men away with them. He says that he was too far away to see who the men were, but that he thought there were at least four.

'Anyway, what small courage he does possess now came to the fore, and he determined to follow the captives and attempt to rescue them. I don't know what was going through his mind, maybe he was concussed, but he seems sincere. I've known him for years. He's persistent, dull, even, but not bold. Somehow, he managed to track the Normans north to a small town that he thinks they've made into a local administrative centre. I've never heard of it, but he says it's called Mammesfeld.'

Edgar stirred. The name of the town was familiar. It took him back to the days of searching for his wife, Godgifu, after her abduction by the Normans. He was headed for Mammesfeld when he and his housecarls were apprehended by the Wildmen – their first meeting with them.

'Mammesfeld? I know that name. We were headed there in our search for my wife. We never got there; we were stopped by the Wildmen.'

'Really?' Osfrith looked intrigued. 'That does lend some weight to Caedmon's story. Is it an administrative centre?'

'I don't know. All I know is that the tax collection parties were meeting there for some reason. The Wildmen told us that about six hundred Normans had descended on the poor place.'

'They could well be using it as a meeting point, then. Caedmon managed to get work on a farm nearby. God knows how. He wouldn't know one end of a shovel from the other. Physical labour's never been one of his strong points. The lifestyle of a land-working peasant did not suit him and didn't provide him with many of the luxuries he was used to as the steward to a king's thegn, but as he says, it allowed him to survive, and to keep an eye open. He's been working the land there for two years now, and I have to admit that it shows. Time and hard work have not been kind to him.'

'I would agree with that, my lord,' said Hallvindur. 'I didn't even recognise the little turd at first.'

'Enough, Hallvindur!' snapped Osfrith. 'Caedmon has done me a great service, without being sure if he would ever see me again or even if I was still alive. He has paid for that service with his health. Now, he tells me that there is a royal hunting lodge in Mammesfeld…'

'Yes, yes there is!' interrupted Edgar. 'I remember that was where the Wildmen told us the tax collectors were gathering when we were on our way there.'

'Good, well that all adds up. It seems that the hunting lodge has been fortified and expanded. There's some Norman henchman there permanently now, in charge of the whole thing. There is, according to Caedmon, a fixed company of about a hundred and fifty footmen and thirty cavalry. If Mammesfeld wasn't an administrative and military centre when you were headed there, Edgar, then it must be now. The lodge also seems to be acting as a clearing-house for captured men and women. The men are sold as labour, the women as…' he paused, caught his breath. 'Sorry, Edgar.'

'I know what happens to the women,' said Edgar, without looking up. 'I just thank the gods that my Gifu had the strength to escape in the only way that she could.'

On the other side of Osfrith, Guthrum stirred and nodded appreciatively. 'And that she took some of the bastards with her,' he said.

Osfrith paused. 'Aye,' he said. 'I think we can all agree on that.' He raised his horn and drank some more ale.

'Anyway, the point of Caedmon's tale is that he believes that my housecarls, those that survived, at any rate, have either been sold into the slavery of Norman barons or killed if they were too… feisty.' His hand tightened around the drinking horn. 'I hope for their sakes that they all died.'

He remained silent for a while. None of the others interrupted his private reverie. They all had them from time to time. Getting lost in the past, soaking up the memories of lost friends and loved ones, was one way of coping with the present, though the indulgence could not be permitted to last too long.

Osfrith took an audible intake of breath. 'My sister-son, Cyneheard, on the other hand, is a different matter. In the early days of his investigations, Caedmon discovered that Cyneheard was indeed amongst the captured men. Since then, Caedmon has seen him half a dozen times, always with the Normans. As I said, he was ever a bright lad, good with his letters. Caedmon seems to think that the Norman thug who's in charge around there has taken a liking to the lad, after a fashion. Cyneheard walks with the party that accompanies this man everywhere. He carries papers, and it looks like he's acting as a translator and interpreter of English documents, which most of the Norman dogs cannot read or understand, ignorant filth that they are.'

Edgar stirred uneasily. An unwelcome thought had occurred to him, and he was sure that the others must have had it, too.

'Forgive me, my lord…'

'Yes, Edgar. I know what you're going to say, but get it out in the open anyway.'

'I'm sorry to say this, but is it possible that your sister-son has been turned? That he is now a willing secretary to this Norman? After all, if as you say he is young and believes that his family and former household have all been killed and that he has no home to go back to, it would probably be a sensible thing to do. You said yourself he was not a great warrior. Nobody could blame the lad for doing what he had to in order to survive.'

'Thank you, Edgar. That had to be said. And thank you for couching it in those terms. But it appears that willingness is not part of the arrangement. Caedmon says that he has never seen Cyneheard without a hobble.'

Guthrum, who had been holding his breath without realising it, let out a gasp of relief.

Edgar smiled, 'Good. That's good.'

'Let's drink to that,' said Brihtwulf, refilling everyone's horn.

They drank and sat in silence as they waited for Osfrith to collect his thoughts.

'I want the lad back,' he said finally.

They all looked intently at him. His face betrayed great strain, and he was struggling to get the words out. 'He's my only kin, the only thread I have that still links me with my family. Let's snatch this one little victory.'

'How?' said Brihtwulf. 'We can't march the army up to this – what was it called? Mammesfeld? – just to rescue one boy. Even sending a small detachment to do the job is unthinkable. If this place Mammesfeld is being turned into an administrative centre and has a decent-sized garrison, it will be a very tough target. Then there's all the stuff we'd have to fight through simply to get there, not to mention get back again. Asbjorn'd never stand for it. Can't be done. I'm sorry.'

Osfrith pursed his lips. 'I wasn't thinking of the whole army going, or even a single detachment. If I could, I'd go myself, on my own if necessary, and bugger what Asbjorn thinks of it. Maybe a very small group? Just to see if there's a way. If it doesn't look like an army, it won't be opposed as one.'

Edgar glanced across at Guthrum. 'If it's just a quick look, then why not release Guthrum and me? We could get there in a couple of days, and just the two of us would arouse no suspicion amongst the enemy. We'll just see what we can see and report back.'

Osfrith was nodding in approval. He looked at Brihtwulf.

'It's your decision, Brihtwulf,' he said. 'Edgar and Guthrum are under your command.'

Brihtwulf thought for a moment. 'Yes, alright. See what you can find out about the situation, then report back to us. If an opportunity to free the lad does present itself, unlikely as that may seem, then take advantage of it.'

Osfrith's eyes were moist. 'Thank you, Brihtwulf. This means everything to me. And thank you, Edgar, and Guthrum, too.'

Behind Osfrith, Hallvindur cleared his throat, the sound deep and rumbling.

'Hallvindur?'

'With your leave, my lord, I would like to go with lord Edgar. Master Cyneheard knows me, and a familiar face may

The Lost Land

be an advantage.'

'Or it may not,' said Brihtwulf. 'If the lad sees you and recognises you, he may inadvertently give you away to his captors.'

'I'll make sure that he doesn't see me until the right time,' said Hallvindur.

'I think it's a good idea,' said Edgar. 'And God knows I would welcome Hallvindur's presence on such a mission.'

'Alright,' said Brihtwulf, decisively. 'You three will go to Mammesfeld to see if anything can be done.'

'May we speak to Caedmon?' Edgar asked Osfrith.

'Yes, of course. Hallvindur, would you?'

'Aye, my lord,' rumbled the big Dane, and headed off towards Osfrith's tent.

'This could be a very dangerous enterprise, Edgar. You know that?' said Brihtwulf.

'Aye. But I'd rather do something like this to help bring about one of the small victories than sit around here kicking my heels waiting for some progress towards the larger ones.'

'Good. Just be careful, that's all.'

Hallvindur returned with Caedmon, who looked much better for the fine meal and the dry clothes Osfrith had procured for him.

'Ah, Caedmon. Feeling better, now?' asked Osfrith.

'Yes, my lord, thanks to your generosity.'

'I want you to meet these men. This is Thegn Edgar, and this is his housecarl, Guthrum. They have volunteered to travel to Mammesfeld to see if there is anything we can do to recover Cyneheard.'

Caedmon's face broke into a huge, relieved smile. He bowed to Edgar.

'Oh, thank you, my lord,' he gushed. 'Thank you. Please

let me know if I can be of any service.'

'You can start by telling us everything you've learned about Mammesfeld. The town, the garrison and of course the fortified lodge.'

'Yes, my lord, of course. Mammesfeld is a market town, or it was. Its nature is being changed by the Normans. The market still happens, but it's smaller than it used to be. The merchants, you see, and the small traders, they don't like the way the Normans treat them. Several have disappeared, and the word around town is that they were killed for no better reason than sport. Soldiers will march into the market and demand money from the merchants. They call it tax. The merchants call it theft.

'There's a lot of building going on in the town, too. Not only is the lodge being turned into a fortified stronghold, but all through the town, the people who live there are being thrown out of their homes. Those houses are being torn down and new buildings, bigger, grander, are being put up in their place. Confusion and bitterness are rife.'

'Sounds pretty much like the rest of the country,' said Edgar. 'Tell us about the lodge. How is it being fortified?'

'A palisade has been thrown up around it. I haven't been inside, but it seems that there's a lot of work going on inside those new walls as well. I wouldn't be surprised if the old lodge had been demolished and something more Norman put up in its place, though I can't say for sure.'

'What of the garrison?'

'Hard to keep a track of them. I'm not in the town most of the time, but I guess there are about a hundred and fifty foot soldiers permanently stationed there. More come and go every day, but others I've spoken to say that's the number that seems to stay there.

'Then there's the horsemen. Thirty or forty, I would say. They're usually out patrolling the woods around the town, but they berth there during the night. I've seen that myself.'

'How many soldiers are out of the fortification and patrolling round the town at any one time, would you say?'

'Hard to be accurate, sir. At least fifty, I guess.'

'Hmm. Alright. Now, what of Cyneheard? How often have you seen him?'

'Six times, my lord. It's definitely him, I swear. Each time he was in the company of the Norman leader. Hobbled, as I told Lord Osfrith.'

'Did he ever see you?'

'No, my lord. I hid in case he saw me. I didn't want to raise his hopes.' He looked forlorn. 'After all, what could I do to help him?'

'Do you know where he's being held?'

'I saw him twice walk back into the fortified lodge with the Norman leader. I can only assume that he's being held there. He isn't the only one in there, by all accounts.'

'I see.' Edgar sat in silence for a moment, rubbing the scars on his face. 'Lord Osfrith tells us that you've been working at a farm. Is that so?'

'Yes, my lord, and damned hard work it is, too.'

Edgar smiled. 'Yes, I imagine it is. Where is this farm that you've been working on? How far from the town?'

'I've mostly been on a farm about a mile north of the town, sir. It's easier to slip into town from there.'

'And how have you explained your absence to the farmer?'

'Oh, there's no need for that, sir. The work is very casual. The farmer there pays by the day. He keeps a tally of all his occasional workers – there's only half a dozen or so of us on any one day. He only pays the penny each fourth day you work. Workers come and go, as several of the local farmers use the same system. These are not big farms and they can't afford a large or regular workforce.'

'Good, then maybe you'll be able to rejoin that workforce. I'd like you to return to Mammesfeld with us. As long as that's acceptable to you, Osfrith?'

Osfrith nodded. 'Of course.'

'Good. Guthrum and I may also have to join the workforce when we get there.'

Guthrum nodded his agreement.

'What of this Norman leader? Do you have his name?'

Caedmon shuddered. 'Indeed I do, my lord, and a nasty piece of work he is, too. His name is Barentin. Baron Roger de Barentin.'

12

Mammesfeld

Edgar and his companions approached Mammesfeld along a narrow lane from the north-east. It had taken a day and a half of walking. The forest had gradually closed in and enveloped them and now, just about a mile from the settlement, the trees crowded close to the side of the road, dense and heavily shadowed.

Caedmon timidly broke the silence. His voice was hushed, partly for fear of being overheard, however unlikely that may have been, and partly because the dense forest seemed to demand it.

'The hunting lodge lies towards the south. It's away from the main centre of the settlement, on a low hill,' he said.

'A hill? How close can we get before being seen?' asked Guthrum.

'When it was just a hunting lodge, the hill was wooded and it stood in a small clearing, but the Normans have cut down all the trees around it. It will be difficult to approach in daylight and not be seen. You could probably only get within a few hundred yards at best.'

'I see. The frontal approach seems to be impractical then.'

'Yes. There's a major road heading south which is overlooked by the lodge. There's a fair amount of foot, hoof and wheel traffic along it. We could walk past without arousing any suspicions as long as we didn't linger or show any unusual interest in the place.'

'Good,' said Edgar. 'That's what we'll do then. I want to approach from the south. The Normans will naturally be less suspicious of traffic coming from the south. They have trouble in the north, and that's where they'll be looking for it coming from.'

'We should leave this road then. There are hunters' paths through the forest that skirt around the town. This close in there should be a few. If we head south-east then turn to the south-west, we should meet the main south road,' said Caedmon.

Sure enough, after a few minutes, a narrow path opened up to their left and meandered into the forest. They followed the path in a roughly south-westerly direction, bypassing the town, then followed another path towards the south-east which, as Caedmon had said, met the main south road some distance from the settlement.

The south road was wide and appeared to be in a fairly good state of repair. The four men waited some way back in the forest until no one was visible along the road.

Caedmon pointed south along the road. 'That way leads to another town, Snotingeham, about a dozen miles away. There's a large market there,' he said.

The Lost Land

'This will be a busy road, then,' said Edgar. 'Come on. Let's carry on.'

They continued walking north, the dense forest still surrounding them on both sides, though many trees had recently been cut back from the verges of the road.

'They're making this road harder for any enemy to attack,' muttered Guthrum. 'I wonder if the Wildmen have been active round here.'

They walked further and soon came to a clearing that had obviously been made recently. Low tree stumps still stood where they had not yet been cleared, and around them were piles of wet sawdust, leaves and small broken branches. The ground raised gently before them. At the top of the rise stood a massive palisade wall, apparently made from the split trunks of the felled trees. A wooden tower rose from behind the wall and in the open-sided top, they could see the figure of a soldier, watching the road they were walking along.

'Alright, everybody keep their wits about them,' said Edgar. 'No staring at the lodge, just walk on by at this pace.'

They looked as intently as they could at the lodge as they passed, peering out of the corners of their eyes as they kept their heads fixed forward. It was formidably defended. They saw only one entrance, and that was guarded by two low raised towers, one on each side of the heavy wooden gate. Edgar counted eight sentries patrolling round the area in front of the gate.

'Shit,' muttered Guthrum. 'We're not going to get in there easily.'

They walked past the lodge-turned-fortress and on into the settlement of Mammesfeld.

'Look at these buildings,' said Edgar quietly. 'Much of

this is newly built. It seems that the Normans are definitely settling in here.'

They walked along the main street, where much building work was going on. The street was full of the sounds of hammers, saws and foremen shouting at labourers.

'We'll need somewhere to spend the night,' said Edgar.

'We can bed down in the forest,' said Guthrum. 'If we go now, Hallvindur and I can catch something to eat before it gets dark.'

'The road ahead of us heads north,' said Caedmon. 'It forks after a few hundred yards. To the right is the north-east road that we walked down, whilst to the left is the north-west road that leads to the farm that I worked at.'

'You go on. Take the north-east road,' said Edgar. 'Leave Wildmen signs so I can track you. I'll be along soon.'

Guthrum nodded. 'Right,' he said, and he, Hallvindur and Caedmon headed off towards the north.

Edgar pulled his hood over his head to disguise his obvious facial scars, slowed his pace and began ambling round the settlement. The building work had apparently been ongoing for some time. New houses lined the main street, which was wide, presumably to accommodate the market that Caedmon had told them about. Some of the houses were large and grand and stood out impressively amongst the more normal wattle and daub low-roofed buildings.

An expensively dressed man rode past on a small horse, a servant following close behind him on foot. The servant was carrying a portable writing table round his neck, and a bulging bag.

That figures, thought Edgar. An official of the Norman

regime, probably associated with the tax-gathering that was robbing so many Englishmen of their landholdings.

As they passed Edgar, the servant stumbled, losing his grip on his bag and dropping it onto the dirt road near Edgar's feet. His master swivelled round in his saddle and squinted through beady eyes at the servant. A torrent of foreign invective poured from his mouth. The servant stood still and stared back miserably. He looked utterly worn out. Edgar stooped and snatched the bag off the ground where it had fallen.

The servant looked terrified and the master pulled his horse round and started shouting in the bastard tongue. Edgar calmly handed the bag back to the servant. The master grunted and barked a command at the browbeaten man, who looked at Edgar with dull eyes and then walked on in pursuit of his superior.

'You're welcome,' muttered Edgar quietly at the pair's retreating backs.

He turned and continued his walk. Against the wall of one of the smaller, older houses was a table on which were a few loaves, evidently for sale.

Edgar approached the table and a grey-haired woman stepped out of the house to greet him.

She nodded suspiciously in cautious greeting. 'Stranger,' she said.

'Yes. I'm just passing through. I'd like to buy two loaves, please.' He reached for his scrip, which hung off his belt.

'What's a warrior like you doing "just passing through" a place like this?' asked the woman, screwing her eyes almost shut.

'Warrior?' said Edgar. 'Why do you think I'm a warrior?'

She chuckled. 'You didn't get a face like that herding sheep.'

'I'll just take the loaves, please,' insisted Edgar.

'How many of you are there?' She asked. 'Two loaves is a lot for your meal alone, isn't it?'

Edgar exhaled, trying to sound like his patience was growing thin.

The old woman glanced up and down the street.

'Come inside,' she said, pushing open the door behind her.

'What?'

'Just do it!' she hissed.

He followed her through the door and into the single-roomed house. A ladder at one end led up to a sleeping platform. At the other end of the room, to Edgar's left, a man sat in a chair by an open fire pit in which a few small twigs were burning feebly.

'This what you want?' asked the woman.

The man looked up. He was old and haggard, and his face carried a disfiguring wound similar to Edgar's own, though not so severe. His thin white hair hung lankly around his face. He looked closely at Edgar.

'Aye, woman. He'll do,' he rumbled. His voice was deep and sounded too powerful for such an apparently old, weak man.

'I'll do for what?' asked Edgar, his hand reaching for the long dagger that hung out of sight under his cloak.

The man sighed wearily. 'Just sit down, lad. I'm not the enemy.'

'Then who is the enemy?' asked Edgar.

'Them lot,' said the man, jutting his chin towards the door. His eyes suddenly filled with venom and he stiffened

The Lost Land

in his chair as if he was going to rise and fight them all single-handedly. Just as quickly, he collapsed back into his chair and the fire left his eyes.

'I can't do it any more,' he muttered, mainly to himself, Edgar guessed. 'Just can't do it. Day was when I'd be up and at 'em. No holding me back, there wasn't.' He stared dully into the fire. He spat into it.

'What do you want with me?' said Edgar, more gently.

'Sit, lad. Please sit.' He pointed at a wooden stool opposite him on the other side of the fire pit.

Edgar walked forward and sat. The old man nodded and closed his eyes, swallowing hard.

'My name is Frithlac. I'm a baker, though now I'm so ill my wife does most of the work.' He indicated the old woman with a slight wave of his finger.

'I'll be outside,' said the woman, slipping out of the door.

'Although not a born warrior, I've fought my share of battles.' He indicated the sinuous scar on the side of his face. 'As have you, I see.'

'I got this at Stanford when Harald Sigurdson attempted to take this land,' said Edgar, touching his own scar-tissued wound with the middle finger of his left hand.

'Ah, yes. Might have turned out better if he'd won,' mused the man. 'No disrespect to you, lad, but maybe these nasty bastards wouldn't have been here if the Norse had arrived in strength.'

'We can't live on maybes,' answered Edgar.

'No, no. 'Spose not,' he sighed. 'I got this thirty years ago,' he said, livening up a bit. 'It was only a skirmish. It should never have amounted to anything, really. A bit of cattle rustling. The thegn was away, and his housecarls with him. Otherwise, I wouldn't have been there.'

Edgar looked puzzled.

'Burwarran,' explained the man. 'Over thirty years I was in the local burwarran, ready to be called up by the thegn if ever he needed us. And he did,' the man smiled at private recollections.

'Anyway, these cattle rustlers needed dealing with quick, like. The thegn's steward called for volunteers from the burwarran to round 'em up. I was there with knobs on, I can tell you.'

He paused and stared at his paltry fire. 'There were about fifty of the turds,' he continued. 'And only twenty of us. Gave us quite a shock. But we fought like the very demons of Hell, we did. Killed most of 'em and the rest ran away. We lost five of ours and six more rendered useless.' He pointed at his scar again.

'Point is, though, I've never felt so alive as I did during that fight.'

He stopped talking abruptly and looked up at the roof of his house. It was dark up amongst the beams.

'Alright. That fight – I killed three men. Three! And me a baker! What a day!'

Edgar stirred uncomfortably in his chair. 'Well done. That's very good. Now, what do you want with me?'

'Sorry, lad. Yes. This rabble,' he pointed towards the door of his home, 'have forbidden any Englishman to carry a sword in the town or even to possess one. There was a big collection of weapons six months ago. But I didn't hand mine over, see. I hid it. I...' he faltered. 'I *couldn't* hand it over. It represented a part of me. The best part. The strong part that wouldn't take no for an answer. Now, if I were a younger man and if my legs and back didn't give me such terrible pain as they do, I'd be at that lot like a mad dog. But I can't. I just can't.'

He looked at Edgar and Edgar saw the lines of pain etched there, both physical and emotional.

'I know there's a big Danish army not two or three days from here. I think you either have something to do with it or you're on your way to join it. Am I right?'

Edgar was instantly on his guard. Who was this man? 'Why do you think there's a Danish army here?' he asked.

'Ah! Everyone knows. It's the talk of the town. It's fair got these bastards shitting their pants, too.'

Edgar remained silent.

'Alright, alright. Stay quiet. But I think I know my man. I think you're on our side.'

He peered closely at Edgar, but Edgar kept his features completely blank.

'Help me up,' said the old man. Edgar stood and reached down to him. Putting his hands under his arms, he lifted the man from his chair. He was surprisingly heavy for one so thin and wasted. The man groaned as he stood and rubbed his hands up and down over the lower part of his back. 'Grab that ladder, lad. It's not fixed. Put it against the wall just here.'

Edgar did as he was bid and placed the ladder against the wall where Frithlac had indicated.

'Now I need to do this,' said the man, gently moving Edgar away from the ladder. Grunting with pain, Frithlac cautiously ascended. He reached up and felt along one of the roof beams until Edgar heard something thump against the beam.

'Ah,' said Frithlac, with some satisfaction. He took hold of the bundle he had found and brought it down the ladder, which he descended even more slowly than he had climbed.

Once at the bottom of the ladder, he held the bundle of rags before him and blew some dust off it. He carefully unwrapped it. Within was a sword. He ran the palm of his hand lovingly up and down the flat of the blade. Then, smiling at it one last time, he handed it over to Edgar.

'Here,' he said. 'I think you'll know what to do with this.'

Edgar took the weapon and held it by its handle. It was nicely balanced but was otherwise an unremarkable piece of work. The blade was clean and had a decent edge, and the handle had recently been re-wrapped in soft hide.

Edgar nodded. 'It's a nice sword,' he said.

'I think you're going to need one of these,' said Frithlac. 'And I can't keep it. I'm not giving it to no Norman scum, that's for sure. Do some good with it, eh?'

Edgar nodded and rewrapped the sword in its rags. He slipped it down the inside of the left leg of his leggings and secured the bundle around his belt.

'I'll see what I can do,' he said, finally.

The old man hobbled back to his chair and sat down heavily. Edgar turned for the door.

'Do one of them for me, eh, lad?' said Frithlac without looking at Edgar. He returned his stare to the fire and closed his eyes.

Edgar adjusted the sword within his leggings and slipped quietly out of the door, closing it gently behind him.

Outside, he found the old woman holding four loaves out to him.

'Take them,' she said.

'How much do you want?' asked Edgar, reaching for his scrip.

The Lost Land

She smiled tiredly at him. 'You've already paid,' she said.

Walking along the north-east road, Edgar spotted a tree with a faint mark on its trunk. The mark told him that Guthrum could be found two hundred paces in a straight line from the tree.

What he actually found was Caedmon, building a small pile of twigs.

He looked up as Edgar approached. 'I'm expecting them back at any time,' said the steward. 'I thought I'd start the fire in preparation for the bounteous feast they are sure to return with.'

Edgar smiled and handed over the four loaves. 'Here, add these to our pantry.'

Caedmon's eyes lit up. 'Oh, nicely done, my lord,' he exclaimed. 'A feast indeed.'

As he spoke, Hallvindur stepped out from the brush, two game birds dangling from his hand. Guthrum followed with two hares. Caedmon sniffed with reluctant respect.

As they ate round the small fire, they discussed their observations and options.

'There's no way we're getting into that fortified lodge,' grumbled Hallvindur, chewing on a hare's haunch. 'It looks unassailable, at least by the three of us.'

Caedmon looked up. 'The four of us,' he said.

Hallvindur grunted. 'The three of us,' he said.

'I might suggest looking at who does go into the lodge,' Caedmon said quietly.

Edgar stopped chewing his meat at Caedmon's words.

'What are you saying, Caedmon?' he asked, eyeing the steward carefully.

'Just this, my lord; as you have noticed, there is a great deal of construction going on in the town at the moment. This means that there are many strangers and off-landers walking about within the town. They go unchallenged because they're there at the command of the Norman baron. There is also a great deal of construction going on at the lodge, from what I hear. The defences in place now, those that we saw today, are just temporary, in my opinion, impressive though they are. Workmen are going in there every day. There are carters with their waggons loaded with food, not just for the baron and his garrison, but for all the men who are working there. There are priests, monks and nuns who occasionally visit. Norman monks and clerics are taking over many parishes and administrative posts. They see Mammesfeld as a safe haven on their journeys. The point is, my lord, that many, many people walk in and out of that place every day, and they are only lightly challenged by the guards.'

Edgar was astounded. It was obvious, but only this little steward, with no fighting experience, had seen it.

He threw a bone onto the fire. 'Dear God, you're right. We've done this before, right, Guthrum?'

Guthrum nodded. In the search for Edgar's wife, Godgifu, abducted by this same Norman baron, Edgar and his housecarls had infiltrated the work gangs building a Norman motte and bailey to obtain information. Whilst the operation failed, Godgifu already having killed herself before Edgar arrived, they had managed to infiltrate the hall being used by the Normans and had eventually burned it down.

'Edgar, if...' began Guthrum.

'No, it's alright, Guthrum. This is a different situation.

I am of course aware of the possibility of getting revenge on de Barentin, but I'm also very conscious that a young man's life is at stake here. That life is paramount. We owe it to Lord Osfrith, if nothing else.'

'Let Hallvindur and I make the first attempt at infiltration. Don't forget that de Barentin knows your face. He'll remember that it was you who killed his thug de Caen. You probably still have a price on your head.'

Edgar nodded slowly. 'Alright. First thing tomorrow I want you to check out the possibilities of getting in. Don't just tag along with a group of workmen like we did at Redford. We need to be in the gang legitimately.'

'What about me, my lord?'

Edgar paused and looked thoughtfully at Caedmon.

'Can you cook?'

Caedmon sighed. 'Yes,' he said. 'I worked in Thegn Osfrith's kitchens for four years before becoming a steward.'

'Good. See if the baron needs any help in his kitchens. Yes?'

Caedmon brightened up. 'Yes, my lord, of course.'

'Go gently, Caedmon. Not too enthusiastic. Just ask to be pointed to the kitchens. Ask for a job and ask nothing else. Clear?'

'Of course, sir.'

'You know that my wife was killed by this man, don't you, Caedmon?'

'I... I had heard something to that effect, sir.'

'She died by poisoning herself.'

'Oh, sir, I...'

'Before she went, she took some of them with her.'

'That is good, my lord.'

'What do you know of poisons, Caedmon?'

Caedmon's face drained white. 'Nothing, sir. I'm sorry, my duties never...'

'It's alright, Caedmon. I fear that the three of us who accompany you are men of less subtle means. I need to find out more. I think I know where to start my enquiries.'

Guthrum looked keenly at Edgar.

'Don't worry, Guthrum. I know to be careful. The fact is, I've already been contacted by a disgruntled tenant here. Look,'

He reached behind him and pulled the bundle from where he had covered it with fallen leaves. He unwrapped the sword and held it out for inspection.

'It is death for an Englishman to own a sword in Mammesfeld,' said Caedmon.

'So I gather. I was given this blade by an old man who could not bear to give it to what he called "Norman scum". He asked only that I use it to kill Normans.'

'He could have been killed for that,' said Caedmon.

'That's why I think I'll be safe talking to him. Or to his wife, whose bread, freely given, you have just eaten.'

'I thought you stole it,' rumbled Hallvindur, looking disappointed.

'I am no thief, Hallvindur,' said Edgar mildly. 'But I do now have contacts.' He smiled and took a bite out of a loaf.

Guthrum, Hallvindur and Caedmon were all up well before dawn and headed into town, each from a different direction. Edgar took his time, waiting until the sun made its presence known, albeit through a thick layer of dark grey cloud. A cold wind whipped about him as he walked towards the town. He pulled the hood of his cloak up and tightened it around his face. As he walked along the main street, he noticed many men and women apparently going about their business, some walking fast, others dawdling. He assumed the pace of a dawdler and made his way slowly towards the house where he had previously met the old couple. The table was outside the house again, with just a few poor loaves scattered untidily on it.

He picked one up and thrust it into his face, sniffing deeply.

'Don't snot all over it!'

The door of the house had opened and the old woman was peering out. He kept his hood tight round his face.

'I'll have it,' he said. 'And do you have any ale to wash it down?'

'Aye, I have ale. Would you drink it here?'

'I'd rather come inside,' he said, opening the hood slightly.

'It costs more inside,' she said.

'I have silver,' he replied.

She stepped back and held the door open for him. He slipped past her and she closed the door behind him.

'Didn't think to see you again so soon,' she said.

Across the room, her husband raised his head at her voice.

'Come, sit,' the woman said.

Edgar sat. He looked at the old couple before him. Years of toil were etched on their leathery faces and gnarled hands.

'I wanted to thank you for your gift,' said Edgar.

'You can thank us by making good use of it, lad,' said the old man. Edgar remembered his name as Frithlac.

'I intend to. But first I need some information.'

He looked at the old woman. 'Do you know much of herbs?' he asked.

She blinked as if taken aback by the question.

'Herbs? You want to learn how to cook?' she asked, mild contempt in her voice.

'Not exactly, no. Herbs are medicinal. They can cure certain ills and speed recovery, can't they? Some of them?'

'Of course.'

'But others you must keep clear of, especially if mixed with other ingredients?'

The woman's face cleared.

'Oh, I see. Yes, some can be very dangerous. And mushrooms, especially mushrooms. I suppose you want instruction on which things that grow in the forest you should avoid?'

'That's it,' agreed Edgar. 'I wouldn't want any of the bad ones to get into any cooking, for example.'

The old man and woman looked at each other a moment. Almost imperceptibly, the old woman nodded.

Frithlac turned to face Edgar. 'My Helga has a sister, Aegytha, who is well versed in such matters. She lives in a small house about a mile south of here, a few hundred yards off the main road, in a clearing in the forest. She helps in childbirth and such things, and has a reputation for being wise in healing.'

'How will I find her house?' asked Edgar.

'There's a large yew tree on the main road on your left as you head south. There's only one, you can't miss it. Turn off the road there. You'll find it.'

Edgar rose. 'Thank you. You have helped more than you can possibly know.'

He turned to leave the house.

'Young man,' said the woman, rising to follow him. 'I wonder if you would be so good as to take my sister some bread whilst you are going that way?'

'Of course.'

At the door, she wrapped some bread in a linen wrap and tied it with a short length of cord.

'Thank you,' she said, and was gone indoors again.

As Frithlac had promised, the yew tree was obvious. It stood wide and gnarled, and nothing grew beneath its needle covered branches. He looked carefully around to see that he was unobserved and stepped off the muddy road and into the undergrowth. He walked in the way the Wildmen had taught him, leaving no broken grass or plants behind him to give any indication that he had passed that way. Where he could, he followed animal tracks and the natural gaps between plants.

After a short while, he spotted a small hovel, sitting to one edge of an airless clearing, no more than thirty paces across. He approached carefully but openly, not wishing to alarm anyone nearby. The hut was low-walled and the thatched roof came down almost to the ground, where a deep gully had formed by the action of rain dripping off the thatches. There were no windows, but at one end a flimsy wicker door was closed against the elements.

'Hello?' called Edgar at the door. 'Anybody here? I'm looking for the wise woman, Aegytha.'

After a few moments, the door creaked open and a face, smutted with soot, appeared in the crack.

'Who wants her?' said the face.

'My name is Edgar. I seek help. I come from your sister.'

'My sister, eh? Did she send anything with you? She normally sends me a small gift.'

Edgar dangled the linen wrap in front of the woman's face.

The door opened a little further and the woman stood back from the door.

'You'd better come in out of the cold,' she said.

It was dark inside. A large fire burned in the middle of the hovel, with a cooking pot hanging over it. Smoke from the fire hung from the ceiling almost to the top of Edgar's head. It was suffocatingly close.

'Sit down,' said the woman, indicating a low bench along one wall. 'Give,' she held her hand out to receive the wrap. She sat opposite Edgar and carefully unwrapped the bundle on her lap.

Edgar was surprised to see that Helga had only sent her sister quarter of a loaf.

'Ah,' said Aegytha. 'All is well.'

She stood and took a ladle, pouring out two cups of a steaming brew from the pot.

'Drink,' she said.

Edgar looked dubiously at the hot liquid in the cup.

'It's just a warming brew,' said Aegytha, sipping from her cup. 'I should tell you that if you had brought me a full loaf, you would be drinking it from a different cup.'

The menace in Aegytha's voice made Edgar look up sharply.

'That cup's safe,' she said. 'Have no fear.'

Edgar sipped the brew. It was slightly astringent and earthy, but not unpleasant, and it did send warmth coursing through his body.

'Helga trusts you. We have a code.'

'I see. You have to be cautious these days, I understand that.'

'So how can I help you?'

Edgar looked carefully at her. Behind the sooty film on her face, he could see that she was nowhere near as old as Helga.

'Pardon me for asking,' he said. 'But you must be twenty years younger than Helga. Are you really her sister?'

'"Sister" does not always need to have a strictly familial meaning,' said Aegytha. 'I have a few sisters, but no living siblings.'

'I see, but how did you know I came from Helga and not one of your other "sisters"?'

Aegytha sighed. 'Who else would send me bread?' she asked, as if to a child.

'Oh. Of course.'

'Now what do you want from me?'

'I understand you are wise in the lore of herbs and mushrooms.'

'I have some knowledge of them, yes.'

'I have a… problem. An… infestation.'

'Rats?'

'You might say so. It's a large infestation, not far from here. I know I won't be able to eradicate it completely, but removal of a few rats would help me in my long-term plans considerably.'

'You want to kill some Normans,' she said.

Edgar's breath caught. 'Well…'

'Look, warrior, you need to be open with me if I am to help you. Killing Normans is quite a different business from killing rats.'

'I know, killing people is not easy.'

'No. They need bigger doses than rats, normally.'

'Alright. I need to make the garrison in the fortified lodge at Mammesfeld very sick. If some of them die, all the better. I'm trying to get a man into the kitchens, he can administer whatever's necessary.'

She frowned. 'Are you only trying to get rid of the higher-ups?'

'I need as many as possible to be incapacitated or dead. The guards, mostly.'

'In that case, the kitchens are not the place to administer the poison. The kitchens cater only for the higher-ups.'

'That might not be enough,'

'They all drink the same water, though. At least in the lodge. They have their own well.'

'We need to poison the well?'

'I would say so, wouldn't you?'

Edgar nodded thoughtfully. 'By the end of today, I will have three men working within the new fortifications. It shouldn't be too difficult to get something into the well.'

'Don't be too confident, warrior. The well is vital to them. It will be fiercely guarded.'

'Yes, of course, you're right. What shall I use?'

Aegytha stood up and walked across to a low table on the other side of her hut. She selected a plain-looking round-bottomed pot and handed it to him. Then she held a small beaker out.

'You see this beaker?' she asked.

'Yes.'

'Place that much water – no more – in this pot. Then you will need to fill it with a mushroom that I'm going to show you. Fill it right to the top with these mushrooms. Boil it for as long as it would take you to walk five miles. As the mushrooms reduce, add more and keep adding more until half-way through the boil. Seal the top. You must then drop the pot down the well. When it breaks at the bottom, the job will be done.'

'That's it? Mushrooms and water?'

'Come with me.'

She wrapped a heavy woollen shawl around her shoulders and led Edgar into the forest. She walked straight to another, even gloomier clearing where a fallen tree lay.

'You should look in an area like this,' she said. 'See, oak trees.'

Edgar looked around, there were several oaks in the immediate area.

'Now. Look at these,' said Aegytha. She pointed at the ground where some white mushrooms with flat, olive-green caps grew.

'Note that the stems grow out of what looks like a sack.'

She pointed at the feature, visible close to the ground level.

'See also that it looks wet, even though it isn't. Inspect them very carefully so you know what you're looking for. Don't let anyone catch you picking them.'

Edgar reached out to take one of the mushrooms.

'No!' she said, urgently. 'When you pick them, wear gloves.'

'Alright.'

'Then burn the gloves.'

'I see,' said Edgar.

Edgar stood for a few moments, contemplating the fungus growing around the dead tree. He committed its appearance carefully to memory. Somewhere above him in the canopy, a small bird chirruped softly.

'Are you content?' asked Aegytha.

'I'm content with what you have told me. Thank you.'

He reached under his tunic to where his small scrip lay. He pulled out two silver pennies and handed them over to Aegytha.

'Woden be with you,' she said and headed off back to her hovel.

Unconsciously, Edgar's hand went to the small raven amulet he wore around his neck. It had been given to him by another strange female, a very old woman who lived in a cave beneath the great forest close to the Wildmen's Paddock. She, too, had spoken of Woden, the old one-eyed chief of the gods. Edgar watched Aegytha's back retreating into the forest. He shook his head and headed back to camp.

13

Disillusionment

A lone heron grunted gutturally as the three mounted men forded the river and passed the sentries at Hakrholme. It unfurled its ungainly wings and hauled itself out of the shallow water, flying low over the reed beds, croaking as it went.

The sentries acknowledged Halfdene, Harek and Alaric as they passed.

The three riders made their way at a leisurely pace along the narrow, muddy lanes towards the army's camp. They heard it and smelt it before it came into sight. The first sign of the camp was a series of wooden sheds, hastily erected when the army first landed. Within them, a team of blacksmiths had built furnaces large enough to provide the ironwork demanded by the army. As they passed, one of the blacksmiths was pounding on a bar of red-hot iron, sparks flying with every impact of his hammer. The bar bent smoothly round his anvil before he pulled it away and plunged it into the searing heat of the furnace.

Beyond the smithy was the bakers' area, dotted with the beehive ovens in which the army's daily bread was baked. A tub of flour, its surface heaving with weevils, had been carelessly left open next to one of the ovens.

The soldiers' tents came into view, a milling town of leather. Towards the centre stood the larger tents of the commanders, and above all of them rose the pointed tops of Asbjorn's huge tent.

They climbed down from their horses and passed them on to a young stable hand, who made clicking noises to the horses and with practised ease walked them away to one of the fields put aside for them.

The three men walked, a little stiffly, up the field towards Osfrith's tent.

'Look,' said Harek, pointing towards Asbjorn's tent. 'Asbjorn's banner has gone.'

'What does that mean?' asked Halfdene.

'It means Asbjorn isn't here. Maybe he's gone back to the ships.'

They arrived at Osfrith's tent just as the king's thegn was coming out.

'Harek!' he cried. 'You're back, excellent! Good news?'

'I would say so, yes,' replied Harek.

'Good, good. Come in, all of you.'

He motioned them inside his tent. They sat down around the rough table.

'I take it that you found the Wildmen, then?' asked Osfrith as he lowered himself cautiously onto a stool. He looked eagerly at each man in turn.

'I wouldn't quite say that, but they found us.'

A servant stepped forward from within the depths of

The Lost Land

the tent, carrying a large jug of ale and four beakers.

Harek picked the jug up and began pouring.

'I tell you what, Osfrith, the tales we have been told about these men barely scratch the surface. They are utterly incredible. They look like the forest; they sound like the forest. I can barely credit what I've seen these past few days.'

'They look and sound like the forest?' asked Osfrith, looking puzzled. 'How so?'

'They wear outfits that disguise the fact that they are man-shaped. There is foliage blurring the outlines, their faces are painted to match the greenery they inhabit. I swear that when one stands still, he simply becomes a part of the forest – a bush, a tree stump, it's truly remarkable. And the calls they use to communicate with each other. Bird song, bird calls, that's all. They've made an entire language. You look sceptical. I don't blame you, but I swear to you it's true. It's no wonder the Normans are afraid to enter the forest, or that the people living in the nearby villages now believe the woods to be haunted.'

'You spoke with them, then? Of our plan?'

'We met with Alfweald, their leader. He's a most remarkable man, as Edgar and his companions have told us in the past. We spoke with the council of the Wildmen and they are very keen indeed to assist in any way they can.'

'Excellent!' cried Osfrith, clearly delighted at the outcome.

'They are even more formidable now than they were when these lads were with them.' He waved his beaker at Alaric and Halfdene. 'I believe that it's quite possible that not a single Norman we send into the forest will ever come out again. The Normans are now very aware of them, however, and even have special patrols, trained similarly to the Wildmen, but not nearly so well. Alaric, tell Osfrith what happened.'

Alaric bowed his head briefly to Harek.

'Whilst on watch on our first night in the forest, I happened to hear a sound that could only be made by a man. I investigated and discovered a troop of five Normans. I listened in to their conversation and learned that they were a special patrol. I guessed that their quarry could only be the Wildmen. From what they said, I could tell that they were one of several highly trained units searching the forest at that time.

'Armed with this information, I advised Halfdene to stop using the Wildmen calls as we searched for them. It occurred to me that the Normans might well have learned some, in which case the "Friend" call that we knew may now be interpreted by the Wildmen as "I'm a Norman, come and shoot me."

'As it happened, I was right. I searched ahead of Halfdene and Harek. I nearly ran into one of the Norman patrols as I did, but before they saw me, they were all dead, killed simultaneously by Wildmen archers. I find it hard to believe, still, and yet I was standing right next to one of the Wildmen when it happened. It's only because he recognised me from my time with them that I didn't fall with the Normans. The Wildman who recognised me told me that there were actually fourteen Norman patrols in the forest at that time. Not a single man of them came out of the forest again.'

Osfrith was listening intently.

'Dear God,' he said. 'With men like that at our back, we'd be unstoppable.'

He stopped, looking thoughtfully at the door-flap of his

tent. He drew breath. 'The situation here, however, may be changing.'

'What do you mean?' said Harek.

'Jarl Asbjorn has left the camp.'

'Yes, we noticed his banner was missing. Where's he gone?'

'He's gone to a meeting. With the Bastard himself.'

'What?'

'Messengers came to the ships a few days ago under a flag of truce. They didn't come here, you notice. Maybe the Bastard doesn't know where we are yet. An invitation was sent to Asbjorn to meet in person with the Bastard, under promise of his protection.'

'Where?'

'I was not made privy to that information. He took a party of one hundred of his toughest Danes with him to ensure that the Bastard's protection was not violated.'

Halfdene snorted.

Alaric coughed discreetly. Osfrith looked at him.

'You have something to say, Alaric?'

'By your leave, my lord. The Jarl took only Danes with him?'

Osfrith and Harek exchanged a glance.

'He did. Do you have a point?'

'If there are negotiations proceeding, then I think that a satisfactory outcome for the Danes might not be in accordance with what the English contingent would find acceptable.'

Harek grunted.

'What does that mean?' asked Halfdene.

'What our long-winded friend is saying is that Asbjorn may have different goals than the Englishmen may like.

Maybe Asbjorn is going to allow the army to be paid off.'

Halfdene's face fell. 'No, surely not…'

'Look,' said Harek. 'Let's just wait and see what happens when Asbjorn gets back, eh?'

'But…'

'Alright, Halfdene. Settle down. We're getting a little ahead of ourselves,' said Osfrith.

Halfdene subsided, looking troubled.

'The important thing is that you have secured the cooperation of the Wildmen, and that's got to be what we concentrate on. Once Asbjorn knows that, he may see that we now have an even bigger advantage than we did before. We don't even know what he'll be saying to the Bastard. He may well be delivering an ultimatum from Sweyn-king. We'll just have to wait and see, as Harek says. Let's not assume the worst just yet.'

'We do need to let Asbjorn know the full story, though,' said Harek. 'The Normans are now fully aware of the Wildmen and their capabilities. They are adapting their tactics to counter the effectiveness of the Wildmen. Look at those special patrols we encountered. Those men were no clodhopping Norman burwarran, they were trained troops, almost as good as the Wildmen themselves.'

'And yet you say they were all killed?'

'That's true, they were, but we mustn't underestimate the Bastard's forces. They are adapting, rather more quickly than I would like to see.'

'I still think that the Wildmen are far ahead of the Normans. Even though they are adapting, the Wildmen are adapting at the same rate, maybe even faster, and are staying well ahead of the enemy,' offered Halfdene.

'Let's hope that's true,' said Osfrith.

They sat for a while, drinking their ale and staring at the fire.

'Where's Edgar?' asked Halfdene.

'Ah, yes. Edgar, Guthrum and Hallvindur are on a special intelligence-gathering sortie for me.'

'Oh?'

'A member of my old household came to the camp to find me, at much risk, I may say. This man used to be my steward. I thought him dead along with everyone else, my family included, but he brought me information that my sister-son still lives and is a captive of the Normans at a place called Mammesfeld.'

Alaric stirred.

'Yes, Alaric, you know of the place, Edgar told me. He, Guthrum and Hallvindur have travelled to Mammesfeld to see if they can find out more and if there's any way that he could be rescued. It's a slim chance, I know, but he's my only remaining family, and I would dearly love to have him restored to me.'

Halfdene looked alarmed. 'I should be with Edgar,' he said. 'He's my thegn. My axe should be at his side.'

Alaric nodded. 'If I may venture to suggest it, my lord, this assignment seems to be one to which my particular talents are well suited.'

'Yes, I agree with you both. I'd be grateful if you could travel to Mammesfeld, find Edgar and give him whatever help you can, but you've only just got back. You need to eat and rest. It's getting late already. Stay here tonight and set off in the morning. You won't be able to ride horses; you'll have to walk there.'

'I would accompany you, too,' said Harek. 'But I think

I need to remain here, as one of Asbjorn's council, I should be here when he returns. I can't say that I'm altogether happy about this meeting he's having with the Bastard.'

'Agreed,' said Osfrith. Alaric and Halfdene looked at each other and then nodded their accord.

'With that in mind, my lord, might Alaric and I withdraw for the night?' said Halfdene.

'Of course, and thank you for all you've done and are going to do.'

Outside, Alaric stood for a moment, staring into the sky.

'You alright?' asked Halfdene.

'Yes. Yes, I'm fine. You return to our tent and I'll join you shortly.'

Halfdene turned and strode away. Alaric peered at the crowded tents around him. He headed off towards the centre of the camp, where Asbjorn's tent stood, his banner conspicuously absent. Halfway there he found what he was looking for.

The holy men who had accompanied the army from Denmark shared half a dozen tents, pitched close to each other within easy reach of the Jarl's tent.

A couple of monks sat next to a fire and looked up as Alaric approached.

'I seek Lord Osfrith's chaplain,' he said.

'That would be me,' said a gruff voice behind him. Alaric turned to see a short, grizzled man in the coarse robes of a cleric. 'How can I help you?'

Alaric told him.

The priest stood in silence. He shook his head as if to clear it. 'You are not serious, surely?'

'Quite serious.'

The priest spluttered in indignation. 'Certainly not! Who do you think you are to make such a request of me?'

'I think I am a man who has a task to perform which will require what I ask of you.'

'I shall see what Lord Osfrith has to say about this! The insolence!'

The cleric strode away towards Osfrith's tent and Alaric followed him at a more sedate pace. At Osfrith's tent, the priest shoved past the sentry and flung the door-flap open, barging in.

Alaric strolled up to the tent but remained outside as the angry voice of the priest rose in protest. The sentry lifted an eyebrow at Alaric, who smiled back.

Alaric heard Osfrith's voice quietly trying to placate the priest, who simply shouted back in fury.

'Silence!' Osfrith's voice cut through the bluster, and it stopped instantly. Osfrith's voice continued again, more quietly but with determination. Although the words could not be made out, the outcome of the argument was clear. The sentry looked back at Alaric and smiled happily.

The flap of Osfrith's tent snapped open and the priest, red-faced and furious, stepped out. He looked at Alaric with disgust.

'You may have what you ask for,' he said.

14

The Lodge

Joining the work gangs for the fortification was easier than Edgar could have hoped. The clerks taking on the workers were overworked and unenthusiastic.

Guthrum and Hallvindur had been drafted into the work gang with no questions the previous day, and when Edgar arrived looking for work, he was virtually waved through without a second look.

'We'll spend today doing proper work as part of the workforce,' said Edgar as they walked across the muddy ground inside the outer palisade.

There were several gangs of men working on different projects. Two gangs were working on two more towers at the corners of the palisade, one group was building a large stable block whilst a fourth was busy demolishing part of the old lodge and replacing it with a far larger and more imposing building.

Edgar gravitated towards the partly demolished central

building. A harassed looking foreman was shouting at some men. Edgar couldn't tell what the issue was, but the men clearly did not understand what the Norman foreman was saying.

Edgar, Guthrum and Hallvindur walked up to the demolition gang, and soon were heaving hods of rubble away to a designated tipping point. The work was heavy and repetitive, but at least it allowed them to watch what was going on in some detail.

Around mid-morning, Edgar caught sight of Caedmon, standing by the main gate next to a sentry, who was pointing towards the far side of the lodge. Edgar quickly looked down and hissed at Guthrum and Hallvindur to do the same. He had a nightmare vision of the untrained Caedmon spotting them and waving. Fortunately, Caedmon didn't even attempt to look for them. Something must have got through to him, thought Edgar.

At midday, the order went up for men to take their food break. Guthrum produced a small sack containing some of the bread and meat from the previous evening, and the three of them sat and ate hungrily.

A young woman in a stained smock pushed a heavy-looking cart around on which were several jugs of water and some beakers.

Edgar nudged Guthrum. 'Look, water.'

Guthrum nodded. 'That cart looks very heavy for such a slip of a lass. Maybe I should offer some help,' he said.

'Good idea,' agreed Edgar. He leaned over and whispered something into Hallvindur's ear. The giant Dane nodded slightly and stood up.

As the cart approached, Hallvindur careered heavily into it, knocking the girl down into the mud and spilling the contents of the cart over the ground.

The girl squealed.

'Hey!' shouted Guthrum, leaping to his feet.

The heads of nearby men swivelled to find the source of the commotion.

Guthrum ran over to the struggling girl and offered her his hand. She took it and pulled herself back to her feet.

'You oaf!' shouted Guthrum at Hallvindur. 'Look where you're going!'

Hallvindur growled back, but said nothing and returned sullenly to his seat next to Edgar.

Guthrum stooped to right the cart and he began picking up the jugs and beakers from where they had fallen.

'You'll need to get more water, I'm afraid,' he said to the girl, who stared at him with a look of confusion.

'It's alright, I'll help you,' he smiled.

She stared at him. She was thin with short, thick, curly brown hair. Her face was plain and freckled, with eyes that did not quite look in the same direction.

'You won't get nothing back,' replied the girl, angrily. Her voice was thin and squeaky.

'I don't want anything,' said Guthrum.

'That ain't what men say round here,' she said.

'I'm new round here. I just want to help.'

'Well, alright. But that's it.'

Guthrum picked up the handles of the cart and pushed it after the girl, who stomped off away from the lodge.

She approached a corner of the palisade where no building work was going on at present, but a soldier stood, fully armoured, holding a shield and a spear, a long sword hanging from his waist. As he saw Guthrum approaching, he stiffened, dropping his spear to threaten Guthrum.

'Stop! No go!'

The girl tutted loudly. 'It's alright, Stan, he's helping me,' she said.

The man said something in his Norman gibberish, but Guthrum didn't understand. The girl tutted again.

'He,' she said, a little more loudly, pointing at Guthrum, 'is with me,' pointing at herself.

'Oh!' The guard grinned. 'Pokey-pokey!'

In a remarkably familiar manner, the girl swatted the soldier with the flat of her hand, giggling childishly as she did so. 'No pokey-pokey you Norm pig!'

The soldier laughed.

Guthrum joined in the laughter.

The soldier's helmeted head signalled them both to carry on. The girl strode on. As he passed the soldier, Guthrum muttered out of the side of his mouth. 'Pokey-pokey!'

The soldier laughed again and Guthrum winked at him. He followed the girl to a low wall, behind which was a water tank, open to the sky. Guthrum looked on with interest. 'Is this the well?' he asked.

'No, silly. The well's behind. The Norms pull up water all the time and put it in this tank. It's easier to get a lot out at one go then. Didn't matter so much before all you worky men came along. The water in the tank gets a bit green and scummy, but the Norms don't care about that. They have theirs straight from the well.'

Guthrum peered round the tank. There, a few yards away was the well, roughly walled. Three heavy wooden buckets on ropes stood beside it. The soldier the girl had called Stan turned towards them on his slow patrol, and Guthrum walked casually away from the well.

Guthrum nodded towards the soldier.

'You called him "Stan",' he said.

'Yeah. His name sounds a bit like Stan. I can't get me tongue round them fancy foreign names. I call 'em all Stan. I used to know a boy once, and he were called Stan.'

'I see,' nodded Guthrum, as if highly enlightened. He picked up one of the water jugs from the cart and scooped it in the water tank. He did this with all the others whilst the girl looked on.

'You did that quite well,' she said. 'But I do it the other way.'

'The other way?'

'Yeah, look.' She picked up one of the jugs, emptied it into the tank and scooped it through the water from left to right.

Guthrum must have looked puzzled because the girl rolled her eyes – again Guthrum was struck by the way that they ended up looking in slightly different directions – and put her hands on her hips.

'See?'

'Not really,' Guthrum admitted.

'You did it this way,' she imitated scooping from right to left. 'And I do it this way,' she mimed scooping from left to right.

'I see. And that's better, is it?'

"Course, silly,' she said, slapping him feebly across the upper arm.

Guthrum refrained from asking why.

'We should get back to the thirsty men,' he said.

They walked back towards the men. As they passed Stan, Guthrum winked at him again, and he replied with a thumbs-up gesture and a leer.

Guthrum dropped down back between Edgar and Hallvindur. As he did so, the girl stopped in her tracks and turned to him.

'They call me Penta. I said you weren't getting nothing but you might get just a bit if you want.'

She turned and fled. Hallvindur was shaking with silent laughter, and Edgar was struggling to keep a smile from his face.

'Aw,' he said. 'She's sweet.'

Hallvindur erupted with raucous laughter and punched Guthrum in the arm.

'Your babies will be beautiful,' he managed to say, through the laughter. He looked straight into Guthrum's face and crossed his eyes, sticking his tongue out of one side of his mouth.

Guthrum snorted and joined in the laughter.

'Actually, she was quite useful,' he said. 'She gave me an introduction to the well guard. He's called Stan.'

'Stan?' said Edgar. 'That's not a very Norman name.'

'Well, apparently it's something like Stan. That's what she calls him because she once knew a boy called Stan.'

Hallvindur rolled over, clutching his sides.

'Alright, don't draw attention to yourself,' said Edgar.

Hallvindur sat up and wiped his eyes, still hiccupping with spasms of mirth.

Guthrum continued, unmoved. 'There's a tank for water just in front of the well itself. Apparently, it's been installed only since there have been so many workmen here. She tells me that the holding tank is just for water for the workforce, the Normans get their water directly from the well. It's clearer. The well itself is fairly standard, there's a low circular wall around it. From the length of the ropes attached to the buckets, I'd say the water is only about ten feet down.'

'Good, Guthrum, that's useful information, particularly about the fact that the Normans and the local workforce effectively have a different water supply, at least for a short time.'

Shouts were coming from all over the site now. 'Looks like break time is over. We'd better get back to work.'

That evening, the four men convened again at their campsite in the forest, well away from the road.

Caedmon was inordinately pleased with himself.

'I am now an official scullion in the baron's kitchen,' he said.

'Excellent, Caedmon. Did you manage to get the items I asked for?'

Caedmon reached round and picked up his bag. From it, he produced a small hessian sack, a rough pot and a pair of heavy working gloves.

'Caedmon, you have excelled yourself.'

The little steward glowed with pride.

'Thank you, my lord.'

Hallvindur rolled his eyes and Guthrum grinned.

'Right. We need to find the mushrooms that Aegytha told me about,' said Edgar. 'They are particularly poisonous, so nobody must touch them without the gloves on, clear?'

They all nodded their agreement.

'We'll start together, and when I find a crop, I'll point it out then we'll split up and try to find more.'

They set off deeper into the forest, Edgar stopping

them every now and then to examine a sprouting of fungus.

'We need to find oak trees, I think,' he said. 'The crop I was shown was growing near one. Spread out and see if you can spot one. There was also a fallen tree. I don't know if that was important, but it might help. A good, well-rotted one would be best, I think.'

They spread out and soon Edgar heard a low whistle, quite birdlike. A Wildman signal. He followed the sound and found Guthrum sitting on a huge fallen oak, covered with overgrowth.

'This do?' asked the housecarl.

'Let's see.' Edgar walked around the trunk, poking in the overgrowth with a stick.

'Ah,' he said. 'Here, look, lads,' he pointed at the olive-capped, white mushrooms.

'See if you can find any more and I'll harvest these. He pulled on the work gloves and picked the mushrooms carefully, one by one, placing them in the hessian sack.

Hallvindur found the next crop. These too went into the sack. Caedmon found a spot where three oak trees grew together. The forest floor around them was thick with the right mushrooms.

'This should be enough, I think,' said Edgar.

Returning to the campsite, Caedmon set about building a small fire. Hallvindur and Guthrum set off in search of more game.

Edgar took the rough beaker that Caedmon had purloined and poured water into it to the level that Aegytha had indicated to him.

Carefully, and still wearing the gloves, Edgar picked the mushrooms out of the sack and placed them into the pot.

He kept putting them in until they reached the rim. Then with a stick, he forced them down until there was room for more at the top. He did this three times. When he was satisfied that the little pot was quite crammed with the mushrooms, he placed it over the fire.

After a few minutes, he heard it beginning to fizz as the water began to boil.

Caedmon had been watching with interest.

'Now what, my lord?'

'Now we wait. It must boil for some time – as long as it takes to walk five miles, I was told.'

'The water will all boil away by then, my lord.'

'Maybe that's the idea. I don't really know. All we can do is follow the instructions I was given. Meanwhile, I'd like you to go to the brook and collect enough clay to seal the top of this beaker once the boil is over.'

'Right away, my lord,' said Caedmon, jumping to his feet and heading off towards the small brook from which they gathered their water.

The pot boiled and gave off a smell that began quite pleasantly, but gradually grew more and more pungent, sickeningly sweet. The four men were forced to sit upwind of it.

'No one will ever drink water that smells like that,' grumbled Hallvindur. 'It's evil.'

After the allotted time, the pot was removed from the fire and gingerly placed upright between a few rocks to cool down. During the last few minutes of the boil, the smell had completely gone away. Edgar had grinned triumphantly at Hallvindur.

'See?' he said. 'We just follow the instructions and everything turns out as it should. You lack faith, Hallvindur.'

Hallvindur snorted and peered into the cooling beaker. The liquid within was thick, full of small pieces of broken-down mushroom, but it no longer smelled anywhere nearly as bad as it had done.

Once the beaker had cooled enough, Edgar plastered over the top with a thick layer of clay. To reduce risk to himself, he kept the gloves on whilst doing so, despite it being difficult and awkward.

When the beaker was tightly sealed, Edgar placed it securely at the base of a tree and cautiously removed the gloves. He flung them in the fire, along with the hessian sack that he had collected the mushrooms in.

At the end of their second day in the fortification, the three men were sitting around their fire chewing on the roasted meat of a game bird that Hallvindur had shot with his bow earlier.

Caedmon was late, and the bird was almost gone when he arrived back.

'Oh thanks,' he muttered, looking at the stripped carcase.

'You've been in a kitchen all day,' growled Hallvindur. 'Don't tell me you haven't been helping yourself to it.'

'Well,' said Caedmon, sitting down and pulling half a roast chicken out of his sack. 'I have news.'

'Go on,' encouraged Edgar.

'I was late this evening because I managed to get myself volunteered for feeding the prisoner.'

They all sat up immediately.

Caedmon preened at the attention.

'Yes?' said Edgar.

'Beneath what looks to be the oldest part of the original

lodge, there's a storeroom. It's lined with daub, though I think it's just cut into the ground. It may be stone-lined, I couldn't tell. It's certainly damp and musty. It's cool, and I think it must have been used for food storage originally. It now houses a single prisoner.'

'Is it Cyneheard?'

'It is.'

'Did he recognise you?'

'I thought he did, he looked surprised, to say the least, when I walked in, but he quickly hid it. The look was gone from his face before my guard escort got through the door.'

'That's as well. If he let slip that he knew you, I doubt we'd have any chance at all of getting near him again.'

Edgar paused, pondering. 'I don't want you to go down to see him again if you can possibly avoid it. I may need you to see him when and if we're ready to attempt to free him, you may need to warn him not to drink the water, but not before. He's probably given water from the holding tank, which should give us some grace time. The risk of discovery if you see him again is just too great.'

'Understood.'

'Was he chained? What condition is he in?'

'He wasn't chained, in fact not tied at all, but he's been kept in that damp, airless room for some time. He doesn't look as fit as he was. He's dirty, unshaven, his hair was tangled. He looks thin.'

'At least he's not collaborating then,' said Guthrum.

'We can be grateful for that,' agreed Edgar. 'I've been thinking that I really would like to get him out if we possibly can. It's all very well being sure that he's here, but if we just return to Osfrith and tell him that, then what's the point? Much better to bring him back with us. What do you say?

It's a big risk.'

'We need to see the effect of your mushroom soup,' said Guthrum. 'If that has anything like the effect that you were told, then it might provide an opportunity for us to snatch him.'

'Agreed. Hallvindur?'

'I'm with you, my lord. After Lord Osfrith, my first duty is to Master Cyneheard.'

'Good. We're all agreed, then. We will make a bid to rescue Cyneheard if it is at all possible.'

Edgar, Guthrum and Hallvindur arrived early for work the following morning. Work was progressing apace with the demolition of the former king's hunting lodge. In its place, a massive stone-built fortress was appearing.

'The question is,' Edgar muttered to Guthrum as they laboured. 'How do we get to the well and leave our gift?'

'I could try helping the girl again,' said Guthrum, glancing around him to make sure they could not be overheard.

'I think that might look suspicious. Any chance you could get chatting to Stan, the guard?'

'Doubt it. He has a twinkle in his eye for the girl, I think. He probably sees me as a rival for her affections. Anyway, his English was very limited.'

'Alright. Let's all think about it during the day.'

The day passed with unrelenting drudgery. Norman overseers kept a wary eye on all their conscripted English labourers.

The demolition of the lodge, a large and complicated building, was progressing in an orderly manner, with the building being demolished one section at a time. Half of the old building was down now, the wattle and daub between solid wooden uprights succumbing to the blows of heavy hammers and two-man saws.

As Edgar hammered away at a wall, he kept looking at the wall to his right-hand side, not yet due for demolition. It looked wrong, uneven and irregular, not matching the walls around it, as if it had been damaged and hurriedly or carelessly repaired.

Under the guise of resting, he leaned against it and felt along the wall, his hands behind his back. The wall was thin and flexed slightly under pressure. He cautiously withdrew his short seax from under his tunic and still leaning against the wall, he picked gently at the wall with the seax behind his back. Feigning dropping something, he knelt on one knee and turned to examine his handiwork. He had made a small hole in the wall. It was indeed very thin. There was a cavity behind the wall, and stale air drifted out.

Edgar resumed his official demolition work but sidled over to Guthrum.

'The wall to our right is very thin. I think it's a repair job done rather cheaply. There seems to be a cavity of some sort behind. Do you think we could get in there and hide?'

'Let me look,' muttered Guthrum.

He made his way to the thin wall and followed it back and round a corner. He tapped inconspicuously as he went, noticing that it sounded hollow throughout.

Round the corner, he found himself in a tight nook, out of sight of everyone else. He carefully examined the wall at the back of the nook. It was made up of small panels underneath a limy wash. One of the lower panels gapped slightly. He kicked it hard, and the panel flew off. Dropping to his knees, Guthrum peered inside the hole. There was indeed a usable cavity within.

Guthrum pulled himself through the hole that he had made. As he did, the ground seemed to give way beneath him, and he found himself falling, thumping against hard stone as he fell.

He reached the bottom. Not too far. Peering up, he could see daylight streaming in through the hole, just about four feet above his head. He'd fallen into a pit. He stood up. The pit was cold and damp, the walls rough and unfinished. An unhealthy-smelling sludge sucked at his boots.

It was probably an old midden-pit, built over as the lodge was expanded. It would likely be a smelly, cold and uncomfortable night but that didn't matter. They had their hiding place.

Guthrum scrambled up the side of the pit and re-emerged at the top. He crawled through the hole and carefully replaced the panel that he had kicked out. He backed out of the nook and noted that he had not been observed, so he casually strolled back to Edgar and continued hammering at the partly-demolished wall.

He explained what he had found. Edgar nodded in acknowledgement.

'Let's make sure we're round here as it begins to get dark. I'll go and tell Hallvindur. He'll have to stay on the outside.'

They had only a short while to wait until the foreman called out for them to stop work and pack up for the day. The previous day's foreman had been replaced by one with a much better grasp of English.

'Shift your arses!' he shouted.

Edgar and Guthrum moved towards the nook, out of

sight of the foreman and the rest of the work gang.

Guthrum pulled the loose panel away and he and Edgar quickly squeezed their way in through the narrow opening. Guthrum carefully replaced the panel and the two of them descended to the bottom of the pit.

From within their hiding-hole, Edgar and Guthrum could hear the voices of the foremen, shouting at the workforce to hurry up and get out.

'Did you notice anyone counting us in this morning?' Edgar asked Guthrum.

'No, and I particularly looked for someone doing that,' he replied.

'Good, I did the same.'

They sat at the bottom of the pit in silence and listened to the sounds of the men leaving their work for the night. The odd loud shouts from the foremen gradually died down until they could hear nothing more.

After a good while had passed since they heard the last shouts of the departing workmen, Edgar whispered in Guthrum's ear.

'How far do you think we are from the room where they're holding Cyneheard?'

'Well the part of the lodge where he's being held is close to the kitchens, according to Caedmon, and they're on the far side of the building from where we are.'

'No chance of digging through and rescuing Caedmon through a tunnel, then?'

Guthrum smiled at the deliberately pleading note Edgar had put into his voice. 'No. Not today.'

'I'm going to scout,' whispered Edgar. He reached into his scrip and removed a ball of clay and a stick of heavily burnt wood. He rubbed the clay over his face and hands, adding dark, broken lines with the charcoal stick.

'How's that?' he said, once finished.

'Who said that?' asked Guthrum.

'Alright, here I go.'

'Careful,' said Guthrum, unnecessarily.

Edgar climbed silently up towards the top of the pit and, wincing at every tiny noise he made, removed the loose panel at the top.

He crawled through the space and once outside lay flat on his belly, listening for the footfalls of guards.

All remained quiet. He heard a distant voice calling out, but it was so distant he could not even tell if it was Norman or English, from within the palisade or without. He pulled himself forward, keeping flat to the ground, and rounded the corner so that he had a better view across the enclosure.

The sky was still bright in the west but was darkening quickly. Low down in the sky, a crescent moon grinned lopsidedly at him as it blindly followed the Sun below the horizon. The ground beneath him was cold and damp. It was mid-November, and the weather may well get frosty before long. He stayed perfectly still for several minutes, scanning the whole of the enclosure. He spotted two guards, one over on the far side, moving slowly, and the other between himself and the well.

Very slowly, he turned and crawled back into their hiding place.

'Two guards at the moment, but I'm sure there'll be more. The Moon won't present a problem for us tonight, it'll be gone soon, but it's clear, so it'll be cold.'

'I don't mind a bit of cold,' grunted Guthrum. 'It's a small price to pay for what we plan to do.'

Edgar nodded. 'We'll wait until full dark, and then a good while longer.'

Guthrum and Edgar emerged into the dark of the night. Edgar looked up and caught his breath.

'The gods are with us!' he whispered.

A heavy fog had fallen and the ground was very wet.

'We're going to leave trails,' muttered Guthrum. 'Quick, move onto the rubble.'

They stepped off the grass and onto the rubble-littered demolition area. The rubble clicked and crunched unless they walked very carefully. Gradually they made their way along the debris pile to the path that led to the main gate. Ahead, a dark shape shifted in the gloom. Both men squatted down as low as they could. The dark shape separated into two, and they saw the indistinct forms of two guards heading off in opposite directions, both away from them.

'Come on,' hissed Edgar. They continued along the path, turning away from it before they reached the gate itself, which was bound to be guarded. Moving diagonally across the enclosure, they reached the palisade wall, still smelling strongly of freshly cut wood. Edgar noted briefly to himself that this confirmed Caedmon's view that this was probably only meant to be a temporary structure, or else they would surely have used seasoned timber.

They crept along the palisade wall slowly and cautiously. Twice, they dimly saw moving shapes. When they did, they froze, crouching low against the wall.

After some time, Guthrum gently squeezed Edgar's arm. He stopped.

'I think we're close to the well now,' breathed Guthrum

into Edgar's ear. 'We can't avoid the grass any more, we need to go right.'

Edgar nodded and set off, crouching as low as he could, towards where they hoped the well would be. Edgar slipped his hand down to his belt, and for the hundredth time reassured himself that the bottle of deadly fluid still lay strapped to his belt. His hand closed round the neck of the beaker. He patted it.

Just ahead of him, Edgar could see a low stone wall emerging from the fog. He slowed down to a stop, and Guthrum stopped behind him.

'You stay here,' he said to Guthrum. 'Out of sight. I'll drop the jar into the well.'

Guthrum patted Edgar's arm and lay down on the ground, making himself virtually invisible.

Edgar stole forwards, crouching almost double, placing each foot very carefully, and not putting the weight on his foot until he was sure that no noise would be made. He first came across the settling tank, where the stagnant water for the workers lay, perfectly still. Remembering Guthrum's description of the area, Edgar moved left.

He stopped suddenly. There was a dark form ahead of him, rocking slightly. A guard, shockingly close. Edgar froze, his hand tightening around his deadly jar. With glacial slowness, Edgar lowered himself down to the ground and lay flat, looking constantly at the sentry, who could be no more than twenty feet away. For what seemed like an eternity, the guard stood quite still, swaying gently. Occasionally he coughed lightly. Just as Edgar's neck was beginning to cramp painfully, another, dimmer shadow appeared and approached the guard. Another guard. They exchanged a few quiet words, then the first guard set off back towards the settling tank and then presumably on to his barracks, his duty over for the night.

The new guard grunted as he thrust something into the ground. His spear, Edgar guessed. Then, coughing more loudly than his colleague, he disappeared into the mist.

Edgar dropped his head to the cold, wet ground. Where had the sentry gone? How long would he be? Did he dare move forward? He pressed his ear hard to the ground in an attempt to hear the sentry's footsteps, but he could hear nothing other than the pounding of his own heart in his ears.

He was just about to move cautiously forward when the sentry returned, pulling his spear out of the ground and disappearing back into the mist. Edgar took his chance and crept forward, straining against the dark and fog to see the sentry. Out of the murk appeared the low wall of the well. He had made it! A cough sounded, but it seemed quite distant. Was it the same man, and was he now far enough away?

Quickly, Edgar fumbled at the tied cord at his waist and pulled the jar of poison off his belt. Without pausing, he threw the jar down the well. He listened carefully and heard a splash as the jar hit the water. There was no cracking, no shattering sound.

Edgar cursed violently under his breath. He turned around and made his way swiftly back to where Guthrum still lay.

'It didn't break!' he hissed.

'What?'

'The bastard pot, it didn't break!'

'Shit. We need to drop some big stones down after it.'

'We passed a pile of building materials about twenty

yards back that way,' said Edgar, pointing into the gloom they had come from.

Guthrum turned and they moved with painful slowness back to the pile of masonry.

There they each selected two large, heavy stones and made their way back to the well. A soft mutter of voices stopped them dead in their tracks about twenty feet from the well. Edgar placed his stones on the ground and motioned Guthrum to stay where he was. Approaching the source of the voices, Edgar made out two dim shapes. The fog seemed to be getting denser. The soft talking continued for some time, then with what sounded like a farewell, the two figures moved apart. One walked away, quickly disappearing into the murk, but the other one was walking straight towards Edgar. Using all the skills in silent movement that he had learned from the Wildmen, he quickly backtracked and skittered off to one side. He hoped that Guthrum noticed the approaching figure in time.

The guard sauntered by, barely visible, but posing a very real threat to Edgar. Edgar held his breath as the guard walked on towards Guthrum. No cry of alarm came, and Edgar breathed a soft sigh of relief. He felt a soft tap on his foot and turned to see Guthrum, flat on the ground. He was dragging the four stones, alternating two with each hand.

Edgar again motioned him to be still and took two of the stones.

Lying on his stomach, he inched towards the well again. No shapes were visible, so he proceeded with caution. Reaching the low wall once more, he carefully lifted one stone and held it over the centre of the well. Whispering a silent prayer to whoever might be listening, he let go.

It seemed to Edgar that the stone fell for a very long

time. When the stone hit the water at the bottom, it made what sounded to Edgar like the loudest noise he had ever heard. It must surely have been heard all over the compound. There was no time to lose. Quickly and with less care, Edgar lifted the other stone and dropped it. Again, this produced a loud splash, but whether the jar below the water had been broken he could not tell. Even if it had cracked open under the impact of one of the stones, there was no way that he could have heard that sound over the splash.

Edgar moved more quickly now, for surely the noise must be attracting the attention of the guards. He dashed back, still stooping low, to where Guthrum had been.

To his left, he heard a startled cry, and then another in front of him. Out of the darkness two large figures loomed before him. Two guards, and they had spotted him.

He turned and dashed away from them, towards the rear palisade, praying with all his might that Guthrum had escaped. The darkness and the fog now came to his aid again, and he reached the rear palisade without any further encounters. Around him, dim glows were beginning to appear. Torches. The guards were now on full alert and were lighting torches to aid them in their discovery of the intruder.

A torch flared to his left, moving towards him. With his back to the wooden stakes of the palisade, he walked sideways, constantly checking on the torch that was approaching him. He glanced ahead. Nothing; no torches. He kept moving, the torch seemed to sway a little and then move off away from him, towards the central building.

Edgar sighed in relief. As he did so, something very hard hit him on the back of the head and he passed out.

15

Captive

Edgar spluttered and coughed. Slimy water splashed in his face as he fought for consciousness. He blinked and looked around. He was lying on a stone floor. His wrists and ankles were tied tightly. Above him a soldier stood, dangling a bucket from his hand. The soldier kicked Edgar in the ribs and he doubled over, gasping for breath.

A harsh word from a corner of the room caused the guard to back away. Edgar looked up and saw a small, dapper man with thinning hair and an aquiline nose. He was sitting on a chair, watching Edgar with evident disgust. He said something which Edgar did not understand.

'What is your name?'

Edgar looked round. In another corner of the room stood an emaciated young man, his eyes darkened with exhaustion and lack of food. He wore a rough-spun tunic and no shoes. His hands were tied and his legs were hobbled.

'Edmund,' said Edgar.

The interrogator spat out some more unintelligible words.

'What are you doing in the Baron's compound?'

Edgar closed his eyes and breathed deeply.

'There was a girl. Pretty girl. She brings the water. Penta, she's called. I was hoping to find her.'

The hobbled youth spoke to the interrogator in his own language. The interrogator replied sharply. Even without understanding the actual words, Edgar could hear the scorn in what he said.

'You expect to find some local peasant girl within the compound after dark? After midnight?'

Edgar shrugged. 'I hoped,' he said, wistfully.

The youth translated.

The interrogator nodded at the soldier, who walked forward and kicked Edgar in the ribs twice and then backed off.

Edgar rolled on the floor in agony. He had felt at least one rib crack.

The interrogator spoke again, and the youth translated.

'You will tell us your true purpose. You are a spy and you will admit it.'

'Does your friend not speak any English?' asked Edgar, running his words together.

'Not a word,' said the translator in a similar way.

'Tell him I was looking for the girl, but I was drunk and fell asleep. Are you the sister-son of a king's thegn?'

The translator spoke to the interrogator who sneered again as he replied.

'He says drinking anything other than water is prohibited for the peasant workforce. Yes, I am, you know him?'

'I didn't want to admit to drinking because I thought I would be forbidden to return and I need the money. He sent me to rescue you.'

The interrogator snorted and replied.

'You are in danger of losing more than your income. And thank you, you're doing a great job.'

'Tell him I'm sorry and I'll never do it again.'

'He says your fate has yet to be decided. The baron must be informed.'

'Beg him not to tell the baron. It is vital that the baron does not see my face.'

The interrogator simply stood up at this and walked out, followed by the guard, who dragged Cyneheard with him.

Guthrum woke from an uneasy sleep. Above him, he could hear the work on the demolition of the lodge proceeding. Last night, he had been close to Edgar when he was taken but had been powerless to intervene. Not only was he greatly outnumbered by the guards, but the only weapon he had was his short seax. No match for the swords and spears of the Normans. He had made his way slowly and silently back to their hiding place, reaching it even as the fog began to lift. He had crawled back into the pit and carefully washed every last trace of the clay and charcoal from his face. This had left him with no drinking water for the night.

He climbed up and eased out of the access panel, replacing it behind him. He stood up and sauntered round the corner.

'You, where the hell did you come from?'

Guthrum looked up to see one of the foremen pointing

angrily at him.

'Just having a piss, Boss,' he called.

'Well stop pissing about and get back to work,' shouted the foreman.

Guthrum jogged back towards the work party, picking up a heavy lump hammer from the ground. He joined the other men battering away at the old walls.

'I want this cleared by the end of the day,' said the foreman.

Guthrum was deeply concerned. He had seen that Edgar had been taken captive, but had no idea what had happened after that. He had to find out where he was being kept, if he was being kept at all and had not simply been executed. The baron knew Edgar from previous encounters, and if he were to recognise him, it would not go at all well for Edgar. Guthrum had to do something, but what? He pounded at the walls, feeling useless.

A deep, familiar voice drifted across the compound. Hallvindur. Guthrum strode across the compound towards him. Hallvindur greeted him with a wave.

'How did you do last night?' said Hallvindur in a low voice.

A foreman was watching them. 'Don't react,' said Guthrum, 'We're being watched. Let's move over to this wall.'

They walked over to the wall and started hitting it with their heavy hammers.

'Well?' asked Hallvindur.

'It's bad. Edgar was taken.'

'What?'

'Easy now, don't react!'

'What happened?'

'Edgar dropped the jar down the well but it didn't break. We had to get heavy stones to drop after it in the hope that one would break the jar. The stones made a loud splash. It alerted the guards. We nearly got away, but there were too many of them. Hopefully, they think Edgar was acting on his own.'

'Where is he?'

'I don't know. I couldn't see anything because of the fog. I heard him go down. I think he must have been taken by surprise and stunned. I'm hoping he was stunned, but we may have to be prepared for the worst.'

'Fuck.'

They hammered at the wall again, large lumps of old plaster and daub falling to the ground around them.

'What about the jar? Did it break?'

'I don't know. We'll just have to wait and see. But if I were you, I wouldn't drink the water if they pull any more out into the holding tank.'

'Do you think they will?'

'The tank was full last night. They'll have no reason to top it up probably for another couple of days.'

'That gives us a little time. We need to get Caedmon looking into where Edgar is. The trouble is, we can't get to speak to him until after we've finished work today.'

'We have to do something,' insisted Guthrum.

Hallvindur fell silent and hammered at a stubborn section of wall, eventually bringing it down with a loud thud.

'The girl,' he said.

'What?'

'Your sked-eyed girlfriend. She probably has a pretty free rein around here. I bet nobody pays any attention to her.'

'Yes, right. You're right. I'll think of something.'
'Let's both think.'

At mid-afternoon, the girl duly came around, pushing her cart full of water jugs. She smiled coyly when Guthrum got up and walked towards her.

'Hello, you,' she said.

'Hello, you,' he replied.

She giggled in delight.

Guthrum helped her pour out the water into the rough clay beakers.

'I've lost my friend,' he said, casually.

'What friend's that?' she asked.

'You know, the man I was sitting next to the day before yesterday, when I helped you with the water. He liked you.'

'Did he?'

'Yes, but I don't know where he's gone.'

'Well I don't know, I'm sure.'

'I think the Normans have got him.'

'Who? Stan?'

'One of the Stans.'

'Do you want me to find out?'

'Do you think you could?'

'I'm good at finding things out,' she smiled confidently.

'Well, alright, but you mustn't let anyone know that I've been asking or I'll get in trouble.'

Her eyes widened. 'Will you? Why?'

'If my friend's in trouble, they'll think I'm trouble too. And then they'll come for me. That's what happens. The friends of people who get into trouble always get picked on and blamed for stuff, too. Even if they've not done anything.'

'I wouldn't want you to get into any trouble,' she said seriously.

'No. I know you wouldn't, because you're my friend, aren't you?'

'Yes.' Her face remained blank for a moment and then Guthrum saw realisation dawn slowly on her.

'You mean if you get into trouble, then I...' she looked terrified.

Guthrum bit down hard on the guilt he felt, but he knew her fear would keep her and all of them safe. He nodded. 'And I don't want that.'

She trembled a little and some water spilled from the jug onto her smock.

Guthrum took her hand in his. He held it gently and looked into her eyes as kindly as he could.

'You must find out about my friend without asking directly about him. Just listen to what other people say. He may be being held in one of the buildings over there.' He nodded towards the remaining sections of the old lodge. 'But you already know that, you being so good at finding things out.'

She stared blankly at him for a moment and then nodded enthusiastically. 'Yes, I did. Listen. Don't ask. I'll do that.'

'Good girl.'

Halfdene and Alaric walked along the road into Mammesfeld. They had set off before dawn, into a foggy, dark grey morning. The fog had thinned to mist and the mist was quickly burned off by the rising sun. Although sunny, the morning was cold; thin rimes of ice had formed around puddles on the road and a glistening frost covered much of the landscape around them. They walked in silence, neither wanting to break the quiet of the road, each lost in his solitary thoughts.

'How are we going to find them?' asked Halfdene as they approached Mammesfeld from the north.

'I don't know yet,' replied Alaric. 'But we must be careful not to appear before them suddenly. They may react in a way that arouses Norman suspicion. We need to see them before they see us.'

Halfdene nodded, thoughtfully.

They walked on for a while in silence. Halfdene watched the road ahead, always aware that they were approaching a centre of Norman activity, on a road that was probably subject to frequent patrols. Glancing constantly to left and right, Halfdene was continually aware of the nearest place to bolt should they need to get off the road in a hurry. A dense bush here, a well-concealed ditch there.

Alaric let out a small, exasperated cry, interrupting Halfdene's thoughts.

'What is it?'

Alaric turned round and walked back ten yards in the direction that they had just come from.

'Look,' said Alaric, pointing at the roadside.

'Gods, how did I miss that?' exclaimed Halfdene.

'The same way everyone else is supposed to miss it. If you're not actively looking for it then you won't see it.'

A thin supple branch in a small tree had been twisted and bent. Deliberately, Halfdene could see now that he looked carefully.

'Come on,' said Alaric, and led Halfdene into the woods at the side of the road. After a couple of hundred yards, they found Edgar's camp, carefully hidden and all but invisible to untrained eyes.

'A fire,' said Alaric, looking at a slightly raised mound of leaf mould. 'Still very slightly warm. This was lit last night.' He swept off the leaf mould and stirred the ashes with a stick. 'What's this?' He reached into the ashes and pulled out a blackened lump.

'What is it?' asked Halfdene.

'Leather, I think,' he replied, dropping it back into the ashes. He re-covered the ashes with the leaf mould to disguise it once again.

'I think we should stay here. All being well Edgar and the others will return here soon. I'm hoping that this is their camp. Who else would put Wildman signs around?'

'Another Wildman?'

'Possibly but unlikely. Most of the Wildmen are located well away from here. It's just possible, though, so we should take precautions.'

Halfdene and Alaric withdrew a little further into the bush, settling down in silence to await the occupants of the camp.

A shout went up from the foremen and the workers started filing towards the gate. Guthrum looked desperately at Hallvindur.

'We've learned nothing,' he hissed.

'I advise patience,' said Hallvindur.

'How can we be patient? Any moment may bring Edgar's death. We must move!'

'And do what? Listen to yourself Guthrum. I've never seen you like this before. You're the calmest and most controlled warrior I know, and yet you're acting like you're still wet behind the ears. Calm down and think like

Guthrum.'

Guthrum inhaled sharply. He held the breath for a moment and then let it out with a noisy gasp.

'You're right. I'm sorry. I'm not… myself.'

'I understand. You look to the lad as a son.'

Guthrum was silent.

'It's alright. We'll get him out.'

'It's just…'

'Yes?'

'I once thought of another man as a son. He was killed. I can't…'

'You can't let it happen again.'

'No, I can't.'

Hallvindur stopped, letting the flow of workers wash around him. 'Then think what would happen if we burst in, slaughtering and shouting. And what would we use as weapons? How would we defeat all these Norman warriors? And when we were dead, which would be very soon, then who would come for Edgar?'

Guthrum remained silent. He turned and followed the workmen as they made their way out of the gate.

Alaric stiffened almost imperceptibly.

'What is it?' breathed Halfdene.

'Approaching footsteps. Untrained. They're not careful enough to be Edgar or Guthrum.'

Halfdene could hear the footsteps now. They were cautious, but he could still hear the crunch of undergrowth and the occasional snap of a twig.

A small man stepped into the cramped clearing in which the camp lay. He sat down and wiped the leaf mould off the fire. Once clear, he started adding little twigs to the remains of the previous fire. He placed some dried moss out of his scrip at the base of them and began rubbing the point of a short stick in a small hole in a dried piece of timber. Smoke began to rise from the wood, and he blew carefully. A couple of sparks blew onto the dried moss and it began to smoulder. Picking the moss up in both hands he blew gently on it and then placed it beneath the pile of twigs, which soon began to burn.

Alaric tapped Halfdene lightly on the elbow and they rose as one and stepped into the clearing.

'Wha…?' Caedmon stood up and stepped backwards in alarm.

'Who are you?' he demanded, his hand going to his seax, hanging from the front of his belt.

'I wouldn't,' warned Halfdene.

'We are friends of Thegn Edgar's,' said Alaric. 'I presume you are Osfrith's man, Caedmon?'

Caedmon nodded vigorously. 'Yes. Yes, I am.'

'Then all is well. Sit, tend your fire.'

Caedmon did as he was told. Halfdene picked up some larger twigs and placed them by the side of the fire,

'Tell us everything that's happened,' said Alaric.

'We've found Master Cyneheard in the Norman fortifications. I have seen him and I know where he's being kept. Hallvindur, Guthrum and Lord Edgar got work within the fortification. There's much building going on. I have a job in the kitchens – that's how I managed to see Master Cyneheard. Lord Edgar made up a poison to put down the well. He and Guthrum stayed in the compound overnight last night – they found a good hiding place, Hallvindur said – so they could drop the poison into the well. Hallvindur and I stayed here last night. I'm hoping to get good news this evening when they return. Lord Edgar planned to rescue Master Cyneheard when the Normans were suffering from the effects of the poison.'

Alaric nodded. 'Good. We'll wait with you. No point in wandering around attracting attention to ourselves.'

Edgar had not eaten or had anything to drink all day. Not eating he could cope with, for a few days at least, but the lack of water was beginning to tell. His mouth was dry and his tongue seemed bigger and rougher than it usually felt. There was no light in the room, underground as it was. He spent most of the time sleeping. It was all that he could do.

He woke to the sound of the heavy iron lock turning. The door opened and Cyneheard and the interrogator from the previous session walked in. Following them was a tall man with black hair, shaved at the back in the Norman fashion. He wore a black studded leather jerkin. Some sort of senior soldier, Edgar assumed.

The interrogator sat in front of Edgar, whilst the soldier stood to one side, leaning casually against the wall of the cell.

The interrogator spoke.

'What is your name?' said Cyneheard.

'I've already told you. Who's your friend?'

'Do not deviate from the answers to the questions,' snapped Cyneheard.

Instantly alert, Edgar realised that the man in black must at least speak a little English. If his English was good, there would be no need for Cyneheard.

'Sorry,' muttered Edgar, looking abashed.

Cyneheard looked at the soldier in black, who nodded

slightly.

'This is Jean de Rouen, Captain of the guards here,' said Cyneheard.

Edgar turned to look at him. 'Hello,' he said.

The man smiled, stepped away from the wall, walked up to Edgar and punched him hard in the face. Edgar fell to the ground. Blood poured from his split lower lip.

'Do not speak to the captain,' said Cyneheard. 'What is your name?'

Edgar remained silent.

'Your name is Edgar.'

Edgar just shrugged.

The captain spoke, and Cyneheard translated. 'You are the grandson of the thegn of Rapendun in Mercia. The thegn failed to pay the rent due to the King and was dispossessed of his land. That land now rightfully, legally and in the eyes of the King and God belongs to my lord the Baron de Barentin.'

Edgar remained silent.

'You will admit this.'

'I will admit nothing.'

Jean de Rouen once again approached Edgar, picked him up and punched him in the face again, and again, and again.

'Your face, it is ruined. But only on the one side. I will be ruining the other side,' he said in heavily accented English.

Cyneheard spoke: 'You are outlawed. You rebel against our lord the King, and you murdered Baron de Barentin's loyal liegeman, Guillaume de Caen.'

'Guillaume de Caen. He was my friend,' said de Rouen, ominously.

Edgar lay on the floor, gasping. He cautiously felt the inside of his mouth with his tongue. A couple of teeth felt loose. He spat blood.

'Your friend was a murderer,' Edgar managed to say between gasps.

'It is war. Much is fair in war.'

'For you, but not for us.'

The soldier simply shrugged. 'We are the victors,' he said. 'If you had won, you would have slaughtered us.'

'We still will,'

De Rouen laughed. 'Maybe so, but not today.'

The door to the cell opened and two more soldiers entered. They were carrying heavy chains and tools. They ignored everyone else in the room and hammered huge nails into the wall of the cell, bending them round the chains.

Once the chains were fixed to the walls, the two soldiers looked at de Rouen, who nodded. They hauled Edgar to his feet and fastened the chains round his wrists, pulling them tight so that his hands were hard against the walls at shoulder level. Then they walked out.

'What is your name?' said the interrogator through Cyneheard.

'You know my name,' said Edgar.

De Rouen stepped forward again and slammed his fist into Edgar's stomach. Edgar gasped and folded forward as far as the chains would allow him. A sickening pain spread to every last fibre of his body. He fought for breath but found it impossible to inhale.

Cyneheard stepped forward, his hands reaching out as if to help Edgar, but de Rouen slapped him back.

'Please!' cried Cyneheard. 'Please tell them what they want!'

'Silence!' shouted de Rouen. 'Or you'll be joining him.'

The floor was swimming in front of Edgar's eyes. His peripheral vision was beginning to shrink, but at last, he managed to inhale slightly, then again.

The interrogator spoke once more, calmly and without emotion.

'One more time,' said Cyneheard, his voice breaking. 'What is your name?'

Edgar swayed from his chains, still looking down at the floor. He didn't have the breath to reply. De Rouen stepped forward and grabbed Edgar's chin. He twisted his head up until he could look into Edgar's eyes. Edgar rolled his eyes up into his head and slumped forward, hanging only by his chains.

De Rouen spat. He let go of Edgar and let him slump. The chains around Edgar's wrists and the full weight of his body on his shoulders caused him a great deal of pain, but the alternative was more beatings, so he stayed down.

At that moment, the door of the cell opened and another man entered. Edgar remained motionless, hanging from his chains, eyes closed. He heard de Rouen stiffen and the interrogator get to his feet, his chair legs dragging on the floor as it pushed backwards.

This could mean only one thing. The baron himself had entered. Edgar felt despair rising within him. He heard a shuffling of feet, then he heard the cell door closing.

There was silence in the cell for a few moments. Then he heard a rustling of clothing very close.

Edgar sensed an approaching presence as he feigned unconsciousness. Fear twisted his gut. He knew who this was.

This was Baron Roger de Barentin, the man who was

responsible for the deaths of his grandfather and his wife. The man who had stolen Rapendun from him. The man who had killed Eric as they fled for Denmark. The man he had met in battle and beaten once before.

A meaty hand lifted his chin.

The Baron looked closely at Edgar's face, taking in the shattered left-hand side, the lumpy scars, the drooping eye. He nodded slightly to himself, clearly satisfied.

'We meet again,' he said.

Edgar kept his eyes closed. The hand dropped his chin and his head lolled back.

'Come on, Edgar. You can fool them, but you can't fool me you know.'

Last time they had met, at the fateful hour of Eric's death, de Barentin had spoken to them through a translator. Edgar wondered if he had at that point already been learning English but now felt confident enough in the language to forgo the intermediary.

De Barentin's voice was soft and lightly tinged with his Norman accent. Edgar reluctantly admitted that the baron had a pleasant voice. It didn't match with anything else about him, and the realisation of this hardened Edgar's heart against the false gentleness of the voice.

He opened his eyes slowly. He could see the baron's richly booted feet and lower legs.

He lifted his head and straightened up. De Barentin looked on approvingly.

'That's better,' he said. 'You killed my man Guillaume de Caen,' he said softly. 'That demands a great and terrible price.'

'You killed my grandfather. You killed my wife.'

'Your wife? Did I?'

Edgar remained silent.

'One filthy English whore looks pretty much like any other to me,' he smiled. 'So I suppose that is possible.'

Edgar felt his anger surge and struggled to keep it in check.

The baron stepped back and stared at Edgar for a few moments.

'What were you doing in my compound last night?'

'I told your creature. I wanted to find the girl Penta, but I got drunk and fell asleep. When I woke up, I went looking for her.'

The Baron chuckled. 'Yes, you did tell him that. But it's a lie. You know it and I know it. Do we have to dance this dance?'

'I am telling the truth.'

'When last we met, you fled England on a Danish ship. Now you return to England to get a job as a builder for the man who killed your wife? Is that right?'

'I returned to England because it is my home. I didn't know you were here in this place.'

'Am I to conclude that it is a pure coincidence that you arrive here at the same time as a Danish army intent on conquering this land and removing its rightful king?'

'I know nothing about any army. I want no more of that.'

'I see.'

The baron reached up and gently touched Edgar's face. Edgar winced.

'You will forgive my men. They are crude and largely uncultured. Me, I have read many books and travelled to many places. I have seen things that have truly amazed me, Edgar. Even here, in this cold northern land, some things have astonished me. Why will you people not accept that you have been conquered? Why will you not just get on with your lives and leave governance to the new rulers? I am genuinely puzzled, Edgar. What difference does it make to you if your king is English or Norman? You have had foreign rulers before; there are many Danes on your king list. What of the great Cnut? You revere his memory as you do the greatest of your native kings. Why not accept William and let him prove to you that he is as great as any of them?'

Edgar looked into de Barentin's eyes. His voice was strained and hoarse as he spoke. 'Cnut was a legitimate king of England. He was lawfully elected to the throne by the Witan. The Bastard was not. Harold was the legitimately elected king. William killed him, a God-anointed king. For that, he is damned forever.'

'But Edgar, your history is littered with kings who gained their crown through the murder of their own kings. Surely you see that?'

Edgar remained silent and his eyes slid to the floor again.

De Barentin said nothing for some time and then said: 'I'm going to let my men back in again now. You must understand that I can't just stop them. It would make me look weak. Think about what I have said.'

With that he walked out of the room, to be replaced by de Rouen, who came in on his own, the interrogator and Cyneheard presumably having been dismissed.

'You will tell me what you were doing in the Baron's compound last night.'

Edgar closed his eyes briefly and then reopened them, looking at de Rouen. 'There's this girl…' he began.

De Rouen's hand, within a studded leather glove, swept

up and caught Edgar on the undamaged side of his face. Edgar's head snapped round and he felt a warmth on his face, trickling down towards his jawline.

'She's called Penta.'

Again, the hand slapped viciously against Edgar's face. Edgar groaned slightly, earning him a further slap.

'About this girl. No more,' said de Rouen.

'She's lovely,' muttered Edgar.

De Rouen's fist plunged into Edgar's stomach once again. This time he did not need to feign passing out, and he woke some time later to find himself alone in his cell.

As he passed through the gate of the compound at the end of the shift, Guthrum felt a tug at his elbow. He looked round to see Penta looking up at him with huge, round eyes.

'I've got news!' she exclaimed.

'Hush, not so loud,' said Guthrum, warily looking at the workmen around him. No one paid any attention to the girl.

He took her by the arm and they walked out together. Guthrum kept a gentle but firm grip on her arm until they were well away from any possible prying ears.

'Well done,' he said kindly, not expecting much from the girl. 'What have you found out?'

She stared pointedly at Hallvindur, who simply smiled his terrifying smile at her.

'It's alright, he's a friend,' said Guthrum.

'He looks frightening,' she said, not taking her eyes off him.

'He frightens our enemies, but not us,' said Guthrum.

She looked slightly mollified then looked around theatrically, making it clear that she was aware of the danger of being overheard.

'Would them Norms call your friend "Scarface"?'

'Yes, they might. He does have a scarred face.'

'Well, there was some talk of Scarface. Is he a friend of the baron?'

Guthrum felt his heart start thudding. 'No,' he said quietly.

'Well this can't be him then, 'cos they call him "the baron's friend".'

'Shit,' said Guthrum. 'That means that the baron's seen him and recognised him.'

'Won't the baron help him, then?'

'No, Penta, he won't. My friend and the baron had… an argument some time ago. They really are not friends. The baron will probably kill him.'

Penta gasped and threw one hand up in horror to cover her mouth.

'But that's awful,' she said through her fingers.

'Yes, it is,' said Guthrum slowly. 'Did you hear anything else, Penta?'

'I know where he is.'

'Really? That's very clever of you. Where is he?'

'He's in the baron's special guest room. That's what they call it. It's in one of them new low buildings by the wall to the left of the gate. I think it's the one with the cellar. That's a new underground room. They want to keep wine in it.'

She said "cellar" and "wine" carefully, hesitating over the unfamiliar words.

'Very good, Penta. That's very good indeed. You have been a great friend to me.'

She smiled happily. 'I promise I won't tell no one, not even Daddy.'

'That would be a very good idea. Keep quiet, keep safe. Thank you.'

She curtsied clumsily to him and started walking home.

'Penta,' called Guthrum softly.

She turned round, looking at him quizzically.

'Here,' he said. He reached inside his tunic and pulled out a small silver cross on a leather thong. 'I'm very sorry if I frightened you. You're a good girl. Keep this,' he said.

Her eyes widened as she gaped at the little treasure. She took it and stood in silence for a moment, gazing at it. She looked up at Guthrum. 'Oh,' was all she managed.

'Go on, off you go.'

She turned and hurried away from him.

Guthrum glanced at Hallvindur, who wasn't laughing this time.

'Right, so we know where he is and we know that the baron has recognised him. Let's get back to the camp and think of a way to get him out.'

Alaric sat by the small fire, his head resting in his hands. He stared at the flicker of the flames and worked at digesting all the information that he had received from Guthrum. He knew it was vital to get Edgar out of his imprisonment as fast as possible. The prospects for him were not good. The added complication was that Osfrith's nephew Cyneheard must now also be rescued. Getting one body out of the compound would be difficult enough, two would be near impossible.

Guthrum stared sullenly at the fire in silence, whilst Halfdene and Hallvindur talked quietly about ever more fanciful rescue plots.

Caedmon sidled up to Alaric and sat beside him.

'The poison,' he started, hesitantly.

'Yes?' replied Alaric.

'If I understand the situation, we have two possibilities. Either the poison beaker was broken and the well will now be blighted, or the beaker did not break, in which case we can look for no assistance from that quarter.'

'Correct,' said Alaric.

'If the beaker did not break, then one option would be to get back in there and break it somehow, ensuring that the water supply will strike the Normans down.'

'Too difficult. After what happened last night, you can be quite sure that the garrison will be ever more vigilant. We must just hope and pray, if you're that way inclined, that Edgar has not told them why he was in the compound. That they don't know about the poison. The worst scenario would be that the jar did not break and the Normans know it is there, in which case they will surely fish it out. And if I know them, feed it to Edgar.'

Guthrum sprang to his feet. 'We must go, now!' he cried, his face contorted in distress.

Halfdene stood and took Guthrum by the shoulders. 'No, Guthrum. There is no hope for a frontal assault. There are too few of us and too many of them. It would be the death of all of us, including Edgar.'

'Halfdene's right, Guthrum,' said Alaric gently. 'I know that Edgar's captivity is tearing you apart, but you must think like the warrior that you are. We need you with a calm head and a clear mind. I don't think we'll be able to get him back without that.'

Guthrum stared wildly at Alaric, his body tense and poised for flight. Halfdene braced himself. He knew that Guthrum was by far the stronger man and if he decided to go, there would be nothing he could do to stop him. Then he felt the tension drain out of Guthrum's limbs. His head dropped and he nodded.

'You're right, Alaric. I'm sorry,' he patted Halfdene on the wrist. Halfdene dropped his hands from Guthrum's arms.

'Good lad. Thanks,' muttered Guthrum.

He sat down again, but no longer stared at the fire but across it at Alaric. 'We seem to be in your hands, once again, Spy.'

'I'll try not to let you down,' said Alaric.

'You never have. We trust you.'

'Thank you. Now I need to think hard about this. Let's put out the fire and get our heads down.'

Edgar awoke as a hand gently slapped his cheek. He looked up woozily. Two men were in the cell with him. One he recognized immediately as Roger de Barentin. The other seemed to be employed simply to hold a torch. The light from the torch flickered, sending wild shadows around the gloomy room.

'Come on,' said de Barentin. 'Look at me.'

Edgar looked at de Barentin. 'Good,' he said. 'I think you have had enough of my colleagues' tender caresses, have you not?'

Edgar did not reply, his mouth swollen and caked in blood.

'Yes. I see that you have. I did not want this, you know. I am not the cruel man, but certain procedures, they must be followed, no? For appearance's sake, if for nothing else.'

Edgar's head drooped and he stared at the floor.

'Look at me,' repeated de Barentin. 'You know that not

all of your English nobility resists us? No? Many have joined with us. Their lands, they keep. Their titles, they keep. The King extends his generous and protective arms around them.'

He fell silent. Edgar's head dropped against his chest again.

'William is king of England. Your duty is to the king of England. You must not think of him as the duke of Normandy, for he is now risen above that, no? He is your king. He is my king. We share that, do we not? This is a land of great riches. The King is generous to his friends but merciless to his enemies. The King wants you to be his friend. I want you to be my friend. My friends are rich and powerful.'

De Barentin turned and walked slowly across the cell, towards the man holding the torch, blocking the firelight and plunging Edgar into darkness. He turned again and walked back to Edgar.

'Be my friend, Edgar, and all this can stop. Be my friend and you shall be Edgar, Thegn of Rapendun once again. Your lands and titles restored, and who is to know? Maybe more will follow if you find favour with the King. A man of your considerable qualities should have little difficulty in that. Think of it, Edgar.'

Quietly, de Barentin turned and left the room, the torch-bearer following him.

Edgar stared across the blackness of the cell. In his mind's eye, he saw the mead hall at Rapendun. He saw his upbringing there, sparring with wooden swords with his childhood friends, Halfdene and Modbert. He saw the great feasts held at harvest time when the farmers from the area all gathered at the mead hall and ate and drank themselves silly, reward for the months of backbreaking labour needed to sustain the manor.

Could it be like that again? Could he sit at the high table, his friends around him, toasting the harvest, laughing, joking, brawling?

He saw it now; he was sitting at the high table, his friends all gathered together, eating, laughing, drinking. The farmers were sitting at the long tables, devouring the feast that had been prepared for them.

'This is good,' smiled Halfdene. 'Look how content everyone is, Edgar. You've done so well!'

All the hall arose with a great cheer and raised their drinking horns and cups. They hailed him as their thegn and called for his good health and ever-greater wealth. Modbert slapped him on the back. In front of him, Guthrum and Eric began an insulting contest, leaving everyone rolling with laughter. Edda skipped into the hall, carrying a great jug of the sweetest mead he had ever tasted. She happily poured out more mead for everyone. His grandfather smiled broadly at Edgar.

'I am so proud of you,' he said.

Godgifu wrapped her arm around his waist and kissed him on the cheek.

'Gifu,' he whispered.

Guthrum issued a startled cry. Edgar looked up. An arrow point was protruding from the front of Eric's neck. Blood gushed down his front, soaking his leather shirt.

The smile faded from Edgar's grandfather's face as his skin took on the pallor of a dead man. Gifu faded away, beyond his reach, and Edda trembled with fear beneath an upturned cart as her entire village was slaughtered around her.

Edgar awoke with a gasp of pain. Not the pain of his body, but the deeper pain of his soul. The pain that could never fully heal.

His dream was vivid in his memory. He was strongly tempted to close his eyes and return to it, if just for a moment.

He forced the caked-on blood around his mouth to split, painfully opening barely closed wounds. He panted with the effort.

'Fuck you,' he gasped to the black cell.

At that moment he determined that he was going to die in this cell. He would resist no longer. This was the final chapter of his short life. He would die but he would not give in.

He would never give in.

16

Rescue

Alaric and Halfdene travelled along the muddy lane towards Mammesfeld. Before they set off, Alaric had opened his pack and shaken out the clerical robe that he had obtained from Osfrith's outraged chaplain. He pulled it on and tied the cord around his waist.

'Very fetching,' said Halfdene.

'Not complete, though. I need one more thing. We passed one about half a mile back up the road on our way in yesterday. Please fetch it for me, my son.'

Halfdene grinned. He too had noticed the solitary donkey standing forlornly in a field yesterday. He liked donkeys, they always looked so gentle, yet sad.

Alaric spurred the reluctant donkey up the muddy path to the gate of the compound. Halfdene walked ahead of him, head down, clutching Alaric's travel pack to his chest. It contained some water, a small amount of bread, a wooden plate and cup. Not sacred items, but quite indistinguishable from them.

They had agreed that Halfdene should play the part of Alaric's servant, a lay brother atoning for some long distant sin.

As they approached the gate of the palisade, a guard stepped forward and held his hand outwards, commanding them to stop. Behind him, a steady stream of workmen and traders was being waved through into the interior of the fortification. Alaric pulled back on the donkey's reins and the animal came abruptly to a halt. Halfdene stopped as well, looking humble as the soldier approached.

'Can I be of help, Father?' asked the guard.

Alaric replied in perfect Norman French. 'It is not you who can be of help to me, son, it is I who can be of great service to your immortal soul.'

'Yes, Father, of course, but in this instance, how may I assist you?'

'You can direct me to the Baron be Barentin.'

'What is your business with the baron, Father?'

'It is not my business, my son, it is God's business, and you are starting to be in the way.'

The guard looked across at one of the other guards and indicated that he was going into the compound.

'I'll take your beast, Father, and make sure that it is fed and watered.'

'Thank you, my son.' He dismounted the donkey, without showing the relief that he felt. 'Would you please give my servant some food, also? He has walked far and is not strong.'

'Of course,' nodded the guard.

'Now, the baron?'

'This way, Father.' He handed the donkey to a passing boy. 'Take this to the stable and then take that to the kitchen,' he ordered, indicating Halfdene with a stab of his index finger. The boy headed off towards the stable with the donkey and Halfdene grudgingly following him.

The guard led Alaric to the centre of the compound, where part of the old lodge was still standing amid the rubble of other demolished buildings. New construction was growing all around this central core.

Alaric was shown into a small anteroom, where a harassed clerk was shuffling sheets of parchment, quietly muttering to himself.

'Priest,' said the guard to him, unceremoniously. The clerk barely looked up, merely pointing to a few chairs against the wall.

'Sit, Father, I will be with you shortly.'

The guard stepped out and Alaric watched the clerk with interest as he tried to get the parchments into some sort of order. After a few minutes, Alaric spoke.

'I can see that you are a busy man, my son. Should I just go through and see the baron?'

'The baron?' asked the clerk, appearing momentarily confused. 'Oh, no, he's not there. Don't know where he is. If you wait, I'm sure he'll be back some time.'

'Maybe I should just go about the Lord's business, then?'

'Yes, please. I'm sure the baron would not mind. He is a God-fearing man.'

'Thank you, my son.' Alaric made a sign of the cross towards the man, who bowed briefly.

Alaric walked out of the door and into the busy compound. He spoke to some guards, blessing them as he left.

Where was this cellar that Guthrum's girl had informed him of? He continued to walk slowly around the compound, blessing anyone who stopped in front of him.

There. He saw it now, against the far wall of the compound. A new block of rooms, single-storied.

As he watched, a guard ran out of the block, stumbled and vomited violently on the ground.

Alaric smiled to himself. A wave of relief washed over him. The beaker had been broken! The Normans must not know about it. That meant either that Edgar had not been broken and told all, or that he was already dead. There had been time for the poison to take effect. There must have been a new drawing of water this morning for the guards. Fortunately, it was unlikely that the workmen would have the benefit of fresh water for some time, their water mostly being from the settling tank. He hoped it would be so.

Alaric approached the guard with deep concern on his face.

'My son, what is wrong?'

The guard looked up at him, sweat pouring from under the rim of his helmet. He shook his head, then vomited again. Alaric stood upright and shouted at the top of his voice.

'Demons! This man is afflicted by demons! Keep away!'

Heads were turning towards him and men were stopping in their tracks to look.

Alaric pointed at the stricken guard.

'The Devil is on his back, see how his evil talons dig into the man's very soul!'

The guard obligingly threw up even more violently at this, collapsing down onto his knees and elbows.

The Lost Land

'I have seen this before!' cried Alaric to the stupefied crowd. 'None of you are safe! The devil is amongst you. The only solution is prayer. Pray now! Pray for your lives and your souls!'

Amongst the crowd, another guard suddenly keeled over onto his back, vomit spewing from his mouth as he fell. The second victim convinced the onlookers. They fell to their knees and began praying loudly and expressively.

Alaric ran towards the building from which the first guard had come.

'I will seek out and destroy the demons!' he called to anyone who was still paying him any attention.

He burst into the building, to find two more guards unconscious on the floor. A door stood open in front of him. He stepped through. It was dark, but a small lantern flickered in a niche to one side of the door. He took it and walked carefully down the steps.

At the bottom was another door. It was unlocked. He opened it and slipped through. Inside was a guard chamber, where a single guard sat, picking his fingernails with a short dagger.

'Do not rise, my son,' said Alaric, although the man had shown no signs of intending to do so. 'Is this where the prisoner is kept?'

'What's it to you?' grunted the guard.

'He is to die this afternoon. The baron has ordered me to minister to his spiritual needs.'

The guard looked blankly at Alaric then shrugged and stood. He walked to a heavy door to one side of the chamber, and with a key hanging from a ring at his belt, he opened it and swung it open.

'I'll have to come in with you,' said the guard, evidently

annoyed at having his finger-picking disturbed.

They stepped in and Alaric held up the lantern. He had to suppress the urge to gasp as he saw Edgar hanging from his chains. His face was a mess of blood that had run down and soaked the sweat-stained shirt that hung in rags from his shoulders. Edgar did not move nor make any sign that he was aware of their presence or was even awake.

'Just as well we're getting rid of him,' said the guard. 'He stinks, and I don't think he could stand much more anyway.'

'I know nothing about him. Is he English?' Alaric asked the guard.

'Far as I know,' he replied. 'They use a translator or Lord de Rouen speaks to him.'

Alaric shook his head. 'My English is not very good. I have not been here long. Do you know his name?'

'Nah. Don't care really.'

Alaric cleared his throat.

'My son?' he said, in English.

No response.

'My son? Look at me, my son.'

Edgar didn't move.

'Look at me, my son. Really, really look at me.'

Edgar's shoulders twitched a little. His head craned slightly upwards, and his eyes opened, crusty blood stringing across his eyelids.

'Do you see me?' asked Alaric. 'Do you know who I am?'

Edgar straightened himself up slightly.

'This idiot can't understand what we say. Do you know me?'

Edgar's voice was weak and cracked. 'I know you, Spy,' he whispered.

'Good.'

Alaric turned to the guard. Switching back to Norman French, he said 'I must take his confession. You must stand outside.'

'I can't go out; I'd get into all sorts of trouble.'

'And when you stand before God on Judgement Day and explain to the Almighty that you listened to another man's confession because you thought you'd get into trouble; how much trouble do you think you will be in then?'

'I can't even understand what he's saying,' he whined.

'It doesn't matter. I must also stand before the Almighty on that day, and if I tell him that I thought it was alright to break one of my most sacred vows because the man I was with was too stupid to understand, where will we be then? We will both be thrown into the pit of eternal despair. There to consider the consequences of this moment for all eternity. Eternal damnation and the most terrible sufferings possible. It all hinges on this moment, on your decision, here and now.'

The guard looked perplexed, then sulkily, he stepped out of the door, closing it behind him.

Alaric smiled, holding the key ring up where Edgar could see it. Edgar was too far gone to share in Alaric's triumph.

'How did...' he began.

'Misdirection,' said Alaric. 'He was envisioning himself burning forever in the pit of Hell whilst he should have been looking after these.'

'How will we get out?' whispered Edgar.

'Well, I've not worked that bit out yet, my lord, but with a little luck...'

There was a heaving sound followed by a splash from

outside the door.

'There we are,' smiled Alaric.

He quickly unlocked the chains round Edgar's wrists and supported him as they staggered to the cell door. Alaric opened the door a crack and peered out. The guard was doubled over on his chair, coughing and dribbling vomit. He looked up as Alaric stepped out. Alaric slashed out with his right foot, catching the man on the side of the head. He groaned and slid to the floor.

'Come on,' said Alaric urgently. Edgar could barely walk, but he staggered along beside Alaric up the stairs and out onto a sight of carnage. Dozens of people lay moaning on the ground as the poison took hold.

'Here,' said Alaric, lowering Edgar to the ground. 'Just lie still out here for a while. You'll be quite inconspicuous amongst this lot.'

He eased Edgar down onto the ground and hurried away towards the work gangs.

Guthrum looked up keenly as Alaric approached.

'Any luck?' he asked.

'He's out. I've left him lying with the poisoned. Nobody will spot him amongst them. Now, Cyneheard. Lead me to the kitchens.'

Guthrum and Hallvindur dropped their tools and ran towards the kitchens. Guthrum kicked open the door and stood back as Alaric marched in.

Halfdene sat with his back to the wall, chewing on a piece of stale bread. Caedmon was standing next to him. Halfdene stood as Alaric entered.

Reverting to Norman French, Alaric began shouting. 'The Devil is in this place! The Devil is here! Run for your lives!'

A fat man turned on Alaric. 'What is this?' he shouted. 'Who are you to come barging into my kitchen?'

'Look outside,' cried Alaric, 'You can see how the Devil possesses so many here. You will be possessed too if you do not flee!'

'What nonsense,' shouted the cook, as he pushed past Alaric to look outside.

'My God!' he called. 'You're right. Everyone flee! This place is cursed!'

The kitchen staff scrambled for the door, leaving Alaric alone with Halfdene and Caedmon.

'Take us to Cyneheard,' ordered Alaric, sharply.

Outside the kitchen, the scene was appalling. It seemed the entire garrison had been debilitated. Unconscious men lay in pools of their own vomit, whilst the workforce looked on in disbelief and fear.

Caedmon took Alaric and Halfdene to the cell where Cyneheard was being kept. A guard lay unconscious on the flagging outside the door.

Cyneheard backed himself into a corner of his cell when Alaric kicked the door open.

'What's going on?' he demanded.

'You're coming with us. We'll take you to your uncle.'

Alaric sliced through the ropes at Cyneheard's ankles and pulled the boy upright. He was weak and unsteady.

'Come on,' insisted Alaric.

Glancing at the young man's bare feet, he added to Halfdene, 'Get the boots off that guard, we need them here.'

Halfdene pulled the boots off the guard and threw them to Cyneheard.

'Quickly,' Alaric said. We must go. Now.'

The young man swiftly pulled on the guard's boots and

staggered forward.

Halfdene placed Cyneheard's right arm over his own shoulder and took the weight, half dragging him out into the open.

'Dear God,' exclaimed Cyneheard. 'What happened here?'

'Never mind that,' said Halfdene. 'Caedmon, get horses from the stables, can you saddle them?'

'Yes, I think so.'

'I can saddle horses too,' said Cyneheard.

'Good lad. We need four. Fast as you can.'

Halfdene, Caedmon and Cyneheard headed towards the stable. Guthrum and Hallvindur ran up to Alaric.

'We've found where you left Edgar. He doesn't look good,' said Guthrum.

'I know. We must get away from here as fast as possible. There will be patrols out from here, and they may be back at any time. It would appear that we have missed de Barentin once again. He's not here.'

'Do you know how far he's gone?'

'No idea, even his clerk seemed not to know.'

'Right. I'll go and get Edgar. Hallvindur, I'll need your help.'

The two housecarls set off to where Edgar was lying. Alaric hurried over to the stables. Halfdene, Cyneheard and Caedmon were fitting saddles to horses, so Alaric grabbed a fourth and threw it onto the back of a large black mare. He finished the task as Guthrum and Hallvindur returned, carrying Edgar between them, each with an arm round his shoulders.

Edgar looked up briefly, through slitted and blood-encrusted eyes. Then he seemed to fade away, drooping between the two housecarls.

'Come on, let's be going,' said Alaric. Guthrum climbed onto one horse. Hallvindur and Alaric passed the semi-conscious Edgar up in front of Guthrum who then held tightly onto him.

Alaric leaped sprightly onto the back of the black mare and Hallvindur helped Cyneheard up in front of him.

Halfdene had already mounted a horse and finally, Hallvindur climbed on the fourth horse and Caedmon climbed on behind him.

Kicking the horses' sides, they galloped out of the compound and towards the town. The guards at the gate did not even look up from their misery as the horses thundered by. Alaric pulled up short beside a small group of astonished English workers.

'What's happening, Father?' called one. 'They're saying that the Devil is here, is that true?'

Alaric snorted. 'Devils are indeed here,' he said. 'But you know that already, don't you?'

They muttered amongst themselves.

'Don't drink the water,' said Alaric emphatically, and kicked his horse into a gallop.

They hurtled through the town and out along the forest road. In front of Guthrum, Edgar stirred.

'Guthrum, where are we?'

'Heading away from Mammesfeld, lad. We're going back to Hakrholme.'

'Guthrum, listen,' gasped Edgar. 'I won't make it. I need rest. Please.'

Guthrum held tightly to Edgar with one hand and felt the young man slipping sideways in the saddle. He slowed the horse.

Hallvindur brought his horse alongside.

'Why are you slowing?' he asked.

'Edgar needs rest. We must stop for a while.'

'What? That would be foolish. The Normans will be after us in no time. We can't stop.'

'Look, I can't gallop with Edgar's dead weight. He can't stay awake. We'll head back to the camp just for a few hours. We won't be found there.'

They carefully led their horses off the road and into the forest. There they tied the horses to the low branches of a wide-spread oak.

Edgar was near to complete exhaustion, so Guthrum lowered him gently to the ground.

'He just needs to sleep,' said Guthrum anxiously.

Alaric pored over Edgar, examining the wounds on his face.

'Some of these wounds are deep, and I fear that his cheek is broken. He will need some tending. Caedmon, fetch water, please.'

Caedmon rushed off to gather water from the nearby stream.

Hallvindur and Halfdene, seeing that there would be no further travel for some time, crept away to keep watch on the road.

Once he had had his wounds washed, Edgar slept peacefully. There seemed no hope of moving him for some hours.

'I have dried meat,' said Caedmon. 'And some bread and cheese. I've been hoarding it for a while, bringing some back with me every night. I thought it may be useful.'

The Lost Land

Alaric looked up at him. 'Well done, Caedmon. That was good thinking. Now might be a good time for us all to eat.'

Caedmon reached under a low bush and pulled out several small leather packages. He opened them carefully, revealing an array of meats, bread, cheese and some raw vegetables.

'I think we should have maybe a quarter of this between us now,' he said. 'To give us a head start when we set off again. Who knows when we'll be able to hunt?'

They agreed and ate the meagre fare in silence. Edgar stirred and opened his eyes. 'Guthrum?'

'I'm here lad. Stay still, you'll be fine. Here, have some cheese and some water.'

He passed Edgar a piece of cheese and his water bottle. Edgar swallowed a little and drank some water. He handed back the remains of the cheese to Guthrum, nodding his thanks and closed his eyes again.

As Caedmon was wrapping up his food packets again, Halfdene suddenly motioned for silence. He turned his head slightly, straining to hear.

'Horses,' he whispered. 'Maybe four or five. Coming this way.'

Hallvindur grunted quietly, and soon all of them could hear the sound of hooves. They were not galloping, but perhaps at a canter.

'It has to be a Norman patrol from Mammesfeld,' said Guthrum. 'They're looking for us.'

'We weren't that careful coming off the road,' said Alaric. 'We may have left a followable trail.'

'Right,' said Guthrum. 'Hallvindur, Halfdene, come with me. We'll get on the horses and gallop out of here making as much noise as possible. That should distract them away from the camp. The rest of you, stay with Edgar.'

Guthrum, Halfdene and Hallvindur slipped silently into the brush to retrieve the horses.

Alaric stood up at a crouch. 'I'm going to get closer to the road, hopefully they'll just walk on by, but we may need as much notice as we can get.' He loped off quietly towards the road.

The sound of the horses' hooves was getting closer. A cry went up from one of the riders, still some distance away, but the sound of snapping branches made it clear that the riders were off the road and coming towards them. Edgar opened his eyes again, aware of the movement around him.

Caedmon put a hand lightly on Edgar's chest. 'Shh,' he whispered. Edgar froze. His eyes opened wider and he glanced around him, taking in the absence of his men.

'Master Cyneheard,' hissed Caedmon. 'Move deeper into the forest. Lie low and don't move.'

'But what of Edgar?'

'I'll look after Edgar. It's because of you that we're here. I found you, I came to rescue you for your father. You must save yourself.'

'You can't defend Edgar on your own,' he said.

'And what will you do? Look at yourself. You're weak and underfed. You have no strength and no weapons. Go. Hide, I beg of you.'

Cyneheard paused just a moment, looking at Edgar, who nodded at him. He turned and crept further onto the bush.

Another cry went up, this time from behind them. Guthrum, Halfdene and Hallvindur were kicking their horses into a gallop, crashing through the undergrowth and shouting as they went.

An answering cry came from the Norman horsemen as they took up the pursuit.

Caedmon cowered low, covering Edgar, as the Norman horsemen crashed past, within fifty feet of where they lay.

Caedmon remained still, hovering low over Edgar, his hand resting lightly on Edgar's chest, as the sound of the horsemen faded away into the distance. He breathed out slowly and stood up. 'I think they're gone, my lord,' he said. Edgar pushed himself up on his elbows. As he did, he heard the sound of a horse whickering.

Caedmon whirled round at the sound. It was close. Edgar strained his ears. There - the sound of a footstep, human, not equine. One of the horsemen had remained behind and was now dismounted and walking towards them.

Into the clearing, not twenty feet from where Edgar lay, stepped Jean de Rouen. He was sweating, his long dark hair plastered to his forehead. His eyes lit up when he saw Edgar. He spoke, but Edgar could not understand what he said. With a shrug of his shoulders, he cast off the heavy woollen riding cloak that he was wearing and advanced on Edgar, pulling his sword out of its scabbard. Caedmon cried out, 'No!' and flung himself between Edgar and de Rouen. De Rouen barely broke stride as he contemptuously sideswiped Caedmon's head with the flat of his sword, hardly even flicking his eyes towards him. Caedmon fell to the ground, stunned.

De Rouen strode purposefully towards Edgar, slashing his sword in front of him. Edgar scrabbled backwards, leaning on his elbows and pushing with his heels.

De Rouen laughed cruelly as he stood over Edgar.

Edgar pushed himself back again. De Rouen brought his sword down in a mighty swing. Adrenalin pumping through his veins, Edgar overcame his fatigue and pain and rolled quickly out of the way. De Rouen's sword sliced down into the earth where Edgar had been lying less than a second before.

The Norman laughed delightedly and pulled his sword out of the ground. Edgar pushed himself backwards again towards the base of a tree and as he did so, he felt something hard in the leaves under his right hand. Frithlac's sword! Edgar had completely forgotten about it. His fingers closed automatically around the hilt.

De Rouen swung his sword backwards, preparing to strike. Gathering every last ounce of his strength, Edgar thrust upwards. Frithlac's sword, still in its linen wrappings, burst out from under the wet leaves.

As de Rouen's sword slashed down, the baker's blade thrust upwards beneath the Norman captain's ribs and up into his chest.

The power in Norman's swing dropped immediately, and his sword clanged onto the ground next to Edgar's head. De Rouen fell forward, towards Edgar. The sword embedded in his chest bent and snapped at the hilt. De Rouen collapsed and lay still on top of Edgar.

Alaric sprinted into the clearing as fast as he could run. He saw de Rouen and Edgar and ran across, grabbing de Rouen by the collar of his leather jerkin and dragging him back with all his might.

Edgar was covered with blood. Alaric thrust de Rouen aside, and he fell heavily to the ground, his eyes and mouth open in the shock of death.

Alaric fell to his knees next to Edgar and started feeling

for wounds.

'It's alright, Alaric. The blood's not mine,' gasped Edgar.

'But what happened?'

Edgar held up the broken hilt of the sword.

'What? Where did you get that from?' said Alaric.

'It was given to me by a proud man in Mammesfeld. He couldn't possibly have known that it would save my life. The blade's still inside him,' he pointed at de Rouen.

'Thank the gods!' cried Alaric.

Behind him, Alaric heard a moan. He turned and for the first time saw Caedmon, lying on the ground, hands to his head.

'Caedmon! Let me look at you,' said Alaric, leaping over.

Caedmon's head was sore, and a small cut was bleeding down the side of his temple.

'Nothing serious. You're lucky. Where's Cyneheard?'

'I sent him to hide. He couldn't have helped.'

'Very wise. We could have lost him here.'

'Now what?' asked Caedmon.

'Now we wait here for the others to return. If they do return.'

Edgar shook his head. 'No, as soon as we're ready we'll start moving. Through the forest though, and away from the road. We'll use Wildman contact calls.'

Alaric held up a hand. 'When we went to find the Wildmen, we found that they were being hunted by specialised Norman patrols, who seem to have learned the Wildman calls that we knew. As a result, they now have a different set of calls. Anyone using the old calls will now be killed by any Wildman who hears them. We can't use the old calls we know. I'll teach you the new one that Alfweald taught me. Halfdene also learned it so he and the others should be safe.'

'Alright, agreed,' said Edgar, wearily. 'Now, let's hide this body as best we can.'

'Caedmon and I will deal with that. You must rest now.'

Edgar did not reply. He was already asleep.

17

Shelter

Some considerable time later, whilst Edgar was still asleep, Guthrum, Halfdene and Hallvindur returned to the camp on foot.

'We abandoned the horses and sent them off along the road. With any luck, the Normans will lose them and think we've got away.'

Alaric had stripped off his priestly robe and bundled it up to make a pillow for Edgar's head. He had also gathered up de Rouen's riding cloak and wrapped it around Edgar.

'How's he doing?' asked Guthrum.

'He'll be alright, given time, but any extended travelling now will be stressful and will slow down the healing process.'

'That's not good, because we can't stay here. Those Normans will be coming back this way before long, and who knows how many other patrols will be sent out in search of us? If we stay here, we'll be found. We must go.'

Alaric looked at him.

'Now,' said Guthrum emphatically.

'Alright,' said Alaric. 'May I suggest that we head west, away from the road but not obviously following it? The Normans will assume that we will continue along the road, or along the line of it, to head back north, where we appeared to be fleeing in the first place.'

'Yes, good. Come on, let's get him up.'

Guthrum and Alaric gently roused Edgar from his sleep. He woke slowly, staring around at them, initially with incomprehension.

'Where are we?' he asked.

'Still at the camp,' said Guthrum. 'We have to move now. I'm sorry but you have to get up and walk.'

'That's alright. I can do that.'

Edgar heaved himself into a sitting position, gasping at the pain in his abused ribs. He sat there, panting, for a few moments.

'Here,' said Alaric, handing him de Rouen's boots. 'Yours seem to have been removed. You'll need these.'

Edgar took the boots and pulled them onto his feet.

'Nice of him to come all this way with such a fine pair of boots for me,' said Edgar, admiring his new footwear.

With a hand from Guthrum and Alaric, he stood up. He staggered backwards a little when they let go of him, but Guthrum caught him before he could fall.

'I'm alright. Just a little dizzy,' said Edgar, patting Guthrum absently on the forearm.

'Come on,' said Guthrum, and the six men started walking, slowly and with many pauses, further into the woods.

Heading west, they crossed three minor roads through the forest. Before each one, Alaric, Hallvindur and Halfdene walked on ahead, crouching low and moving very slowly, to ensure that the road was clear before they attempted crossing it. Once they saw a single horseman, riding leisurely in a southerly direction, but otherwise they saw no one.

As the sun approached the horizon, dark clouds gathered, casting the world into deeper and deeper gloom.

'It's not going to be a pleasant night,' said Guthrum. 'We need to stop and make camp. Halfdene, Hallvindur, check the area, see if you can snatch something to eat.'

The two housecarls set off in search of food, water and any potential threats.

'Come on, Edgar, sit down.' Guthrum and Alaric helped Edgar down onto the ground in the shelter of a broad-branched tree. It would afford little protection if it rained, having no leaves, but it was at least something substantial to lean against.

Alaric took out his priest's robe and rolled it up for Edgar to use as a pillow. Edgar closed his eyes and leaned back against the solid trunk of the tree. He pulled the heavy cloak closed around him and within moments he was asleep.

Halfdene and Hallvindur returned empty-handed.

'Never mind,' said Guthrum. 'We still have Caedmon's stash to keep us going for a couple of days.'

Caedmon obligingly opened his bag, removed the food parcels and carefully divided small portions between them.

It was cold that night, and the following morning was dull and overcast. Thick grey clouds hung sulkily overhead, giving no indication of which direction the sun lay in.

'We need to get some warmer clothing for Edgar and

Cyneheard,' said Alaric quietly to Guthrum. The weather's about to take a turn for the worse, I'm sure of it. Neither of them has the energy to survive without better clothing.'

'You're right,' agreed Guthrum. 'We need to make that a priority. That and finding somewhere better to shelter. We can't stay in the open much longer, it's not just Edgar and Cyneheard who will suffer if the snows come.'

They woke Edgar and Cyneheard and gave them more generous portions of food than they had eaten themselves the night before.

As soon as the food had been eaten, they began walking in the same direction that they had travelled the previous day. It was not taking them closer to Hakrholme and the army, but it was more likely to be taking them away from Norman patrols.

The forest was dense here, and only by being very careful could they make their way through the heavy undergrowth without leaving an obvious trail. Edgar staggered a little every now and then. His face was swollen and red. Alaric tended it as best he could with the few useful herbs he found along their way, but it was obvious that the damage was not healing quickly enough, and that the danger of it turning bad was ever-present.

Towards the middle of the day, as far as they could tell under the dark overcast, they found themselves walking along a deep cleft in the forest floor. The ground underfoot was soft and wet, whilst to their left was a ridge of rising ground with crumbling, jagged rocks poking through the low-lying scrub. To their right, the ground also rose, but more gently.

'I don't like being down here, we should strike up the slope. At least we'll get out of this nasty boggy ground,' said

Guthrum.

They turned and began to ascend the gentler slope to their right.

Cyneheard was breathing heavily as they climbed, the depredations of his three years as a Norman prisoner taking its toll even on the relatively shallow incline.

Edgar was struggling even more. Half-way up he just stopped, unable to proceed. Guthrum stood beside him, his hand holding Edgar's upper arm. He looked at Edgar with deep concern on his face.

'Come on, Edgar, we need to get up there,' he said gently.

Edgar remained motionless, panting and staring at the ground, too winded even to speak.

Hallvindur stepped up to Guthrum.

'Guthrum, I know Edgar is your charge, but this is where I can help.'

Gently, he gathered Edgar into his strong arms and seemingly without any effort picked him up and carried him like a babe.

'Let's get up there,' he said.

They reached the top of the slope and found themselves in a thicket of closely packed alder trees. The ground was dry here, and a thick layer of brown leaves provided some insulation. Hallvindur placed Edgar on a deep pile of the leaves.

Cyneheard sat down with a gasp and he rolled over onto his side, breathing heavily.

'Alright,' said Guthrum. 'We'll make a temporary camp here. Halfdene, Alaric and Hallvindur, I want you to scout the area thoroughly. I want to know if there is any sign of Norman presence or any other for that matter. I want to find better shelter and I want you to get food. There must be something around here that we can eat. Caedmon, you stay with me and look after Cyneheard. I'll build a fire. It may give our position away, but we'll have to risk it, we need to warm these two up as best we can.'

Within a short time, Guthrum had constructed a low fire made of the driest twigs he could find. The wetter the wood, the more smoke the fire would produce. He built a hearth around the fire with stones to keep the damp leaves out. He moved Edgar closer to it, and Cyneheard shuffled himself round to the other side. It was an inadequate thing, providing barely enough heat to warm their fingers, but it gave a little focus.

Caedmon produced four portions of his dwindling food supply. He gave one each to Edgar and Cyneheard, then passed one to Guthrum. Guthrum shook his head, refusing the food. Caedmon took it back, looked regretfully at the portion he had cut for himself and then placed both portions back in his satchel. Quietly, Guthrum noticed the act and felt a rush of approval for the former steward.

By mid-afternoon, snow had started to fall. Halfdene returned with two hares, which he had gutted and skinned. Caedmon took them from him and wrapped them in the linen wrappings left over from the food he had purloined from Roger de Barentin's kitchens. They would need cooking soon, but the fire they had at the moment was nowhere near large or hot enough to roast the hares over.

Alaric returned an hour later, reporting that he could detect no trace of Norman activity, or any other human presence within a mile in any direction of their position. Guthrum felt himself relax at the news, thinking that maybe he could now make the fire bigger.

Finally, Hallvindur also returned with a wood pigeon and with the best news of all.

'I've found a cave. It's small and the entrance is cramped and almost hidden behind a thick bush, but it should just about do for us, for a short while, at least. It's on the other side of this wet valley,' he pointed to the boggy ground they had climbed up out of. 'The rocky side gets steeper and steeper the further down you go until it finally becomes a sheer wall. Down near the base of the wall about quarter of a mile from here, the cliff is covered in thick growth - hazel, I think. Behind this is a small opening that leads into a larger chamber. It will be cramped, but at least it's dry and we'll be warmer than if we stay here.'

'Excellent work, Hallvindur,' said Guthrum. 'We move at once.'

He picked up a handful of leaves and dumped them on top of the fire, adding more and more handfuls until it was completely smothered.

Satisfied that the fire was not smouldering and would produce no smoke, he stood up and held his hand out for Edgar.

Edgar took the hand and heaved himself to his feet. He made no noise, but his face betrayed the pain that he felt. Hallvindur stepped forward but Edgar shook his head.

'No, I'll walk. I can do it.'

Cyneheard also stood up, unsteadily, but more securely than Edgar.

Guthrum led the way and they walked along the ridge until Hallvindur pointed across the boggy valley to the now sheer cliff on the other side.

'There. The cave is somewhere behind those bushes.'

The cliff face rose about twenty feet. At the top, there was a thick overhang of rock, with long tendrils of ground-hugging plants cascading over it. At the base was a large hedge of hazel and brambles. There was no sign of any opening or cave.

'Excellent,' muttered Alaric, standing next to Guthrum.

Guthrum nodded. 'Come on, then. Edgar, will you be alright going down here?'

'We'll soon find out,' grinned Edgar, feebly.

'Alright. Hallvindur, you go on ahead. I'll stay close to Edgar and make sure he doesn't fall.'

The snow was beginning to fall in large flakes now, which settled on the ground and formed a thin white blanket over everything.

They made their way down the incline to the boggy ground below without incident. Edgar seemed to be keeping up well, and Guthrum felt relief flooding through him. Seeing his young thegn being carried like a child had struck an icy spike of fear into his heart.

They crossed the wet ground, Caedmon cursing noisily as the near-freezing black water oozed into his boots. He received a sharp rebuke from Guthrum to be quiet.

Hallvindur walked on ahead, Halfdene behind him.

'Here,' he said, squeezing round the back of the hazel bush. Halfdene followed. Hallvindur had vanished from sight.

In front of him was an opening, no higher than waist-height and wide enough for two men to squeeze in side by side. Halfdene bent over and pushed his head and shoulders through the opening. It was dark inside, but he wriggled further in. With his feet still sticking outside, he felt the wall veer away to his right as the cave turned a corner. He forced himself up onto his hands and knees and followed it round.

'It's a bit tight, but I think it's better in than out,' said Hallvindur's voice from the far side of the hollow.

Halfdene's eyes were getting used to the dark in the cave and he could make out the shape of the big man about fifteen feet away, against the far wall.

'Yes, I see what you mean. If we build a fire in the opening, we'll be quite warm in here.'

He turned round and emerged again from the cave, pressing himself between the hazel bush and the rock wall to report back to Guthrum.

'It's small but Hallvindur's right, it will do.'

'Good. Caedmon, come with me and we'll gather firewood. Halfdene, get Edgar and Cyneheard settled in. We'll be back in a while.'

Guthrum walked back across the wet gully bottom and towards the higher ground on the other side of the narrow valley. A fallen tree lay part-way up the slope and Guthrum began hacking at its branches with his seax.

Caedmon followed suit, choosing the branches that were off the ground, the lower ones looking too wet.

'Guthrum,' he began.

'Hmm?' said Guthrum, twisting a small branch off.

'I want to apologise.'

Guthrum stopped what he was doing and looked up, surprise on his face.

'Whatever for?'

'I know I've been a hindrance to you on this expedition. I'm sorry. I was not brought up to be a warrior like you, Halfdene and Hallvindur. I've endangered you many times. I'll try to do better in future.'

Guthrum shook his head. 'Caedmon, you astonish me.

It was your information that led us here in the first place. You identified where Cyneheard was being kept, and your handy pilfering of supplies has kept us in food at a time when we couldn't get anything else. Far from endangering this expedition, you have brought it success. I believe that without you, we would probably have failed, and you can be sure that Thegn Osfrith will learn of your contribution when next we see him.'

Caedmon's mouth sagged open. 'Really? You think that?'

'I do. Look, you're not used to the occasional hardship of life on journeys like this. It's part of our upbringing and training that we know how to act in circumstances that simply don't happen in the life that you're used to. We know how to survive. And we're used to having freezing mucky water in our boots.'

Caedmon smiled.

'Thank you,' he stammered. 'You don't know how much it means to me to hear you say that. Hallvindur thinks I'm an idiot.'

'And you think that Hallvindur is a brainless brute.' Guthrum recalled how tenderly Hallvindur had carried Edgar. 'You're both wrong. Now come on and let's gather these branches.'

The snow was building up as they hacked away at the branches. There was no way to disguise the fact that branches had been removed from the tree, a fact that would inform any decent tracker that someone nearby was building a fire. Even worse, as they walked back to the cave, they left unavoidable footprints in the snow as they went, leading right to the cave entrance.

The Lost Land

Night fell early, as it does when the sky is thickly overcast. The snow continued to fall heavily throughout the evening until a deep blanket lay over the forest.

Sitting at the mouth of the cave, Halfdene peered out into the gloom outside. The fire within was low and cast a faint ruddy glow around the corner of the cave. Whatever light seeped out of the cave was well concealed by the overgrowing bushes.

Guthrum had been worried, he knew, by the tracks left by himself and Caedmon as they ferried firewood into the cave from the fallen tree, but Halfdene was confident that by now those tracks would be deeply buried beneath the fresh snow.

Outside the cave was silence, apart from the gentle swishing of fat snowflakes falling all around. Halfdene stuck his hand out into the snowfall, feeling the pinpricks of cold as the snow fell onto it. He pulled his hand back and licked it. The snow tasted clean and fresh. At least they would not suffer from lack of water. He planned to scoop up large quantities of snow to melt into their water bags. They were reasonably well off for food as well. Caedmon's rations would last another day, then they had two hares and a pigeon, which would see them fed, if rationed well, for another three days.

By then, Halfdene felt sure, Guthrum would approve a hunting party. Guthrum's obsession with safety, he felt sure, was due to concern for Edgar. Guthrum was hugely protective towards the thegn. He could understand that. He felt much the same way. He allowed his mind to drift back to their boyhood days, when he, Edgar and Modbert had played and learned together. Guthrum had taught them all how to fight with sword and axe. They had practised long and hard together, forming the sort of bond that would last a lifetime. He paused, thinking of their friend Modbert – dead, Halfdene was sure, these three years since the great battle at Stanford where Edgar had nearly died. Halfdene unconsciously rubbed his leg, where he too bore the scars of that terrible day. Like Edgar's, his wounds had been tended that day by the Lady Godgifu.

A shuffling sound brought Halfdene out of his reverie. He turned to see Guthrum, bent over in a crouch, coming round the corner of the cave.

'Anything?' he whispered.

'Not a thing,' replied Halfdene. 'I think we're well away from any regular paths.'

'I hope so.'

'How's Edgar?'

'He's sleeping. Today took a lot out of him, but there seems no sign of his wounds going bad. Alaric's been rubbing a paste made of dried leaves of some sort over them. It seems to be helping.'

'Is there nothing that man can't do?' asked Halfdene.

'He's a strange one alright. I'm just glad that he's with us.'

Halfdene nodded. He remembered when Alaric had first been 'captured' whilst Edgar and his companions were on the trail of the Normans who had taken Godgifu. Like Edgar, Halfdene was sure now, knowing Alaric as he did, that he had deliberately allowed himself to be captured. There was simply no way that a man as sneaky and intelligent as that could have been captured by them otherwise. He felt some embarrassment that he had urged Edgar to kill Alaric at that time. What would the future have held for them if that had happened? He didn't want to contemplate it. Instead, he said 'Edgar is strong, Guthrum. Remember Stanford?'

'I do, and I'm pinning my hopes on that. You should get some sleep. I'll take over the watch for now.'

Halfdene squeezed past Guthrum and into the interior of the cramped cave. It was much warmer inside here, and the gentle snoring of his companions soon lulled him into a restful sleep.

He was awoken by his foot being shaken. He opened his eyes, and years of training stopped him from speaking. Early morning light filtered around the bend of the cave.

He looked up. Guthrum crouched by his feet, shaking them. He had a finger across his lips. Seeing Halfdene's eyes open, he tilted his head towards the cave entrance, indicating that Halfdene should follow him.

Squatting in the cave mouth, Halfdene could hear muffled noises.

Voices.

He looked at Guthrum. The voices were still distant. Halfdene turned and went back into the cave, where he woke everybody silently, placing his hand over Caedmon's mouth as he shook him awake. Predictably, the steward tried to cry out, but Halfdene's hand muffled the sound. The last thing they needed was for one of them to wake up noisily as someone passed their hideout.

Everyone was staring at Halfdene, Caedmon looking frightened. Halfdene placed his finger on his lips and then indicated that they should all stay where they were. Then he returned to Guthrum.

Outside, the snow had stopped falling and an almost palpable stillness lay over the little valley, broken only by the voices, which were clearer now, definitely Norman by the cadence. From the right they appeared, a party of eight horsemen, all armoured. They were moving casually, not caring about being silent or of maintaining a military formation. They were strung out loosely in twos, and several of the men were chatting loudly with their companions.

'They're not looking for us,' breathed Guthrum in Halfdene's ear.

Halfdene nodded and continued watching.

The horsemen rode on by, never even glancing towards the hidden cave mouth where Guthrum and Halfdene were crouching.

Once the sound of the men had faded completely, the two men returned to the inner cave.

'Eight horsemen, Normans of course. They seemed quite relaxed and were obviously not looking for us, or for anyone else for that matter,' reported Guthrum.

'That's good, then,' said Edgar.

'As far as it goes, yes. But it does mean that we're not as safe as we imagined. This snow is now a big problem. We won't be able to go out without leaving obvious trails. I suspect that if those eight horsemen had seen the trails that Caedmon and I left in the snow yesterday, then they would have investigated further. We can't be complacent.'

'We have food to last us a couple of days, and water will be no problem with all the snow around, we can just scoop it up from around the cave mouth,' said Edgar. 'Having said that, we should be prepared to move as soon as we can.'

They all mumbled their agreement.

'I suggest that you and Cyneheard take this opportunity to rest and recover,' said Guthrum. 'Our little enforced stay may prove a blessing after all.'

'It's warm and dry here at least,' said Edgar. 'Let's make the best of it.'

Caedmon prepared one of the hares and roasted it over the fire. He dismembered it first, the fire was not large enough to cook the animal whole.

As they ate their food, Edgar turned to Cyneheard. 'How do you know the Norman tongue so well?' he asked.

'As a boy, I was sent to the court of the Bastard. I spent two years there, learning the language and something of their culture, if you can call it that.'

Edgar nodded. It had not been unusual for aristocratic youths to be sent to a foreign court as part of their training for the life ahead. Old Edward-king himself had spent much of his young life in the court of William's father Robert and his grandfather Richard.

'Did you know the Bastard himself whilst you were there?'

'I was presented to him when I first arrived, as were several other newly-arrived brats. He was deep in discussion with someone as we were paraded in front of him. He never even looked up. I remember thinking that even if he was a duke, he was a very ill-mannered one. Sometimes he was present at feasts, but I wouldn't say that he showed any particular interest in the pups who were sent over. I didn't enjoy my time there and returned when the opportunity first presented itself. If I hadn't gone, though, I might not be alive today. My usefulness as a translator outweighed the fun they could have had killing me.'

He paused, staring into the low fire.

'Edgar, you said that my uncle sent you. Is that true? Is he still alive?'

Edgar was taken aback. But of course, Cyneheard would not have seen his uncle since Osfrith set off for the great battle against the Normans. It would have been perfectly natural, if painful, for Cyneheard to assume that as a king's thegn, Osfrith would have died at the side of Harold-king.

'Yes, he's still alive. He sent us when Caedmon here discovered your whereabouts. He thought you dead as well.'

'How? How is he alive when our king is dead?'

Edgar drew breath. When he had met Osfrith himself for the first time, before he had left England for the Danish court, he had wondered the same. How can a man sworn to protect the life of the king with his own life still be alive when the king is dead?

'When I first met your uncle, over a year ago, I asked him the same. I will give you the answer that he gave me. He was at that time travelling with four other king's thegns, who had also all survived the great battle. They had not survived well, though. They were damaged men. Your uncle was gravely wounded during the battle and was taken from the field for treatment of his wounds. Whilst he was still incapable, the battle was lost. All the thegns in your uncle's party were in the same condition, and all feel the burning shame, though the fault is not theirs. Your uncle fought bravely, Cyneheard. He has a badly wounded leg, and cannot now walk without a stick.'

Cyneheard turned to Hallvindur.

'Hallvindur, you're my uncle's man. Is this true? Did my uncle fight well? Did he do his duty?'

'He did, Master Cyneheard. I was at the great battle with him. I saw him fight; I saw him go down. I have even more respect for your uncle now than I did before the battle. He could have done no more.'

Cyneheard was silent, still staring at the fire.

'And he is near here?'

'He is. He left England to seek the assistance of Sweyn-king. We all did. Except for Caedmon, of course,' replied Edgar. 'We're back now with a Danish army. We will take back the kingdom.'

Cyneheard looked up. 'I had heard rumours. They had reached me even in my cell,' he said. 'The Normans were getting worried by the stories they heard. Where is the army? How are matters progressing?'

'We took Eoforwic but had to abandon it. The Normans had razed it to the ground and it was indefensible. The army is now based in a place called the Isle of Hakrholme, just south of the Humbre.'

Halfdene cleared his throat.

'Halfdene?'

'I haven't had the chance to tell you this yet. When Alaric, Harek and I returned to the army camp after our visit to the Wildmen, Jarl Asbjorn was absent. Lord Osfrith told us that he had a meeting with the Bastard himself.'

'What was there to discuss?' asked Edgar.

Halfdene indicated Alaric. 'Alaric suggested that the Bastard was going to pay off the army.'

'What?'

Alaric shrugged. 'I suggested that it was one possibility. It would not be inconsistent with past Danish tactics.'

'But Sweyn-king said we were to take the kingdom in his name,' said Guthrum, puzzled. 'How can this be?'

Edgar closed his eyes. 'Shit,' he said.

'What is it?' asked Guthrum.

'I was warned about this. Loki tried to tell me. He had

been dubious about the invasion right from the start. He told me that Asbjorn was untrustworthy and that this would turn out to be nothing more than a glorified Viking raid. Shit. Shit, shit, shit! I refused to listen to him. I thought he was being cynical, annoyed because he had to put off his long-awaited trading trip to Micklagard in order to carry us over here.'

'I think we should wait to see what's become of the invasion force before we draw any hasty conclusions,' said Alaric. 'But I fear that the invasion may not happen as we might wish it.'

'Who knows what private arrangements Sweyn and Asbjorn made between themselves? The King may well say publicly that he is claiming the throne of England, but who knows the mind of a king, really?' said Halfdene.

'All the more reason for us to get away from here as soon as we can, then,' said Edgar.

Two days later, the food was running low, but no more snow had fallen.

'I think we should move on today,' said Edgar as they finished the last of the meat they had caught when they first arrived in the valley.

'How are you feeling?' asked Halfdene.

'It's difficult to tell, being cooped up inside the cave. I need to get out and walk.'

'If we go, we'll leave trails. That's alright if we don't come back. It doesn't matter if the cave gets found now,' said Guthrum. 'As long as you and Cyneheard are fit enough to travel, we can walk in the trail left by the Normans' horses.'

The snow that had fallen remained on the ground; the

temperature never having risen enough to melt it.

They filed out of the cave, Hallvindur in the lead, and hopped and slid down the valley side to the tracks in the valley bottom. The boggy ground had frozen, making walking a little easier. Once in the tracks left by the Norman horsemen, their own footprints were not easy to detect, and in any event, could have been made by a party of infantry accompanying the horsemen. There was nothing they could do about the tracks leading down from the cave, but hopefully they would not be spotted by any pursuing party before the snow melted or another snowfall concealed them.

It felt good to be out of the fug of the cave and breathing the crisp, clean air of the forest, but there was no denying the fact that it was very cold. Edgar and Cyneheard were inadequately dressed, though Edgar had de Rouen's boots and cloak, and Cyneheard wore Alaric's borrowed priestly robe over his tunic.

Alaric had walked on ahead, and a little over an hour later, they saw him trotting back towards them.

'There's a narrow road up ahead. From the tracks, I would say it's not much used, but there has been some traffic recently. Mostly on foot, but I can also make out the tracks of a cart and an ox. Maybe we're approaching a settlement.'

Edgar paused, his breath condensing in clouds around his head.

'What do you think? Should we risk it?'

'Let me and Halfdene go on ahead and see if we can see where the road leads. You get some shelter here if you can.'

'Agreed. Don't take too long though, staying still in this cold could be dangerous.'

Alaric quickly pulled off his tunic and handed it to Cyneheard, who gave him the priest's robe.

Alaric and Halfdene walked on for about a mile and a half along the narrow road. It was muddy but frozen, so walking was not difficult.

'There,' said Halfdene, clutching Alaric's arm. 'Smoke.'

'Alright, nice and easy now, we're travellers and we seem to be a bit lost. You're my manservant.'

'Yeah, yeah, been here before,' muttered Halfdene.

They continued walking towards the smoke, which hung as if caught in the stark, leafless branches of the overhanging trees.

To their right, there was a clearing, in which stood a small mead hall. It was not as large or impressive as the one at Rapendun had been before the Normans burnt it down, but large enough to mark it out as the home of at least a village headman, if not a minor thegn.

'Looks like we're not the only visitors here,' murmured Alaric out of the corner of his mouth. Eight horses were being tended by a couple of young lads to the side of the hall, where a compact stable stood.

'It will almost certainly be a Norman patrol, so keep your head,'

'Yes, Father,' muttered Halfdene in a cowed voice.

Alaric strode up to the door of the hall and stepped inside. Halfdene followed him in, his heart pounding.

It took a few moments for Halfdene's eyes to adapt to the dimness within the hall. Torches guttered on the upright pillars. A long table was placed down the left-hand side of the hall with benches on either side.

At the far end was a group of Norman horsemen,

appearing relaxed as they ate from wooden plates. One of them looked up as they entered, but seeing no threat, returned to his food.

Alaric strode up to the centre of the hall, where a fire burned warmly.

He held his hands up to the fire and rubbed them together.

In a loud voice, he made a comment in Norman French. The soldiers looked up. Halfdene held back in the shadows, wondering nervously what Alaric had planned.

One of the soldiers rose from the table and approached Alaric. To Halfdene's surprise, the man appeared to be quite deferential. He spoke with Alaric in quiet tones. Alaric replied likewise, with anger at first and then in a more mollified voice.

The soldier returned to his colleagues and began talking with them.

Alaric signalled Halfdene to join him and they sat down at the other end of the hall.

'My first words were "It is well when a man of God from Normandy is robbed of his possessions on the road whilst the soldiers of the king are at their leisure."'

'Ah. How well did that go down?'

'The captain there was quite contrite. I had to explain why I had no trappings of a priest and why I was on foot. Being robbed seemed an obvious choice, and it put them on the back foot. The captain explained that this is an outlying hall of a large estate, currently run by a Norman steward, the thegn having "run away", by which I suppose he means killed. This is a regular resting place for patrols along this road. The captain has promised to seek out the filthy English criminals, whom I placed a day's walk away to the south. He also promised to appropriate a donkey or horse for me from the estate's property. I think we can do better than that, though. I'm going to spend some time with my "countrymen" there. I want you to sneak back to the others and bring them here quickly and quietly, and ready for a scrap. Yes?'

'Alright. What excuse do I have for sneaking out?'

'I'll give you a signal. I'll drop my beaker on the floor when I judge the time to be right. Just walk up to me and ask, in humble terms, to be allowed to step outside to relieve yourself. Leave the rest to me.'

'I can do that. Are you expecting us to take on eight fully mailed horsemen with our little seaxes?'

'You may have to deal with a couple. The rest will be in no fit state, I promise.'

At that moment, a young man approached the table. He brought a jug of mead and a single beaker. He placed them in front of Alaric and walked away.

'Thanks very much,' muttered Halfdene to the youth's retreating back.

'It's good. You're invisible to them,' said Alaric. 'Now, I'm going carousing. Watch for my sign, but otherwise remain here, still and silent.'

Halfdene nodded and Alaric picked up the jug and beaker and walked over to the Normans.

He said a single word, and the Normans all stood up. Alaric began reciting prayers that were familiar to Halfdene, though the exact words, in Latin, meant little to him. At the end of his recitation, the Normans all muttered 'Amen', and Alaric made a sign of the cross in the air above their bowed heads.

Halfdene watched the performance in wonder. Good

The Lost Land

God, that man's got some balls, he thought.

Bringing his arms down beside him in a sign of finality, Alaric made another comment. The Normans all laughed and sat down, chatting animatedly with Alaric and each other.

Halfdene remained quiet and unseen in the shadows at the far end of the hall from the carousing soldiers.

As time progressed and Alaric continued making merry with the Normans, Halfdene was again struck by Alaric's powers of deception. He apparently drank as much as any of them, and his voice got louder in time with theirs, and yet he was sure that very little of the drink had actually gone down his throat. What was he doing with it? Jug after jug was brought to the table for the noisy men.

At one point, the captain pointed at one of his men and issued what was clearly an order. The man looked put out but nevertheless tightened his sword belt and walked none too steadily to the door. He pulled it open, and an icy blast blew around Halfdene's legs.

A serving girl walked through the hall with more food. Once she had delivered it to the table, the young man who was also serving told her to go home. At that moment, Alaric noisily dropped his beaker, cursing loudly. The mead splashed all over the bottom of his priestly robe.

Halfdene took his cue, walked up to Alaric, head bowed and whispered in his ear. Alaric looked angrily at him, spat some sort of curse and then nodded curtly.

Halfdene wasted no time. He hurried across the hall and out of the door. The guard who had been sent outside was nowhere to be seen, so Halfdene quickly took to the road and headed south, pausing first to urinate loudly just in case the guard was about.

The light was fading quickly, so Halfdene hurried lest he miss the spot in the forest where he and Alaric had joined the road. He would not have missed it, for Hallvindur was waiting, concealed behind a stand of trees at the correct point. He handed back to Halfdene the seax that he had left behind.

Hallvindur guided Halfdene back to the party, which had moved closer to the road in anticipation of Alaric and Halfdene's return.

Edgar was shivering with the cold, and Cyneheard looked very pale.

'Alaric's playing the priest again. There are eight Norman horsemen in a mead hall about a mile and a half from here. When I left, one of them had been sent outside, presumably to guard, though I didn't see him. Seven are getting drunk with Alaric. If they've carried on at the rate they were drinking, they should be quite easy by now. We'll have to approach fairly silently. I'll go on ahead, see if I can spot the guard, then signal the rest of you.'

'Where has that manservant of yours got to?' asked the captain.

'He said he wanted to piss,' replied Alaric. 'But that was a lie.'

The captain frowned slightly. 'What do you mean?' he said, concern sounding in his slurred voice. He tried to sit up a bit straighter.

'Did you see that trollop who brought you the meat?'

'Aye, I did.'

'That's where he went. He can't keep it in his britches. I allow it because it keeps him quiet, and being English he is already doomed to eternity in hell. How can a little fornication make matters any worse?'

The men laughed.

'You, as good Normans and good Christians know that fornication is a mortal sin and that any indulgence will commit you to eternal damnation in the infernal pit, which is why you behave as you do.' He buried his face in his beaker as the soldiers looked uncertainly at each other. Two had already fallen off their seats and were snoring loudly.

'Of course, English women don't count. That's just like tupping a sheep or a goat. I mean real Christian women.'

'Erm…' said one.

'Come on, we've got plenty more mead here,' said Alaric, spilling mead onto the table as he slopped good quantities into the beakers of his companions.

'So, is it alright with a goat?' asked one, tentatively.

'Maa,' said the soldier next to him. They all fell into fits of uncontrollable laughter.

Halfdene approached the hall cautiously. It was nearly dark now and he had to strain to make out the road ahead. A smell of woodsmoke alerted him to the proximity of the hall, and soon he could see faint candlelight round the door. He quietly extracted his seax from its scabbard and held it backwards along his forearm, so as not to show any glint of metal.

As he neared the hall, a small sound came from his right. There on a tree stump sat the Norman guard. He stood up as Halfdene approached and his hand fell to the hilt of his sword. Halfdene stepped back, ducked low, and as his seax dropped down from its hidden position, he brought his hand up in a powerful blow, driving the blade up under the guard's chin. The Norman dropped to the ground without uttering a sound. Halfdene dragged him a little way off the road.

Turning back, he whistled quietly, and Hallvindur, Guthrum and Edgar appeared out of the gloom. Caedmon held back, staying with Cyneheard who was plainly unfit to fight.

'Are you sure about this Edgar?' asked Halfdene with concern.

'I'm sure. Let's do it.'

'Right. I'll go back into the hall. They won't suspect Alaric's manservant.'

He opened the door of the hall and peered round.

At the far end of the hall, in the dying light of the fire, he could see that six of the Normans were on the floor, sleeping, whilst Alaric and the captain still sat at the table. Both were holding their heads low over the tabletop and were mumbling at each other. Occasionally they would both start giggling. Halfdene leaned back outside the hall and indicated that the others should enter.

He walked towards the drunken men, and as he did so, Alaric stood up straight, grabbing the jug of mead and smashing it into the side of the captain's head. The man fell off his bench and was still. One of the sleeping soldiers muttered something incomprehensible and turned over. Otherwise, there was no reaction.

Edgar, Guthrum and Hallvindur crossed the hall to where Alaric and Halfdene stood.

'Out for the night, I would say,' said Alaric, cheerfully.

'Have you pissed yourself?' asked Hallvindur.

The front of Alaric's robe was drenched from the waist down.

'Twelve beakers of mead will do that to a man,' replied

Alaric.

Hallvindur looked on in distaste.

'Especially if he doesn't drink them but still has to get rid of them.'

Hallvindur's face broke into a grin.

'What do we do with this lot?' asked Halfdene.

'What we have to,' said Edgar. 'Get them outside, make sure they're unconscious first so they don't make any noise, then finish them off. Get their armour and clothing. We can make good use of that, I think.'

As he spoke, the young man who had been serving them entered the hall from a back door. He stopped and stared in disbelief at what he saw.

'Guthrum,' said Edgar.

Guthrum ran up to the lad and grabbed him before he could flee.

'Have you killed 'em?' the young man asked.

'No,' said Edgar.

'Pity.'

'Oh yes? Why's that?'

'They're fucking Normans, that's why. They killed our thegn. He was a good man. Don't even know why they killed him.'

'These Normans?' said Edgar, pointing at the insensible men on the floor around him.

The lad peered carefully at them. He shrugged.

'Dunno. They're fucking Normans. They all look the fucking same.'

'And yet you happily serve them mead all night?'

'Happily? Who said happily? And it's not just mead.'

'What do you mean?'

'It's mead and piss. My piss, mine and my mate's,' he

said proudly. He looked at Halfdene. 'That's why I didn't give you a beaker, mate. I could tell you was English.'

Hallvindur laughed. 'Makes your deception all the more believable, little spy,' he said to Alaric.

Alaric, unperturbed, simply shrugged. 'All part of the plan,' he smiled.

'What're you going to do with the buggerers?' asked the lad.

'How often do patrols stop in here?' asked Edgar.

'Every three or four days, I suppose. The Norman steward comes along once a week or so to check on supplies.'

'When are you next expecting him?'

'Couple of days.'

'Then we need to get rid of them quickly. Do you have a midden nearby?'

The lad grinned. 'Oh, yes. A big stinking one.'

'You good with a shovel?'

'Good enough, sir. Good enough.'

'Good lad. We'll deliver them to the midden and start the digging with you. If you're asked, these men had a good night's sleep here and then headed south at daybreak, alright?'

'Yes, sir. Thank you, sir.'

18

Journey North

Dressed in the Normans' clothes and mail, they took the horses and headed north first thing the following morning. Although too large for him, Alaric was given the captain's helmet with its small plume of horsehair. If they were challenged anywhere along the way, Alaric could be their spokesman, fluent as he was in the Normans' language.

Guthrum was positively ebullient as he rode alongside Edgar.

'I feel a whole lot better in mail and with a sword by my side,' he said to Edgar. 'I don't think I'll ever get used to skulking and hiding. Face the bastards head-on, I say.'

Edgar smiled. The mood of the party had lifted considerably that morning. At last, they felt as though they had a little control over their destinies.

Caedmon was making it very obvious that he was uncomfortable in his mail coat.

'It's so heavy!' he exclaimed as it was pulled on over his

head.

'Of course it's heavy, idiot. It's made of iron. You won't be complaining if someone tries to stab you or shoot you with an arrow,' said Hallvindur as he struggled to pull the mail shirt over the wriggling Caedmon's head. 'Stand still!' he ordered, as if to a small child.

Caedmon sighed and grunted sulkily as the shirt fell onto his shoulders.

He complained even more when Hallvindur threaded Caedmon's left arm through the straps of the long cavalry shield.

'It's too cumbersome,' he complained.

'It's just a bit of wood and leather. Keep hold and don't complain so much,' grunted Hallvindur as he adjusted the shield on Caedmon's arm.

The others, even Cyneheard, were used to wearing the mail armour and felt better for its reassuring weight. They were unused to the long cavalry shield, but after feeling the weight and adjusting its position against their legs and bodies when in the saddle, they all agreed that the rounded top and long, pointed bottom were ideally shaped to provide maximum protection to a rider's body and left leg.

The Norman swords were indistinguishable from the ones the fighting men had used all their lives, but they keenly felt the absence of axes, the Englishman's weapon of choice.

Heavy clouds had rolled in from the west, bringing with them the very real threat of more snow to come. Dressed in the Normans' heavy tunics, though, they were less fearful of the cold than they had been. Inside the Norman helmets were bonnets of linen padded with wool. They made the

The Lost Land

helmets fit more comfortably and also pulled out for use as warm hats when the helmets were not being worn. This they did and now all rode along feeling warm and secure.

The snow started falling around mid-morning. At first, it fell like a thin, icy drizzle; small hailstones bouncing off their heads and stinging their noses, but soon the hail turned to light flakes of snow which grew thicker, heavier and wetter as time went by.

Despite the feeling of elation at being able to travel openly, the mood of the party sank as they became wetter and colder.

Ahead of them spread a thick blanket of trees, but without their leaves, they would offer precious little protection from the snow. The road stretched on ahead, a thick ribbon of white.

'At least we don't have to try to hide our tracks,' said Halfdene, brushing snow from his leggings before it could melt and wet him even more.

'We're very conspicuous,' replied Edgar. 'Come on, let's get under those trees.'

He dug his spurs lightly into the horse's flank and it quickened its pace to a canter. They all followed.

As they approached the trees, Guthrum spoke to Edgar. 'We should eat. It will help keep the cold at bay for a while.'

'Agreed,' said Edgar. 'Once we reach the trees, we'll halt for food.'

Under the scant cover of the trees, the six men dismounted and Caedmon, in charge of the large quantity of food donated by the Norman-hating young man at the mead hall, doled out six generous helpings of bread, cheese and meat, along with a skin of mead that the lad promised he had not yet pissed in.

They ate and drank in companionable silence. No birds were singing and all that could be heard was the gentle hiss of the falling snow.

Alaric paused, a handful of food part-way to his mouth.

'Riders,' he said. 'Many of them.'

'Mount!' called Edgar, 'Let's get off the road.'

'With respect, sir, we shouldn't do that. Our tracks are all too visible, and if we try to hide it will look far more suspicious. Leave any talking to me.'

They could all hear the riders now. Not a heavy gallop, but the low thudding of horses at a canter. Edgar and the others stepped back from the roadside, behind their horses, whilst Alaric strode boldly into the road.

The horsemen appeared out of the swirling snow, huddled low in their saddles. Alaric estimated there to be about thirty of them. The horsemen, Normans clearly, rode past, hardly sparing Alaric a sideways glance, until one man peeled off from the column and approached him.

He wore a heavy blue cloak over his shoulders and his helmet trailed a long white horsehair plume.

'Are you headed north to join the army?' asked the man without preamble.

'We are, sir,' replied Alaric without hesitation.

'Then you'd better come with us. We've heard that there are some of those damned hairy rebels about. You'll be safer with us. Follow on and catch up with us.'

'Yes, sir. Thank you, sir.'

With that, he wheeled his horse round and set off in pursuit of his men.

'What was that?' asked Edgar.

'We're joining them.'

'What? That's just asking for trouble. We can't talk with them.'

'It's alright, we'll keep to the rear. Cyneheard and I can stay closest to them so if there are any questions, we'll be able to answer.'

'Where are we going?'

'North, to join an army, apparently.'

'We'll be joining the army that's been gathered to fight our army!' said Guthrum.

'We'll drop out before then, don't worry,' said Alaric. 'By the way, you should know that he also said that there have been reports of what he calls the "damned hairy rebels" around.'

'Wildmen!' said Edgar enthusiastically. 'It must be.'

'Yes, I agree, and heaven help us if they catch us with a Norman patrol.'

'Shit. I hadn't thought of that.'

'If there's any Wildman activity, I suggest that we all use the Wildman "friend" call. Don't forget not to use the one we used last year. That will almost guarantee an arrow in an uncomfortable place. Use the one I taught you. Just show me that you all remember it.'

Not until they could all repeat the call accurately did Alaric permit them to remount their horses and head off in pursuit of the Normans.

The weather was getting worse as they reached the rear of the Norman column. The snowflakes were thicker and heavier, falling so densely that it was impossible to see more than about twenty paces ahead.

Whilst the weather did nothing for Edgar's aches, he was still somewhat relieved by it. The Norman horsemen were all hunched over in their saddles, trying to keep the snow out of their faces. Most had put on their helmets in an attempt to keep their heads dry. With their shoulders hunched and heads down, none of them was inclined to attempt small talk with the newcomers.

Edgar held his head down against the storm and allowed himself to drift into an almost sleepy state. His ribs and cheek were aching fiercely, and the cold was penetrating the older wounds on the left-hand side of his face, reawakening the deep, gnawing pain that went with them. It took a considerable effort simply for him to stay upright in the saddle.

He glanced across at Cyneheard. The lad was staring stoically ahead, but exhaustion was etched onto his grey face. Edgar knew that Cyneheard would take many weeks, maybe months, to return to the strength that he should have. He'd been near-starved for almost three years. He could not simply return to a normal diet, it would take a long time, slowly increasing the amount of food he ate until he was eating what a young man of his age should be.

The trees, which had offered meagre protection from the snow were thinning out again, and soon they were trudging across a wildly open area with no protection from the wind, which had picked up enormously whilst they were under the trees. The road was passing along an exposed ridge, and the wind whipped up the snow violently. The falling snow was flying past them almost horizontally, and snow that had already settled on the ground was being ripped up and thrust along by the howling wind.

Edgar felt despondent. Everything had gone wrong on this expedition. The expedition leader, Jarl Asbjorn, was apparently only interested in overseeing a huge looting party, with no thought of regaining the kingdom, which was the understanding on which Edgar and all the other English thegns and carls had joined the Danish invasion force. Whilst he felt satisfaction at having rescued Cyneheard, here they were, riding along with a large Norman patrol, where a slip of the tongue could undo them in an instant. They were still a long way from a successful conclusion to the rescue mission. Now it seemed that the country itself had turned against them, lashing them with whips of ice.

Edgar tried to clench his fists, but the cold prevented his fingers from moving except very sluggishly. His face felt immobile, too. He tried sticking his lower lip out, something he used to do as a child to determine how cold it was, but it wouldn't move. Very cold, then.

The column was moving down from the ridge now, heading towards a seemingly endless expanse of trees. Edgar just caught glimpses of leafless branches stretching away into the distance. He had lost all track of where they were and felt too cold even to think about how they were going to get away from these Normans.

He glanced around at his companions. They were all in the same state as himself – cold, wet and hunched over. Unable to call out to them, he looked down again.

Once more under the trees, the wind dropped a little and the snow became a little thinner. One or two of the Normans began shouting over at each other, though the banter seemed anything but good-natured.

Edgar, head down, staring ahead of his horse's front hooves, did not notice anything was amiss until he saw the body of one of the Normans as his horse walked past it. He looked up quickly to see that the column ahead of him was in some disarray. Men were drawing swords and looking frantically around them, trying to locate the source of the arrows that were picking them off one by one.

'Wildmen!' hissed Edgar to his companions. 'Drop back, get some distance between us.'

He wheeled his horse round and began attempting to whistle the Wildman call that Alaric had taught them less than two hours before. His lips would not cooperate, and no sound emerged.

Alaric was having more luck, he whistled loudly, falling back to be in the centre of his five companions. Guthrum and Halfdene had also managed to coax their frozen lips into cooperation and were echoing Alaric's call.

Ahead of them, men were swarming out of the undergrowth, attacking the horsemen with swords and axes. A large horseman, who had been riding just ahead of Edgar, was slashing around him with his long cavalry sword. Edgar saw three Wildmen go down before the man was felled from his horse. Even then he didn't give up, swinging his sword around him with grim determination until a white-feathered arrow slammed into his neck and he spun violently to the ground and did not move again.

By this time, Edgar, Guthrum and Halfdene had drawn their swords and were attacking the rear of the Norman column, apparently to the confusion of both the Normans and the Wildmen.

Cyneheard, Alaric and even Caedmon followed their example, adding to the weight of the Wildmen's attack on the Normans.

Edgar called to a nearby Wildman as he readied his bow, pointing the arrow at Edgar.

'Six of us are with you!'

The Wildman switched his aim immediately and felled

a horseman.

Horses were screaming as they were shot from beneath their riders. A horseman was nowhere near as intimidating without his horse.

Mostly grounded now, the Normans formed a circle, their shields coming together to form a shield wall.

The Wildmen surrounded them, rushing forward, hacking and thrusting with their swords and axes. The Normans were well-trained, however, and were managing to repulse the Wildmen's attacks. Arrows rained down on them from hidden archers amongst the trees.

Edgar joined one of the onrushes, but a sharply out-thrust shield caught him in the damaged ribs and he fell to the floor, his vision clouding as the pain crushed him.

He felt himself being dragged away.

'Stay down!' he heard Halfdene call to him. The din of blade hitting shield continued for some time, punctuated by screams from dying men.

When Edgar finally managed to sit up, the Normans were heaped in their circle, all dead.

Cyneheard and Caedmon had withdrawn from the fight and were standing some distance away. Alaric, Guthrum and Halfdene were standing over the dead Normans.

'Get up, you,' said a voice behind Edgar. He turned round painfully. A Wildman was standing behind him, axe raised, ready to strike.

Edgar stood, with difficulty.

'Who are you?' said the Wildman.

'I am Edgar, thegn of Rapendun. I spent time last year with the Wildmen, and now I'm here with the Danish army.'

'Oh yes?' snarled the Wildman. 'The Danish army that was coming here to rid us of the Norman swill?'

Edgar nodded, panting.

'So where is your precious army?' demanded the Wildman. More of his Wildmen colleagues were gathering around Edgar.

'To the North. A place called Hakrholme.'

'When were you last with them?'

'A week, maybe ten days. What's the matter?'

'What's the matter?' the Wildman snorted. 'They've gone, that's what's the matter. Your conquering heroes have pissed off, that's what the fucking matter is, pal.'

Edgar dropped his head. It was true, then. Nothing but a glorified Viking raid.

'Shit,' he whispered. He closed his eyes and exhaled. He looked up at the axe-wielding Wildman. 'I think we've all been lied to,' he said.

'Well we certainly fucking have. We were told to prepare for a real invasion, to be ready to finish the Normans off once and for all. Only that's not what happened, is it?'

He looked up and called over to his colleagues. 'Take their weapons, bind their wrists.'

Edgar began to protest, but the man lashed out and punched him in the face.

Guthrum, Halfdene and Alaric started towards Edgar, but with a shout, they were surrounded by blades and nocked arrows.

'Alright,' said Guthrum quietly. He dropped his sword to the ground. 'Put your weapons down. We'll sort this out.'

Alaric and Halfdene followed Guthrum's lead and dropped their swords.

He turned to the leader of the Wildmen. 'Alfweald will vouch for us. Take us to him.'

'Shut up!'

The six companions were swiftly tied at the wrist and hobbled.

The Wildmen's camp was very close to the road, and it took them only twenty minutes to get there. Edgar stumbled along, fresh pain blossoming in his face from the punch, adding to the older hurt.

They were pushed unceremoniously to the ground in a circle cleared of brush where the snow lay thinly.

'What do we do with them?' asked one of the Wildmen.

'I haven't decided yet,' growled the leader. 'Just don't let them move.'

The leader stalked away, leaving four angry Wildmen, brandishing axes, to stand guard over them.

They lay, cramped, cold and wet. Edgar looked askance at the faces of his companions. Cyneheard stared dully at the ground next to his face. Edgar was worried about him. The lad was nearly broken. He would offer no resistance if the Wildmen decided that they must die.

Caedmon looked terrified. His eyes, wide and bleary, looked round constantly, flitting from one Wildman to the next.

On the other side of him, Alaric appeared to have dozed off, as calm and unperturbed by the events as he ever was. Halfdene looked angry and prepared to fight. Guthrum winked at Edgar. Edgar drew surprising reassurance from the small gesture. Guthrum was here. Everything would be alright.

A disturbance in the surrounding undergrowth caught Edgar's attention. Two men strode into the clearing. One was the leader of the band that had attacked the Normans, but the other was a newcomer. The band leader was trying, unsuccessfully, to hold back the other man.

'I will see them!' exclaimed the newcomer, pushing the leader aside.

He moved close up to the prisoners and examined them.

'I know these men. Why are they tied up like this?' he demanded of the band leader.

'They wear Norman mail and helms, carry Norman swords, and were riding with a party of Norman horsemen. Which part of that picture don't you understand?' replied the leader angrily.

'Yet they said they were with the Danes?'

'Yes, there's another good reason to kill them.'

'You'll not do that until we've found out exactly what's happening here,' said the newcomer forcibly.

'Says you?'

The newcomer grabbed the band leader by the front of his shirt. 'Says me. I am a member of the Wildmen's council. You will do as I say or you will suffer the consequences. Do you understand?'

The man remained defiantly silent. In an instant, a seax was at his throat, a thin stream of blood already beginning to trickle down the wicked blade.

'I will put you down, right here, right now. Do. You. Understand?'

The leader slowly nodded.

Shoving the now submissive band leader away, the man walked over to the prisoners.

'Sit up,' he ordered.

Carefully and with difficulty, the six men shuffled into a sitting position.

'Now then,' he began in a calm but cold voice. 'I

recognise four of you. I can name Thegn Edgar, Guthrum and Halfdene, and this one,' he nudged Alaric with his foot, 'I recall as a spy who provided us with some useful information. Thegn Edgar, will you speak for your men?'

Edgar nodded, 'I will,' he said.

'Right. Firstly, who are these other men?'

Indicating each man with a nod of his head, Edgar introduced them. 'Cyneheard is the sister-son of King's Thegn Osfrith Edwinsson, Hallvindur is Thegn Osfrith's housecarl and Caedmon here was Osfrith's steward before the thegn's household were all murdered by the Normans.'

'None of you have any reason to collaborate with the Normans, so why were you doing so?'

'We were not.'

'You were riding with them. You were armed as they were, dressed as they were.'

'About ten miles behind us is a small mead hall, an outlier of a large thegnly estate. It is currently used to provide refreshment and overnight shelter for Norman patrols.'

The man looked at the subdued band leader, who nodded sullenly.

'Very well, go on.'

'At the rear of the hall is a large midden. Buried within that midden you will find the bodies of the eight men who originally wore these clothes and bore these weapons. Only one of them will still be wearing his armour.'

The man looked again at the band leader, who shrugged his shoulders.

'We can check that.' He looked once more to the band leader who turned to leave.

'There's a young lad there who helped us bury them. He

serves the Normans mead mixed with piss,' called Edgar.

'I think you'd better start at the beginning,' said their interrogator.

Edgar drew a breath. He told of Sweyn-king's plans to claim the throne of England for himself, of the battle at Eoforwic, of the camp at Hakrholme, and of the apparent treachery of Jarl Asbjorn.

'We had planned to involve the Wildmen in the invasion. As you know, four of us here spent some months with the Wildmen. Halfdene and Alaric were part of a deputation sent to persuade Alfweald to go along with the plan. As I heard it, he was more than willing.'

'That he was.'

'Whilst they were with Alfweald, Caedmon here was caught by our guards. He was looking for his old master. He had found that Cyneheard had not been killed but instead was a prisoner of the Normans. Lord Osfrith sent us to attempt a rescue. We succeeded to some extent, but I was captured.'

'How did you rescue the lad?'

'We poisoned the well with a strong infusion of a mushroom, whose properties were revealed to me by a cunning-woman at Mammesfeld.'

The man nodded and Edgar continued.

'Thanks to the excellent impersonation skills of Alaric, my men also managed to rescue me. I was beaten badly during my incarceration, and have not yet fully recovered my strength. We hid for some time in the forest, in a small hidden cave. When we came across the mead hall I have already mentioned, Alaric's impersonations once again provided us with an escape route.'

'How?'

The Lost Land

Alaric spoke up. 'I speak their language. I was dressed as a priest. I got them drunk. We slit their throats,' he said simply.

'I see.'

'Then as we were riding away on their horses and in their mail and with their weapons, we were gathered into the larger force by a captain who didn't bother to check our credentials. I suppose we got lucky.'

'Right. I can't release you until my man returns with confirmation of your story, but let's assume for the moment that I believe you. Where were you heading?'

'North, back to Hakrholme.'

'That won't do you any good. Our information is that the Danes have left.'

Edgar dropped his head. 'I think we've all been duped by this Danish expedition. I was there when Sweyn-king announced his plans. The only reason the English lords agreed to it was that Sweyn promised to wrest the crown from the Bastard's head. Maybe he never planned to do that, but simply to grab as much loot as he could whilst the kingdom was in turmoil. Or maybe Asbjorn's working his own plan. I understood he had a personal meeting with the Bastard himself.'

'We heard that too.'

'I'll be truthful with you; I fear that Jarl Asbjorn has no intention of carrying through with the invasion. I think he has his booty and will return now. From the attitude of your man, I think he and probably all of you feel the same way. I'm sorry. It wasn't supposed to happen like this.'

'No, I don't suppose it was. I'm Ascwin, I was in the Paddock for a short while when you were there, though I left before the burning. It's fortunate for you that I recognised you, otherwise Raddo would probably have hanged you.'

'And I probably wouldn't have blamed him.'

19

Last Stand

The six companions had lost their horses during the battle. Now they walked with the ragged gang of Wildmen towards the north, where they were hoping to meet with other scattered Wildman groups. Edgar and Cyneheard were still suffering from their times at the mercy of the Normans, but the relatively slow pace of the Wildmen through the woodlands was not too taxing for them.

It was slightly warmer under the trees, and the wind was more broken, with fewer snow flurries. The temperature remained low, though, as did the men's spirits.

Stopping for the night, Ascwin permitted fires to be lit. The danger of being spotted by the now rare Norman patrols was far outweighed by the dangers of freezing to death.

There was little food available and all had to make do with meagre rations. Caedmon had lost the rations given to them by the lad at the mead hall when he had lost his horse.

The conversation was muted and desultory. The victory over the Norman column felt small and insignificant compared with the treachery of the Danes.

The man Raddo, who had previously been so keen to execute Edgar and his companions, now sat with them. He had seen the bodies of the Norman horsemen buried under the midden at the mead hall and had been impressed with the young servant's account of how they had been defeated, even if he thought that the lad had overblown his own part in the action.

For the first time, Edgar began to hear men speak openly of what they would do if it proved impossible to prise the Normans out of England.

'I don't want to think about it,' said Raddo. 'But I think we need to consider what the future might hold.'

'What were you before joining the Wildmen?' asked Edgar.

'Farmer. Held a few fields from my thegn. Some wheat, some barley, some sheep. When the Normans ousted my thegn, they burned the surrounding area fairly thoroughly. My house was burned down, the fields trampled and my sheep taken off to feed the invaders. Those they didn't eat they killed anyway, then burned the carcases so that the locals had no food source.

'I could rebuild. Come to some sort of arrangement with whatever fat bastard ends up taking the land. A man's got to live, even if it means having to live with the Normans.'

Hallvindur rumbled something that Edgar didn't quite catch.

'I wish it wasn't so, but the man's right,' said Edgar. 'We've exhausted all our possibilities.'

'The Wildmen fight on,' said Guthrum.

'Aye. There's that,' said Edgar, smiling grimly.

Edgar's disappointment felt physical, like a yawning emptiness. Along with all the English thegns thrown off their rightful land by the invaders, he still held a fervent wish to reclaim that land, to strike back at the cursed Norman. They had done everything they could, but had been let down at the last moment by what had at first seemed like their greatest hope.

Edgar's personal disappointment was coloured largely by his own refusal to listen to Loki's warnings about this very eventuality. He feared that his friendship with the ship's captain could now be lost, that Loki would no longer confide in and trust him. Edgar had given him no reason to.

Guthrum was looking intently at Edgar. 'It's not over until it's over,' he said gently.

The Wildmen slept huddled together, whilst duty sentries were stationed around a circle about two hundred yards across, centred on the lowering fire. There were no alarms during the night, and Edgar slept through almost the full dark.

'We should make contact with most if not all of our people today,' said Ascwin as they cleared away the signs of the night's stop.

'We're gathering together to discuss tactics for dealing with the Normans in the light of the Danish withdrawal. We have a great deal to talk about. Alfweald will be there and all the other council members, with only a few Wildmen still keeping guard in other parts of the forest.'

As Ascwin predicted, early in the afternoon, whistles

and calls from the advance scouts had announced that they, in turn, had heard contact calls from other groups.

Now the council of the Wildmen sat in a wide circle, with all the other Wildmen surrounding them. All had the right to speak at this extraordinary meeting.

Edgar was surprised to notice that it was not only the fighting men who had turned up for this conclave. The women and children who had had no option but to follow their menfolk into the wild woods were also present in great number. Altogether there must have been nearly five hundred souls present, very nearly the entire number of the Wildmen.

Former king's reeve Alfweald stood in the centre of the circle and turned round slowly to see everyone gathered there.

'My friends,' he began, his great greying beard wagging as he spoke. 'We have gathered together today to discuss a matter of immense importance. As most of you know, an invading army sent by Sweyn-king of Denmark has recently been campaigning to wrest the crown of this kingdom from the accursed Bastard of Normandy. We held great hopes of what we could achieve together. We were even contacted directly by representatives of the Danish army, to agree a course of action that we could undertake to ensure the greatest possible success of the Danish invasion.

'Now it appears that all our hopes are dashed. Despite some initial successes, notably at Eoforwic and in other places throughout Northumbria, the great Danish host has withdrawn. I understand from informants that the leader of the host, Jarl Asbjorn, brother of Sweyn-king, has met with the Bastard and has accepted his gold to cease hostilities.'

The gathered Wildmen muttered angrily, some even shouting out. Alfweald held his hand up to still them.

'I know, I know,' he said. 'But there is nothing that we can do to reverse the Danish treachery. What is done is done. I have heard others speak of days of old, when marauding Danish armies were paid vast sums by English kings to keep them at bay, and how that never really worked. Why walk away from a source of gold? The Danes always came back for more, looting and burning. Maybe this will happen again. Maybe the Danes will not truly go away, and maybe they will return for more gold. But there's the core of the matter. They may come back for more gold. Not to eject the Normans, but simply to get them to pay more. If we had learned from our own history with the Danes, then maybe we would not have been so optimistic about this army. We must accept that our salvation is not going to come from Denmark. Perhaps all we can expect from them is more burnings, lootings and killings to add to the burden of our misery.'

He paused and looked round at all the faces.

'We have gathered here to decide what we are going to do in the future. The first and most fundamental question is this: Do we fight on? Yes or no?'

Silence hung over the forest glade as the import of Alfweald's question sunk in. Was this really to be the end of all they had fought for and suffered over the last three years?

'Now I know that there are arguments on both sides, so we will listen to anyone who wishes to speak for fighting on, and also from anyone who wishes to propose that we stop. We will not surrender, but we can melt away back into the population without the Normans even knowing that we've gone. With luck, they will fear the forests for many years to come, even if we are no longer in them.'

He looked around again. A gust of wind sent flurries of snow cascading off the branches of the trees. Alfweald's beard streamed out towards his right shoulder.

'So, my friends. Who will be heard? Who will speak? Whatever the decision arrived at by this great council today, no reprisals of any kind will be made against those whose opinion does not prevail. You may speak openly and without fear.'

There were awkward shufflings of feet. Many looked down at the ground, unwilling to catch the reeve's eye.

Eventually, a council member stood.

'Fordred,' said Alfweald. 'Speak and be heard.'

Fordred bowed slightly to Alfweald, then turned to address the gathering.

'Most of you know me,' he said. 'I have been with the Wildmen for these three years. You all know why; my story is no different from anyone else's. I have fought hard beside you and I have never wavered from doing what I was asked to do.'

Heads were nodding, and there were cries of 'Aye,' from the gathered Wildmen.

'We have fought hard and we have killed many invaders. We have stayed ahead of the Normans in our knowledge of the land and our ability to disappear into it. Before the Danes came, many of us feared that the Normans were learning our skills too quickly. We were still ahead but by a noticeably reducing margin.'

Some of the Wildmen muttered agreement.

'The arrival of the Danes caused us great optimism. The Normans would have more on their hands than they could handle. We would continue our efforts; we were ready to

The Lost Land

step them up to a level we had never before worked at. It would have been hard – and for many of us fatal – work. But we were prepared to do that if it was to achieve for us our aim of ridding this land of the Norman pestilence. It was something we were coming to recognise that we would likely not be able to do on our own. At last, here was our deliverance.

'Now where are we? Right back where we were before the Danes arrived. You may say that therefore we should carry on as before. We can still damage them. But we have lost something. We have lost something vital, critical to our cause.

'Before, we had hope. Hope that a Danish army would come to our aid. Now we no longer have that hope. Now Christ and all His saints know that I do not want this struggle to end except with our victory, but we have reached a point where we have to consider going back to our fields. I know that I'm not the only one here to feel like this. To remain in arms against the Norman will lead only to death. Ours.

'I hear what Lord Alfweald says about freedom to speak today. I have spoken freely, but I will abide by whatever decision the great council comes to today. You need never fear that my words are those of cowardice.'

'No!' shouted several voices.

'Thank you,' said Fordred and resumed his seat.

Alfweald rose again.

'I thank you for your typically eloquent argument, Fordred. We never fear for your courage, I assure you. You have given us much to ponder. Especially those amongst us who still have living family. Will anyone else speak?'

In amongst the standing Wildmen, a hand was raised

hesitantly.

'Who's that?' asked Alfweald. 'Step forward.'

A short, stocky man with thinning hair stepped through the press of bodies.

'Gelfwine, isn't it?' asked Alfweald.

'Aye, my lord,' answered the man.

'Speak and be heard, Gelfwine,' said Alfweald, sitting down.

Gelfwine looked nervously at the Wildmen gathered around him. He cleared his throat.

'Like Fordred, many of you know me. I've not been with you for as long as him, just over two years. Unlike Fordred, I'm just a simple farmer. I held two small fields from my thegn before he was killed. I have no family, so never had to face the loss of them. Maybe that makes me less willing to return to my fields, I don't really know.

'I do not relish working for a Norman lord. I have heard tales of their cruelty and harshness. If I'm honest, I don't know if this is true, but from what I have seen of the Normans, then I want no part of them. They killed our king, they killed our thegns, they killed our families, they burned our houses, they killed our livestock, they burned our fields. How can we forgive and forget that? How can we return to our fields which these wicked men now claim to own? How can we accept the gifts of lords who have done these things to gain our lands? How can we bend the knee to a man who would not flinch at killing everyone in what he thinks of as his kingdom?

'Are we to give up now? After we have suffered so much and after we have achieved so much as the Wildmen? Was it all for nothing? We can't give up. We just can't.

'I said before that I had no family. That was certainly

true when I was driven off my fields. But it isn't true now. I have found a family right here, in all of you. That is a family that I would, and will, fight to the death for.'

A cheer arose from the Wildmen, and several of his colleagues patted Gelfwine on the back.

Alfweald lifted his hand for silence.

'Well spoken, Gelfwine. Very well spoken. You also have given us a great deal to consider. Does anyone else have anything to add to what has been so finely said by these two men?' He looked round, but nobody raised a hand or a voice.

'Right. We need to think and discuss amongst ourselves. We will prepare a meal, and after we have all eaten, we will come to our decision. I remind you that in this decision, every man and woman shall have a vote. This is not a matter for the council.'

As the assembled Wildmen dispersed to find and prepare their food, Alfweald turned to Edgar.

'Edgar, will you sit with me?' he asked.

'Of course,' replied Edgar.

He sat down next to Alfweald and accepted a waterskin from the former reeve.

'What do you think, Edgar?'

Edgar shook his head. 'I hardly know what to think. I cannot bear the thought of giving up the fight against the Norman, but at the same time, I think our cause is probably hopeless. We are too few, and as we have found time after time, communicating effectively with other groups is well-nigh impossible.'

Alfweald sighed. 'You know, Edgar, we must take most of the blame for this situation.'

'We?'

'Us, the thegns, the lords. And above us the earls. Remember what happened after the death of Harold? Infighting. The earls all shuffling for position. They would rather see the country burn than assist some other earl with whom they had a petty rivalry. The earls would not work together. You told me yourself of your attempts to form a coalition of thegns in your part of Mercia. That didn't go well, did it?'

Edgar remembered it well. Under his grandfather's instruction, he had arranged a meeting of a dozen local thegns to discuss an appropriate response to the massive tax demands made by the Normans following their victory over Harold-king. He had been faced with indifference and a deep-seated parochialism. The thegns would not help each other, and each was interested only in his own well-being. One thegn had even been strongly suspected of using the crisis to rid himself of some neighbours and thereby increase the size of his own lands. What was his name? Edgar thought back to that depressing meeting. Dudda, that was it. He briefly wondered if Dudda had made the moves he was suspected of planning, and if he was now toadying up to a greasy Norman lord, or whether he was, like so many thegns, dead in an unmarked grave.

He shook his head to clear it of the unwelcome images.

'No, my lord, it did not go well.'

In a confusing change of direction, Alfweald suddenly asked 'Where is Harek?'

'Harek?'

'Yes, the Danish king's thegn who visited us along with Halfdene and Alaric. Where is he?'

'He remained at Hakrholme when my men and I went

to Mammesfeld to rescue Cyneheard.'

'Did he now?'

'What about Harek?'

'Oh, probably nothing. Don't worry about it.'

'He remained in Hakrholme because he feared that Asbjorn was going to do exactly what he ended up doing. I don't think Harek trusted Asbjorn.'

'It would appear that none of us should have.'

Once more, Alfweald stood in the centre of the circle of Wildmen. They stood in silence, all eyes on him, the man who had led them for three years.

The sky was darkening, night was falling. Alfweald looked around at his people, trying to gauge their mood.

'You have had time to think, time to discuss this most weighty of matters with your friends, some of you with your families. I will ask you just one question. The answer that you give me to that question will lead to further questions, which we must debate tomorrow.

'I will ask you now simply to answer the question: Do we continue to fight the Normans? I will ask first for Ayes, and then for Nays. If you say Aye, then we must decide how we are to continue, and what tactics we should adopt. If you say Nay, then we must decide how we disband, and how we can re-enter normal life with as little disruption as possible. For now, are you all ready to answer the first question?'

He turned round, looking at every face that he could see. Every one of the adults had turned out for the vote. The men looked grim, the women no less so.

Alfweald raised his voice. 'Then I ask you – do we continue to fight the Normans? Those who wish, say Aye.'

As a single voice, the cry "Aye!" came back at him.

Alfweald smiled slightly and nodded.

'And those who wish, say Nay.'

The crowd remained silent. Even those who had spoken against continuing decided in the end that fighting on would be the only acceptable course of action.

'Thank you for your show of confidence, my friends,' said Alfweald. 'Tomorrow we must speak of many things. Tonight, I want you all to think of ways in which we can still face the Normans, even without the backing of a great host. How can we hurt them? How can we get under their skin? How can we get to their leaders? Think hard, my friends, think long. All ideas will be given a hearing. Don't be afraid if you think your idea sounds outlandish. The Wildmen *are* outlandish.'

The Wildmen cheered and began to disperse.

It would be another cold night in the forest.

The heavily overcast dawn took a long time in arriving. So it was that the Wildmen were finished with their breakfast when the first light began to penetrate through the deep, roiling clouds.

Edgar, Guthrum and Halfdene were preparing to join one of the hunting parties to gather food for later in the day. Edgar looked up as a scout ran into the glade and straight up to Alfweald.

Edgar watched with interest as Alfweald listened to what the scout had to say, then patted him on the arm. The scout ran back the way he had come. Alfweald whistled a shrill whistle and immediately the group commanders ran to gather round him. Edgar joined the dash.

'There is a small Norman foot patrol coming towards us,' said Alfweald. 'They are only about half a mile distant.

This is a golden opportunity to do a bit of damage. Gather your groups and form ambushes. Edgar, I'm glad you're here. Gather your people and do the same, I want you near the rear. You know what to do.'

Edgar ran back to Halfdene and Guthrum. Hallvindur and Alaric moved closer to hear what he had to say.

'A bit of action,' said Edgar. 'There's a Norman patrol headed this way. Infantry. We're going to take them out. They're coming from that direction,' he pointed. 'And so we need to go that way,' he pointed in the opposite direction. 'We need to be at the rear.'

'The rear?' asked Hallvindur. 'I don't like being in the rear.'

'When you fight with the Wildmen, you do what Alfweald tells you to do,' replied Edgar. 'We all do.'

Edgar ran over to where Caedmon and Cyneheard were sitting, clearing up the remains of their fire.

'There are some Normans coming and there's going to be some fighting,' said Edgar. 'Caedmon, I want you to take Cyneheard south, away from where the trouble will be. Both of you keep low and hidden. We'll meet up afterwards. Just stay out of sight.'

'Edgar,' said Cyneheard. 'I can fight. I want to fight.'

'No, I'm sorry. You're in no fit state to fight. The best thing you can do is stay hidden. Give yourself the chance to fight another time.'

Cyneheard looked disappointed, but he gave Edgar no argument.

'Come on, Master Cyneheard,' said Caedmon. 'We'll find somewhere to lie low, just for now.'

'Alright, I'm coming.'

With Caedmon still gently supporting Cyneheard, the

odd couple moved off towards the south and away from the glade.

Edgar rejoined his companions and they withdrew to the rear of the already invisible Wildman lines. Nothing could be done about the scars on the ground left by the morning's fires, but that didn't matter. The Wildmen were ready for an engagement.

The bustle of the Wildmen's morning activities had vanished completely. The women and children had melted away into the forest, moving quickly and silently to get as far away from the fighting as possible.

Small bird sounds rippled around the forest. Some of them Edgar knew would be the Wildmen, communicating information about the movement of the Normans, but he could not interpret them, new as they were.

Then, seen clearly through a narrow gap in the trees, there stood a Norman footman. He held his sword in his right hand and a shield covered his left arm. A long chain mail tunic hung down just below his knees. His helmet reflected the dull light from the cloudy sky as he stood and looked around as if lost.

A quiet, bird-like twitter came from a stand of undergrowth fifty feet ahead of him.

'Sounds like "Wait", to me,' whispered Guthrum.

Edgar nodded. Some of the calls obviously had not changed. Probably only the recognition calls, making it harder for the Normans, who somehow seem to have learned at least some of the Wildmen's communication.

The Norman looked to his right, and another joined him, dressed identically. He walked slowly and carefully.

A muted call emanated from the same undergrowth, and immediately the two Normans fell, white-feathered arrows protruding from their unguarded throats.

A cry went up, other Normans began to rush forward, holding their shields up in front of their faces, only too aware of their comrades' fate. Several more appeared now, moving forward across a broad front.

'Why are they moving through the forest like this?' whispered Guthrum. 'Why aren't they using the roads?'

Edgar frowned. It made no sense, unless…

'They're coming for us,' he replied.

Edgar's mind was racing. Even if the patrol was specifically looking for them, still it made little sense. Why so few? Such a small patrol would surely be wiped out, the Norman captains would know that.

'Shit!' hissed Edgar.

'What is it?' asked Guthrum.

'It's a trap. This is a throw-away advance unit. There are probably several of them spread across the forest. There'll be a larger force bringing up the rear, probably much larger.'

Guthrum swore. 'You're right. That makes sense. We need to warn Alfweald.'

As he spoke, the newly arrived Norman footmen began shouting.

'Too late. We're discovered,' said Edgar.

Without any call that Edgar could hear, arrows began whistling out of the forest. Some found their mark above or below incautiously held shields, others thudded uselessly into them. Still they continued shouting, bringing their colleagues in what Edgar imagined would be a very large force down on the Wildmen.

The advance party was now in great difficulty. Without being able to see where the arrows were coming from, they had stumbled into the middle of the Wildmen's firing range. Arrows whispered out all around them, from in front, behind and from both sides. The Normans all fell.

As the last man fell, Alfweald stood up from his hiding place, whistling loudly.

The calls were unknown to Edgar and his companions, so Edgar, crouching low, ran over to another group of Wildmen nearby.

'What does he say?' demanded Edgar of the group's leader.

'Prepare for attack,' said the man, looking around him.

All around, archers were clambering up trees and hunkering down in undergrowth. Others were drawing swords and axes and although not in their usual camouflage, were doing their best to blend in with the wintry treescape around them.

Edgar sped back to his companions. 'This is going to be bad. This isn't the type of fighting the Wildmen are good at. Shit. Shit, shit, shit.'

Guthrum drew his sword, Halfdene and Hallvindur already had theirs at the ready, and Alaric was looking curiously at the sword in his hand.

'Alaric,' hissed Edgar. 'Try to get away from the fight. You're not trained for this.'

The spy shook his head.

'No, sir. If we have to stand, then we stand together.'

He waved the sword around clumsily. 'After all, how hard can it be?'

Silence had fallen around the forest again. The dead Normans lay close together, Wildmen secreted all around.

Edgar strained to hear anything that could give away the positioning of the Normans he was sure must be advancing towards them.

He realised that he was gripping the sword too tightly. He eased his grip a little, trying to relax and prepare himself for battle. He knew he was not in full fighting form. His ribs still ached, and pain shot through his side when he moved his arm in certain ways. He would have to adapt his fighting technique accordingly, though as he knew from his training sessions with Harek, any competent swordsman would recognise that he was protecting a wound and would take full advantage of it.

Distantly, though not distantly enough for comfort, Edgar could now hear men shouting. The Normans were advancing.

Whistles from advanced scouts reported the progress of the Normans as they closed in on the Wildmen.

He could hear the sounds now of a great many men hacking their way through the undergrowth and bushes.

Warning cries came from the forward Wildman scouts as they were cut down.

'Here they are,' said Guthrum grimly as about thirty infantrymen burst through the last bushes.

A loud whistle sounded, from Alfweald, Edgar thought.

Arrows flew from hiding places, and a few of the Normans fell or staggered. Then, where there had been thirty, there were hundreds. Still widely separated from each other, the Norman army looked like an armoured wall, shields held firmly in front of them as they walked sideways-on into the part of the forest where the Wildmen hid. The Normans slashed at any possible cover, sometimes making contact with a hidden Wildman.

'Alfweald's out of options,' said Guthrum.

As he spoke, Alfweald burst out of his hiding place,

brandishing a large battleaxe.

'Wildmen!' he yelled.

All around, the Wildmen stepped from their hiding places. The air was thick with white-flighted arrows, and Normans began to fall in greater numbers.

Seeing the Wildmen in front of them, the Normans advanced more quickly now.

The first hand to hand engagements began. The Normans had the advantage from the outset. The Wildmen were greatly outnumbered, and very few had any armour, dressed for stealth as they usually were.

'Come on,' said Edgar to his companions.

They stood and advanced towards the nearest skirmish, where a number of Normans were making pretty short work of a small group of lightly-armed Wildmen.

The Normans paid them little heed as they approached, dressed as they were in stolen Norman armour.

The desperate Wildmen looked on in despair as Edgar and his companions approached.

'Wildmen!' cried Edgar and swung his sword down on the arm of a Norman who was about to dispatch a fallen unarmoured man.

The Norman screamed, his right arm shattered between elbow and wrist.

All Edgar's crew now attacked the party of Normans. They were taken off guard and it didn't take long to finish them all off.

Edgar took the hand of the fallen Wildman and pulled him to his feet.

There was no time for words, another party of Norman infantry advanced towards them, cautiously, but with determination.

The foremost of the Normans fell suddenly, an arrow piercing his cheek and penetrating deep into his head.

One of his colleagues stared at him as he fell and Guthrum leaped forward, bringing his sword down across the man's head. The sword bit deeply into the bottom of his helmet, dislodging it and rendering the man unconscious, at best.

The fight was now engaged, each of Edgar's men picking an opponent and battling them, each killing his man.

More arrows found their targets amongst the Normans, but more kept coming.

A stout soldier with tightly fitting mail squared up to Edgar, plunging his sword forward with dizzying speed. Edgar sidestepped quickly, feeling the stab of pain from his damaged ribs, but fortunately not from the Norman's sword.

Edgar brought his sword down to catch the Norman's arm, but the sword was withdrawn as quickly as it had been thrust forward, and Edgar's blade found only thin air. He spun to prevent himself from staggering and found the Norman's sword slicing towards his shoulder. He ducked away again, bringing his sword up and forward to find the vulnerable area beneath the Norman's arm. He felt the sword bite, and he followed it through with a hard push. The sword split the mail coat and sank a few inches into the Norman's side.

The man looked into Edgar's face and pulled himself off the sword. He dropped his own sword and shook his head at Edgar. It was an odd moment, but Edgar knew exactly what the man was trying to communicate – I'm stopping now.

Edgar withdrew his sword and the Norman turned to

walk away from the fight.

Edgar had no time to see what happened to him, as another Norman stepped up and thrust his shield into Edgar's face. Edgar leaned back and using a technique taught to him by Harek what seemed like years ago, he used the flat of his sword to force the Norman's shield up. As it went up, Edgar thrust forward. He felt his sword make hard contact with something, and his opponent staggered away, falling on his face.

Edgar glanced around. They were now surrounded by Normans. He had become detached from his companions, but he could see Halfdene hacking away with his sword. Beyond him, the giant Hallvindur was swinging an axe he had found in great sweeps, a small mound of dead Normans at his feet.

Edgar snapped his attention back to his immediate surroundings. A tall swordsman was approaching him. Edgar braced himself, wishing he had a shield.

His opponent began a head-spinning attack. Edgar only just managed to fend off the first assault, but as he staggered back, the man began another attack, even more quickly.

Edgar felt hot pain searing along his side. He felt the slickness beneath his mail and knew that he'd been sliced by the Norman's sword, though how badly he didn't know and had no time to investigate. He staggered back, exaggerating the effect of the wound.

His opponent stepped forward, dropping his shield to deliver the finishing blow, and Edgar summoned up all his remaining strength to slash horizontally across the man's now unprotected midriff.

The man grunted and fell back a couple of paces. His mail had held, but a broad swathe across his stomach was seeping blood. The man looked down at himself, dazed. Edgar stepped forward and thrust his sword as hard as he could toward the man's wound.

This time the links of his chain mail split, and the sword thrust carried through into the man's guts. He moaned and fell backwards.

Edgar withdrew his sword and gasped. The wound in his side was red hot, and he took advantage of a lull in the action in his immediate area to examine himself carefully. The wound did not appear too deep, but he was losing blood at an uncomfortably fast rate.

Looking around, he began to appreciate the scale of what was happening. The Wildmen were losing.

About fifty yards away, he saw Alfweald, standing amid a pile of his dead colleagues and enemies, swinging his mighty battleaxe, dispatching Norman after Norman. As Edgar watched, half a dozen Normans closed in on him. His colleagues were all dead, he stood alone.

'No,' gasped Edgar, trying to run towards Alfweald. His legs responded only slowly to his desire. He tripped and stumbled. Looking up, he saw Alfweald disappear under a rain of sword slashes.

Just when Edgar feared Alfweald must surely have perished, he saw the reeve's head appear once more above the Normans. It was covered in blood. One of the Normans spun away and crashed to the ground.

The rest of them repeated their attack, sword slash after sword slash hacking down on the big man. With despair, Edgar saw him go down, blood spurting from his mouth.

He felt the edges of his vision begin to contract. No, he thought, not now. My friends...

Then he collapsed into unconsciousness.

20

After the Battle

'Edgar.'

Slowly, painful light began to penetrate Edgar's eyes. He opened them slightly, squinting at the light, dull and feeble as it was.

'Edgar.'

Guthrum was leaning over him, his face creased in a worried frown.

'Guthrum,' said Edgar. 'What's happened?'

'You've lost a lot of blood, but I've staunched the flow. You'll be alright. Just lie still.'

'The battle... the Wildmen?'

'Hush. Lie still.'

Edgar felt himself slipping into unconsciousness again, and allowed himself to go.

He slowly became aware of movement around him. Guthrum was putting short branches onto a compact fire that he'd started.

'Guthrum?' whispered Edgar.

Guthrum turned. 'Edgar,' he said and smiled.

Edgar closed his eyes but felt no desire to go back to sleep. He tried to sit up, but stabbing pain coursed through his body and he gasped.

'Whoa, whoa,' said Guthrum, leaning over and supporting him, lifting him gently into a sitting position.

Edgar looked around him. They were still on the battlefield. All around were the bodies of the combatants. The snow was liberally splashed with red, and the sky glowered an unhealthy yellow above them.

'How did we do?' asked Edgar.

'Not well, lad. Not well.'

'The others?'

Guthrum shook his head. 'I don't know, I've been here with you. The battle went past us, the Normans just kept on advancing, slashing and hacking as they went. Their lines were fairly loosely arranged, and they didn't pay any attention to just two more bodies as they passed.'

'You played dead, Guthrum? You?'

'It was the only way I could stay with you. If I hadn't, then I would be dead by now. And so would you.'

Edgar closed his eyes and allowed his head to hang down.

'I think the battle is continuing, but it's moved well away from us now, and there can't be much still going on.'

'The Wildmen?'

'Done.'

'We must find our friends.'

'You need rest.'

'I need to find my friends. I must know what happened

to them. I don't need any more Modberts in my life. Help me up, we search.'

Guthrum stood and held out a hand for Edgar. Edgar winced as he stood, and held tightly onto his side.

'Are you alright?' asked Guthrum.

'I'll be fine. Come on. Halfdene and Hallvindur were over here when I last saw them.'

They walked slowly across the field of carnage. Whatever snow was left after the trampling of so many feet was coloured throughout in various shades of pink and red. Edgar found the stout man he had stabbed and then allowed to withdraw from the fight. He was sitting with his back to a tree, his sightless eyes still staring out across the battle site.

Edgar dropped painfully to his knees. He gently reached out and closed the man's eyes.

'I'm sorry,' he whispered.

He stood up again and surveyed the scene of devastation around him. 'Yesterday, Guthrum, you said to me that it isn't over until it's over.'

'Yes, I did.'

'Well, it's over now.'

'Aye,' whispered Guthrum.

They walked on, to a pile of bodies four or five deep.

'This is the work of our two,' said Edgar. 'Halfdene was here and Hallvindur was there.'

'Edgar,' said Guthrum, quietly.

Edgar crossed over to where Guthrum had dropped to his knees. He was pulling a body out of the way. Underneath were two more. The one on top was huge. It could only be Hallvindur.

'Oh, no,' muttered Edgar.

Guthrum turned the body over. His helmet had come

off, and his long straggling blonde hair was plastered with sweat across his face, but there was no doubt who it was.

Edgar knelt, his pain forced into some remote part of his consciousness, and turned over the body beneath Hallvindur. The shoulder was caked in coagulating blood, and a lot had splashed up into the man's face.

'Oh, sweet Jesus,' said Edgar. It was Halfdene. 'Oh God, Guthrum, we've lost them both.'

Guthrum didn't respond. His eyes were closed and he was rocking back and forth very gently.

They stayed with the bodies of their friends, not daring to move on to seek out the remaining three members of their company. Edgar felt hot tears stinging his eyes as he stared unseeingly into the forest around them. Guthrum remained silent for a long time.

'My lord!'

Edgar didn't even hear the cry from some way behind him.

'My lord!'

Footsteps were falling behind Edgar. He didn't look up. He couldn't have cared less if a Norman was marching up to him to kill him. He felt total desolation. He had failed his friends, his dependents. This entire enterprise had been a fool's outing, and it had cost his friends their lives.

'My lord, it's you, thank the sweet Christ that we've found you!'

A hand fell gently onto Edgar's shoulder, and only then did he look up to find Caedmon looking down at him.

'Thank God you survived, I… Oh, no.'

Caedmon looked down at the bodies next to where Edgar slumped.

'Caedmon,' said Edgar, acknowledging the steward's presence.

'Oh, my lord,'

Behind him, Cyneheard stepped forward. 'Edgar, I…' he faltered. 'I wanted to fight.'

Edgar straightened himself up, and stood, painfully. He grabbed Cyneheard to him and hugged him tightly.

'Then let us thank the gods that you didn't,' he said.

'Hallvindur?' Caedmon was bending over the giant.

'Caedmon…' Edgar began.

'Hallvindur, that's a nasty bump on your head, but you need to get up now.'

'Caedmon, please…'

'Come on you big lummock, rest time's over.'

Edgar was about to pull the disturbed Caedmon away from the body of Hallvindur when he heard a low groan. Edgar gasped. Hallvindur was moving slightly.

'Get up, you oaf,' said Caedmon.

Hallvindur's eyes opened slightly. 'What's that, you little turd?' He groaned loudly and put his hand to the back of his head. 'Who hit me?'

'Hallvindur!' cried Edgar.

'My lord? Did we win?'

'No.'

'Ah.'

'My lord!' said Caedmon, urgently, tugging at Edgar's mail shirt. 'Halfdene still breathes. He needs immediate attention. Where's Alaric?'

'What? Halfdene? Alaric? I don't know.'

Confusion raged through Edgar's mind. Hallvindur and Halfdene still both alive? How had he not seen it? Gods, he hadn't even checked them for signs of life. So deep was his desolation that he could not even conceive that the worst had not happened.

'Help me,' commanded Caedmon.

Guthrum and Edgar moved to help the little steward as he pushed other bodies away from Halfdene.

Carefully, Caedmon began stripping the armour away from Halfdene's shoulder. He pulled the mail coat over his head, then, removing a domestic seax from his belt, sliced away at the padded leather tunic Halfdene wore underneath his mail.

'Hold him,' said Caedmon as he stripped the tunic away. Underneath was an ugly wound. A sword had obviously crashed down on Halfdene's shoulder, causing a deep wound which was still oozing blood and in which Edgar could see the pearly whiteness of bone. Some of the bone was in situ, some was in little chips, shattered away from the shoulder.

'Without Alaric's expertise, I'm afraid I will have to tend this,' said Caedmon. 'I need water, clean water. Cold to start with but I'll need some heated as well. Collect snow, clean snow only, we'll melt it.'

'In what?' asked Cyneheard.

'Use some helmets, there are enough about.'

The three men set off collecting helmets and filling them from drifts of clean snow. Guthrum expanded the small fire he had made and the helmets were placed around it.

Caedmon meanwhile pushed clean cloths from his scrip into Halfdene's wound. He gently felt inside the wound and removed what splinters of bone he could find.

When the water was ready, he poured large quantities of it into the wound, repeating the process with the hot water once it had reached a temperature he considered adequate.

'A travelling healer once told me, whilst I was working in Lord Osfrith's household, that wounds should always be cleaned as a first step. I don't know why that should be, but I have done it with every wound I've tended since then. It doesn't always guarantee a clean heal, it doesn't even always guarantee survival, but it does seem to be a contributing factor.'

'When you were wounded at Stanford, the first thing Godgifu did was to spend a long time cleaning your wounds,' said Guthrum to Edgar. 'Then she applied salves and herbs,' he added.

'The next stage is that. The application of herbs and salves. I don't have any, and I lack Alaric's expertise in identifying the correct plants to use. I wouldn't know what to use in summer when they're in leaf and flower, but now…' he looked round at the desolate snowy forest.

'We'll just have to hope that my cleaning of the wound was good enough. I'll clean it again soon, and keep doing that. It may help. It's all I can do.'

'It's plenty, Caedmon. You're a life-saver,' said Edgar, genuinely impressed with the little man.

'Well, we'll see, my lord. Let's hope so.'

Halfdene was still unconscious, probably as well considering the pain that he would have had to endure during Caedmon's treatment of his wound.

'He will be asleep for some time, I would think,' said Caedmon.

Edgar stood up. 'We need to find Alaric. We have to know one way or the other whether he survived. Hallvindur, can you walk?'

The Lost Land

'Yes, it's just my head that hurts, and I'm a little dizzy.'

'Well take it gently. Come on Cyneheard. Caedmon, you stay with Halfdene.'

'Aye, my lord.'

The four men set off on the grisly task of checking every corpse on the battlefield, sometimes having to dig through piles of bodies to get to the ones at the bottom. The snow was slick underfoot, and the stink of blood and ordure filled their nostrils.

Edgar found himself close to Cyneheard. 'Where did you find to hide?' he asked.

Cyneheard snorted. 'I take no pride in this, Edgar.'

'I know, but if you had fought, I very much doubt you would have survived. You're still weak from your abuses by the Normans. It was better to hide and be fit to fight another day, believe me. No shame attaches to you. A wise warrior knows when to fight and when not to.'

'Brock hole,' said Cyneheard quietly.

'Brock hole?'

'Yes, when it became obvious that a large number of Normans were involved and not just the few we first thought, Caedmon found an abandoned one and pushed me down it.'

'Good gods! I wouldn't go down a brock hole!'

'Caedmon assured me that it was an old one.'

'That's just as well, if you'd found a brock down there it would have ripped your face off.'

'Caedmon was right. The sett was empty but deep. Small enough to make breathing an effort, but long enough for him to crawl in after me. He came in feet first and pulled a pile of snow and leaves over the opening. Then he kept watch. Meanwhile, I was down at the far end, wondering how long the air would last.'

Edgar laughed briefly. 'Caedmon is quite a remarkable man when it comes down to it, isn't he?'

Cyneheard nodded. 'He is, indeed.'

They found the remains of Alfweald, his body showing the ferocity of the attack on him. He was covered all over with fierce sword wounds. Edgar gently wiped the blood from his face. He laid him out, and folded his hands around the handle of his great battleaxe.

Edgar and Guthrum stood over his body for a while in silence.

Edgar caught sight of a movement from the corner of his eye. In the distance, a figure was moving towards the site of the carnage. It was a woman, staring in horror at what was before her. As he spotted her, another appeared close to her. The Wildmen women were returning from their hiding places, to face the terrifying prospect of life in the aftermath of the Wildmen's defeat.

All around Alfweald were the bodies of the Normans he had killed.

Guthrum grunted. He leaned over Alfweald's body and removed the battleaxe from his hands.

'Guthrum, what are you doing?' asked Edgar.

'Just this,' he replied. He pulled the Norman bodies away from the reeve and systematically hacked off all their heads. He then piled the severed heads underneath Alfweald's feet and returned the bloody axe to his hands.

After an hour of searching, none of the party had found any trace of Alaric.

'He does that,' said Guthrum. 'He's done it before. When he judges the moment to be right, he just disappears.

We can't find any trace of him, so I believe that he slipped away at some opportune moment and is probably right now making his way back to us, probably after having inflicted some massive inconvenience on the Normans.'

Edgar grinned. 'Gods, I hope you're right, Guthrum. I couldn't cope with another disappearing companion.'

They stood in silence for a while.

A movement caught Edgar's eye. Away in the distance, through the trees, two enormous ravens were flapping around the edge of the battlefield.

With a start, Edgar's thoughts went to the vision he had had when being tended by the strange old woman in a small cave beneath the forest when he was first involved with the Wildmen. He had been unhorsed and knocked out by an ill-placed tree branch.

Under the influence of a herbal concoction she had brewed for him, he had relived the point in the Battle of Stanford when he had received his massive facial wound. He had seen himself, somehow detached from his near-dead body. A strange robed man with one eye had approached him in his dream. The old woman had told him that the man was Woden One-eye, the chief of the old gods, who walked among the dead of battle, releasing their souls to fly to their eternal feasting hall. With him were two huge ravens.

And now, over another battlefield, were two huge ravens. He looked about, eager to see if he could catch a sight of the Old One once again.

'Are you alright, Edgar?' asked Guthrum.

'What? Yes, yes. I'm fine. Come on, let's get back to Caedmon and the fire.'

They found Caedmon rewashing Halfdene's wound. He had collected a lot more snow and filled several helmets, and all were now standing in or very near to the fire.

'He's breathing steadily,' said Caedmon. 'There's no immediate danger, I think. We just have to wait for him to wake up, and he'll do that in his own time.'

'Thank you, Caedmon,' said Edgar.

'Any sign of Alaric?'

'No. We'll have to wait and see if he turns up. In the meantime, we appreciate what you're doing for Halfdene.'

Caedmon made a shallow bow with his head towards Edgar, and turned back to his patient, embarrassed by the trust placed in him.

The night was drawing in. The fire was built up to last until the dawn, and Edgar ordered that they should all sleep.

'I'll take watch,' said Guthrum.

'No need, Guthrum. The Normans are gone. We won't be disturbed tonight.'

'There are other things in the forest besides Normans,' said Guthrum.

'We have a good fire. We'll be safe.'

Guthrum nodded, too tired to continue the argument.

Edgar woke the following morning stiff and sore. He opened his eyes and saw that the fire had gone out during the night.

A small movement caught his eye and he stiffened.

Moving his eyes only, he looked around the camp. Someone was squatting next to Halfdene, looking at him intently.

Very slowly and in complete silence, Edgar moved his hand across to where his sword lay in the leafy snow next to him. His hand closed around the hilt.

'I wouldn't, if I were you, sir, I may be the only one who can save Halfdene's arm.'

'Alaric!'

'Indeed, sir.'

'Where did you go?'

'If that can wait until later, sir, I'd be grateful. Right now, I need to tend this wound. You've cleaned it well, but it needs treatment.'

'I didn't clean it, Caedmon did.'

Alaric half turned towards Edgar. 'Caedmon?'

'Yes.'

'There is more to that man than initially meets the eye.'

'I agree. What needs to be done for Halfdene?'

'I have a small pot of an unguent made from a few different herbs. It isn't fresh, but it was made late this last summer. I need to get it into the wound. You may have to hold Halfdene down because it will hurt like nothing he's felt so far. Not only will I have to get my fingers right into the wound, but the unguent also stings very strongly.'

'He's unconscious,' said Edgar.

'No I'm not,' grunted Halfdene. 'And I can't say I like the sound of Alaric's words. Come on Edgar, get hold of me. I'll try not to struggle too much.'

Alaric unbuckled his belt, pulled it off and folded it in two. He held it out to Halfdene.

'Here,' he said. 'Bite down on this. It helps. Trust me, I know what I'm talking about.'

Halfdene took the belt and clamped down on it with his teeth.

'Ready sir?'

Edgar nodded his assent.

'Halfdene?'

Halfdene paused a moment, then nodded, grunting around the belt in his mouth.

'Alright, here we go.'

Alaric dipped two fingers in the pot and pulled out a thick, green paste. He quickly pulled apart the sides of Halfdene's wound and plunged his fingers in as far as they would go. Halfdene screamed around the belt, his teeth clamping down hard. He bucked, trying to get away from the pain, but Edgar held him firmly. Alaric worked quickly and efficiently, pulling some more paste out of the pot and working it thoroughly into the wound. Halfdene squirmed and screamed, saliva dribbling from the sides of his mouth and sweat pouring from his brow.

Alaric finished his grim task and sat back, wiping his bloodied fingers on a rag.

Halfdene moaned and his eyes rolled wildly.

'I'm sorry, my friend. It gives me no pleasure to cause you so much pain, but I wish to save your arm. This will help.'

Halfdene did not reply. He had passed out.

Edgar turned round to see Guthrum, Hallvindur, Caedmon and Cyneheard all sitting up and watching the proceedings in a mixture of fascination and horror.

Alaric grinned at them.

'This wound will need stitching once the stinging has faded. That should take a couple of hours. Meanwhile, I need to clean my needle. Caedmon, would you be so good as to boil some water? I've found that the hotter the water, the lower the chances of the wound going bad.'

'Of course,' stammered Caedmon.

Hallvindur was staring at Alaric.

'Where the fuck have you been?' he asked.

'Ah. You aren't going to like this bit, Hallvindur, and I apologise in advance.'

'What do you mean?'

'I was fighting behind you when I saw Halfdene fall. I could see the wound would be bad, if not immediately fatal. The men he was fighting, for there were three of them, had turned towards you. You'd just finished off one Norman, but I thought three might be too much for you, and more were approaching. I hit you very hard at the base of your skull, where your helmet was slipping forward. You went down very quickly, and I made it look from a distance like I had run you through with the sword instead of merely hitting you with the pommel. On the ground and unconscious, you'd be safe. I turned to the men who were closing in on you and smiled at them. They thought I was one of them, I was, after all, wearing a Norman captain's helmet. I then joined the Norman side, not actually engaging in any combat, and occasionally slipping a blade into the back of one of them while nobody was watching. I followed the Normans for a mile or so, but when it became clear that the Wildmen were spent, I quietly joined the dead of the field, sneaking away once darkness had fallen. I found your fire easily enough, and here I am.'

Hallvindur stared at Alaric, his face red with anger. He was breathing deeply, and Edgar prepared himself for trouble.

'You knocked me out? During a battle?'

'Yes. I was... worried for you.'

'It really hurts!' yelled Hallvindur.

'I am truly sorry. I was making you safe in the fastest way I could think.'

Hallvindur snorted but sat back.

'Turd,' he muttered.

There was a short moment of silence. Then Edgar spoke.

'Alright. It seems that against all the odds, we have all survived the last stand of the Wildmen. We need to move on, to get back to the fleet. Treacherous dogs though they are, we need to get back to Denmark. It's the only place that's safe for us now. We have to put aside our feelings for Jarl Asbjorn and all those who promised so much and delivered so little. They disgust me, as they do you. I hold Asbjorn personally responsible for the deaths of all our comrades here, and if there was any way to revenge ourselves on him, I would pursue it. But we need to put that aside, at least for the present. We just can't keep trying to wreak vengeance on those who offend us in some way. Let this stop now. Let's return to Denmark and pick up new lives there.'

They were all looking intently at him.

'I will suffer no deviation from my wishes. Do I make myself perfectly clear to everyone?'

Slowly, they all agreed, and Edgar said nothing until he had received everyone's assent.

Snow began to fall again. Edgar sighed.

'Good. It's time we looked after ourselves for a while. I've had enough of this place, and I think it's clear that it's had enough of us.'

He caught Guthrum's eye. The housecarl gave him the barest of nods and the tiniest hint of a smile. It cheered Edgar more than he could have believed. He had earned the approval of his old tutor.

The Lost Land

They stayed around their fire until they had eaten their midday meal, a rough collection of some dried berries and some very stale bread. Caedmon had a small lump of cheese left over, which he insisted Halfdene eat.

Alaric stitched Halfdene's wound neatly and declared him fit to travel.

The snow was beginning to cover the bodies of the fallen around them, and they picked their way carefully through the battlefield and away through the forest to the north. They soon came across a wide path, making the journey easier. Hallvindur scouted ahead, keeping in touch with whistles.

They passed into a wide clearing, about quarter of a mile across, which exposed them to the full harshness of the weather. Large banks of snow had drifted across the path and made the going more difficult.

Suddenly, Hallvindur raced back towards them.

'Down, down!' he called. They all dropped down behind the nearest snow bank.

Hallvindur leaped over the bank and slid down next to Edgar.

'What is it?' asked Edgar.

'Wolves, a large pack. They must have caught the scent of the blood from the battle and now we lie between them and their dinner.'

Edgar motioned to Guthrum and the two of them crept carefully up the lee side of the drift until their eyes were just above its crest.

Circling not twenty yards in front of them was the wolf pack. At their head was a huge white male, his startling golden eyes staring straight at Edgar and Guthrum.

The rest of the pack stopped their circling and followed

their leader's gaze.

'I think they know we're here,' whispered Edgar.

'They always do. God knows how.'

'Look at the size of that one,' said Edgar in awe.

'Aye, he's a big lad. Wouldn't want to have to scrap with him.'

'Could we take them on?'

'Maybe a few at a time. Probably not all together.'

Edgar stared through the swirling snow at the wolf pack. They remained motionless, just stretching their necks forward to catch the scent of their prey.

Then, through the dimness of the snowstorm, way over on the far side of the clearing, beyond the wolves, Edgar glimpsed two large, black, ragged, circling birds. The ravens were back.

Suddenly very aware of the small raven amulet around his neck, he put his hand reassuringly on Guthrum's shoulder and stood up.

'Edgar!' hissed Guthrum urgently.

Edgar strode up to the top of the snowdrift and stared at the big male wolf. Its golden eyes remained fixed on him, its ears pricked forward in concentration. It leaned slightly forward, catching Edgar's scent even from this distance. Its gaze was intense, and Edgar found himself feeling immense admiration for the magnificent animal.

Edgar and the wolf stared at each other in complete stillness for what seemed an age to Edgar.

The dog wolf took four paces towards Edgar, then stopped and huffed. It turned round and led its pack away to the west.

'Sweet Jesus. What the hell was that about?' asked Guthrum, scrabbling to join Edgar at the top of the drift.

'I… I'm not sure. It felt the right thing to do.'
'It was bloody stupid if you ask me!'
'I didn't ask you, Guthrum.'
'No, well.'
'Come on. We've got a way to go yet.'

21

Christmas

There was no guard at the crossing point onto the Isle of Hakrholme. They went unchallenged amongst the fields and narrow lanes that crossed the Isle. They passed only a single local inhabitant, who looked at them suspiciously and then turned back to his business.

The camp field, which previously had been filled with the tents and campfires of the Danish army now stood abandoned.

'Not everyone's gone,' said Guthrum. 'Look, there's a tent still standing.'

'It's Osfrith,' said Edgar. 'He must be waiting for us, or for Cyneheard.'

They walked over to the tent. All around them was the detritus left by the horde as they left. Black smudges marked the positions of campfires, churned ground where horses had stood.

The snow had fallen more thinly here, not providing the

thick ground cover they had previously travelled through.

The wind whipped the banner on top of Osfrith's tent, making it snap loudly.

'No guards,' observed Guthrum as they approached the tent. He stepped up to the door flaps and pulled them open. 'Nobody home. I don't think they've gone far. There's still furniture in there and a couple of chests. I think it's probably just a temporary absence.'

'So we either go looking for them or we wait for them to return,' said Edgar.

'Or we could split,' suggested Guthrum. 'You, Halfdene and Cyneheard wait here and rest, whilst the rest of us search.'

Edgar nodded. He was feeling weak and incredibly tired. All he wanted to do was to lie down on a comfortable pallet and sleep for hours. Yet he fought to resist the urge. It felt close to giving up, and he was not yet ready to do that.

'Could this be a trap?' said Hallvindur.

'No,' said Alaric immediately. 'It's too contrived. We've made good progress over the last few days. As far as we're aware, the Normans did not know that the army was camping here. It's a hidden island in a lot of ways. There's no way they could have seen us. How did they clear everyone else away? How did they know that the one tent we would be looking for was Osfrith's?'

Hallvindur grunted. Alaric's answer made sense, though the thought of a trap had been in everyone's mind.

'Alright,' said Edgar. 'Alaric and Hallvindur, you go and search for signs of where Osfrith could have gone to, or the rest of the army for that matter. The rest of us will remain here in case Osfrith returns soon. I want you back by nightfall, so don't go too far.'

'We'll check the river banks first,' said Alaric. 'That's the most likely direction they would have gone.'

Alaric and Hallvindur set off to investigate the river.

Guthrum remained outside the tent on lookout duty whilst Caedmon searched the area for any food that might have been left behind.

Edgar, Halfdene and Cyneheard moved inside the tent. Despite his resolution to remain awake, Edgar fell asleep almost immediately.

The sound of loud voices woke him. He looked around, unsure at first as to where he was. Osfrith's tent. It was dim inside the tent; dusk must have fallen. He remembered his words to Alaric and Hallvindur about returning before dark. Looking across the tent, he could see the dishevelled form of Cyneheard, who had obviously also been asleep, looking across at him.

Halfdene was nowhere to be seen.

'Edgar!' The tent door flap was pulled open and Guthrum looked in. 'It's Osfrith, he's back with Alaric and Hallvindur.'

Edgar stood up immediately, wincing at the pain in his side. He pulled back the flap, to see Osfrith limping up the hill, with Alaric and Hallvindur and three other armed men with him.

Halfdene stood beside Guthrum, looking pale and drawn but resolute.

'Edgar!' shouted Osfrith, 'Edgar!'

'Here!' called back Edgar.

Edgar felt Cyneheard step up beside him and pull the tent flap further open.

'Uncle!' cried Cyneheard, and ran out of the tent and

down the incline towards Osfrith.

'Cyneheard!' exclaimed Osfrith. 'Cyneheard, my dear boy! I thought you dead for sure.'

The two men faced each other, each appraising the appearance of the other. Neither had fared well over the past three years.

After a few moments, they moved together and fell into each other's arms.

Edgar turned away and went back into the tent.

That evening, they all sat together in the tent, bar Osfrith's housecarls, who stood outside keeping watch.

Osfrith and the three carls who had remained with him had been down at the river catching fish. They had caught enough for everyone to have their fill.

'I needed to stretch my leg,' explained Osfrith. 'I was sick of sitting alone in this tent waiting for news. Let me tell you what's happened here, and then you can tell me how you rescued my sister-son.'

He put his emptied food bowl down on the ground beside him.

'You'll probably have heard, or at least surmised, that Asbjorn has apparently accepted William's geld and has withdrawn to the ships. Most of them are still anchored in the estuary, and so far there's no sign that Asbjorn has ordered the fleet back home. Some ships still patrol along the river. I can't make it out. I don't know what he's up to. Not what we were hoping, that's all I'm certain about.

'I think we can conclude that the Danish invasion is over, at least for now. Asbjorn seems to be trying to relive the glory days of Viking raids, when they raided, were paid off with gold and then raided again. There seems to be no intention to wrest the kingdom from this shitty upstart. If Sweyn really had his sights set on the English crown, then I think he will be very disappointed.

'I don't know what else to add. The facts are there, stark as they are.'

'There's more bad news.'

Osfrith looked up at Edgar. 'What?' he asked.

'It would seem that Asbjorn's little deal allowed the Bastard to reassign some of his troops. We met with some Wildmen on our return and were present at a gathering of all the Wildmen. Alfweald was asking whether they should go on fighting now that the Danes have withdrawn, and if so, how. The Wildmen voted unanimously to continue fighting, but before the second question could be debated, a Norman army, presumably released from duties further north, attacked. There was a fierce battle, where Halfdene and I were wounded.'

He paused, looking at the ground in front of his feet.

'Go on,' urged Osfrith, his face grim.

'The Wildmen put up a brave and ferocious fight, but they are finished. There can't be more than a few tens of them left.'

'Then it is truly over,' muttered Osfrith.

'For our part,' Edgar looked round, indicating his companions, 'We have decided to return to Denmark, to put this behind us, to do nothing about Asbjorn's treachery.'

Osfrith remained silent, looking ahead of him, deep in thought.

'Asbjorn will pay for his failure. Of that, I can assure you. You're right that you can do nothing about it yourselves, but Asbjorn will have to account for his actions to Sweyn-king. The King will also take evidence and advice from those of us who were there. As a king's thegn, I will be part of that. The reckoning will come, I promise you.'

Cyneheard suddenly slumped against his uncle. Osfrith reached round and held onto the young man's shoulders.

'I'm sorry,' muttered Cyneheard. 'I'm just so tired.'

Osfrith released his hold.

'We need to stay here a while longer yet,' he said. 'Wounds need to heal, and Cyneheard needs to build up his strength. Those bastards…'

Guthrum spoke up. 'Lord Osfrith is right. We need to allow Cyneheard, Edgar and Halfdene to heal. Maybe we should move somewhere less conspicuous than where we are. We should take down the tent. If we're going to be here for any length of time, may I suggest that we modify the tent to make it easier to hide?'

'Good idea, Guthrum. Where do you suggest we move to?'

'There are woodlands about a mile inland from here. Some of us hunted there before we went to Eoforwic. It's a small wood, rarely visited by the locals. There are easier hunting grounds nearby. As the Jarl had ordered that we did not interfere with the locals any more than necessary, we had to find less frequented hunting areas.'

'Excellent. We'll move first thing in the morning.'

'Might I also suggest, sir, that we make efforts to contact the fleet. We will at some time want to rejoin if we are to return to Denmark.'

Osfrith nodded. 'I'll see to that. As I mentioned before, some ships are still patrolling. It should be just a matter of attracting the attention of one as it passes.'

'Very good, sir,' said Guthrum.

With that, they wrapped themselves in blankets and

settled down for the night.

Edgar lay for a while, his eyes unwilling to close despite the weariness that he felt. His ribs were still aching, though being honest with himself, he knew that they were healing rapidly. Yet still, an almost overwhelming tiredness was constantly hanging over him. He needed rest, lots of it. The failure of the expedition had left him with an almost physical sense of disappointment.

His mind wandered back to happier days in Rapendun, where his grandfather had been thegn. In his mind's eye, he vividly saw the mead hall, his grandfather's house, the church and the bell tower. He recalled the last time he had visited Rapendun, as a fugitive. He had visited the grave of his grandfather in the crypt below the church, where the sacred bones of St Wystan and two Mercian kings had lain.

His thoughts switched to services held in the church. Happy services; services tinged with sadness. Funerals. One funeral stood out in his mind. An old housecarl of his grandfather's, Thurstan by name. He had been struck by a wasting disease of some kind. The herbalists and the priests could do nothing to prevent its relentless spread. Thurstan had grown thinner and thinner, a once large, strong man reduced to little more than thinly stretched skin over a skeleton.

Edgar, about thirteen years old at the time, had found Thurstan sitting on a fallen tree trunk by the river.

'Young Master Edgar, what a pleasant surprise,' the old housecarl had said with a warm smile.

Edgar had sat down next to him.

'What are you doing here, Thurstan? You should be at home, getting better, not walking around out here all alone.'

Edgar had felt a genuine concern for his grandfather's

old retainer.

'Ah, Edgar. I appreciate your concern, but I'm afraid that no amount of sitting around at home is going to make me better.'

'Well walking around out here isn't going to, either,' insisted Edgar with youthful stubbornness.

'I'm not going to get better, Edgar. I'm dying. I know it and everyone around me knows it. I'd rather sit here and watch the kingfishers than moulder away in a dark house.' He smiled happily.

'You're not going to die, Thurstan,' Edgar said, his voice wavering.

'I'm sorry Edgar. We all have to die at our appointed time, and mine is very close.' He smiled again.

'Then why do you look so happy? Why are you not sad?'

Thurstan sighed and looked back across the river to where a heron stood motionless on its stilt-like legs, waiting to stab its beak down at an unsuspecting fish.

'I am sad, in a way. But I've had a good life. I've lived well, fought well. Loved and been loved. I have done my duty and had duty done by me. I am content. I accept what is to come. There is great comfort in acceptance, you know.'

'But you'll be dead.'

'Yes, I will, but what comes next? There's a whole other life ahead of me. Some say that we go to a great banqueting hall to feast, drink, hunt and fight with our ancestors forever. Others that we'll go to be with the Christ forever. Who knows? I don't. I'm looking forward to finding out, though.'

Thurstan had died two days later, and his funeral had been a much less sad occasion than Edgar had thought it was going to be. His two sons led the drinking after he had been buried, and the night was full of song and laughter. During the festivities, Edgar's grandfather had turned to Edgar and said, his eyes shining, 'Thurstan would have loved this. What a fine send-off.'

Several things stayed with Edgar afterwards. The joy in a person's life could outweigh the sadness of their death, and those words of Thurstan's; 'There is great comfort in acceptance.'

Edgar closed his eyes, hearing the sides of the tent flap and snap around him. The air moved strangely in the tent, shoved to and fro by the shifting side panels.

Acceptance. A pleasant lightness descended on Edgar. Acceptance. He groaned quietly as he drifted off into a restful sleep.

The following morning, as Edgar, Cyneheard and Halfdene stood around, ordered to do nothing, Guthrum, Caedmon, Alaric and Osfrith's housecarls dropped the tent to the ground, and under Guthrum's guidance began slicing the tent panels down to smaller sizes.

When they were happy with their work, the tent was bundled up into four parcels and they all set off for the small woodland that Guthrum had spoken about the night before.

The three invalids were ordered to sit beneath a tree whilst the healthier members of the party selected a suitable place to pitch the modified tent.

'I feel like a child,' grumbled Halfdene.

'It's for our own good,' said Edgar. 'How's the shoulder?'

'It's absolutely fine.'

'No. Really.'

'It hurts like a bastard.'

'Let it heal, Halfdene. You'll be no use to anyone if it doesn't heal properly. And then God help you, 'cause you're nothing to look at.'

Halfdene guffawed. 'Alright. Point made. I'll sit like a good little boy.'

Caedmon emerged from the bushes with a smile on his face.

'My lord, Master Cyneheard, the tent is prepared.'

'Come on, fellow invalids,' said Edgar as he stood up, wincing only slightly at the stab of pain from his side.

Halfdene got up awkwardly, twisting to avoid having to use his injured shoulder.

They followed Caedmon a short way into the brush until they came to a low mound of bracken and small branches. From a distance, it was well disguised, but close up there was no mistaking the shelter.

'It's a bit low, isn't it?' asked Halfdene dubiously.

'It's only for lying down in,' said Guthrum. 'We can't afford anything big enough to stand up in, or even sit upright. It would be too visible. We just need to be invisible for a few days.'

Edgar nodded his approval. 'It's good, Guthrum. Thank you.'

'Ah, Edgar, there you are,' Osfrith hobbled from around the back of the shelter. 'Now you three are to go in there and rest,' he said. 'No argument now. We'll make a meal in a couple of hours, but until it's ready, you should try to sleep.'

'Not sleepy,' muttered Halfdene.

'Halfdene,' warned Edgar.

Halfdene grunted unhappily.

'Come on,' said Edgar, dropping to his hands and knees

to enter the camouflaged tent.

Inside, the shelter was more spacious than Edgar had imagined it would be. Although lower than in its previous incarnation, the tent panels had been reworked to provide a greater floor surface area and heaps of small branches and twigs had been piled up to make comfortable bedding. Edgar was grateful for the opportunity to do nothing for a while, and soon he was sleeping soundly.

The following days passed peacefully. Edgar, Halfdene and Cyneheard all showed good signs of recovery, though it became obvious that Edgar's previous observations were correct and that a full recovery for Cyneheard would take many months, possibly years. Nevertheless, he started to take part in short hunting expeditions, and his painfully thin body began to thicken slightly.

One evening, as they sat, huddled around a low campfire, Caedmon cleared his throat. Everyone turned to look at him.

'My lords, gentlemen. I have been calculating the time of year. From the last date that I definitely know, I have carefully counted the days by events that occurred in them until I reached today. It's obvious that we are in Midwinter,' he held his palm upwards to indicate the weather around them. 'More specifically, I believe that tomorrow will be Christmas Eve.'

Everyone gasped. The normal cycle of religious observances had been completely broken for them all. Events had pushed all other considerations into the background, where they had been forgotten. And now Christmas had sneaked up on them.

'We need a feast, then,' said Guthrum decisively. 'We have no priest to celebrate the sacrament for us, so we must do what we can to mark the occasion.'

It was agreed. At first light, everyone would go out in hunting parties. Caedmon and Alaric would tour the nearest farmsteads and buy such foodstuffs as they were unlikely to be able to find themselves at this time of year.

They split into pairs. Edgar and Halfdene walked about a mile to the east of their camp, to an area that seemed uninhabited and wild. There they began to hunt. Little was moving in the cold weather.

'They're all hiding,' whispered Halfdene.

'No, wait. Look,' Edgar said, indicating with the top end of his hunting bow.

Fifty yards ahead of them, a lone roe deer stood, its head, wreathed in steamy breath, turned away from them. It stood like a statue, unmoving, but clearly wary and listening for the first sounds of approaching danger.

Halfdene slowly withdrew an arrow from his quiver and nocked it to the drawstring of his bow.

'No, not yet. We need to get closer,' said Edgar, almost under his breath.

The deer seemed to relax and put its head down to the ground again, eating.

'Carefully now,' said Edgar. He began to move slowly around the deer in one direction, whilst Halfdene crept silently away in the other direction.

Edgar carefully placed his feet between twigs and other detritus, attempting to be as quiet as possible. The deer continued eating, apparently unaware of the two hunters slowly closing in on it.

Above them, a roost of jackdaws suddenly exploded out of the trees, responding to some unseen danger. The deer looked up and instinctively began to bolt away from the jackdaws, away from the two men.

Halfdene whistled to Edgar and indicated that they should follow it, carefully. Edgar signalled his agreement and they quickened their pace, following the deer into a large, open meadow, sloping down to their left towards a river. The deer stopped some way across the meadow, then walked slowly to its right for a few paces before looking cautiously around and stooping its head down to feed again.

Edgar and Halfdene slowed down and bent double, then slowly began advancing on the deer once more.

They had covered just over half the distance between the cover of the trees and the deer when they heard a shout to their right, up the hill. A horseman had caught sight of the deer and was beginning to accelerate down the slope towards the animal, which now looked up and bolted.

'Drop!' called Edgar.

Over the brow of the hill, another dozen riders had now appeared. They were armoured and were carrying shields and spears.

Edgar and Halfdene threw themselves flat to the ground, but the short, winter-starved grass did little to shield them. With another shout, the riders wheeled away from their pursuit of the deer and turned towards the two men.

In seconds they were on them, circling them. More riders had appeared from over the brow and now about thirty armed soldiers encircled them, spears pointing towards them.

'Drop your bows and weapons!' one of them barked, in heavily accented English.

Edgar and Halfdene stood up, dropping their bows.

Halfdene's hand moved towards his hidden seax.

'Halfdene, no! They'll kill you.'

Halfdene withdrew his seax slowly and dropped it to the ground in front of his feet. Edgar did the same, never taking his eyes off those of the man who had ordered them to disarm.

They stood in the middle of the circle of horses, their arms held wide, away from their belts. The armed men all looked at them, stony in their silence. Then between the legs of two of the horses, a huge grey dog snaked into the circle.

'No,' whispered Edgar. 'Sweet Jesus, no.'

The dog approached them, teeth bared.

Edgar heard a command being barked at the dog, which immediately lay down where it stood, without taking its eyes off the two men and still with bared teeth.

Two horses in the circle drew aside and another rider entered the circle. Dressed in his rich, bearskin cloak, Roger de Barentin pulled his horse to a stop just in front of Edgar and Halfdene.

He swung down from his horse and approached Edgar.

When face to face with him, de Barentin took Edgar's chin roughly in his hand and twisted his head from side to side, carefully examining the wounds on Edgar's face through slitted eyes.

The rider who had ordered Edgar and Halfdene to disarm asked something of the Baron.

After a moment, the Baron released Edgar's chin and replied in the same language, adding in English 'This is not the man I seek. Now do something useful and bring me that deer.'

The rider shouted a string of orders and the riders

galloped off in pursuit of the deer.

The Baron stood impassively in front of Edgar.

'This land is ours now,' he said. 'It is lost to you. Go and live your life in peace, Edgar. Just not here.'

He turned and remounted his horse. As he turned the horse away from them, he whistled loudly, and the great grey hound stood and followed its master.

Edgar and Halfdene stood in the suddenly empty and silent clearing. They were quiet for a moment, allowing their heartbeats to calm down.

Eventually, Halfdene stammered, 'What the fuck…?'

Edgar didn't reply.

'What the fuck just happened, Edgar? Was that de Barentin?'

'Yes, it was. And I don't know what just happened.'

Halfdene sat down heavily on the grass. He was panting slightly. Edgar joined him.

'I don't understand,' said Halfdene. 'He said "This is not the man I seek," and yet you must be. He knew who you were. And he just let you go.'

'He did. We should not ignore his gift, Halfdene, whatever his reasons behind it. Come on, let's get back to the camp. I've lost my appetite.'

Edgar and Halfdene did not speak to each other for the whole journey back to their camp, each lost in his own confused thoughts.

On their arrival back at the camp, they found that most of the hunting parties had returned, all more successfully than them.

'Edgar?' asked Guthrum, looking up from a grouse he was plucking, and instantly aware of Edgar's strange

The Lost Land

demeanour. 'What's wrong? What's happened?'

Edgar and Halfdene looked at each other in silence.

'What?' demanded Guthrum, starting to look worried.

The others around the camp closed in to listen to the conversation.

'We were captured by a party of about thirty Norman riders,' said Edgar.

Guthrum looked shocked.

'Roger de Barentin himself was with them. They were searching for me, I think, and probably others. De Barentin recognised me, even called me by name when his men couldn't hear him. Then he let us go.'

'What? Why?'

Edgar shrugged, looking perplexed. 'I have no idea. No idea at all.'

Frustrated, Guthrum turned to Halfdene. 'Halfdene?'

Halfdene shook his head. 'It's as Edgar says. I don't know. His exact words were; "This land is ours now. It is lost to you. Go and live your life in peace, Edgar. Just not here."'

'There's one thing we can be sure of,' said Edgar. 'Roger de Barentin never does anything without good reason. From personal experience, I know him to be intelligent, wily and ruthless. He's playing some bigger game that we don't know about. I would recommend that we take his suggestion that we leave seriously.'

'We'll attempt to make contact with the fleet first thing tomorrow,' said Osfrith firmly. 'We need to clear out as soon as we can. I think you three are all fit to go now.'

The three injured men nodded in agreement.

At that moment, Alaric and Caedmon returned from their foraging expedition with several loaves of bread in a sack.

'We managed to bag a couple of grouse, which we swapped for this bread,' said Caedmon enthusiastically. 'What? What's the matter?'

Guthrum related the tale succinctly to Alaric and Caedmon.

'We saw no one. Nothing of any Normans,' said Alaric, clearly distressed that something was happening of which he had no knowledge.

'They must be searching for us, or at least for Edgar,' said Osfrith. 'There's likely more than one party of horsemen around, and they've found their way onto Hakrholme. We're not as secure as we thought we were. Are we all back now? No. I see Hallvindur is still absent. Anyone know where he went to?'

'He was heading down to the river. He wanted to spear some fish for tomorrow. He took your man Grim with him,' said Guthrum.

'Good. Alright, let's prepare our food for tomorrow, at least we should be able to have our final Christmas here in peace.'

By the following morning, Hallvindur and Grim had still not arrived back, and Osfrith was getting worried about them.

'Those Normans were headed down towards the river when they went after the deer,' said Halfdene. 'Maybe they came across Hallvindur and Grim whilst they were chasing it.'

'That's unlikely,' said Guthrum. 'I got the impression that Hallvindur was intending to make use of the fishing spot he had used whilst the army was encamped. That

The Lost Land

would be some way further north than where you had your encounter with the Normans.'

'It's still a worrying point,' said Edgar. 'Let's spread out and head towards the river. If we split into pairs again, we should be able to cover quite a lot of ground. I want to find them.'

Osfrith nodded. 'We'll head out straight away. Caedmon and Cyneheard, you remain here and start the food cooking. We'll still want to eat, no matter what we find.'

They set off, all in an easterly direction, towards the river along which they had first arrived at Hakrholme. They travelled cautiously, ever mindful of the possible presence of Norman search parties. Edgar felt confident that de Barentin would by now have led his party far away from here. The threat of possible other groups served to keep him careful, though.

In the distance, Edgar heard a sound like a loud deer bark, but with a slight squeal at the end.

Edgar and Halfdene looked at each other.

'Guthrum,' said Halfdene. It was the Wildman call for widely dispersed hunting parties to converge.

They first saw Guthrum standing in an open area a few hundred yards back from the riverbank. Next to him was a very tall man who could only have been Hallvindur. Edgar let out a gasp of relief when he saw the giant Dane safe and well. With them were several other men.

As they approached, Edgar could see the other men standing with Guthrum and Hallvindur. One was Osfrith's carl, Grim. One other stood out to him. Short and neatly dressed in a rich crimson quilted coat, it could only be Loki, and with him, two hardened members of his crew, battle axes slung across their backs.

'Edgar!' called Guthrum. 'All is well, and it looks like we'll be able to rejoin the fleet today.'

'Good. That's good. Loki, I'm pleased to see you.'

The captain turned to face Edgar. 'Thegn Edgar. I'm glad you survived,' he said formally, bowing slightly at the waist.

The cool response was as good as Edgar could have expected. He would have to work to regain Loki's trust and friendship.

The other parties were now arriving.

'It looks like you all survived. Against the odds,' said Loki.

'Captain Loki, it is good to see you!' said Osfrith with real enthusiasm as he hobbled up to the captain. 'We need to rejoin the fleet as soon as possible. Can you arrange for us to return?'

'I can, my lord. The fleet is moored in the mouth of the great river, a short sail from where we stand.'

'Excellent. We have plenty of food for a feast on this holy day. Do we have time to enjoy it? We also have two more of our party at our camp, preparing the food.'

'That sounds most agreeable, my lord.'

Loki turned to his two crew and gave them swift orders. They turned and hurried back towards the river, where Stormleaper must have been lying, beyond the thick reed beds.

They began walking at a leisurely pace back towards the camp. After a short while, Loki's two crewmen returned, each carrying a large flagon and two wide-brimmed metal drinking cups.

The Lost Land

The smells of the cooking meat met them before they arrived back at the camp. Caedmon and Cyneheard had been hard at work, and plates of meat were set out, with half a loaf on each plate, and a thin sauce that Caedmon had brewed from the meat juices and some dried herbs he had procured.

Caedmon and Cyneheard were introduced to Loki, who was particularly interested to hear Cyneheard's tale of survival against the odds for over three years.

The feast was greatly enjoyed by all. Loki's ale was poured out into the two big cups, which were passed round and round the company.

'I can take you back to the fleet with the high tide, which should have risen sufficiently about an hour before sundown,' said Loki. 'Unfortunately, you will not be able to remain on my ship, as I have business elsewhere. I will make sure you are all berthed on good vessels.'

Edgar felt his heart sink. He had hoped that he would be able to remain with Loki, to patch up their differences. He did not relish the thought of starting from scratch with a new captain and a new crew.

After the meal, they all sat back and finished off the last of the ale that Loki had provided.

Osfrith lay back and soon began to snore gently. Cyneheard sat protectively next to him.

'Thank you for that meal Cyneheard, Caedmon. It was a fine feast indeed,' said Edgar, rubbing his full stomach.

'Aye!' agreement came from around the campfire.

From his cross-legged position, Loki stood up in a single, graceful motion.

'Walk with me, Edgar,' he said.

Edgar stood up and followed Loki as he walked through

the trees. They wandered in silence until they reached the site of the army's camp. Ahead of him, Loki looked down at his feet, stooped, and retrieved something from the ground.

'Penny,' he said to Edgar, showing him the small silver coin. He inspected it closely. 'Danish. One of our boys will be regretting dropping this.'

They walked on, over the crest of the low hill and down the other side. A roughly metalled track crossed their way, and Loki turned right to follow it. It wound between ditches, marking the boundaries of fields filled with autumn's stubble. They would be ploughing soon, Edgar thought. Despite everything that had happened, the cycles of ploughing, seeding and harvesting would go on as it ever had.

'Where are we going?' said Edgar.

'Hmm? Oh, nowhere in particular. I just like walking when I'm not at sea. Keeps me in touch with the land.'

The boundary ditches petered out at this point, and open, uncultivated land lay to either side of the track. Shallower ditches ran alongside the road, highlighted by the melting snow.

'My name isn't really Loki, you know,' began Loki.

'I guessed.'

'My father was a senior thegn in the household of Jarl Ulf of Orkney.'

'Sweyn-king's father?'

'Aye, that's the one. You know that the King came to his throne through his mother, not his father?'

'I'd heard something like that. How did that happen?'

'Ulf's wife – Sweyn's mother, was the daughter of Sweyn Forkbeard, king of the Danes, and, briefly, of the

English. Estrith Sweyndattir is therefore also the sister of Cnut the Great, king of most places round here,' Loki grinned briefly at Edgar.

'Yes, we all know of him,' replied Edgar.

'Ulf was appointed Jarl of Denmark by Cnut, but eventually rebelled against him. Cnut stamped the rebellion out and Ulf was killed.'

Loki looked across the fields ahead of him, where two young boys were running around in the distance, chasing each other.

'The marriage of Ulf and Estrith was not what you would call a happy one. It had served its political purpose for Cnut but had made life miserable for Estrith. She had done her duty well, giving Ulf four children.

'My father and Estrith became close during those unhappy years, and although they both risked death, they became lovers.'

'Dear God, Loki, what are you telling me?'

The two boys were running towards them now, laughing and trying to trip each other up. They fell to the ground, panting and laughing, twenty paces from Loki and Edgar.

The boys picked themselves up.

'Hey!' called one. 'Are you with all them men?'

'Which men?' asked Loki.

'All them men what was here?'

'You mean the army of the king of Denmark?'

'Is that what they was? Wow.'

'They've gone now.'

'Where've they gone?'

'Not far. You may see them again.'

'Wow,' said the lad, his eyes bright and eager. 'D'you

think we could join them?'

'Maybe in six or seven years, by the look of you,' laughed Loki. 'Here,' he held out the shiny silver penny that he had picked up on the camp field.

'Woah! Thanks mate!'

'Now bugger off, the pair of you.'

The two lads ran off towards the trees at the far side of the field, beyond which could be seen a thin curl of smoke, probably rising from a dwelling.

'Asbjorn is the King's brother through his mother, and my brother through his father,' said Loki, not looking at Edgar.

'Jesus, Loki.'

'He knows it. I don't think the King does, though. And nobody else must.'

'I understand.' Edgar paused. 'How does Asbjorn know?'

'I don't know. Maybe his mother told him. It was my mother who told me. My father has been dead many years. My mother still lives.'

'I still don't understand why you hate him so much.'

'I don't hate him, but I do know him. He will never acknowledge me as kin, and so he tries to remove me. He can't have me killed; I'm too well known at court. The King himself gives me tasks that he knows I can perform well. I'm too useful to the King to be simply disposed of.'

'What does Asbjorn do, then?'

'He finds me the most dangerous missions to perform. Singing my praises into the King's ear, he will happily recommend me for jobs I am unlikely to survive because only I could possibly do them.'

'We need to get you away from the court,' said Edgar.

'If you remember, I did have plans for that, before all this began.'

'Micklagard.'

'Micklagard. I had a woman once, you know. We were to be married.'

With a sinking feeling, Edgar asked, 'What happened?'

'Asbjorn saw to it that she was removed from my presence. She was a thegn's daughter, and he persuaded the King to send the thegn away on some perilous task on the German border. He was killed, and Asbjorn made sure that he inherited. The thegn had no sons, you see.'

'What happened to the daughter?'

'She's in a convent, somewhere, I believe. Asbjorn laughed when he told me.'

'And still you don't hate him?'

'He's a child. This farcical expedition shows that.' Loki smiled. 'I'll find her some day. She's still young. Plenty time yet.'

'But first, to Micklagard?'

'I think so, don't you?'

'Loki, I'm really very sorry for my behaviour towards you at the start of this expedition. I didn't listen to what you were saying, and I should have done.'

'You had a lot personally invested in the outcome. Of course you wanted to believe that it was going to be successful.'

'I'm a fool.'

'You're no fool, Edgar. Your only problem is that you believe that everyone else is as honourable as you are. You'll learn.'

'I've learned, I think.'

'Good. Then you and your men will come with us to

Micklagard?'

'If you'll have us, it would be an honour and a pleasure.'

'I have orders to remain with the fleet. I believe, however, that the fleet will lie at anchor over the winter before raids are resumed. I do not intend to be part of that. The crews will go through desperate hardship, spending the whole of the winter aboard their vessels. I will not subject my crew to the whims of my idiot half-brother.

'Now, if I read the signs correctly, and I usually do, then we have a run of at least three good, clear days ahead of us. The winds are steady from the west, we should be able to make Roskilde within a week. Few ship's captains would dare the crossing at this time of year, but Stormleaper is strong, and I am confident of the weather.'

'Sounds like a plan.'

'Then it's settled. Come on, let's get back and pack everything up. We'll leave tonight and slip past the other ships in the darkness. For us, my friend, this expedition is over.'

Together, they walked along the gritty path, back to their companions.

Historical Note

Little is written about the Danish invasion of 1069, and what has been written by later commentators is lacking in detail and often contradictory.

The Anglo-Saxon Chronicle describes an immense army, swelled by forces from all over the north of England. The capture of York is mentioned, and that the Normans had burned the city and completely plundered the minster.

William's response to the taking of York was to march swiftly north, only to find that the Danes had retreated to their ships at the mouth of the Humber, where he couldn't reach them. He spent Christmas in the ruins of York, having paid off the Danes.

The following year, 1070, Sweyn's forces once again began raiding, this time in East Anglia. Peterborough was burned and the minster there looted. It is at this point that one of the most famous resistance fighters appears in the records – Hereward of Bourne, who since the 14th century has been known as Hereward 'the Wake'. This epithet was probably given to him by the Wake family, who claimed descent from him.

The account given by the Anglo-Saxon Chronicle suggests that the Danish invasion was no more than a glorified raid. The Chronicle does hint strongly, though, that England was in a state of near-anarchy at this time. Resistance to the Norman usurper was very strong and widespread. Sweyn may have merely taken advantage of that fact to make a quick and easy pillaging of the country, but it is likely that he also saw an opportunity to claim the English throne for himself. His claim on the throne, whilst not exactly watertight, was better than William's.

After the sacking of Peterborough, the Danes and the Normans came to an agreement, and the Danes returned home. There would be other Danish raids in the succeeding years, but nothing on the scale of the 1069/70 invasion.

During the writing of this book, I visited many of the places mentioned in it. The place that I particularly remember is Roskilde, a very pleasant town sitting at the end of Roskilde Fjord just 20 miles, and an easy train journey, from Copenhagen. At Roskilde is the great brick-built cathedral, the Roskilde Domkirke, Denmark's most important church. It is the equivalent of England's Westminster Abbey, being the burial location for very many Danish kings and queens, including Sweyn Estrithson. Sweyn's memorial, built into a pier flanking the apse, proclaims him to be king of the Danes, English and Norwegians. This is a truly magnificent and beautiful church, and worth a day of anybody's time.

Roskilde is also home to the Viking Ship Museum

(Vikingskibs museet), where the remains of five scuttled Viking ships of various types, excavated in 1962 at Skuldelev, about ten miles up the fjord from Roskilde, can be seen close up.

The museum sits at the water's edge, and has a dock on the fjord where five reconstructed ships can be seen and boarded. These include the magnificent *Sea Stallion of Glendalough*, a reconstruction of the Skuldelev 2 longship, which was very similar in design to my fictional *Stormleaper*.

Gazetteer

Eleventh-century place names used in the book and their modern equivalent.

Barnestaple	Barnstaple, Devon
Bebbanburg	Bamburgh, Northumberland
Bortone	Burton Agnes, Yorkshire
Brycgstowe	Bristol
Colton	Fictional
Defenscir	Devonshire
Deorby	Derby, Derbyshire
Dunholm	Durham, County Durham
Eoforwic	York, Yorkshire. Known to the Danes as Jorvik. 'Eoforwic' and 'Jorvik' have almost identical pronunciations.
Gerultoft	Garthorpe, Axholme, Lincolnshire
Hakrholme	Axholme, Lincolnshire
Heldernesse	Holderness, Yorkshire
Hrafn's Spur	Spurn Head, Yorkshire
Humbre	The River Humber
Jorvik	York. See Eoforwic
Mammesfeld	Mansfield, Nottinghamshire
Micklagard	Constantinople, capital of the Eastern Roman Empire, now Istanbul.
Nordfolc	Norfolk
Pridby	Fictional. Neighbouring settlement to Colton.
Roskilde	Roskilde, at this time capital of Denmark.

Senlac	The location of the battlefield of Hastings.
Snotingeham	Nottingham, Nottinghamshire
Stanford	Stamford Bridge, Yorkshire
Swaddleton	Fictional. Neighbouring settlement to Colton.
Warwic	Warwick, Warwickshire
Wuelle	Wells-Next-the-Sea, Norfolk

Acknowledgements

A big thank you to all the readers of *Thegn*, who have passed on such positive and enthusiastic comments.

Special thanks to Mum, Dee, Karl and all the beta-readers. To Vladimir Shvachko for his beautiful artwork and to Ken Leeder for his brilliant cover design. Also to Theo Moorfield, for the outstanding website.

Very special thanks to Toni for her continued support and technical expertise.

For more information and to download a free novella (a prequel to the Thegn Edgar series), please visit

www.ThegnEdgar.com

Thegn Edgar will return in

THE SILVER SEEKERS

Printed in Great Britain
by Amazon